Praise for Murr[...]

Also by Murray Leinster:

GOLDEN AGE
MASTERWORKS

Sidewise in Time

MURRAY LEINSTER

This edition first published in Great Britain in 2020 by Gollancz
an imprint of the Orion Publishing Group Ltd
Carmelite House, 50 Victoria Embankment
London EC4Y 0DZ

An Hachette UK Company

1 3 5 7 9 10 8 6 4 2

A CIP catalogue record for this book is available from the British Library.

ISBN 978 1 473 22739 2

Typeset at The Spartan Press Ltd, Lymington, Hants

Printed in Great Britain by Clays Ltd, Elcograf S.p.A.

www.gollancz.co.uk
www.sfgateway.com

CONTENTS

SIDEWISE IN TIME

FOREWORD

Looking back, it seems strange that no one but Professor Minott figured the thing out in advance. The indications were more than plain. In early December of 1934 Professor Michaelson announced his finding that the speed of light was not an absolute – could not be considered invariable. That, of course, was one of the first indications of what was to happen.

A second indication came on February 15th, when at 12:40 p.m., Greenwich mean time, the sun suddenly shone blue-white and the enormously increased rate of radiation raised the temperature of the earth's surface by twenty-two degrees Fahrenheit in five minutes. At the end of the five minutes, the sun went back to its normal rate of radiation without any other symptom of disturbance.

A great many bids for scientific fame followed, of course, but no plausible explanation of the phenomenon accounted for a total lack of after disturbances in the sun's photosphere.

For a third clear forerunner of the events of June, on March 10th the male giraffe in the Bronx Zoological Park, in New York, ceased to eat. In the nine days following, it changed its form, absorbing all its extremities, even its neck and head, into an extraordinary, egg-shaped mass of still-living flesh and bone which on the tenth day began to divide spontaneously and on the twelfth was two slightly pulsating fleshy masses.

A day later still, bumps appeared on the two masses. They grew, took form and design, and twenty days after the beginning of the phenomenon were legs, necks, and heads. Then two giraffes, both male, moved about the giraffe enclosure. Each was slightly less than half the weight of the original animal. They were identically marked. And they ate and moved and in every way seemed normal though immature animals.

An exactly similar occurrence was reported from the Argentine Republic, in which a steer from the pampas was going through the same extraordinary method of reproduction under the critical eyes of Argentine scientists.

Nowadays it seems incredible that the scientists of 1935 should not have understood the meaning of these oddities. We now know something of the type of strain which produced them, though they no longer occur. But between January and June of 1935 the news services of the nation were flooded with items of similar import.

For two days the Ohio River flowed upstream. For six hours the trees in Euclid Park, in Cleveland, lashed their branches madly as if in a terrific storm, though not a breath of wind was stirring. And in New Orleans, near the last of May, fishes swam up out of the Mississippi River through the air, proceeded to 'drown' in the air which inexplicably upheld them, and then turned belly up and floated placidly at an imaginary water level some fifteen feet above the pavements of the city.

But it seems clear that Professor Minott was the only man in the world who even guessed the meaning of these – to us – clear-cut indications of the later events. Professor Minott was instructor in mathematics on the faculty of Robinson College in Fredericksburg, Va. We know that he anticipated very nearly every one of the things which later startled and frightened the world, and not only our world. But he kept his mouth shut.

Robinson College was small. It had even been termed a 'jerkwater' college without offending anybody but the faculty and certain sensitive alumni. For a mere professor of mathematics to make public the theory Minott had formed would not even be news. It would be taken as stark insanity. Moreover, those who believed it would be scared. So he kept his mouth shut.

Professor Minott possessed courage, bitterness, and a certain cold-blooded daring, but neither wealth nor influence. He had more than a little knowledge of mathematical physics and his calculations show extraordinary knowledge of the laws of probability, but he had very little patience with problems in ethics. And he was possessed by a particularly fierce passion for Maida Hayns, daughter of the professor of Romance languages, and had practically no chance to win even her attention over the competition of most of the student body.

So much of explanation is necessary, because no one but just such a person as Professor Minott would have forecast what was to happen and then prepare for it in the fashion in which he did.

We know from his notes that he considered the probability of disaster as a shade better than four to one. It is a very great pity that we do not have his calculations. There is much that our scientists do not understand even yet. The notes Professor Minott left behind have been invaluable, but there are obvious gaps in them. He must have taken most of his notes – and those the most valuable – into that unguessed-at place where he conceivably now lives and very probably works.

He would be amused, no doubt, at the diligence with which his most unconsidered scribble is now examined and inspected and discussed by the greatest minds of our time and space. And perhaps – it is quite probable – he may have invented a word for the scope of the catastrophe we escaped. We have none as yet.

There is no word to describe a disaster in which not only the earth but our whole solar system might have been destroyed; not only our solar system but our galaxy; not only our galaxy but every other island universe in all of the space we know; more than that, the destruction of all space as we know it; and even beyond that, the destruction of time, meaning not only the obliteration of present and future but even the annihilation of the past so that it would never have been. And then, besides, those other strange states of existence we learned of, those other universes, those other pasts and futures – all to be shattered into nothingness. There is no word for such a catastrophe.

3

It would be interesting to know what Professor Minott termed it to himself, as he coolly prepared to take advantage of the one chance in four of survival, if that should be the one to eventuate. But it is easier to wonder how he felt on the evening before the fifth of June, in 1935. We do not know. We cannot know. All we can be certain of is how we felt – and what happened.

I

It was half past seven a.m. of June 5, 1935. The city of Joplin, Missouri, awaked from a comfortable, summer-night sleep. Dew glistened upon grass blades and leaves and the filmy webs of morning spiders glittered like diamond dust in the early sunshine. In the most easternly suburb a high-school boy, yawning, came somnolently out of his house to mow the lawn before schooltime. A rather rickety family car roared, a block away. It backfired, stopped, roared again, and throttled down to a steady, waiting hum. The voices of children sounded among the houses. A colored washerwoman appeared, striding beneath the trees which lined this strictly residential street.

From an upper window a radio blatted: '—*one, two three, four! Higher, now! – three, four! Put your weight into it! – two, three, four!*' The radio suddenly squawked and began to emit an insistent, mechanical shriek which changed again to a squawk and then a terrific sound as of all the static of ten thousand thunderstorms on the air at once. Then it was silent.

The high-school boy leaned mournfully on the push bar of the lawn mower. At the instant the static ended, the boy sat down suddenly on the dew-wet grass. The colored woman reeled and grabbed frantically at the nearest tree trunk. The basket of wash toppled and spilled in a snowstorm of starched, varicolored clothing. Howls of terror from children. Sharp shrieks from women. '*Earthquake! Earthquake!*' Figures appeared running, pouring out of houses. Someone fled out to a sleep-ing porch, slid down a supporting column, and tripped over a rosebush in his pajamas. In seconds, it seemed, the entire population of the street was out-of-doors.

And then there was a queer, blank silence. There was no earthquake. No house had fallen. No chimney had cracked. Not so much as a dish or window-pane had made a sound in smashing. The sensation every human being had felt was not an actual shaking of the ground. There had been movement, yes, and of the earth, but no such movement as any human being had ever dreamed of before. These people were to learn of that movement much later. Now they stared blankly at each other.

And in the sudden, dead silence broken only by the hum of an idling car and the wail of a frightened baby, a new sound became audible. It was the tramp of marching feet. With it came a curious clanking and clattering noise. And then a marked command, which was definitely not in the English language.

Down the street of a suburb of Joplin, Missouri, on June 5, in the Year of Our Lord 1935, came a file of spear-armed, shield-bearing soldiers in the short, skirtlike togas of ancient Rome. They wore helmets upon their heads. They peered about as if they were as blankly amazed as the citizens of Joplin who regarded them. A long column of marching men came into view, every man with shield and spear and the indefinable air of being used to just such weapons.

They halted at another barked order. A wizened little man with a short sword snapped a question at the staring Americans. The high-school boy jumped. The wizened man roared his question again. The high-school boy stammered, and painfully formed syllables with his lips. The wizened man grunted in satisfaction. He talked, articulating clearly if impatiently. And the high-school boy turned dazedly to the other Americans.

'He wants to know the name of this town,' he said, unbelieving his own ears. 'He's talking Latin, like I learn in school. He says this town isn't on the road maps, and he doesn't know where he is. But all the same he takes possession of it in the name of the Emperor Valerius Fabricius, emperor of

Rome and the far corners of the earth.' And then the school-boy stuttered: 'He – he says these are the first six cohorts of the Forty-second Legion, on garrison duty in Messalia. That – that's supposed to be two days' march up that way.'

He pointed in the direction of St. Louis.

The idling motor car roared suddenly into life. Its gears whined and it came rolling out into the street. Its horn honked peremptorily for passage through the shield-clad soldiers. They gaped at it. It honked again and moved toward them.

A roared order, and they flung themselves upon it, spears thrusting, short swords stabbing. Up to this instant there was not one single inhabitant of Joplin who did not believe the spear-armed soldiers were motion-picture actors, or masquer-aders, or something else equally insane but credible. But there was nothing make-believe about their attack on the car. They assaulted it as if it were a strange and probably deadly beast. They flung themselves into battle with it in a grotesquely reck-less valor.

And there was nothing at all make-believe in the thorough-ness and completeness with which they speared Mr Horace B. Davis, who had only intended to drive down to the cotton-brokerage office of which he was chief clerk. They thought he was driving this strange beast to slaughter them, and they slaughtered him instead. The high-school boy saw them do it, growing whiter and whiter as he watched. When a swordsman approached the wizened man and displayed the severed head of Mr Davis, with the spectacles dangling grotesquely from one ear, the high-school boy fainted dead away.

II

It was sunrise of June 5, 1935. Cyrus Harding gulped down his breakfast in the pale-gray dawn. He had felt very dizzy and sick for just a moment, some little while since, but he was him-self again now. The smell of frying filled the kitchen. His wife cooked. Cyrus Harding ate. He made noises as he emptied his plate. His hands were gnarled and work-worn, but his expression was of complacent satisfaction. He looked at a calendar hung on the wall, a Christmas sentiment from the Bryan Feed & Fertilizer Co., in Bryan, Ohio.

'Sheriff's goin' to sell out Amos today,' he said comfortably. 'I figger I'll get that north forty cheap.'

His wife said tiredly: 'He's been offerin' to sell it to you for a year.'

'Yep,' agreed Cyrus Harding more complacently still. 'Comin' down on the price, too. But nobody'll bid against me at the sale. They know I want it bad, an' I ain't a good neighbor to have when somebuddy takes somethin' from under my nose. Folks know it. I'll git it a lot cheaper'n Amos offered it to me for. He wanted to sell it t'meet his int'rest an' hol' on another year. I'll git it for half that.'

He stood up and wiped his mouth. He strode to the door.

'That hired man shoulda got a good start with his harrowin',' he said expansively. 'I'll take a look an' go over to the sale.'

He went to the kitchen door and opened it. Then his mouth dropped open. The view from this doorway was normally that of a not especially neat barnyard, with beyond it farmland flat as a floor and cultivated to the very fence rails, with a promising crop of corn as a border against the horizon.

Now the view was quite otherwise. All was normal as far as the barn. But beyond the barn was delirium. Huge, spreading tree ferns soared upward a hundred feet. Lacy, foliated branches formed a roof of incredible density above sheer jungle such as no man on earth had ever seen before. The jungles of the Amazon basin were parklike by comparison with its thickness. It was a riotous tangle of living vegetation in which growth was battle, and battle was life, and life was deadly, merciless conflict.

No man could have forced his way ten feet through such a wilderness. From it came a fetid exhalation which was part decay and part lush, rank growing things, and part the overpowering perfumes of glaringly vivid flowers. It was jungle such as paleobotanists have described as existing in the Carboniferous period; as the source of our coal beds.

'It – it ain't so!' said Cyrus Harding weakly. 'It – ain't so!'

His wife did not reply. She had not seen. Wearily, she began to clean up after her lord and master's meal.

He went down the kitchen steps, staring and shaken. He moved toward this impossible apparition which covered his crops. It did not disappear as he neared it. He went within twenty feet of it and stopped, still staring, still unbelieving, beginning to entertain the monstrous supposition that he had gone insane.

Then something moved in the jungle. A long, snaky neck, feet thick at its base and tapering to a mere sixteen inches behind a head the size of a barrel. The neck reached out the twenty feet to him. Cold eyes regarded him abstractedly. The mouth opened. Cyrus Harding screamed.

His wife raised her eyes. She looked through the open door and saw the jungle. She saw the jaws close upon her husband. She saw colossal, abstracted eyes half close as the something gulped, and partly choked, and swallowed. She saw a lump in the monstrous neck move from the relatively slender portion just behind the head to the feet-thick section projecting from the jungle. She saw the head withdraw into the jungle and instantly be lost to sight.

Cyrus Harding's widow was very pale. She put on her hat and went out of the front door. She began to walk toward the house of the nearest neighbor. As she went, she said steadily to herself:

'It's come. I'm crazy. They'll have to put me in an asylum. But I won't have to stand him any more. I won't have to stand him any more!'

It was noon of June 5, 1935. The cell door opened and a very grave, whiskered man in a curious gray uniform came in. He tapped the prisoner gently on the shoulder.

'I'm Dr Holloway,' he said encouragingly. 'Suppose you tell

8

me, suh, just what happened t'you? I'm right sure it can all be straightened out.'

The prisoner sputtered: 'What – why – dammit,' he protested, 'I drove down from Louisville this morning. I had a dizzy spell and – well – I must have missed my road, because suddenly I noticed that everything around me was unfamiliar. And then a man in a gray uniform yelled at me, and a minute later he began to shoot, and the first thing I knew they'd arrested me for having the American flag painted on my car! I'm a traveling salesman for the Uncle Sam Candy Bar Co.! Dammit, it's funny when a man can't fly his own country's flag—'

'In your own country, of co'se,' assented the doctor comfortingly. 'But you must know, suh, that we don't allow any flag but ouah own to be displayed heah. You violated ouah laws, suh.'

'Your laws!' The prisoner stared blankly. 'What laws? Where in the United States is it illegal to fly the American flag?'

'Nowheah in the United States, suh.' The doctor smiled. 'You must have crossed ouah border unawares, suh. I will be frank, an' admit that it was suspected you were insane. I see now that it was just a mistake.'

'Border – United—' The prisoner gasped. 'I'm not in the United States? I'm not? Then where in hell am I?'

'Ten miles, suh, within the borders of the Confederacy,' said the doctor, and laughed. 'A queer mistake, suh, but theah was no intention of insult. You'll be released at once. Theah is enough tension between Washington an' Richmond without another border incident to upset ouah hot-heads.'

'Confederacy?' The prisoner choked. 'You can't – you don't mean the Confederate States—'

'Of co'se, suh. The Confederate States of North America. Why not?'

The prisoner gulped. 'I – I've gone mad!' he stammered. 'I must be mad! There was Gettysburg – there was—'

'Gettysburg? Oh, yes!' The doctor nodded indulgently. 'We are very proud of ouah history, suh. You refer to the battle in the War of Separation, when the fate of the Confederacy rested on ten minutes' time. I have often wondered what would have been the result if Pickett's charge had been driven back. It was Pickett's charge that gained the day for us, suh. England recognized the Confederacy two days later, France in another week, an' with unlimited credit abroad we won out. But it was a tight squeeze, suh!'

The prisoner gasped again. He stared out of the window. And opposite the jail stood an unquestionable courthouse. Upon the courthouse stood a flagpole. And spread gloriously in the breeze above a government building floated the Stars and Bars of the Confederacy!

It was night of June 5, 1935. The postmaster of North Centerville, Massachusetts, came out of his cubby-hole to listen to the narrative. The pot-bellied stove of the general store sent a comfortable if unnecessary glow about. The eyewitness chuckled.

'Yeah. They come around the cape, thirty or forty of 'em in a boat all o' sixty feet long with a crazy square sail drawin'. Round things on the gunnel like – like shields. An' rowin like hell! They stopped when they saw the town an' looked s'prised. Then they hailed us, talkin' some lingo that wa'n't American. Ole Peterson, he near dropped his line, with a fish on it, too. Then he tried to talk back. They hadda lotta trouble understandin' him, or made out to. Then they turned around an' rowed back. Actors or somethin', tryin' to play a joke. It fell flat, though. Maybe some of those rich folks up the coast pullin' it. Ho! Ho! Ole says they was talkin' a funny, old-fashioned Skowegian. They told him they was from Leifsholm, or somethin' like that, just up the coast. That they couldn't make out how our town got here. They'd never seen it before! Can y'imagine that? Ole says they were wikin's, an' they called this place Winland, an' says – What's that?'

A sudden hubbub arose in the night. Screams. Cries. A shotgun boomed dully. The loafers in the general store crowded out on the porch. Flames rose from half a dozen places on the water front. In their light could be seen a full dozen serpent ships, speeding for the shore, propelled by oars. From four of their number, already beached, dark figures had poured. Firelight glinted on swords, on shields. A woman screamed as a huge, yellow-maned man seized her. His brazen helmet and shield glittered. He was laughing. Then a figure in overalls hurtled toward the blond giant, an ax held threateningly.

The giant cut him down with an already dripping blade and roared. Men rushed to him and they plunged on to loot and burn. More of the armored figures leaped to the sand from another beached ship. Another house roared flames skyward.

III

And at half past ten a.m. on the morning of June 5th, Professor Minott turned upon the party of students with a revolver in each hand. Gone was the appearance of an instructor whose most destructive possibility was a below-passing mark in mathematics. He had guns in his hands now, instead of chalk or pencil, and his eyes were glowing even as he smiled frostily. The four girls gasped. The young men, accustomed to seeing him only in a classroom, realized that he not only could use the weapons in his hands, but that he would. And suddenly they respected him as they would respect, say, a burglar or a prominent kidnaper or a gang leader. He was raised far above the level of a mere mathematics professor. He became instantly a leader, and, by virtue of his weapons, even a ruler.

'As you see,' said Professor Minott evenly, 'I have anticipated the situation in which we find ourselves. I am prepared for it, to a certain extent. At any moment not only we, but the entire human race may be wiped out with a completeness of which you can form no idea. But there is also a chance of survival. And I intend to make the most of my survival if we do live.'

He looked steadily from one to another of the students who had followed him to explore the extraordinary appearance of a sequoia forest north of Fredericksburg.

'I know what has happened,' said Professor Minott. 'I know also what is likely to happen. And I know what I intend to do about it. Any of you who are prepared to follow me, say so. Any of you who object – well – I can't have mutinies! I'll shoot him!'

'But – professor,' said Blake nervously, 'we ought to get the girls home—'

'They will never go home,' said Professor Minott calmly. 'Neither will you, nor any of us. As soon as you're convinced that I'm quite ready to use these weapons, I'll tell you what's happened and what it means. I've been preparing for it for weeks.'

Tall trees rose around the party. Giant trees. Magnificent trees. They towered two hundred and fifty feet into the air, and their air of venerable calm was at once the most convincing evidence of their actuality, and the most improbable of all the things which had happened in the neighborhood of Fredericksburg, Virginia. The little group of people sat their horses affrightedly beneath the monsters of the forest. Minott regarded them estimatingly – these three young men and four girls, all students of Robinson College. Professor Minott was now no longer the faculty member in charge of a party of exploration, but a definitely ruthless leader.

At half past eight a.m. on June 5, 1935, the inhabitants of Fredericksburg had felt a curious, unanimous dizziness. It passed. The sun shone brightly. There seemed to be no noticeable change in any of the facts of everyday existence. But within an hour the sleepy little town was buzzing with excitement. The road to Washington – Route One on all road maps – ceased abruptly some three miles north. A colossal, a gigantic forest had appeared magically to block the way.

Telegraphic communication with Washington had ceased. Even the Washington broadcasting stations were no longer on the air. The trees of the extraordinary forest were tall beyond the experience of any human being in town. They looked like the photographs of the giant sequoias on the Pacific Coast, but – well, the thing was simply impossible.

In an hour and a half, Professor Minott had organized a

party of sightseers among the students. He seemed to pick his party with a queer definiteness of decision. Three young men and four girls. They would have piled into a rickety car owned by one of the boys, but Professor Minott negatived the idea.

'The road ends at the forest,' he said, smiling. 'I'd rather like to explore a magic forest. Suppose we ride horseback? I'll arrange for horses.'

In ten minutes the horses appeared. The girls had vanished to get into riding breeches or knickers. They noted appreciatively on their return that besides the saddles, the horses had saddlebags slung in place. Again Professor Minott smiled.

'We're exploring,' he said humorously. 'We must dress the part. Also, we'll probably want some lunch. And we can bring back specimens for the botanical lab to look over.'

They rode forth – the girls thrilled, the young men pleased and excited, and all of them just a little bit disappointed at finding themselves passed by motor cars which whizzed by them as all Fredericksburg went to look at the improbable forest ahead.

There were cars by the hundreds where the road abruptly ended. A crowd stared at the forest. Giant trees, their roots fixed firmly in the ground. Undergrowth here and there. Over it all, an aspect of peace and utter serenity – and permanence. The watching crowd hummed and buzzed with speculation, with talk. The thing they saw was impossible. It could not have happened. This forest could not possibly be real. They were regarding some sort of mirage.

But as the party of riders arrived, half a dozen men came out of the forest. They had dared to enter it. Now they returned, still incredulous of their own experience, bearing leaves and branches and one of them certain small berries unknown on the Atlantic coast.

A State police officer held up his hand as Professor Minott's party went toward the edge of the forest.

'Look here!' he said. 'We been hearin' funny noises in there. I'm stoppin' anybody else from goin' in until we know what's what.'

Professor Minott nodded. 'We'll be careful. I'm Professor Minott of Robinson College. We're going in after some botanical specimens. I have a revolver. We're all right.'

He rode ahead. The State policeman, without definite orders for authority, shrugged his shoulders and bent his efforts to the prevention of other attempts to explore. In minutes, the eight horses and their riders were out of sight.

That was now three hours past. For three hours, Professor Minott had led his charges a little south of northeast. In that time they saw no dangerous animals. They saw some – many – familiar plants. They saw rabbits in quantity, and once a slinking gray form which Tom Hunter, who was majoring in zoology, declared was a wolf. There are no wolves in the vicinity of Fredericksburg, but neither are there sequoias. And the party had seen no signs of human life, though Fredericksburg lies in farming country which is thickly settled.

In three hours the horses must have covered between twelve and fifteen miles, even through the timber. It was just after sighting a shaggy beast which was unquestionably a woodland buffalo – extinct east of the Rockies as early as 1820 – that young Blake protested uneasily against further travel.

'There's something awfully queer, sir,' he said awkwardly. 'I don't mind experimenting as much as you like, sir, but we've got the girls with us. If we don't start back pretty soon, we'll get in trouble with the dean.'

And then Minott drew his two revolvers and very calmly announced that none of them would ever go back. That he knew what had happened and what could be expected. And he added that he would explain as soon as they were convinced he would use his revolvers in case of a mutiny.

'Call us convinced now, sir,' said Blake.

He was a bit pale about the lips, but he hadn't flinched. In fact, he'd moved to be between Maida Haynes and the gun muzzle.

'We'd like very much to know how all these trees and plants, which ought to be three thousand miles away, happen to be growing in Virginia without any warning. Especially, sir, we'd like to know how it is that the topography underneath all this brand-new forest is the same. The hills trend the same way they used to, but everything that ever was on them has vanished, and something else is in its place.'

Minott nodded approvingly. 'Splendid, Blake!' he said warmly. 'Sound observation! I picked you because you're well spoken of in geology, even though there were – er – other reasons for leaving you behind. Let's go on over the next rise. Unless I'm mistaken, we should find the Potomac in view. Then I'll answer any questions you like. I'm afraid we've a good bit more of riding to do today.'

Reluctantly, the eight horses breasted the slope. They scrambled among underbrush. It was queer that in three hours they had seen not a trace of a road leading anywhere. But up at the top of the hill there was a road. It was a narrow, wandering cart track. Without a word, every one of the eight riders turned their horses to follow it. It meandered onward for perhaps a quarter of a mile. It dipped suddenly. And the Potomac lay before and below them.

Then seven of the eight riders exclaimed. There was a settlement upon the banks of the river. There were boats in harbor. There were other boats in view beyond, two beating down from the long reaches upstream, and three others coming painfully up from the direction of Chesapeake Bay. But neither the village nor the boats should have been upon the Potomac River.

The village was small and mud-walled. Tiny, blue-clad figures moved about the fields outside. The buildings, the curving lines of the roofs, and more especially the unmistakable outline of a sort of temple near the center of the fortified hamlet said these were Chinese. The boats in sight were junks, save that their sails were cloth instead of slatted bamboo. The fields outside the squat mud walls were cultivated in a fashion altogether alien. Near the river, where marsh flats would be normal along the Potomac, rice fields intensely worked spread out instead.

Then a figure appeared near by. Wide hat, wadded cotton-padded jacket, cotton trousers, and clogs – it was Chinese peasant incarnate, and all the more so when it turned a slant-eyed, terror-stricken face upon them and fled squawking. It left a monstrously heavy wooden yoke behind, from which dangled two buckets filled with berries it had gathered in the forest.

The riders stared. There was the Potomac. But a Chinese village nestled beside it, Chinese junks plied its waters.

'I – I think,' said Maida Haynes unsteadily, 'I – think I've – gone insane. Haven't I?'

Professor Minott shrugged. He looked disappointed but queerly resolute.

'No,' he said shortly. 'You're not mad. It just happens that the Chinese happened to colonize America first. It's been known that Chinese junks touched the American shore – the Pacific coast, of course – long before Columbus. Evidently they colonized it. They may have come all the way overland to the Atlantic, or maybe around by Panama. In any case, this is a Chinese continent now. This isn't what we want. We'll ride some more.'

The fleeing, squawking figure had been seen from the village. A huge, discordant gong began to sound. Figures fled toward the walls from the fields round about. The popping of firecrackers began, with a chorus of most intimidating yells.

'Come on!' said Minott sharply. 'We'd better move!'

He wheeled his horse about and started off at a canter. By instinct, since he was the only one who seemed to have any definite idea what to do, the others flung after him.

And as they rode, suddenly the horses staggered. The humans on them felt a queer, queasy vertigo. It lasted only for a second, but Minott paled a little.

'Now we'll see what's happened,' he said composedly. 'The odds are still fair, but I'd rather have had things stay as they were until we'd tried a few more places.'

IV

That same queasy vertigo affected the staring crowd at the end of the road leading north from Fredericksburg. For perhaps a second they felt an unearthly illness, which even blurred their vision. Then they saw clearly again. And in an instant they were babbling in panic, starting their motor cars in terror, some of them fleeing on foot.

The sequoia forest had vanished. In its place was a dreary waste of glittering white; stumpy trees buried under snow; rolling ground covered with a powdery, glittering stuff.

In minutes dense fog shut off the view, as the warm air of a Virginia June morning was chilled by that frigid coating. But in minutes, too, the heavy snow began to melt. The cars fled away along the concrete road, and behind them an expanding belt of fog spread out – and the little streams and runlets filled with a sudden surplus of water, and ran more swiftly, and rose.

The eight riders were every one very pale. Even Minott seemed shaken but no less resolute when he drew rein.

'I imagine you will all be satisfied now,' he said composedly. 'Blake, you're the geologist of the party. Doesn't the shore line there look familiar?'

Blake nodded. He was very white indeed. He pointed to the stream.

'Yes. The falls, too. This is the site of Fredericksburg, sir, where we were this morning. There is where the main bridge was – or will be. The main highway to Richmond should run' – he licked his lips – 'it should run where that very big oak tree is standing. The Princess Anne Hotel should be on the side of that hill. I – I would say, sir, that somehow we've gone back in time or else forward into the future. It sounds insane, but I've been trying to figure it out—'

Minott nodded coolly. 'Very good! This is the site of Fredericksburg, to be sure. But we have not traveled forward or back in time. I hope that you noticed where we came out of the sequoia forest. There seems to be a sort of fault along that line, which it may be useful to remember.' He paused. 'We're not in the past or the future, Blake. We've traveled sidewise, in a sort of oscillation from one time path to another. We happen to be in a – well, in a part of time where Fredericksburg has never been built, just as a little while since we were where the Chinese occupy the American continent. I think we better have lunch.'

He dismounted. The four girls tended to huddle together. Lucy Blair's teeth chattered.

Blake moved to their horses' heads. 'Don't get rattled,' he said urgently. 'We're here, wherever it is. Professor Minott is going to explain things in a minute. Since he knows what's what, we're in no danger. Climb off your horses and let's eat. I'm hungry as a bear. Come on, Maida!'

Maida Haynes dismounted. She managed a rather shaky smile. 'I'm – afraid of – him,' she said in a whisper. 'More than – anything else. Stay close to me, please!'

Blake frowned.

Minott said dryly: 'Look in your saddlebags and you'll find sandwiches. Also you'll find firearms. You young men had better arm yourselves. Since there's now no conceivable hope of getting back to the world we know, I think you can be trusted with weapons.'

Blake stared at him, then silently investigated his own saddle-bags. He found two revolvers, with what seemed an abnormally large supply of cartridges. He found a mass of paper, which turned out to be books with their cardboard backs torn off. He glanced professionally at the revolvers and slipped them in his pockets. He put back the books.

'I appoint you second in command, Blake,' said Minott, more dryly than before. 'You understand nothing, but you wait to understand. I made no mistake in choosing you despite my reasons for leaving you behind. Sit down and I'll tell you what happened.'

With a grunt and a puffing noise, a small black bear broke cover and fled across a place where only that morning a highly elaborate filling station had stood. The party started, then relaxed. The girls suddenly started to giggle foolishly, almost hysterically. Minott bit calmly into a sandwich and said pleasantly:

'I shall have to talk mathematics to you, but I'll try to make it more palatable than my classroom lectures have been. You see, everything that has happened can only be explained in terms of mathematics, and more especially certain concepts in mathematical physics. You young ladies and gentlemen being college men and women, I shall have to phrase things very simply, as for ten-year-old children. Hunter, you're staring. If you actually see something, such as an Indian, shoot at him and he'll run away. The probabilities are that he never heard the report of a firearm. We're not on the Chinese continent now.'

Hunter gasped, and fumbled at his saddlebags. While he got out the revolvers, Minott went on imperturbably:

'There has been an upheaval of nature, which still continues. But instead of a shaking and jumbling of earth and rocks, there has been a shaking and jumbling of space and time. I go back to first principles. Time is a dimension. The past is one extension of it, the future is the other, just as east is one extension of a more familiar dimension and west is its opposite.

'But we ordinarily think of time as a line, a sort of tunnel, perhaps. We do not make that error in the dimensions about which we think daily. For example, we know that Annapolis, King George courthouse, and – say – Norfolk are all to the eastward of us. But we know that in order to reach any of them, as a destination, we would have to go not only east but north or south in addition. In imaginative travels into the future, however, we never think in such a common-sense fashion. We assume that the future is a line instead of a co-ordinate, a path instead of a direction. We assume that if we travel to futureward there is but one possible destination. And that is as absurd as it would be to ignore the possibility of traveling to eastward in any other line than due east, forgetting that there is northeast and southeast and a large number of intermediate points.'

Young Blake said slowly: 'I follow you, sir, but it doesn't seem to bear—'

'On our problem? But it does!' Minott smiled, showing his teeth. He bit into his sandwich again. 'Imagine that I come to a fork in a road – I flip a coin to determine which fork I shall take. Whichever route I follow, I shall encounter certain landmarks and certain adventures. But they will not be the same, whether landmarks or adventures.

'In choosing between the forks of the road I choose not only between two sets of landmarks I could encounter, but between two sets of events. I choose between paths, not only on the surface of the earth, but in time. And as those paths upon earth may lead to two different cities, so those paths in the future may lead to two entirely different fates. On one of them may lie opportunities for riches. On the other may lie the most prosaic of hit-and-run accidents which will leave me a mangled corpse, not only upon one fork of a highway in the State of Virginia, but upon one fork of a highway in time.

'In short, I am pointing out that there is more than one future we can encounter, and with more or less absence of deliberation we choose among them. But the futures we fail to encounter, upon the roads we do not take, are just as real as the landmarks upon those roads. We never see them, but we freely admit their existence.'

Again it was Blake who protested: 'All this is interesting enough, sir, but still I don't see how it applies to our present situation.'

Minott said impatiently: 'Don't you see that if such a state of things exists in the future, that it must also have existed in the past? We talk of three dimensions and one present and one future. There is a theoretic necessity – a mathematical necessity – for assuming more than one future. There are an indefinite number of possible futures, any one of which we would encounter if we took the proper "forks" in time.

'There are any number of destinations to eastward. There are any number to futureward. Start a hundred miles west and come eastward, choosing your paths on earth at random, as you do in time. You may arrive here. You may arrive to the north or south of this spot, and still be east of your starting point. Now start a hundred years back instead of a hundred miles west.'

Groping, Blake said fumblingly: 'I think you're saying, sir, that – well, as there must be any number of futures, there must have been any number of pasts besides those written down in our histories. And – and it would follow that there are any number of what you might call "presents".'

Minott gulped down the last of his sandwich and nodded. 'Precisely. And today's convulsion of nature has jumbled them and still upsets them from time to time. The Northmen once colonized America. In the sequence of events which mark the pathway of our own ancestors through time, that colony failed. But along another path through time that colony throve and flourished. The Chinese reached the shores of California. In the path our ancestors followed through time, nothing developed from the fact. But this morning we touched upon the pathway in which they colonized and conquered the continent, though from the fear that one peasant we saw displayed, they have not wiped out the Indians.

'Somewhere the Roman Empire still exists, and may not improbably rule America as it once ruled Britain. Somewhere, not impossibly, the conditions causing the glacial period still obtain and Virginia is buried under a mass of snow. Somewhere even the Carboniferous period may exist. Or to come more closely to the present we know, somewhere there is a path through time in which Pickett's charge at Gettysburg went desperately home, and the Confederate States of America is now an independent nation with a heavily fortified border and a chip-on-the-shoulder attitude toward the United States.'

Blake alone had asked questions, but the entire party had been listening open-mouthed.

Now Maida Haynes said: 'But – Professor Minott, where are we now?'

'We are probably,' said Minott, smiling, 'in a path of time in which America has never been discovered by white men.

That isn't a very satisfactory state of things. We're going to look for something better. We wouldn't be comfortable in wigwams, with skins for clothing. So we shall hunt for a more congenial environment. We will have some weeks in which to do our searching, I think. Unless, of course, all space and time are wiped out by the cause of our predicament.'

Tom Hunter stirred uncomfortably. 'We haven't traveled backward or forward in time, then?'

'No,' repeated Minott. He got to his feet. 'That odd nausea we felt seems to be caused by travel sidewise in time. It's the symptom of a time oscillation. We'll ride on and see what other worlds await us. We're a rather well-qualified party for this sort of exploration. I chose you for your trainings. Hunter, zoology. Blake, engineering and geology. Harris' – he nodded to the rather undersized young man, who flushed at being noticed – 'Harris is quite a competent chemist, I understand. Miss Ketterling is a capable botanist. Miss Blair—'

Maida Haynes rose slowly. 'You anticipated all this, Professor Minott, and yet you brought us into it. You – you said we'll never get back home. Yet you deliberately arranged it. What – what was your motive? What did you do it for?'

Minott climbed into the saddle. He smiled, but there was bitterness in his smile. 'In the world we know,' he told her, 'I was a professor of mathematics in a small and unconsidered college. I had absolutely no chance of ever being more than a professor of mathematics in a small and unconsidered college. In this world I am, at least, the leader of a group of reasonably intelligent young people. In our saddlebags are arms and ammunition and – more important – books of reference for our future activities. We shall hunt for and find a world in which our technical knowledge is at a premium. We shall live in that world – if all time and space is not destroyed – and use our knowledge.'

Maida Haynes said: 'But again – what for?'

'To conquer it!' said Minott in sudden fierceness. 'To conquer it! We eight shall rule a world as no world has been ruled since time began! I promise you that when we find the environment I seek, you will have wealth by millions, slaves by thousands, every luxury, and all the power human beings could desire!'

Blake said evenly: 'And you, sir? What will you have?'

'Most power of all,' said Minott steadily. 'I shall be the emperor of the world! And also' – his tone changed indescribably as he glanced at Maida – 'also I shall have a certain other possession that I wish.'

He turned his back to them and rode off to lead the way. Maida Haynes was deathly pale as she rode close to Blake. Her hand closed convulsively upon his arm.

'Jerry!' she whispered. 'I'm – frightened!'

And Blake said steadily: 'Don't worry! I'll kill him first!'

V

The ferryboat from Berkeley plowed valorously through the fog. Its whistle howled mournfully at the regulation intervals.

Up in the pilot house, the skipper said confidentially: 'I tell you, I had the funniest feelin' of my life, just now. I was dizzy an' sick all over, like I was seasick an' drunk all at the same time.'

The mate said abstractedly: 'I had somethin' like that a little while ago. Somethin' we ate, prob'ly. Say, that's funny!'

'What?'

'Was a lot o' traffic in the harbor just now, whistlin'. I ain't heard a whistle for minutes. Listen!'

Both men strained their ears. There was the rhythmic shudder of the vessel, itself a sound produced by the engines. There were fragmentary voice noises from the passenger deck below. There was the wash of water by the ferryboat's bow. There was nothing else. Nothing at all.

'Funny!' said the skipper.

'Damn funny!' agreed the mate.

The ferryboat went on. The fog cut down all visibility to a radius of perhaps two hundred feet.

'Funniest thing I ever saw!' said the skipper worriedly. He reached for the whistle cord and the mournful bellow of the horn resounded. 'We're near our slip, though. I wish—'

With a little chugging, swishing sound a steam launch came out of the mist. It sheered off, the men in it staring blankly at the huge bulk of the ferry. It made a complete circuit of the big, clumsy craft. Then someone stood up and bellowed unintelligibly in the launch. He bellowed again. He was giving an order. He pointed to the flag at the stern of the launch – it was an unfamiliar flag – and roared furiously.

'What the hell's the matter with that guy?' wondered the mate.

A little breeze blew suddenly. The fog began to thin. The faintly brighter spot which was the sun overhead grew bright indeed. Faint sunshine struggled through the fog bank. The wind drove the fog back before it, and the bellowing man in the steam launch grew purple with rage as his orders went unheeded.

Then, quite abruptly, the last wisps of vapor blew away. San Francisco stood revealed. But – San Francisco? This was not San Francisco! It was a wooden city, a small city, a dirty city with narrow streets and gas street lamps and four monstrous, barracklike edifices fronting the harbor. Nob Hill stood, but it was barren of dwellings. And—

'Damn!' said the mate of the ferryboat.

He was staring at a colossal mass of masonry, foursquare and huge, which rose to a gigantic spiral fluted dome. A strange and alien flag fluttered in the breeze above certain buildings. Figures moved in the streets. There were motor cars, but they were clumsy and huge.

The mate's eyes rested upon a horse-drawn carriage. It was drawn by three horses abreast, and they were either so trained or so checkreined that the two outer horses' heads were arched outward in the fashion of Tsarist Russia.

But that was natural enough. When an interpreter could be found, the mate and skipper were savagely abused for entering the harbor of Novo Skevsky without paying due heed to the ordinances in force by the ukase of the Tsar Alexis of all the Russias. These rules, they learned, were enforced with special rigor in all the Russian territory in America, from Alaska on south.

The boy ran shouting up to the village. 'Hey, grandpa! Hey, grandpa! Lookit the birds!' He pointed as he ran.

A man looked idly, and stood transfixed. A woman stopped, and stared. Lake Superior glowed bluely off to westward, and the little village most often turned its eyes in that direction. Now, though, as the small boy ran shouting of what he had seen, men stared, women marveled, and children ran and shouted and whooped in the instinctive excitement of childhood at anything which entrances grown-ups.

Over the straggly pine forests birds were coming. They came in great dark masses. Not by dozens, or by hundreds, or even by thousands. They came in millions, in huge dark clouds which obscured the sky. There were two huge flights in sight at the boy's first shouting. There were six in view before he had reached his home and was panting a demand that his elders come and look. And there were others, incredible numbers of others, sweeping onward straight over the village.

Dusk fell abruptly as the first flock passed overhead. The whirring of wings was loud. It made people raise their voices as they asked each other what such birds could possibly be. Daylight again, and again darkness as the flocks poured on. The size of each flock was to be measured not in feet or yards, but in miles of front. Two, three miles of birds, flying steadily in a single enormous mass some four miles deep. Another such mass, and another, and another.

'What are they, grandpa? There must be millions of 'em!'

Somewhere, a shotgun went off. Small things dropped from the sky. Another gunshot, and another. A rain of bird shot went up from the village into the mass of whirring wings. And crazily careening small bodies fell down among the houses.

Grandpa examined one of them, smoothing its rumpled plumage. He exclaimed. He gasped in excitement. 'It's a wild pigeon! What they used to call passenger pigeons! Back in '78 there was these birds by billions. Folks said a billion was killed in Michigan that one year! But they're gone now. They're gone like the buffalo. There ain't any more.'

The sky was dark with birds above him. A flock four miles wide and three miles long made lights necessary in the village. The air was filled with the sound of wings. The passenger pigeon had returned to a continent from which it had been absent for almost fifty years.

Flocks of passenger pigeons flew overhead in thick, dark masses equaling those seen by Audubon in 1813, when he computed the pigeons in flight above Kentucky at hundreds of billions in number. In flocks that were innumerable they flew to westward. The sun set, and still the air was filled with the sound of their flying. For hours after darkness fell, the whirring of wings continued without ceasing.

VI

A great open fire licked at the rocks against which it had been built. The horses cropped uneasily at herbage near by. The smell of fat meat cooking was undeniably savory, but one of the girls blubbered gustily on a bed of leaves. Harris tended the cookery. Tom Hunter brought wood. Blake stood guard a little beyond the firelight, revolvers ready, staring off into the blackness. Professor Minott pored over a topographical map of Virginia. Maida Haynes tried to comfort the blubbering girl.

'Supper's ready,' said Harris. He made even that announcement seem somehow shy and apologetic.

Minott put down his map. Tom Hunter began to cut great chunks of steaming meat from the haunch of venison. He put them on slabs of bark and began to pass them around. Minott reached out his hand and took one of them. He ate with obvious appetite. He seemed to have abandoned his preoccupation the instant he laid down his map. He was displaying the qualities of a capable leader.

'Hunter,' he observed, 'after you've eaten that stuff, you might relieve Blake. We'll arrange reliefs for the rest of the night. By the way, you men mustn't forget to wind your watches. We'll need to rate them, ultimately.'

Hunter gulped down his food and moved out to Blake's hiding place. They exchanged low-toned words. Blake came back to the fire. He took the food Harris handed him and began to eat it. He looked at the blubbering girl on the bed of leaves.

'She's just scared,' said Minott. 'Barely slit the skin on her arm. But it is upsetting for a senior at Robinson College to be wounded by a flint arrowhead.'

Blake nodded. 'I heard some noises off in the darkness,' he said curtly. 'I'm not sure, but my impression was that I was being stalked. And I thought I heard a human voice.'

'We may be watched,' admitted Minott. 'But we're out of the path of time in which those Indians tried to ambush us. If any of them follow, they're too bewildered to be very dangerous.'

'I hope so,' said Blake.

His manner was devoid of cordiality, yet there was no exception to be taken to it. Professor Minott had deliberately got the party into a predicament from which there seemed to be no possibility of escape. He had organized it to get it into just that predicament. He was unquestionably the leader of the party, despite his action. Blake made no attempt to undermine his leadership.

But Blake himself had some qualifications as a leader, young as he was. Perhaps the most promising of them was the fact that he made no attempt to exercise his talents until he knew as much as Minott of what was to be looked for, what was to be expected.

He listened sharply and then said: 'I think we've digested your lesson of this morning, sir. But how long is this scrambling of space and time to continue? We left Fredericksburg and rode to the Potomac. It was Chinese territory. We rode back to Fredericksburg, and it wasn't there. Instead, we encountered

Indians who let loose a flight of arrows at us and wounded Bertha Ketterling in the arm. We were nearly out of range at the time, though.'

'They were scared,' said Minott. 'They'd never seen horses before. Our white skins probably upset them, too. And then our guns, and the fact that I killed one, should have chased them off.'

'But – what happened to Fredericksburg? We rode away from it. Why couldn't we ride back?'

'The scrambling process has kept up,' said Minott dryly. 'You remember that queer vertigo? We've had it several times today, and every time, as I see it, there's been an oscillation of the earth we happened to be on. Hm! Look!'

He got up and secured the map over which he had been poring. He brought it back and pointed to a heavy penciled line. 'Here's a map of Virginia in our time. The Chinese continent appeared just about three miles north of Fredericksburg. The line of demarcation was, I consider, the line along which the giant sequoias appeared. While in the Chinese time we felt that giddiness and rode back toward Fredericksburg. We came out of the sequoia forest at the same spot as before. I made sure of it. But the continent of our time was no longer there.

'We rode east and – whether you noticed it or not – before we reached the border of King George County there was another abrupt change in the vegetation – from a pine country to oaks and firs, which are not exactly characteristic of this part of the world in our time. We saw no signs of any civilization. We turned south, and ran into that heavy fog and the snow beyond it. Evidently, there's a section of a time path in which Virginia is still subject to a glacial climate.'

Blake nodded. He listened again. Then he said:

'You've three sides of an – an island of time marked there.'

'Just so,' agreed Minott. 'Exactly! In the scrambling process, the oscillating process, there seem to be natural "faults" in the surface of the earth. Relatively large areas seem to shift back and forth as units from one time path to another. In my own mind, I've likened them to elevators with many stories.

'We were on the Fredericksburg "elevator", or that section of our time path, when it shifted to another time. We rode off it onto the Chinese continent. While there, the section we started from shifted again, to another time altogether. When we rode back to where it had been – well, the town of Fredericksburg was in another time path altogether.'

Blake said sharply: 'Listen!'

A dull mutter sounded far to the north. It lasted for an instant and died away. There was a crashing of bushes near by and a monstrous animal stepped alertly into the firelight. It was an elk, but such an elk! It was a giant, a colossal creature. One of the girls cried out affrightedly, and it turned and crashed away into the underbrush.

'There are no elk in Virginia,' said Minott dryly.

Blake said sharply again: 'Listen!'

Again that dull muttering to the north. It grew louder, now. It was an airplane motor. It increased in volume from a dull mutter to a growl, from a growl to a roar. Then the plane shot overhead, the navigation lights on its wings glowing brightly. It banked steeply and returned. It circled overhead, with a queer effect of helplessness. And then suddenly it dived down.

'An aviator from our time,' said Blake, staring toward the sound. 'He saw our fire. He's going to try to make a crash landing in the dark.'

The motor cut off. An instant in which there was only the crackling of the fire and the whistling of wind around gliding surfaces off there in the night. Then a terrific thrashing of branches. A crash—

Then a flare of flame, a roaring noise, and the lurid yellow of gasoline flames spouting skyward.

'Stay here!' snapped Blake. He was on his feet in an instant. 'Harris, Professor Minott! Somebody has to stay with the girls! I'll get Hunter and go help!'

He plunged off into the darkness, calling to Hunter. The two of them forced their way through the underbrush. Minott scowled and got out his revolvers. Still scowling, he slipped out of the firelight and took up the guard duty Hunter had abandoned.

A gasoline tank exploded, off there in the darkness. The glare of the fire grew intolerably vivid. The sound of the two young men racing through undergrowth became fainter and died away.

A long time passed – a very long time. Then, very far away, the sound of thrashing bushes could be heard again. The gasoline flare dulled and dimmed. Figures came slowly back. They moved as if they were carrying something very heavy. They stopped beyond the glow of light from the camp fire. Then Blake and Hunter reappeared, alone.

'He's dead,' said Blake curtly. 'Luckily, he was flung clear of the crash before the gas tanks caught. He came back to consciousness for a couple of minutes before he – died. Our fire was the only sign of human life he'd seen in hours. We brought him over here. We'll bury him in the morning.'

There was silence. Minott's scowl was deep and savage as he came back to the firelight.

'What – what did he say?' asked Maida Haynes.

'He left Washington at five this afternoon,' said Blake shortly. 'By our time, or something like it. All of Virginia across the Potomac vanished at four thirty, and virgin forest took its place. He went out to explore. At the end of an hour he came back, and Washington was gone. In its place was a fog bank, with snow underneath. He followed the Potomac down and saw palisaded homesteads with long, oared ships drawn up on shore.'

'Vikings, Norsemen!' said Minott in satisfaction.

'He didn't land. He swept on down, following the edge of the bay. He looked for Baltimore. Gone! Once, he's sure, he saw a city, but he was taken sick at about that time and when he recovered, it had vanished. He was heading north again and his gasoline was getting low when he saw our fire. He tried for a crash landing. He'd no flares with him. He crashed – and died.'

'Poor fellow!' said Maida shakenly.

'The point is,' said Blake, 'that Washington was in our present time at about four thirty today. We've got a chance, though a slim one, of getting back! We've got to get the edge of one of those blocks that go swinging through time, the edge of what Professor Minott calls a "time fault", and watch it! When the shifts come, we explore as quickly as we can. We've no great likelihood, perhaps, of getting back exactly to our own period, but we can get nearer to it than we are now! Professor Minott said somewhere the Confederacy exists. Even that, among people of our own race and speaking our own language, would be better than to be marooned forever among Indians, or among Chinese or Norsemen.'

Minott said harshly: 'Blake, we'd better have this out right now! I give the orders in this party! You jumped quickly when that plane crashed, and you gave orders to Harris and to me. I let you get away with it, but we can have but one leader. I am that leader! See you remember it!'

Blake swung about. Minott had a revolver bearing on his body.

'And you are making plans for a return to our time!' he went on savagely. 'I won't have it! The odds are still that we'll all be killed. But if I do live, I mean to take advantage of it. And my plans do not include a return to a professorship of mathematics at Robinson College.'

'Well?' said Blake coolly. 'What of it, sir?'

'Just this! I'm going to take your revolvers. I'm going to make the plans and give the orders hereafter. We are going to look for the time path in which a Viking civilization thrives in America. We'll find it, too, because these disturbances will last for weeks yet. And once we find it, we will settle down among those Norsemen, and when space and time are stable again I shall begin the formation of my empire! And you will obey orders or you'll be left afoot while the rest of us go on to my destiny!'

Blake said very quietly indeed: 'Perhaps, sir, we'd all prefer to be left to our own destinies rather than be merely the tools by which you attain to yours.'

Minott stared at him an instant. His lips tensed. 'It is a pity,' he said coldly. 'I could have used your brains, Blake. But I can't have mutiny. I shall have to shoot you.'

His revolver came up remorselessly.

VII

To determine the cause of various untoward events, the British Academy of Sciences was in extraordinary session. Its members were weary; bleary-eyed, but still conscious of their dignity and the importance of their task. A venerable, whiskered physicist spoke with fitting definiteness and solemnity.

'And so, gentleman, I see nothing more that remains to be said. The extraordinary events of the past hours seem to follow from certain facts about our own closed space. The gravitational fields of 10^{79} particles of matter will close space about such an aggregation. No cosmos can be larger. No cosmos can be smaller. And if we envision the creation of such a cosmos, we will observe its galaxies vanish at the instant the 10^{79}th particle adds its own mass to those which were present before it.

'However, the fact that space has closed about such a cosmos does not imply its annihilation. It means merely its separation from its original space, the isolation of itself in space and time because of the curvature of space due to its gravitational field. And if we assume the existence of more than one area of closed space, we assume in some sense the existence of a hyper-space separating the closed spaces; hyper-spatial coordinates which mark their relative hyper-spatial positions; hyper-spatial—'

A gentleman with even longer and whiter whiskers than the speaker said in a loud and decided voice: 'Fiddlesticks! Stuff and nonsense!'

The speaker paused. He glared. 'Sir! Do you refer—'

'I do!' said the gentleman with the longer and whiter whiskers. 'It is stuff and nonsense! Next you'd be saying that in this hyper-space of yours the closed spaces would be subject to hyper-laws, revolve about each other in hyper-orbits regulated by hyper-gravitation, and undoubtedly at times there would be hyper-earth tides or hyper-collisions, producing decidedly hyper-catastrophes.'

'Such, sir,' said the whiskered gentleman on the rostrum, quivering with indignation, 'such is the fact, sir!'

'Then the fact,' rejoined the scientist with the longer and whiter whiskers, 'sir, makes me sick!'

And as if to prove it, he reeled. But he was not alone in reeling. The entire venerable assembly shuddered in abrupt, nauseating vertigo. And then the British Academy of Sciences adjourned without formality and in a panic. It ran away. Because abruptly there was no longer a rostrum nor an end to its assembly hall. Where their speaker had been was open air. In the open air was a fire. About the fire were certain brutish figures incredibly resembling the whiskered scientists who fled from them. They roared at the fleeing, venerable men. Snarling, wielding crude clubs, they plunged into the hall of the British Academy of Sciences. It is known that they caught one person – a biologist of highly eccentric views. It is believed that they ate him.

But it has long been surmised that some, at least, of the extinct species of humanity, such as the Piltdown and Neanderthal men, were cannibals. If in some pathway of time they happened to exterminate their more intelligent rivals – if somewhere *pithecanthropus erectus* survives and *homo sapiens* does not – well, in that pathway of time cannibalism is the custom of society.

VIII

With a gasp, Maida Haynes flung herself before Blake. But Harris was even quicker. Apologetic and shy, he had just finished cutting a smoking piece of meat from the venison haunch. He threw it swiftly, and the searing mass of stuff flung

Minott's hand aside at the same instant that it burned it horribly.

Blake was on his feet, his gun out. 'If you pick up that gun, sir,' he said rather breathlessly but with unquestionable sincerity, 'I'll put a bullet through your arm!'

Minott swore. He retrieved the weapon with his left hand and thrust it in his pocket. 'You young fool!' he snapped. 'I'd no intention of shooting you. I did intend to scare you thoroughly. Harris, you're an ass! Maida, I shall discuss your action later. The worst punishment I could give the lot of you would be to leave you to yourselves.'

He stalked out of the firelight and off into the darkness. Something like consternation came upon the group. The glow of fire where the plane had crashed flickered fitfully. The base of the dull red light seemed to widen a little.

'That's the devil!' said Hunter uneasily. 'He does know more about this stuff than we do. If he leaves us we're messed up!'

'We are,' agreed Blake grimly. 'And perhaps if he doesn't.'

Lucy Blair said: 'I – I'll go and talk to him. He – he used to be nice to me in class. And – and his hand must hurt terribly. It's burned.'

She moved away from the fire, a long and angular shadow going on before her.

Minott's voice came sharply: 'Go back! There's something moving out here!'

Instantly after, his revolver flashed. A howl arose, and the weapon flashed again and again. Then there were many crashings. Figures fled.

Minott came back to the firelight, scornfully. 'Your leadership is at fault, Blake,' he commented sardonically. 'You forgot about a guard. And you were the man who thought he heard voices! They've run away now, though. Indians, of course.'

Lucy Blair said hesitantly: 'Could I – could I do something for your hand? It's burned—'

'What can you do?' he asked angrily.

'There's some fat,' she told him. 'Indians used to dress wounds with bear fat. I suppose deer fat would do as well.'

He permitted her to dress the burn, though it was far from a serious one. She begged handkerchiefs from the others to complete the job. There was distinct uneasiness all about the camp fire. This was no party of adventurers, prepared for anything. It had started as an outing of undergraduates.

Minott scowled as Lucy Blair worked on his hand. Harris looked as apologetic as possible, because he had made the injury. Bertha Ketterling blubbered – less noisily, now, because nobody paid her any attention. Blake frowned meditatively at the fire. Maida Haynes tried uneasily not to seem conscious of the fact that she was in some sense – though no mention had been made of it – a bone of contention.

The horses moved uneasily. Bertha Ketterling sneezed. Maida felt her eyes smarting. She was the first one to see the spread of the blaze started by the gas tanks of the airplane. Her cry of alarm roused the others.

The plane had crashed a good mile from the camp fire. The blazing of its tanks had been fierce but brief. The burning of the wings and chassis fabric had been short, as well. The fire had died down to seeming dull embers. But there were more than embers ablaze out there now.

The fire had died down, to be sure, but only that it might spread among thick and tangled underbrush. It had spread widely on the ground before some climbing vine, blazing, carried flames up to resinous pine branches overhead. A small but steady wind was blowing. And as Maida looked off to see the source of the smoke which stung her eyes, one tall tree was blazing, a long line of angry red flames crept along the ground, and then at two more, three more, then at a dozen points bright fire roared upward toward the sky.

The horses snorted and reared.

Minott snapped: 'Harris, Harris! Get the horses! Hunter, see that the girls get mounted, and quickly!'

He pointedly gave Blake no orders. He pored intently over his map as more trees and still more caught fire and blazed upward. He stuffed it in his pocket. Blake calmly rescued the haunch of venison, and when Minott sprang into the saddle among the snorting, scared horses, Blake was already by Maida Haynes' side, ready to go.

'We ride in pairs,' said Minott curtly. 'A man and a girl. You men, look after them. I've a flashlight. I'll go ahead. We'll hit the Rappahannock River sooner or later, if we don't get around the fire first – and if we can keep ahead of it.'

They topped a little hillock and saw more of the extent of their danger. In a half mile of spreading, the fire had gained three times as much breadth. And to their right the fire even then roared in among the trees of a forest so thick as to be jungle. The blaze fairly raced through it as if the fire made its own wind; which in fact it did. To their left it crackled fiercely in underbrush which, as they fled, blazed higher.

And then, as if to add mockery to their very real danger, a genuinely brisk breeze sprang up suddenly. Sparks and blazing bits of leaves, fragments of ash and small, unsubstantial coals began to fall among them. Bertha Ketterling yelped suddenly as a tiny live coal touched the flesh of her cheek. Harris' horse squealed and kicked as something singed it. They galloped madly ahead. Trees rose about them. The white beam of Minott's flashlight seemed almost ludicrous in the fierce red glare from behind, but at least it showed the way.

IX

Something large and dark and clumsy lumbered cumbersomely into the space between Grady's statue and the post-office building. The arc lights showed it clearly, and it was not anything which should be wandering in the streets of Atlanta, Georgia, at any hour of the day or night. A taxicab chauffeur saw it and nearly tore off a wheel in turning around to get away. A policeman saw it, and turned very pale as he grabbed at his beat telephone to report it. But there had been too many queer things happening this day for him to suspect his own sanity, and the *Journal* had printed too much news from elsewhere for him to disbelieve his own eyes.

The thing was monstrous, reptilian, loathesome. It was eighty feet long, of which at least fifty was head and tail and the rest flabby-fleshed body. It may have weighed twenty-five or thirty tons, but its head was not much larger than that of a large horse. That tiny head swung about stupidly. The thing was bewildered. It put down a colossal foot, and water gushed up from a broken water main beneath the pavement. The thing did not notice. It moved vaguely, exhaling a dank and musty odor.

The clang of police-emergency cars and the scream of fire-engine sirens filled the air. An ambulance flashed into view – and was struck by a balancing sweep of the mighty tail. The ambulance careened and crashed.

The thing uttered a plaintive cry, ignoring the damage its tail had caused. The sound was like that of a bleat, a thousand times multiplied. It peered ceaselessly around, seeming to feel trapped by the tall buildings about it, but it was too stupid to retrace its steps for escape.

Somebody screamed in the distance as police cars and fire engines reached the spot where the first thing swayed and peered and moved in quest of escape. Two other things, smaller than the first, came lumbering after it. Like it, they had monstrous bodies and disproportionately tiny heads. One of them blundered stupidly into a hook-and-ladder truck. Truck and beast went down, and the beast bleated like the first.

Then some fool began to shoot. Other fools joined in. Steel-jacketed bullets poured into the mountains of reptilian flesh. Police sub-machine guns raked the monsters. Those guns were held by men of great daring, who could not help noting the utter stupidity of the things out of the great swamp which had appeared where Inman Park used to be.

The bullets stung. They hurt. The three beasts bleated and tried bewilderedly and very clumsily to escape. The largest tried to climb a five-story building, and brought it down in sheer wreckage.

Before the last of them was dead – or rather, before it ceased to move its great limbs, because the tail moved jerkily for a long time and its heart was still beating spasmodically when loaded on a city dump cart next day – before the last of them was dead they had made sheer chaos of three blocks of business buildings in the heart of Atlanta, had killed seventeen men, and the best testimony is that they made not one attempt to fight. Their whole and only thought was to escape. The destruction they wrought and the deaths they caused were due to their clumsiness and stupidity.

X

The leading horses floundered horribly. They sank to their fetlocks in something soft and very spongy. Bertha Ketterling squawked in terror as her mount's motion changed.

Blake said crisply in the blackness: 'It feels like plowed ground. Better use the light again, Professor Minott.'

The sky behind them glowed redly. The forest fire still trailed them. For miles of front, now, it shot up sparks and flame and a harsh red glare which illumined the clouds of its own smoke.

The flashlight stabbed at the earth. The ground was plowed. It was softened by the hands of men. Minott kept the light on as little gasps of thankfulness arose.

Then he said sardonically: 'Do you know what this crop is? It's lentils. Are lentils grown in Virginia? Perhaps! We'll see what sort of men these may happen to be.'

He swung to follow the line of the furrows.

Tom Hunter said miserably: 'If that's plowed ground, it's a damn shallow furrow. A one-horse plow'd throw up more dirt than that.'

A light glowed palely in the distance. Every person in the party saw it at the same instant. As if by instinct, the head of every horse swerved for it.

'We'll want to be careful,' said Blake quietly. 'These may be Chinese, too.'

The light was all of a mile distant. They moved over the plowed ground cautiously.

Suddenly the hoofs of Lucy Blair's horse rang on stone. The noise was startlingly loud. Other horses, following hers, clattered thunderously. Minott flashed down the light again. Dressed stone. Cut stone. A roadway built of dressed-stone blocks, some six or eight feet wide. Then one of the horses shivered and snorted. It pranced agitatedly, edging away from something on the road. Minott swept the flashlight beam along the narrow way.

'The only race,' he said dryly, 'that ever built roads like this was the Romans. They made their military roads like this. But they didn't discover America that we know of.'

The beam touched something dark. It came back and steadied. One of the girls uttered a stifled exclamation. The beam showed dead men. One was a man with a shield and sword and a helmet such as the soldiers of ancient Rome are pictured as having worn. He was dead. Half his head had been blown off. Lying on top of him there was a man in a curious gray uniform. He had died of a sword wound.

The beam searched around. More bodies. Many Roman-accoutered figures. Four or five men in what looked remarkably like the uniform that might be worn by soldiers of the Confederate Army – if a Confederate Army could be supposed to exist.

'There's been fighting,' said Blake composedly. 'I guess somebody from the Confederacy – that time path, say – started to explore what must have seemed a damned strange happening. And these Romans – if they are Romans – jumped them.'

Something came shambling through the darkness. Minott threw the flash beam upon it. It was human, yes. But it was three parts naked, and it was chained, and it had been beaten horribly, and there were great sores upon its body from other beatings. It was bony and emaciated. The insensate ferocity of sheer despair marked it. It was brutalized by its sufferings until it was just human, barely human, and nothing more.

It squinted at the light, too dull of comprehension to be afraid.

Then Minott spoke, and at his words it groveled in the dirt. Minott spoke harshly, in half-forgotten Latin, and the groveling figure mumbled words which had been barbarous Latin to begin with, and through its bruised lips were still further mutilated.

'It's a slave,' said Minott coldly. 'Strange men – Confederates, I suppose – came from the north today. They fought and killed some of the guards at this estate. This slave denies it, but I imagine he was heading north in hopes of escaping to them. When you think of it, I suppose we're not the only explorers to be caught out of our own time path by some shift or another.'

He growled at the slave and rode on, still headed for the distant light. 'What – what are you going to do?' asked Maida faintly.

'Go on to the villa yonder and ask questions,' said Minott dryly. 'If Confederates hold it, we'll be well received. If they don't, we'll still manage to earn a welcome. I intend to camp along a time fault and cross over whenever a time shift brings a Norse settlement in sight. Consequently, I want exact news of places where they've been seen, if such news is to be had.'

Maida Haynes pressed close to Blake. He put a reassuring hand on her arm as the horses trudged on over the soft ground. The firelight behind them grew brighter. Occasional resinous, coniferous trees flared upward and threw fugitive red glows upon the riding figures. But gradually the glare grew steadier and stronger. The white walls of a rambling stucco house became visible – outbuildings – barns. A monstrous structure which looked startlingly like a barracks.

It was a farm, an estate, a Roman villa transplanted to the very edge of a wilderness. It was – Blake remembered vaguely – like a picture he had once seen of a Roman villa in England, restored to look as it had been before Rome withdrew her legions from Britain and left the island to savagery and darkness. There were small mounds of curing hay about them, through which the horses picked their way. Blake suddenly wrinkled his nostrils suspiciously. He sniffed.

Maida pressed close to him. Her lips formed words. Lucy

Blair rode close to Minott, glancing up at him from time to time. Harris rode beside Bertha Ketterling, and Bertha sat her horse as if she were saddle sore. Tom Hunter clung close to Minott as if for protection; leaving Janet Thompson to look out for herself.

'Jerry,' said Maida, 'what – what do you think?'

'I don't like it,' admitted Blake in a low tone. 'But we've got to tag along. I think I smell—'

Then a sudden swarm of figures leaped at the horses – wild figures, naked figures, sweaty and reeking and almost maniacal figures, some of whom clanked chains as they leaped. A voice bellowed orders at them from a distance, and a whip cracked ominously.

Before the struggle ended, there were just two shots fired. Blake fired them both and wheeled about. Then a horse streaked away, and Bertha Ketterling was bawling plaintively, and Tom Hunter babbled hysterically, and Harris swore with a complete lack of his customary air of apology.

Minott seemed to be buried under a mass of foul bodies like the rest, but he rasped at his captors in an authoritative tone. They fell away from him, cringing as if by instinct. And then torches appeared suddenly and slaves appeared in their light – slaves of every possible degree of filth and degradation, of every possible racial mixture, but unanimous in a desperate abjectness before their master amid the torchbearers.

He was a short, fat man, in an only slightly modified toga. He drew it close about his body as the torchbearers held their flares close to the captives. The torchlight showed the captives, to be sure, but also it showed the puffy, self-indulgent, and invincibly cruel features of the man who owned these slaves and the villa. By his pose and the orders he gave in a curiously corrupt Latin, he showed that he considered he owned the captives, too.

XI

The deputy from Aisne-le-Sur decided that it had been very wise indeed for him to walk in the fresh air. Paris at night is stimulating. That curious attack of vertigo had come of too much champagne. The fresh air had dispelled the fumes. But it was odd that he did not know exactly where he was, though he knew his Paris well.

These streets were strange. The houses were unlike any that he remembered ever having seen before. In the light of the street lamps – and they were unusual, too – there was a certain unfamiliar quality about their architecture. He puzzled over it, trying to identify the peculiar *flair* these houses showed.

He became impatient. After all, it was necessary for him to return home sometime, even though his wife – the deputy from Aisne-le-Sur shrugged. Then he saw bright lights ahead. He hastened his steps. A magnificent mansion, brilliantly illuminated.

The clattering of many hoofs. A cavalry escort, forming up before the house. A pale young man emerged, escorted by a tall, fat man who kissed his hand as if in an ecstasy of admiration. Dismounted cavalrymen formed a lane from the gateway to the car. Two young officers followed the pale young man, ablaze with decorations. The deputy from Aisne-le-Sur noted subconsciously that he did not recognize their uniforms. The car door was open and waiting. There was some oddity about the car, but the deputy could not see clearly just what it was.

There was much clicking of heels – steel blades at salute. The pale young man patiently allowed the fat man to kiss his hand again. He entered the car. The two bemedaled young officers climbed in after him. The car rolled away. Instantly, the cavalry escort clattered with it, before it, behind it, all around it.

The fat man stood on the sidewalk, beaming and rubbing his hands together. The dismounted cavalrymen swung to their saddles and trotted briskly after the others.

The deputy from Aisne-le-Sur stared blankly. He saw another pedestrian, halted like himself to regard the spectacle. He was disturbed by the fact that this pedestrian was clothed in a fashion as perturbingly unfamiliar as these houses and the spectacle he had witnessed.

'Pardon, m'sieu,' said the deputy from Aisne-le-Sur, 'I do not recognize my surroundings. Would you tell me—'

'The house,' said the other caustically, 'is the hotel of Monsieur le Duc de Montigny. Is it possible that in 1935 one does not know of Monsieur le Duc? Or more especially of Madame la Duchesse, and what she is and where she lives?'

The deputy from Aisne-le-Sur blinked. 'Montigny? Montigny? No,' he admitted. 'And the young man of the car, whose hand was kissed by—'

'Kissed by Monsieur le Duc?' The stranger stared frankly. '*Mon dieu!* Where have you come from that you do not recognize Louis the Twentieth? He has but departed from a visit to madame his mistress.'

'Louis – Louis the Twentieth!' stammered the deputy from Aisne-le-Sur. 'I – I do not understand!'

'Fool!' said the stranger impatiently. 'That was the king of France, who succeeded his father as a child of ten and has been free of the regency for but six months – and already ruins France!'

The long-distance operator plugged in with a shaking hand. 'Number please . . . I am sorry, sir, but we are unable to connect you with Camden . . . The lines are down . . . Very sorry, sir.' She plugged in another line. 'Hello . . . I am sorry, sir, but we are unable to connect you with Jenkintown. The lines are down . . . Very sorry, sir.'

Another call buzzed and lighted up.

'Hello . . . I am sorry, sir. We are unable to connect you with Dover. The lines are down . . .' Her hands worked automatically. 'Hello . . . I am sorry, but we are unable to connect you with New York. The lines are down . . . No, sir. We cannot route it by Atlantic City. The lines are down . . . Yes, sir, I know the telegraph companies cannot guarantee delivery... No, sir, we cannot reach Pittsburgh, either, to get a message through...' Her voice quivered. 'No, sir, the lines are down to Scranton... And Harrisburg, too. Yes, sir... I am sorry, but we cannot get a message of any sort out of Philadelphia in any direction... We have tried to arrange communication by radio, but no calls are answered...'

She covered her face with her hands for an instant. Then she plugged in and made a call herself:

'Minnie! Haven't they heard anything?... Not anything?... What? They phoned for more police?... The – the operator out there says there's fighting? She hears a lot of shooting?... What is it, Minnie? Don't they even know?... They – they're using the armored cars from the banks to fight with, too?... But what are they fighting? What?... My folks are out there, Minnie! My folks are out there!'

The doorway of the slave barracks closed and great bars slammed against its outer side. Reeking, foul, unbreathable air closed about them like a wave. Then a babbling of voices all about. The clanking of chains. The rustling of straw, as if animals moved. Someone screeched; howled above the others. He began to gain the ascendancy. There was almost some attention paid to him, though a minor babbling continued all about.

Maida said in a strained voice: 'I – I can catch a word here and there. He's – telling these other slaves how we were captured. It's – Latin, of sorts.'

Bertha Ketterling squalled suddenly, in the absolute dark. 'Somebody touched me!' she bawled. 'A man!'

A voice spoke humorously, somewhere near. There was laughter. It was the howled laughter of animals. Slaves were animals, according to the Roman notion. A rustling noise, as if in the noisome freedom of their barracks the utterly brutalized slaves drew nearer to the newcomers. There could be sport with new-captured folk, not yet degraded to their final status.

44

Lucy Blair cried out in a stifled fashion. There was a sharp, incisive *crack*. Somebody fell. More laughter.

'I knocked him out!' snapped Minott. 'Harris! Hunter! Feel around for something we can use as clubs! These slaves intend to haze us, and in their own den there's no attempt to control them. Even if they kill us they'll only be whipped for it. And the women will—'

Something, snarling, leaped for him in the darkness. The authoritative tone of Minott's voice was hateful. A yapping sound arose. Other figures closed in. Reduced to the status of animals, the slaves of the Romans behaved as beasts when locked in their monster kennel. The newcomers were hateful if only because they had been freemen, not slaves. The women were clean and they were frightened – and they were prey. Chains clanked ominously. Foul breaths tainted the air. The reek of utter depravity, of human beings brought lower than beasts, filled the air. It was utterly dark.

Bertha Ketterling began to blubber noisily. There was the sudden savage sound of a blow meeting flesh. Then pandemonium and battle, and the sudden terrified screams of Lucy Blair. The panting of men who fought. The sound of blows. A man howled. Another shrieked curses. A woman screamed shrilly.

Bang! Bang! Bang-bang! Shots outside, a veritable fusillade of them. Running feet. Shouts. The bars at the doorway fell. The great doors opened, and men stood in the opening with whips and torches, bellowing for the slaves to come out and attack something yet unknown. They were being called from their kennel like dogs. Four of the whip men came inside, flogging the slaves out, while the sound of shots continued. The slaves shrank away, or bounded howling for the open air. But there were three of them who would never shrink or cringe again.

Minott and Harris stood embattled in a corner of the slave shed. Lucy Blair, her hair disheveled, crouched behind Minott, who held a heavy beam in desperate readiness for further battle. Harris, likewise, held a clumsy club. With torchlight upon him, his air of savage defiance turned to one of quaint apology for the dead slave at his feet. And Hunter and two of the girls competed in stark panic for a position behind him. Maida Haynes, dead white, stood backed against a wall, a jagged fragment of gnawed bone held dagger-wise.

The whips lashed out at them. Voices snarled at them. The whips again. Minott struck out furiously, a huge welt across his face.

And revolvers cracked at the great door. Blake stood there, a revolver in each hand, his eyes blazing. A torchbearer dropped, and the torches flared smokily in the foul mud of the flooring.

'All right,' said Blake fiercely. 'Come on out!'

Hunter was the first to reach him, babbling and gasping. There was sheer uproar all about. A huge grain shed roared upward in flames. Figures rushed crazily all about it. From the flames came another explosion, then two, then three more.

'Horses over here by the stables,' said Blake, his face white and very deadly indeed. 'They haven't unsaddled them. The stable slaves haven't figured out the cinches yet. I put some revolver bullets in the straw when I set fire to that grain shed. They're going off from time to time.'

A figure with whip and dagger raced around an outbuilding and confronted them. Blake shot him down.

Minott said hoarsely: 'Give me a revolver, Blake! I want to—'

'Horses first!' snapped Blake.

They raced into a courtyard. Two shots. The slaves fled, howling. Out of the courtyard, bent low in the saddle. They swept close to the villa itself. On a little raised terrace before it, a stout man in an only slightly modified toga raged. A slave groveled before him. He kicked the abject figure and strode out, shouting commands in a voice that cracked with fury. The horses loomed up and he shook his fists at the riders, purple with wrath, incapable of fear because of his beastly rage.

Blake shot him dead, swung off his horse, and stripped the toga from him. He flung it to Maida.

'Take this!' he said savagely. 'I could kill—'

There was now no question of his leadership. He led the

retreat from the villa. The eight horses headed north again, straight for the luridly flaming forest.

They stopped once more. Behind them, another building of the estate had caught from the first. Sheer confusion ruled. The slaughter of the master disrupted all organization. The roof of the slave barracks caught: Screams and howls of pure panic reached even the fugitives. Then there were racing, maddened figures rushing here and there in the glare of the fires. Suddenly there was fighting. A howling ululation arose.

Minott worked savagely, stripping clothing from the bodies slain in that incredible, unrecorded conflict of Confederate soldiers and Roman troops, in some unguessable pathway of space and time. Blake watched behind, but he curtly commanded the salvaging of rifles and ammunition from the dead Confederates – if they were Confederates.

And as Hunter, still gasping hysterically, took the load of yet unfamiliar weapons upon his horse, the eight felt a certain incredible, intolerable vertigo and nausea. The burning forest ahead vanished from their sight. Instead, there was darkness. A noisome smell came down wind; dampness and strange, overpowering perfumes of strange, colored flowers. Something huge and deadly bellowed in the space before them, which smelled like a monstrous swamp.

The liner *City of Baltimore* plowed through the open sea in the first pale light of dawn. The skipper, up on the bridge, wore a worried frown. The radio operator came up. He carried a sheaf of radiogram forms. His eyes were blurry with loss of sleep.

'Maybe it was me, sir,' he reported heavily. 'I felt awful funny for a while last night, and then all night long I couldn't raise a station. I checked everything and couldn't find anything wrong. But just now I felt awful sick and funny for a minute, and when I come out of it the air was full of code. Here's some of it. I don't understand how I could have been sick so I couldn't hear code, sir, but—'

The skipper said abruptly: 'I had that sick feeling, too

– dizzy. So did the man at the wheel. So did everybody. Give me the messages.'

His eyes ran swiftly over the yellow forms.

'News flash: Half of London disappeared at 2:00 a.m. this morning... S.S. *Manzanillo* reporting. Sea serpent which attacked this ship during the night and seized four sailors returned and was rammed five minutes ago. It seems to be dying. Our bow badly smashed. Two forward compartments flooded... Warning to all mariners. Pack ice seen floating fifty miles off New York harbor... News flash: Madrid, Spain, has undergone inexplicable change. All buildings formerly known now unrecognizable from the air. Air fields have vanished. Mosques seem to have taken the place of churches and cathedrals. A flag bearing the crescent floats... European population of Calcutta seems to have been massacred. S.S. *Carib* reports harbor empty, all signs of European domination vanished, and hostile mobs lining shore...'

The skipper of the *City of Baltimore* passed his hand over his forehead. He looked uneasily at the radio operator. 'Sparks,' he said gently, 'you'd better go see the ship's doctor. Here! I'll detail a man to go with you.'

'I know,' said Sparks bitterly. 'I guess I'm nuts, all right. But that's what come through.'

He marched away with his head hanging, escorted by a sailor. A little speck of smoke appeared dead ahead. It became swiftly larger. With the combined speed of the two vessels, in a quarter of an hour the other ship was visible. In half an hour it could be made out clearly. It was long and low and painted black, but the first incredible thing was that it was a paddle steamer, with two sets of paddles instead of one, and the after set revolving more swiftly than the forward.

The skipper of the *City of Baltimore* looked more closely through his glasses and nearly dropped them in stark amazement. The flag flying on the other ship was black and white only. A beam wind blew it out swiftly. A white death's-head, with two crossed bones below it – the traditional flag of piracy!

Signal flags fluttered up in the rigging of the other ship. The skipper of the *City of Baltimore* gazed at them, stunned.

'Gibberish!' he muttered. 'It don't make sense! They aren't international code. Not the same flags at all!'

Then a gun spoke. A monstrous puff of black powder smoke billowed over the other ship's bow. A heavy shot crashed into the forepart of the *City of Baltimore:* An instant later it exploded.

'I'm crazy, too!' said the skipper dazedly.

A second shot. A third and fourth. The black steamer sheered off and started to pound the *City of Baltimore* in a businesslike fashion. Half the bridge went overside. The forward cargo hatch blew up with a cloud of smoke from an explosion underneath.

Then the skipper came to. He roared orders. The big ship heeled as it came around. It plunged forward at vastly more than its normal cruising speed. The guns on the other ship doubled and redoubled their rate of fire. Then the black ship tried to dodge. But it had not time.

The *City of Baltimore* rammed it. But at the very last moment the skipper felt certain of his own insanity. It was too late to save the other ship then. The *City of Baltimore* cut it in two.

XII

The pale gray light of dawn filtered down through an incredible thickness of foliage. It was a subdued, a feeble twilight when it reached the earth where a tiny camp fire burned. That fire gave off thick smoke from water-soaked wood. Hunter tended it, clad in ill-assorted remnants of a gray uniform.

Harris worked patiently at a rifle, trying to understand exactly how it worked. It was unlike any rifle with which he was familiar. The bolt action was not really a bolt action at all, and he'd noticed that there was no rifling in the barrel. He was trying to understand how the long bullet was made to revolve. Harris, too, had substituted Confederate gray for the loin cloth flung him for sole covering when with the others he was thrust into the slave pen of the Roman villa. Minott sat with his head in his hands, staring at the opposite side of the stream. On his face was all bitterness.

Blake listened. Maida Haynes sat and looked at him. Lucy Blair darted furtive, somehow wistful, glances at Minott. Presently she moved to sit beside him. She asked him an anxious question. The other two girls sat by the fire. Bertha Ketterling was slouched back against a tree-fern trunk. Her head had fallen back. She snored. With the exception of Blake, all of them were barefoot.

Blake came back to the fire. He nodded across the little stream. 'We seem to have come to the edge of a time fault,' he observed. 'This side of the stream is definitely Carboniferous-period vegetation. The other side isn't as primitive, but it isn't of our time, anyhow. Professor Minott!'

Minott lifted his head. 'Well?' he demanded bitterly.

'We need some information,' said Blake. 'We've been here for hours, and there's been no further change in time paths that we've noticed. Is it likely that the scrambling of time and space is ended, sir? If it has, and the time paths stay jumbled, we'll never find our world intact, of course, but we can hunt for colonies, perhaps even cities, of our own kind of people.'

'If we do,' said Minott bitterly, 'how far will we get? We're practically unarmed. We can't—'

Blake pointed to the salvaged rifles. 'Harris is working on the arms problem now,' he said dryly. 'Besides, the girls didn't take the revolvers from their saddlebags. We've still two revolvers for each man and an extra pair. Those Romans thought the saddlebags were decorations, perhaps, or they intended to examine the saddles as a whole. We'll make out. What I want to know is, has the time-scrambling process stopped?'

Lucy Blair said something in a low tone. But Minott glanced at Maida Haynes. She was regarding Blake worshipfully. Minott's eyes burned. He scowled in surpassing bitterness. 'It probably hasn't,' he said harshly. 'I expect it to keep up for probably two weeks or more of – of duration. I use that term to mean time elapsed in all the time paths simultaneously. We can't help thinking of time as passing on our particular time path only. Yes. I expect disturbances to continue for two weeks or more, if everything in time and space is not annihilated.' Blake sat down.

Insensibly Maida Haynes moved closer to him. 'Could you explain, sir? We can only wait here. As nearly as I can tell from the topography, there's a village across this little stream in our time. It ought to be in sight if our time path ever turns up in view, here.'

Minott unconsciously reassumed some of his former authoritative manner. Their capture and scornful dismissal to the status of slaves had shaken all his self-confidence. Before, he had felt himself not only a member of a superior race, but a superior member of that race. In being enslaved he had been both degraded and scorned. His vanity was still gnawed at by that memory and his self-confidence shattered by the fact that he had been able to kill only two utterly brutalized slaves, without in the least contributing to his own freedom. Now, for the first time, his voice took on a semblance of its old ring.

'We – we know that gravity warps space,' he said precisely. 'From observation we have been able to discover the amount of warping produced by a given mass. We can calculate the mass necessary to warp space so that it will close in completely, making a closed universe which is unreachable and undetectable in any of the dimensions we know. We know, for example, that if two gigantic star masses of a certain combined mass were to rush together, at the instant of their collision there would not be a great cataclysm. They would simply vanish. But they would not cease to exist. They would merely cease to exist in our space and time. They would have created a space and time of their own.'

Harris said apologetically: 'Like crawling in a hole and pulling the hole in after you. I read something like that in a Sunday supplement once, sir.'

Minott nodded. He went on in a near approach to a class-room manner. 'Now, imagine that two such universes have been formed. They are both invisible from the space and time in which they were formed. Each exists in its own space and time, just as our universe does. But each must also exist in a certain – well, hyper-space, because if closed spaces are separated, there must be some sort of something in between them, else they would be together.'

'Really,' said Blake, 'you're talking about something we can infer, but ordinarily can't possibly learn anything about by observation.'

'Just so,' Minott nodded. 'Still, if our space is closed, we must assume that there are other closed spaces. And don't forget that other closed spaces would be as real – are as real – as our closed space is.'

'But what does it mean?' asked Blake.

'If there are other closed spaces like ours, and they exist in a common medium – the hyper-space from which they and we alike are sealed off – they might be likened to, say, stars and planets in our space, which are separated by space and yet affect each other through space. Since these various closed spaces are separated by a logically necessary hyper-space, it is at least probable that they should affect each other through that hyper-space.'

Blake said slowly: 'Then the shiftings of time paths – well, they're the result of something on the order of tidal strains. If another star got close to the sun, our planets would crack up from tidal strains alone. You're suggesting that another closed space has got close to our closed space in hyper-space. It's awfully confused, sir.'

'I have calculated it,' said Minott harshly. 'The odds are four to one that space and time and universe, every star and every galaxy in the skies, will be obliterated in one monstrous cataclysm when even the past will never have been. But there is one chance in four, and I planned to take full advantage of it. I planned – I planned—'

Then he stood up suddenly. His figure straightened. He struck his hands together savagely. 'By Heaven, I still plan! We have arms. We have books, technical knowledge, formulas – the cream of the technical knowledge of earth packed in our saddlebags! Listen to me! We cross this stream now. When the next change comes, we strike across whatever time path takes the place of this. We make for the Potomac, where that aviator saw Norse ships drawn up! I have Anglo-Saxon and early Norse vocabularies in the saddlebags. We'll make friends with them. We'll teach them. We'll lead them. We'll make ourselves masters of the world and—'

Harris said apologetically: 'I'm sorry, sir, but I promised Bertha I'd take her home, if it was humanly possible. I have to do it. I can't join you in becoming an emperor, even if the breaks are right.'

Minott scowled at him.

'Hunter?'

'I – I'll do as the others do,' said Hunter uneasily. 'I – I'd rather go home.'

'Fool!' snarled Minott.

Lucy Blair said loyally: 'I – I'd like to be an empress, Professor Minott.'

Maida Haynes stared at her. She opened her mouth to speak. Blake absently pulled a revolver from his pocket and looked at it meditatively as Minott clenched and unclenched his hands. The veins stood out on his forehead. He began to breathe heavily.

'Fools!' he roared. 'Fools! You'll never get back! Yet you throw away—'

Swift, sharp, agonizing vertigo smote them all. The revolver fell from Blake's hands. He looked up. A dead silence fell upon all of them.

Blake stood shakily upon his feet. He looked, and looked again. 'That—' He swallowed. 'That is King George courthouse, in King George County, in Virginia, in our time I think – Hell! Let's get across that stream.'

He picked up Maida in his arms. He started.

Minott moved quickly and croaked: 'Wait!'

He had Blake's dropped revolver in his hand. He was desperate, hunted; gray with rage and despair. 'I – I offer you, for the last time – I offer you riches, power, women, and—'

Harris stood up, the Confederate rifle still in his hands. He brought the barrel down smartly upon Minott's wrist.

Blake waded across and put Maida safely down upon the shore. Hunter was splashing frantically through the shallow water. Harris was shaking Bertha Ketterling to wake her. Blake splashed back. He rounded up the horses. He loaded the salvaged weapons over a saddle. He shepherded the three remaining girls over. Hunter was out of sight. He had fled toward the painted buildings of the courthouse. Blake led the horses across the stream. Minott nursed his numbed wrist. His eyes blazed with the fury of utter despair.

'Better come along,' said Blake quietly.

'And be a professor of mathematics?' Minott laughed savagely. 'No! I stay here!'

Blake considered. Minott was a strange, an unprepossessing figure. He was haggard. He was desperate. Standing against the background of a Carboniferous jungle, in the misfitting uniform he had stripped from a dead man in some other path of time, he was even pitiable. Shoeless, unshaven, desperate, he was utterly defiant.

'Wait!' said Blake.

He stripped off the saddlebags from six of the horses. He heaped them on the remaining two. He led those two back across the stream and tethered them.

Minott regarded him with an implacable hatred. 'If I hadn't chosen you,' he said harshly, 'I'd have carried my original plan through. I knew I shouldn't choose you. Maida liked you too well. And I wanted her for myself. It was my mistake, my only one.'

Blake shrugged. He went back across the stream and remounted.

Lucy Blair looked doubtfully back at the solitary, savage figure. 'He's – brave, anyhow,' she said unhappily.

A faint, almost imperceptible, dizziness affected all of them. It passed. By instinct they looked back at the tall jungle. It still stood. Minott looked bitterly after them.

'I've – I've something I want to say!' said Lucy Blair breathlessly. 'D– don't wait for me!'

She wheeled her horse about and rode for the stream. Again that faint, nearly imperceptible, dizziness. Lucy slapped her horse's flank frantically.

Maida cried out: 'Wait, Lucy! It's going to shift—'

And Lucy cried over her shoulder: 'That's what I want! I'm going to stay—'

She was halfway across the stream – more than halfway. Then the vertigo struck all of them.

XIII

Everyone knows the rest of the story. For two weeks longer there were still occasional shiftings of the time paths. But gradually it became noticeable that the number of time faults – in Professor Minott's phrase – were decreasing in number. At the most drastic period, it has been estimated that no less than twenty-five per cent of the whole earth's surface was at a given moment in some other time path than its own. We do not know of any portion of the earth which did not vary from its own time path at some period of the disturbance.

That means, of course, that practically one hundred per cent of the earth's population encountered the conditions caused by the earth's extraordinary oscillations sidewise in time. Our scientists are no longer quite as dogmatic as they used to be. The dialectics of philosophy have received a serious jolt. Basic ideas in botany, zoology, and even philology have been altered by the new facts made available by our travels sidewise in time.

Because of course it was the fourth chance which happened, and the earth survived. In our time path, at any rate. The survivors of Minott's exploring party reached King George courthouse barely a quarter of an hour after the time shift which carried Minott and Lucy Blair out of our space and time forever. Blake and Harris searched for a means of transmitting the information they possessed to the world at large. Through a lonely radio amateur a mile from the village, they sent out Minott's theory on short waves. Shorn of Minott's pessimistic analysis of the probabilities of survival, it went swiftly to every part of the world then in its proper relative position. It was valuable, in that it checked explorations in force which in some places had been planned. It prevented, for example, a punitive military expedition from going past a time fault in Georgia, past which a scalping party of Indians from an uncivilized America had retreated. It prevented the dispatch of a squadron of destroyers to find and seize Leifsholm, from which a Viking foray had been made upon North Centerville, Massachusetts. A squadron of mapping planes was recalled from reconnaissance work above a Carboniferous swamp in West Virginia, just before the time shift which would have isolated them forever.

Some things, though, no knowledge could prevent. It has been estimated that no less than five thousand persons in the United States are missing from their own space and time, through having adventured into the strange landscapes which appeared so suddenly. Many must have perished. Some, we feel sure, have come in contact with one or another of the distinct civilizations we now know exist.

Conversely, we have gained inhabitants from other time paths. Two cohorts of the Twenty-second Roman Legion were left upon our soil near Ithaca, New York. Four families of Chinese peasants essayed to pick berries in what they considered a miraculous strawberry-patch in Virginia, and remained there when that section of ground returned to its proper *milieu*.

A Russian village remains in Colorado. A French settlement in the – in their time undeveloped – Middle West. A part of the northern herd of buffalo has returned to us, two hundred thousand strong, together with a village of Cheyenne Indians who had never seen either horses or firearms. The passenger pigeon, to the number of a billion and a half birds, has returned to North America.

But our losses are heavy. Besides those daring individuals who were carried away upon the strange territories they were exploring, there are the overwhelming disasters affecting Tokyo and Rio de Janeiro and Detroit. The first two we understand. When the causes of oscillation sidewise in time were removed, most of the earth sections returned to their proper positions in their own time paths. But not all. There is a section of Post-Cambrian jungle left in eastern Tennessee. The Russian village in Colorado has been mentioned, and the French trading post in the Middle West. In some cases sections of the oscillating time paths remained in new positions, remote from their points of origin.

That is the cause of the utter disappearance of Rio and of Tokyo. Where Rio stood, an untouched jungle remains. It is of our own geological period, but it is simply from a path in time in which Rio de Janeiro never happened to be built. On the site of Tokyo stands a forest of extraordinarily primitive type, about which botanists and paleontologists still debate. Somewhere, in some space and time, Tokyo and Rio yet exist and their people still live on. But Detroit—

We still do not understand what happened to Detroit. It was upon an oscillating segment of earth. It vanished from our time, and it returned to our time. But its inhabitants did not come back with it. The city was empty – deserted as if the hundreds of thousands of human beings who lived in it had simply evaporated into the air. There have been some few signs of struggle seen, but they may have been the result of panic. The city of Detroit returned to its own space and time untouched, unharmed, unlooted, and undisturbed. But no living thing, not even a domestic animal or a caged bird, was in it when it came back. We do not understand that at all.

Perhaps if Professor Minott had returned to us, he could have guessed at the answer to the riddle. What fragmentary papers of his have been shown to refer to the time upheaval have been of inestimable value. Our whole theory of what happened depends on the papers Minott left behind as too unimportant to bother with, in addition, of course, to Blake's and Harris' account of his explanation to them. Tom Hunter can remember little that is useful. Maida Haynes has given some worthwhile data, but it covers ground we have other observers for. Bertha Ketterling also reports very little.

The answers to a myriad problems yet elude us, but in the saddlebags given to Minott by Blake as equipment for his desperate journey through space and time, the answers to many must remain. Our scientists labor diligently to understand and to elaborate the figures Minott thought of trivial significance. And throughout the world many minds turn longingly to certain saddlebags, loaded on a led horse, following Minott and Lucy Blair through unguessable landscapes, to unimaginable adventures, with revolvers and textbooks as their armament for the conquest of a world.

THE RUNAWAY SKYSCRAPER

I

The whole thing started when the clock on the Metropolitan Tower began to run backward. It was not a graceful proceeding. The hands had been moving onward in their customary deliberate fashion, slowly and thoughtfully, but suddenly the people in the offices near the clock's face heard an ominous creaking and groaning. There was a slight, hardly discernible shiver through the tower, and then something gave with a crash. The big hands on the clock began to move backward.

Immediately after the crash all the creaking and groaning ceased, and instead, the usual quiet again hung over everything. One or two of the occupants of the upper offices put their heads out into the halls, but the elevators were running as usual, the lights were burning, and all seemed calm and peaceful. The clerks and stenographers went back to their ledgers and typewriters, the business callers returned to the discussion of their errands, and the ordinary course of business was resumed.

Arthur Chamberlain was dictating a letter to Estelle Woodward, his sole stenographer. When the crash came he paused, listened, and then resumed his task.

It was not a difficult one. Talking to Estelle Woodward was at no time an onerous duty, but it must be admitted that Arthur Chamberlain found it difficult to keep his conversation strictly upon his business.

He was at this time engaged in dictating a letter to his principal creditors, the Gary & Milton Company, explaining that their demand for the immediate payment of the installment then due upon his office furniture was untimely and unjust. A

59

young and budding engineer in New York never has too much money, and when he is young as Arthur Chamberlain was, and as fond of pleasant company, and not too fond of economizing, he is liable to find all demands for payment untimely and he usually considers them unjust as well. Arthur finished dictating the letter and sighed.

'Miss Woodward,' he said regretfully, 'I am afraid I shall never make a successful man.'

Miss Woodward shook her head vaguely. She did not seem to take his remark very seriously, but then, she had learned never to take any of his remarks seriously. She had been puzzled at first by his manner of treating everything with a half joking pessimism, but now ignored it.

She was interested in her own problems. She had suddenly decided that she was going to be an old maid, and it bothered her. She had discovered that she did not like any one well enough to marry, and she was in her twenty-second year.

She was not a native of New York, and the few young men she had met there she did not care for. She had regretfully decided she was too finicky, too fastidious, but could not seem to help herself. She could not understand their absorption in boxing and baseball and she did not like the way they danced.

She had considered the matter and decided that she would have to reconsider her former opinion of women who did not marry. Heretofore she had thought there must be something the matter with them. Now she believed that she would come to their own estate, and probably for the same reason. She could not fall in love and she wanted to.

She read all the popular novels and thrilled at the love scenes contained in them, but when any of the young men she knew became in the slightest degree sentimental she found herself bored, and disgusted with herself for being bored. Still, she could not help it, and was struggling to reconcile herself to a life without romance.

She was far too pretty for that, of course, and Arthur Chamberlain often longed to tell her how pretty she really was, but her abstracted air held him at arms' length.

He lay back at ease in his swivel chair and considered, look-ing at her with unfeigned pleasure. She did not notice it, for she was so much absorbed in her own thoughts that she rarely noticed anything he said or did when they were not in the line of her duties.

'Miss Woodward,' he repeated, 'I said I think I'll never make a successful man. Do you know what that means?'

She looked at him mutely, polite inquiry in her eyes.

'It means,' he said gravely, 'that I'm going broke. Unless something turns up in the next three weeks, or a month at the latest, I'll have to get a job.'

'And that means—' she asked.

'All this will go to pot,' he explained with a sweeping gesture. 'I thought I'd better tell you as much in advance as I could.'

'You mean you're going to give up your office – and me?' she asked, a little alarmed.

'Giving up you will be the harder of the two,' he said with a smile, 'but that's what it means. You'll have no difficulty finding a new place, with three weeks in which to look for one, but I'm sorry.'

'I'm sorry, too, Mr Chamberlain,' she said, her brow puck-ered.

She was not really frightened, because she knew she could get another position, but she became aware of rather more regret than she had expected.

There was silence for a moment.

'Jove!' said Arthur, suddenly. 'It's getting dark, isn't it?'

It was. It was growing dark with unusual rapidity. Arthur went to his window, and looked out.

'Funny,' he remarked in a moment or two. 'Things don't look just right, down there, somehow. There are very few people about.'

He watched in growing amazement. Lights came on in the streets below, but none of the buildings lighted up. It grew darker and darker.

'It shouldn't be dark at this hour!' Arthur exclaimed.

Estelle went to the window by his side.

'It looks awfully queer,' she agreed. 'It must be an eclipse or something.'

They heard doors open in the hall outside, and Arthur ran out. The halls were beginning to fill with excited people.

'What on earth's the matter?' asked a worried stenographer.

'Probably an eclipse,' replied Arthur. 'Only it's odd we didn't read about it in the papers.'

He glanced along the corridor. No one else seemed better informed than he, and he went back into his office.

Estelle turned from the window as he appeared.

'The streets are deserted,' she said in a puzzled tone. 'What's the matter? Did you hear?'

Arthur shook his head and reached for the telephone.

'I'll call up and find out,' he said confidently. He held the receiver to his ear. 'What the—' he exclaimed. 'Listen to this!'

A small-sized roar was coming from the receiver. Arthur hung up and turned a blank face upon Estelle.

'Look!' she said suddenly, and pointed out of the window.

All the city was now lighted up, and such of the signs as they could see were brilliantly illumined. They watched in silence. The streets once more seemed filled with vehicles. They darted along, their headlamps lighting up the roadway brilliantly. There was, however, something strange even about their motion. Arthur and Estelle watched in growing amazement and perplexity.

'Are – are you seeing what I am seeing?' asked Estelle breathlessly. '*I* see them *going backward*!'

Arthur watched, and collapsed into a chair.

'For the love of Mike!' he exclaimed softly.

II

He was roused by another exclamation from Estelle.

'It's getting light again,' she said.

Arthur rose and went eagerly to the window. The darkness

was becoming less intense, but in a way Arthur could hardly credit.

Far to the west, over beyond the Jersey hills – easily visible from the height at which Arthur's office was located – a faint light appeared in the sky, grew stronger and then took on a reddish tint. That, in turn, grew deeper, and at last the sun appeared, rising unconcernedly *in the west.*

Arthur gasped. The streets below continued to be thronged with people and motorcars. The sun was traveling with extraordinary rapidity. It rose overhead, and as if by magic the streets were thronged with people. Every one seemed to be running at top speed. The few teams they saw moved at a breakneck pace – backward! In spite of the suddenly topsy-turvy state of affairs there seemed to be no accidents.

Arthur put his hands to his head.

'Miss Woodward,' he said pathetically, 'I'm afraid I've gone crazy. Do you see the same things I do?'

Estelle nodded. Her eyes wide open.

'What *is* the matter?' she asked helplessly.

She turned again to the window. The square was almost empty once more. The motorcars still traveling about the streets were going so swiftly they were hardly visible. Their speed seemed to increase steadily. Soon it was almost impossible to distinguish them, and only a grayish blur marked their paths along Fifth Avenue and Twenty-Third Street.

It grew dusk, and then rapidly dark. As their office was on the western side of the building they could not see that the sun had sunk in the east, but subconsciously they realized that this must be the case.

In silence they watched the panorama grow black except for the streetlamps, remain thus for a time, and then suddenly spring into brilliantly illuminated activity.

Again this lasted for a little while, and the west once more began to glow. The sun rose somewhat more hastily from the Jersey hills and began to soar overhead, but very soon darkness fell again. With hardly an interval the city became illuminated, and then the west grew red once more.

'Apparently,' said Arthur, steadying his voice with a conscious effort, 'there's been a cataclysm somewhere, the direction of the earth's rotation has been reversed, and its speed immensely increased. It seems to take only about five minutes for a rotation now.'

As he spoke darkness fell for the third time. Estelle turned from the window with a white face.

'What's going to happen?' she cried.

'I don't know,' answered Arthur. 'The scientist fellows tell us if the earth were to spin fast enough the centrifugal force would throw us all off into space. Perhaps that's what's going to happen.'

Estelle sank into a chair and stared at him, appalled. There was a sudden explosion behind them. With a start, Estelle jumped to her feet and turned. A little gilt clock over her typewriter-desk lay in fragments. Arthur hastily glanced at his own watch.

'Great bombs and little cannonballs!' he shouted. 'Look at this!'

His watch trembled and quivered in his hand. The hands were going around so swiftly it was impossible to watch the minute hand, and the hour hand traveled like the wind.

While they looked, it made two complete revolutions. In one of them the glory of daylight had waxed, waned, and vanished. In the other, darkness reigned except for the glow from the electric light overhead.

There was a sudden tension and catch in the watch. Arthur dropped it instantly. It flew to pieces before it reached the floor.

'If you've got a watch,' Arthur ordered swiftly, 'stop it this instant!'

Estelle fumbled at her wrist. Arthur tore the watch from her hand and threw open the case. The machinery inside was going so swiftly it was hardly visible; relentlessly, Arthur jabbed a penholder in the works. There was a sharp click, and the watch was still.

Arthur ran to the window. As he reached it the sun rushed

up, day lasted a moment, there was darkness, and then the sun appeared again.

'Miss Woodward!' Arthur ordered suddenly, 'look at the ground!'

Estelle glanced down. The next time the sun flashed into view she gasped.

The ground was white with snow!

'What *has* happened?' she demanded, terrified. 'Oh, what *has* happened?'

Arthur fumbled at his chin awkwardly, watching the astonishing panorama outside. There was hardly any distinguishing between the times the sun was up and the times it was below now, as the darkness and light followed each other so swiftly the effect was the same as one of the old flickering motion pictures.

As Arthur watched, this effect became more pronounced. The tall Fifth Avenue Building across the way began to disintegrate. In a moment, it seemed, there was only a skeleton there. Then that vanished, story by story. A great cavity in the earth appeared, and then another building became visible, a smaller, brownstone, unimpressive structure.

With bulging eyes Arthur stared across the city. Except for the flickering, he could see almost clearly now.

He no longer saw the sun rise and set. There was merely a streak of unpleasantly brilliant light across the sky. Bit by bit, building by building, the city began to disintegrate and become replaced by smaller, dingier buildings. In a little while those began to disappear and leave gaps where they vanished.

Arthur strained his eyes and looked far downtown. He saw a forest of masts and spars along the waterfront for a moment and when he turned his eyes again to the scenery near him it was almost barren of houses, and what few showed were mean, small residences, apparently set in the midst of farms and plantations.

Estelle was sobbing.

'Oh, Mr Chamberlain,' she cried. 'What is the matter? What has happened?'

Arthur had lost his fear of what their fate would be in his

absorbing interest in what he saw. He was staring out of the window, wide eyed, lost in the sight before him. At Estelle's cry, however, he reluctantly left the window and patted her shoulder awkwardly.

'I don't know how to explain it,' he said uncomfortably, 'but it's obvious that my first surmise was all wrong. The speed of the earth's rotation can't have been increased, because if it had to the extent we see, we'd have been thrown off into space long ago. But – have you read anything about the Fourth Dimension?'

Estelle shook her head hopelessly.

'Well, then, have you ever read anything by Wells? "The Time Machine", for instance?'

Again she shook her head.

'I don't know how I'm going to say it so you'll understand, but time is just as much a dimension as length and breadth. From what I can judge, I'd say there has been an earthquake, and the ground has settled a little with our building on it, only instead of settling down toward the center of the earth, or sidewise, it's settled in this fourth dimension.'

'But what does that mean?' asked Estelle uncomprehendingly.

'If the earth had settled down, we'd have been lower. If it had settled to one side, we'd have been moved one way or another, but as it's settled back in the Fourth Dimension, we're going back in time.'

'Then—'

'We're in a runaway skyscraper, bound for some time back before the discovery of America!'

III

It was very still in the office. Except for the flickering outside everything seemed very much as usual. The electric light burned steadily, but Estelle was sobbing with fright and Arthur was trying vainly to console her.

'Have I gone crazy?' she demanded between her sobs.

'Not unless I've gone mad, too,' said Arthur soothingly. The excitement had quite a soothing effect upon him. He had ceased to feel afraid, but was simply waiting to see what had happened. 'We're way back before the founding of New York now, and still going strong.'

'Are you sure that's what has happened?'

'If you'll look outside,' he suggested, 'you'll see the seasons following each other in reverse order. One moment the snow covers all the ground, then you catch a glimpse of autumn foliage, then summer follows, and next spring.'

Estelle glanced out of the window and covered her eyes.

'Not a house,' she said despairingly. 'Not a building. Nothing, nothing, nothing!'

Arthur slipped his arm about her and patted hers comfortingly.

'It's all right,' he reassured her. 'We'll bring up presently, and there we'll be. There's nothing to be afraid of.'

She rested her head on his shoulder and sobbed hopelessly for a little while longer, but presently quieted. Then, suddenly, realizing that Arthur's arm was about her and that she was crying on his shoulder, she sprang away, blushing crimson.

Arthur walked to the window.

'Look there!' he exclaimed, but it was too late. 'I'll swear to it I saw the *Half Moon*, Hudson's ship,' he declared excitedly. 'We're way back now, and don't seem to be slacking up, either.'

Estelle came to the window by his side. The rapidly changing scene before her made her gasp. It was no longer possible to distinguish night from day.

A wavering streak, moving first to the right and then to the left, showed where the sun flashed across the sky.

'What makes the sun wabble so?' she asked.

'Moving north and south of the equator,' Arthur explained casually. 'When it's farthest south – to the left – there's always snow on the ground. When it's farthest right it's summer. See how green it is?'

A few moments' observation corroborated his statement.

'I'd say,' Arthur remarked reflectively, 'that it takes about fifteen seconds for the sun to make the round trip from farthest north to farthest south.' He felt his pulse. 'Do you know the normal rate of the heartbeat? We can judge time that way. A clock will go all to pieces, of course.'

'Why did your watch explode – and the clock?'

'Running forward in time unwinds a clock, doesn't it?' asked Arthur. 'It follows, of course, that when you move it backward in time it winds up. When you move it too far back, you wind it so tightly that the spring just breaks to pieces.'

He paused a moment, his fingers on his pulse.

'Yes, it takes about fifteen seconds for all the four seasons to pass. That means we're going backward in time about four years a minute. If we go on at this rate another hour we'll be back in the time of the Northmen, and will be able to tell if they did discover America, after all.'

'Funny we don't hear any noises,' Estelle observed. She had caught some of Arthur's calmness.

'It passes so quickly that though our ears hear it, we don't separate the sounds. If you'll notice, you do hear a sort of humming. It's very high pitched, though.'

Estelle listened, but could hear nothing.

'No matter,' said Arthur. 'It's probably a little higher than your ears will catch. Lots of people can't hear a bat squeak.'

'I never could,' said Estelle. 'Out in the country, where I come from, other people could hear them, but I couldn't.'

They stood a while in silence, watching.

'When are we going to stop?' asked Estelle uneasily. 'It seems as if we're going to keep on indefinitely.'

'I guess we'll stop all right,' Arthur reassured her. 'It's obvious that whatever it was, only affected our own building, or we'd see some other one with us. It looks like a fault or a flaw in the rock the building rests on. And that can only give so far.'

Estelle was silent for a moment.

'Oh, I can't be sane!' she burst out semi-hysterically. 'This can't be happening!'

'You aren't crazy,' said Arthur sharply. 'You're sane as I am.

Just something queer is happening. Buck up. Say your multiplication tables. Say anything you know. Say something sensible and you'll know you're all right. But don't get frightened now. There'll be plenty to get frightened about later.'

The grimness in his tone alarmed Estelle.

'What are you afraid of?' she asked quickly.

'Time enough to worry when it happens,' Arthur retorted briefly.

'You – you aren't afraid we'll go back before the beginning of the world, are you?' asked Estelle in sudden access of fright.

Arthur shook his head.

'Tell me,' said Estelle more quietly, getting a grip on herself. 'I won't mind. But please tell me.'

Arthur glanced at her. Her face was pale, but there was more resolution in it than he had expected to find.

'I'll tell you, then,' he said reluctantly. 'We're going back a little faster than we were, and the flaw seems to be a deeper one than I thought. At the roughest kind of an estimate, we're all of a thousand years before the discovery of America now, and I think nearer three or four. And we're gaining speed all the time. So, though I am as sure as I can be sure of anything that we'll stop this cave-in eventually, I don't know where. It's like a crevasse in the earth opened by an earthquake which may be only a few feet deep, or it may be hundreds of yards, or even a mile or two. We started off smoothly. We're going at a terrific rate. *What will happen when we stop?*'

Estelle caught her breath.

'What?' she asked quietly.

'I don't know,' said Arthur in an irritated tone, to cover his apprehension. 'How could I know?'

Estelle turned from him to the window again.

'Look!' she said, pointing.

The flickering had begun again. While they stared, hope springing up once more in their hearts, it became more pronounced. Soon they could distinctly see the difference between day and night.

They were slowing up! The white snow on the ground

remained there for an appreciable time, autumn lasted quite a while. They could catch the flashes of the sun as it made its revolutions now, instead of its seeming like a ribbon of fire. At last day lasted all of fifteen or twenty minutes.

It grew longer and longer. Then half an hour, then an hour. The sun wavered in midheaven and was still.

Far below them, the watchers in the tower of the skyscraper saw trees swaying and bending in the wind. Though there was not a house or a habitation to be seen and a dense forest covered all of Manhattan Island, such of the world as they could see looked normal. Wherever or rather in whatever epoch of time they were, they had arrived.

IV

Arthur caught at Estelle's arm and the two made a dash for the elevators. Fortunately one was standing still, the door open, on their floor. The elevator-boy had deserted his post and was looking with all the rest of the occupants of the building at the strange landscape that surrounded them.

No sooner had the pair reached the car, however, than the boy came hurrying along the corridor, three or four other people following him also at a run. Without a word the boy rushed inside, the others crowded after him, and the car shot downward, all of the newcomers panting from their sprint.

Theirs was the first car to reach the bottom. They rushed out and to the western door.

Here, where they had been accustomed to see Madison Square spread out before them, a clearing of perhaps half an acre in extent showed itself. Where their eyes instinctively looked for the dark bronze fountain, near which soapbox orators aforetime held sway, they saw a tent, a wigwam of hides and bark gaily painted. And before the wigwam were two or three brown-skinned Indians, utterly petrified with astonishment.

Behind the first wigwam were others, painted like the first

with daubs of brightly colored clay. From them, too, Indians issued, and stared in incredulous amazement, their eyes growing wider and wider. When the group of white people confronted the Indians there was a moment's deathlike silence. Then, with a wild yell, the redskins broke and ran, not stopping to gather together their belongings, nor pausing for even a second glance at the weird strangers who invaded their domain.

Arthur took two or three deep breaths of the fresh air and found himself even then comparing its quality with that of the city. Estelle stared about her with unbelieving eyes. She turned and saw the great bulk of the office building behind her, then faced this small clearing with a virgin forest on its farther side.

She found herself trembling from some undefined cause. Arthur glanced at her. He saw the trembling and knew she would have a fit of nerves in a moment if something did not come up demanding instant attention.

'We'd better take a look at this village,' he said in an offhand voice. 'We can probably find out how long ago it is from the weapons and so on.'

He grasped her arm firmly and led her in the direction of the tents. The other people, left behind, displayed their emotions in different ways. Two or three of them – women – sat frankly down on the steps and indulged in tears of bewilderment, fright and relief in a peculiar combination defying analysis. Two or three of the men swore, in shaken voices.

Meantime, the elevators inside the building were rushing and clanging, and the hall filled with a white-faced mob, desperately anxious to find out what had happened and why. The people poured out of the door and stared about blankly. There was a peculiar expression of doubt on every one of their faces. Each one was asking himself if he were awake, and having proved that by pinches, openly administered, the next query was whether they had gone mad.

Arthur led Estelle cautiously among the tents.

The village contained about a dozen wigwams. Most of them were made of strips of birch bark, cleverly overlapping each other, the seams cemented with gum. All had hide flaps for doors, and one or two were built almost entirely of hides, sewed together with strips of sinew.

Arthur made only a cursory examination of the village. His principal motive in taking Estelle there was to give her some mental occupation to ward off the reaction from the excitement of the cataclysm.

He looked into one or two of the tents and found merely couches of hides, with minor domestic utensils scattered about. He brought from one tent a bow and quiver of arrows. The workmanship was good, but very evidently the maker had no knowledge of metal tools.

Arthur's acquaintance with archeological subjects was very slight, but he observed that the arrowheads were chipped, and not rubbed smooth. They were attached to the shafts with strips of gut or tendon.

Arthur was still pursuing his investigation when a sob from Estelle made him stop and look at her.

'Oh, what are we going to do?' she asked tearfully. 'What *are* we going to do? Where are we?'

'You mean, *when* are we,' Arthur corrected with a grim smile. 'I don't know. Way back before the discovery of America, though. You can see in everything in the village that there isn't a trace of European civilization. I suspect that we are several thousand years back. I can't tell, of course, but this pottery makes me think so. See this bowl?'

He pointed to a bowl of red clay lying on the ground before one of the wigwams.

'If you'll look, you'll see that it isn't really pottery at all. It's a basket that was woven of reeds and then smeared with clay to make it fire-resisting. The people who made that didn't know about baking clay to make it stay put. When America was discovered nearly all the tribes knew something about pottery.'

'But what are we going to do?' Estelle tearfully insisted.

'We're going to muddle along as well as we can,' answered Arthur cheerfully, 'until we can get back to where we started from. Maybe the people back in the twentieth century can send a relief party after us. When the skyscraper vanished it must have left a hole of some sort, and it may be possible for them to follow us down.'

'If that's so,' said Estelle quickly, 'why can't we climb up it without waiting for them to come after us?'

Arthur scratched his head. He looked across the clearing at the skyscraper. It seemed to rest very solidly on the ground. He looked up. The sky seemed normal.

'To tell the truth,' he admitted, 'there doesn't seem to be any hole. I said that more to cheer you up than anything else.'

Estelle clenched her hands tightly and took a grip on herself.

'Just tell me the truth,' she said quietly. 'I was rather foolish, but tell me what you honestly think.'

Arthur eyed her keenly.

'In that case,' he said reluctantly, 'I'll admit we're in a pretty bad fix. I don't know what has happened, how it happened, or anything about it. I'm just going to keep on going until I see a way clear to get out of this mess. There are two thousand of us people, more or less, and among all of us we must be able to find a way out.'

Estelle had turned very pale.

'We're in no great danger from Indians,' went on Arthur thoughtfully, 'or from anything else that I know of – except one thing.'

'What is that?' asked Estelle quickly.

Arthur shook his head and led her back toward the skyscraper, which was now thronged with the people from all the floors who had come down to the ground and were standing excitedly about the concourse asking each other what had happened.

Arthur led Estelle to one of the corners.

'Wait for me here,' he ordered. 'I'm going to talk to this crowd.'

He pushed his way through until he could reach the confectionery and news-stand in the main hallway. Here he climbed up on the counter and shouted:

'People, listen to me! I'm going to tell you what's happened!'

In an instant there was dead silence. He found himself the

center of a sea of white faces, every one contorted with fear and anxiety.

'To begin with,' he said confidently, 'there's nothing to be afraid of. We're going to get back to where we started from! I don't know how, yet, but we'll do it. Don't get frightened. Now I'll tell you what's happened.'

He rapidly sketched out for them, in words as simple as he could make them, his theory that a flaw in the rock on which the foundations rested had developed and let the skyscraper sink, not downward, but into the Fourth Dimension.

'I'm an engineer,' he finished. 'What nature can do, we can imitate. Nature let us into this hole. We'll climb out. In the meantime, matters are serious. We needn't be afraid of not getting back. We'll do that. What we've got to fight is – starvation!'

V

'We've got to fight starvation, and we've got to beat it,' Arthur continued doggedly. 'I'm telling you this right at the outset, because I want you to begin right at the beginning and pitch in to help. We have very little food and a lot of us to eat it. First, I want some volunteers to help with rationing. Next, I want every ounce of food in this place put under guard where it can be served to those who need it most. Who will help out with this?'

The swift succession of shocks had paralyzed the faculties of most of the people there, but half a dozen moved forward. Among them was a single gray-haired man with an air of accustomed authority. Arthur recognized him as the president of the bank on the ground floor.

'I don't know who you are or if you're right in saying what has happened,' said the gray-haired man. 'But I see something's got to be done, and – well, for the time being I'll take your word for what that is. Later on we'll thrash this matter out.'

Arthur nodded. He bent over and spoke in a low voice to the gray-haired man, who moved away.

'Grayson, Walters, Terhune, Simpson, and Forsythe, come here,' the gray-haired man called at a doorway.

A number of men began to press dazedly toward him. Arthur resumed his harangue.

'You people – those of you who aren't too dazed to think – are remembering there's a restaurant in the building and no need to starve. You're wrong. There are nearly two thousand of us here. That means six thousand meals a day. We've got to have nearly ten tons of food a day, and we've got to have it at once.'

'Hunt?' someone suggested.

'I saw Indians,' someone else shouted. 'Can we trade with them?'

'We can hunt and we can trade with the Indians,' Arthur admitted, 'but we need food by the ton – by the ton, people! The Indians don't store up supplies, and, besides, they're much too scattered to have a surplus for us. But we've got to have food. Now, how many of you know anything about hunting, fishing, trapping, or any possible way of getting food?'

There were a few hands raised – pitifully few. Arthur saw Estelle's hand up.

'Very well,' he said. 'Those of you who raised your hands then come with me up on the second floor and we'll talk it over. The rest of you try to conquer your fright, and don't go outside for a while. We've got some things to attend to before it will be quite safe for you to venture out. And keep away from the restaurant. There are armed guards over that food. Before we pass it out indiscriminately, we'll see to it there's more for tomorrow and the next day.'

He stepped down from the counter and moved toward the stairway. It was not worth while to use the elevator for the ride of only one floor. Estelle managed to join him, and they mounted the steps together.

'Do you think we'll pull through all right?' she asked quietly.

'We've got to!' Arthur told her, setting his chin firmly. 'We've simply got to.'

75

The gray-haired president of the bank was waiting for them at the top of the stairs.

'My name is Van Deventer,' he said, shaking hands with Arthur, who gave his own name.

'Where shall our emergency council sit?' he asked.

'The bank has a boardroom right over the safety vault. I dare say we can accommodate everybody there – everybody in the council, anyway.'

Arthur followed into the boardroom, and the others trooped in after him.

'I'm just assuming temporary leadership,' Arthur explained, 'because it's imperative some things be done at once. Later on we can talk about electing officials to direct our activities. Right now we need food. How many of you can shoot?'

About a quarter of the hands were raised. Estelle's was among the number.

'And how many are fishermen?'

A few more went up.

'What do the rest of you do?'

There was a chorus of 'gardener,' 'I have a garden in my yard,' 'I grow peaches in New Jersey,' and three men confessed that they raised chickens as a hobby.

'We'll want you gardeners in a little while. Don't go yet. But the most important are huntsmen and fishermen. Have any of you weapons in your offices?'

A number had revolvers, but only one man had a shotgun and shells. 'I was going on my vacation this afternoon straight from the office,' he explained, 'and have all my vacation tackle.'

'Good man!' Arthur exclaimed. 'You'll go after the heavy game.'

'With a shotgun?' the sportsman asked, aghast.

'If you get close to them a shotgun will do as well as any-thing, and we can't waste a shell on every bird or rabbit. Those shells of yours are precious. You other fellows will have to turn fishermen for a while. Your pistols are no good for hunting.'

'The watchmen at the bank have riot guns,' said Van

Deventer, 'and there are one or two repeating rifles there. I don't know about ammunition.'

'Good! I don't mean about the ammunition, but about the guns. We'll hope for the ammunition. You fishermen get to work to improvise tackle out of anything you can get hold of. Will you do that?'

A series of nods answered his question.

'Now for the gardeners. You people will have to roam through the woods in company with the hunters and locate anything in the way of edibles that grows. Do all of you know what wild plants look like? I mean wild fruits and vegetables that are good to eat.'

A few of them nodded, but the majority looked dubious. The consensus of opinion seemed to be that they would try. Arthur seemed a little discouraged.

'I guess you're the man to tell about the restaurant,' Van Deventer said quietly. 'And as this is the food commission, or something of that sort, everybody here will be better for hearing it. Anyway, everybody will have to know it before night. I took over the restaurant as you suggested, and posted some of the men from the bank that I knew I could trust about the doors. But there was hardly any use in doing it.'

'The restaurant stocks up in the afternoon, as most of its business is in the morning and at noon. It only carries a day's stock of foodstuffs, and the – the cataclysm, or whatever it was, came at three o'clock. There is practically nothing in the place. We couldn't make sandwiches for half the women that are caught with us, let alone the men. Everybody will go hungry tonight. There will be no breakfast tomorrow, nor anything to eat until we either make arrangements with the Indians for some supplies or else get food for ourselves.'

Arthur leaned his jaw on his hand and considered. A slow flush crept over his cheek. He was getting his fighting blood up.

At school, when he began to flush slowly his schoolmates had known the symptom and avoided his wrath. Now he was growing angry with mere circumstances, but it would be none the less unfortunate for those circumstances.

'Well,' he said at last deliberately, 'we've got to – What's that?'

There was a great creaking and groaning. Suddenly a sort of vibration was felt under foot. The floor began to take on a slight slant.

'Great Heaven!' someone cried. 'The building's turning over and we'll be buried in the ruins!'

The tilt of the floor became more pronounced. An empty chair slid to one end of the room. There was a crash.

VI

Arthur woke to find someone tugging at his shoulders, trying to drag him from beneath the heavy table, which had wedged itself across his feet and pinned him fast, while a flying chair had struck him on the head and knocked him unconscious.

'Oh, come and help,' Estelle's voice was calling deliberately. 'Somebody come and help! He's caught in here!'

She was sobbing in a combination of panic and some unknown emotion.

'Help me, please!' she gasped, then her voice broke despondently, but she never ceased to tug ineffectually at Chamberlain, trying to drag him out of the mass of wreckage.

Arthur moved a little, dazedly.

'Are you alive?' she called anxiously. 'Are you alive? Hurry, oh, hurry and wriggle out. The building's falling to pieces!'

'I'm all right,' Arthur said weakly. 'You get out before it all comes down.'

'I won't leave you,' she declared 'Where are you caught? Are you badly hurt? Hurry, please hurry!'

Arthur stirred, but could not loosen his feet. He half rolled over, and the table moved as if it had been precariously balanced, and slid heavily to one side. With Estelle still tugging at him, he managed to get to his feet on the slanting floor and stared about him.

Arthur continued to stare about.

'No danger,' he said weakly. 'Just the floor of the one room gave way. The aftermath of the rock-flaw.'

He made his way across the splintered flooring and piled-up chairs.

'We're on top of the safe-deposit vault,' he said. 'That's why we didn't fall all the way to the floor below. I wonder how we're going to get down?'

Estelle followed him, still frightened for fear of the building falling upon them. Some of the long floorboards stretched over the edge of the vault and rested on a tall, bronze grating that protected the approach to the massive strongbox. Arthur tested them with his foot.

'They seem to be pretty solid,' he said tentatively.

His strength was coming back to him every moment. He had been no more than stunned. He walked out on the planking to the bronze grating and turned.

'If you don't get dizzy, you might come on,' he said. 'We can swing down the grille here to the floor.'

Estelle followed gingerly and in a moment they were safely below. The corridor was quite empty.

'When the crash came,' Estelle explained, her voice shaking with the reaction from her fear of a moment ago, 'everyone thought the building was coming to pieces, and ran out. I'm afraid they've all run away.'

'They'll be back in a little while,' Arthur said quietly.

They went along the big marble corridor to the same western door, out of which they had first gone to see the Indian village. As they emerged into the sunlight they met a few of the people who had already recovered from their panic and were returning.

A crowd of respectable size gathered in a few moments, all still pale and shaken, but coming back to the building which was their refuge. Arthur leaned wearily against the cold stone. It seemed to vibrate under his touch. He turned quickly to Estelle.

'Feel this,' he exclaimed.

She did so.

'I've been wondering what that rumble was,' she said. 'I've been hearing it ever since we landed here, but didn't understand where it came from.'

'You hear a rumble?' Arthur asked, puzzled. 'I can't hear anything.'

'It isn't as loud as it was, but I hear it,' Estelle insisted. 'It's very deep, like the lowest possible bass note of an organ.'

'You couldn't hear the shrill whistle when we were coming here,' Arthur exclaimed suddenly, 'and you can't hear the squeak of a bat. Of course your ears are pitched lower than usual, and you can hear sounds that are lower than I can hear. Listen carefully. Does it sound in the least like a liquid rushing through somewhere?'

'Y-yes,' said Estelle hesitatingly. 'Somehow, I don't quite understand how, it gives me the impression of a tidal flow or something of that sort.'

Arthur rushed indoors. When Estelle followed him she found him excitedly examining the marble floor about the base of the vault.

'It's cracked,' he said excitedly. 'It's cracked! The vault rose all of an inch!'

Estelle looked and saw the cracks.

'What does that mean?'

'It means we're going to get back where we belong,' Arthur cried jubilantly. 'It means I'm on the track of the whole trouble. It means everything's going to be all right.'

He prowled about the vault exultantly, noting exactly how the cracks in the flooring ran and seeing in each a corroboration of his theory.

'I'll have to make some inspections in the cellar,' he went on happily, 'but I'm nearly sure I'm on the right track and can figure out a corrective.'

'How soon can we hope to start back?' asked Estelle eagerly.

Arthur hesitated, then a great deal of the excitement ebbed from his face, leaving it rather worried and stern.

'It may be a month, or two months, or a year,' he answered gravely. 'I don't know. If the first thing I try will work, it won't be long. If we have to experiment, I daren't guess how long we may be. But' – his chin set firmly – 'we're going to get back.'

Estelle looked at him speculatively. Her own expression grew a little worried, too.

'But in a month,' she said dubiously, 'we – there is hardly any hope of our finding food for two thousand people for a month, is there?'

'We've got to,' Arthur declared. 'We can't hope to get that much food from the Indians. It will be days before they'll dare to come back to their village, if they ever come. It will be weeks before we can hope to have them earnestly at work to feed us, and that's leaving aside the question of how we'll communicate with them, and how we'll manage to trade with them. Frankly, I think everybody is going to have to draw his belt tight before we get through – if we do. Some of us will get along, anyway.'

Estelle's eyes opened wide as the meaning of his last sentence penetrated her mind.

'You mean – that all of us won't—'

'I'm going to take care of you,' Arthur said gravely, 'but there are liable to be lively doings around here when people begin to realize they're really in a tight fix for food. I'm going to get Van Deventer to help me organize a police band to enforce martial law. We mustn't have any disorder, that's certain, and I don't trust a city-bred man in a pinch unless I know him.'

He stooped and picked up a revolver from the floor, left there by one of the bank watchmen when he fled, in the belief that the building was falling.

VII

Arthur stood at the window of his office and stared out toward the west. The sun was setting, but upon what a scene!

Where, from this same window Arthur had seen the sun setting behind the Jersey hills, all edged with the angular roofs of factories, with their chimneys emitting columns of smoke, he now saw the same sun sinking redly behind a mass of luxuriant

81

foliage. And where he was accustomed to look upon the tops of high buildings – each entitled to the name of 'skyscraper' – he now saw miles and miles of waving green branches.

The wide Hudson flowed on placidly, all unruffled by the arrival of this strange monument upon its shores – the same Hudson Arthur knew as a busy thoroughfare of puffing steamers and chugging launches. Two or three small streams wandered unconcernedly across the land that Arthur had known as the most closely built-up territory on earth. And far, far below him – Arthur had to lean well out of his window to see it – stood a collection of tiny wigwams. Those small bark structures represented the original metropolis of New York.

His telephone rang. Van Deventer was on the wire. The exchange in the building was still working. Van Deventer wanted Arthur to come down to his private office. There were still a great many things to be settled – the arrangements for commandeering offices for sleeping quarters for the women, and numberless other details. The men who seemed to have best kept their heads were gathering there to settle upon a course of action.

Arthur glanced out of the window again before going to the elevator. He saw a curiously compact dark cloud moving swiftly across the sky to the west.

'Miss Woodward,' he said sharply, 'What is that?'

Estelle came to the window and looked.

'They are birds,' she told him. 'Birds flying in a group. I've often seen them in the country, though never as many as that.'

'How do you catch birds?' Arthur asked her. 'I know about shooting them, and so on, but we haven't guns enough to count. Could we catch them in traps, do you think?'

'I wouldn't be surprised,' said Estelle thoughtfully. 'But it would be hard to catch many.'

'Come downstairs,' directed Arthur. 'You know as much as any of the men here, and more than most, apparently. We're going to make you show us how to catch things.'

Estelle smiled, a trifle wanly. Arthur led the way to the elevator. In the car he noticed that she looked distressed.

'What's the matter?' he asked. 'You aren't really frightened, are you?'

'No,' she answered shakily, 'but – I'm rather upset about this thing. It's so – so terrible, somehow, to be back here, thousands of miles, or years, away from all one's friends and everybody.'

'Please' – Arthur smiled encouragingly at her – 'please count me your friend, won't you?'

She nodded, but blinked back some tears. Arthur would have tried to hearten her further, but the elevator stopped at their floor. They walked into the room where the meeting of cool heads was to take place.

No more than a dozen men were in there talking earnestly but dispiritedly. When Arthur and Estelle entered Van Deventer came over to greet them.

'We've got to do something,' he said in a low voice. 'A wave of homesickness has swept over the whole place. Look at those men. Every one is thinking about his family and contrasting his cozy fireside with all that wilderness outside.'

'You don't seem to be worried,' Arthur observed with a smile.

Van Deventer's eyes twinkled.

'I'm a bachelor,' he said cheerfully, 'and I live in a hotel. I've been longing for a chance to see some real excitement for thirty years. Business has kept me from it up to now, but I'm enjoying myself hugely.'

Estelle looked at the group of dispirited men.

'We'll simply have to do something,' she said with a shaky smile. 'I feel just as they do. This morning I hated the thought of having to go back to my boarding-house tonight, but right now I feel as if the odor of cabbage in the hallway would seem like heaven.'

Arthur led the way to the flat-topped desk in the middle of the room.

'Let's settle a few of the more important matters,' he said in a businesslike tone. 'None of us has any authority to act for the rest of the people in the tower, but so many of us are in a state of blue funk that those who are here must have charge for a while. Anybody any suggestions?'

'Housing,' answered Van Deventer promptly. 'I suggest that we draft a gang of men to haul all the upholstered settees and rugs that are to be found to one floor, for the women to sleep on.'

'M – m. Yes. That's a good idea. Anybody a better plan?'

No one spoke. They all still looked much too homesick to take any great interest in anything, but they began to listen more or less halfheartedly.

'I've been thinking about coal,' said Arthur. 'There's undoubtedly a supply in the basement, but I wonder if it wouldn't be well to cut the lights off most of the floors, only lighting up the ones we're using.'

'That might be a good idea later,' Estelle said quietly, 'but light is cheering, somehow, and everyone feels so blue that I wouldn't do it tonight. Tomorrow they'll begin to get up their resolution again, and you can ask them to do things.'

'If we're going to starve to death,' one of the other men said gloomily, 'we might as well have plenty of light to do it by.'

'We aren't going to starve to death,' retorted Arthur sharply. 'Just before I came down I saw a great cloud of birds, greater than I had ever seen before. When we get at those birds—'

'When,' echoed the gloomy one.

'They were pigeons,' Estelle explained. 'They shouldn't be hard to snare or trap.'

'I usually have my dinner before now,' the gloomy one protested, 'and I'm told I won't get anything tonight.'

The other men began to straighten their shoulders. The peevishness of one of their number seemed to bring out their latent courage.

'Well, we've got to stand it for the present,' one of them said almost philosophically. 'What I'm most anxious about is getting back. Have we any chance?'

Arthur nodded emphatically.

'I think so. I have a sort of idea as to the cause of our sinking into the Fourth Dimension, and when that is verified, a corrective can be looked for and applied.'

'How long will that take?'

'Can't say,' Arthur replied frankly. 'I don't know what tools, what materials, or what workmen we have, and what's rather more to the point, I don't even know what work will have to be done. The pressing problem is food.'

'Oh, bother the food,' someone protested impatiently. 'I don't care about myself. I can go hungry tonight. I want to get back to my family.'

'That's all that really matters,' a chorus of voices echoed.

'We'd better not bother about anything else unless we find we can't get back. Concentrate on getting back,' one man stated more explicitly.

'Look here,' said Arthur incisively. 'You've a family, and so have a great many of the others in the tower, but your family and everybody else's family has got to wait. As an inside limit, we can hope to begin to work on the problem of getting back when we're sure there's nothing else going to happen. I tell you quite honestly that I think I know what is the direct cause of this catastrophe. And I'll tell you even more honestly that I think I'm the only man among us who can put this tower back where it started from. And I'll tell you most honestly of all that any attempt to meddle at this present time with the forces that let us down here will result in a catastrophe considerably greater than the one that happened today.'

'Well, if you're sure—' someone began reluctantly.

'I am so sure that I'm going to keep to myself the knowledge of what will start those forces to work again,' Arthur said quietly. 'I don't want any impatient meddling. If we start them too soon God only knows what will happen.'

VIII

Van Deventer was eying Arthur Chamberlain keenly.

'It isn't a question of your wanting pay in exchange for your services in putting us back, is it?' he asked coolly.

Arthur turned and faced him. His face began to flush slowly. Van Deventer put up one hand.

'I beg your pardon. I see.'

'We aren't settling the things we came here for,' Estelle interrupted.

She had noted the threat of friction and hastened to put in a diversion. Arthur relaxed.

'I think that as a beginning,' he suggested, 'we'd better get sleeping arrangements completed. We can get everybody together somewhere, I dare say, and then secure volunteers for the work.'

'Right.' Van Deventer was anxious to make amends for his blunder of a moment before. 'Shall I send the bank watchmen to go on each floor in turn and ask everybody to come downstairs?'

'You might start them,' Arthur said. 'It will take a long time for everyone to assemble.'

Van Deventer spoke into the telephone on his desk. In a moment he hung up the receiver.

'They're on their way,' he said.

Arthur was frowning to himself and scribbling in a notebook.

'Of course,' he announced abstractedly, 'the pressing problem is food. We've quite a number of fishermen, and a few hunters. We've got to have a lot of food at once, and everything considered, I think we'd better count on the fishermen. At sunrise we'd better have some people begin to dig bait and wake our anglers. They'd better make their tackle tonight, don't you think?'

There was a general nod.

'We'll announce that, then. The fishermen will go to the

river under guard of the men we have who can shoot. I think what Indians there are will be much too frightened to try to ambush any of us, but we'd better be on the safe side. They'll keep together and fish at nearly the same spot, with our hunters patrolling the woods behind them, taking potshots at game, if they see any. The fishermen should make more or less of a success, I think. The Indians weren't extensive fishers that I ever heard of, and the river ought fairly to swarm with fish.'

He closed his notebook.

'How many weapons can we count on altogether?' Arthur asked Van Deventer.

'In the bank, about a dozen riot guns and half a dozen repeating rifles. Elsewhere I don't know. Forty or fifty men said they had revolvers, though.'

'We'll give revolvers to the men who go with the fishermen. The Indians haven't heard firearms and will run at the report, even if they dare attack our men.'

'We can send out the gun-armed men as hunters,' someone suggested, 'and send gardeners with them to look for vegetables and such things.'

'We'll have to take a sort of census, really,' Arthur suggested, 'finding what everyone can do and getting him to do it.'

'I never planned anything like this before,' Van Deventer remarked, 'and I never thought I should, but this is much more fun than running a bank.'

Arthur smiled.

'Let's go and have our meeting,' he said cheerfully.

But the meeting was a gloomy and despairing affair. Nearly everyone had watched the sun set upon a strange, wild landscape. Hardly an individual among the whole two thousand of them had ever been out of sight of a house before in his or her life. To look out at a vast, untouched wilderness where hitherto they had seen the most highly civilized city on the globe would have been startling and depressing enough in itself, but to know that they were alone in a whole continent of savages and that there was not, indeed, in all the world a single community of people they could greet as brothers was terrifying.

Few of them thought so far, but there was actually – if Arthur's estimate of several thousand years' drop back through time was correct – there was actually no other group of English-speaking people in the world. The English language was yet to be invented. Even Rome, the synonym for antiquity of culture, might still be an obscure village inhabited by a band of tatterdemalions under the leadership of an upstart Romulus.

Soft in body as these people were, city-bred and unaccustomed to face other than the most conventionalized emergencies of life, they were terrified. Hardly one of them had even gone without a meal in all his life. To have the prospect of having to earn their food, not by the manipulation of figures in a book, or by expert juggling of profits and prices, but by literal wresting of that food from its source in the earth or stream was a really terrifying thing for them.

In addition, every one of them was bound to the life of modern times by a hundred ties. Many of them had families, a thousand years away. All had interests, engrossing interests, in modern New York.

One young man felt an anxiety that was really ludicrous because he had promised to take his sweetheart to the theater that night, and if he did not come she would be very angry. Another was to have been married in a week. Some of the people were, like Van Deventer and Arthur, so situated that they could view the episode as an adventure, or, like Estelle, who had no immediate fear because all her family was provided for without her help and lived far from New York, so they would not learn of the catastrophe for some time. Many, however, felt instant and pressing fear for the families whose expenses ran always so close to their incomes that the disappearance of the breadwinner for a week would mean actual want or debt. There are very many such families in New York.

The people, therefore, that gathered hopelessly at the call of Van Deventer's watchmen were dazed and spiritless. Their excitement after Arthur's first attempt to explain the situation to them had evaporated. They were no longer keyed up to a high pitch by the startling thing that had happened to them.

Nevertheless, although only half comprehending what had actually occurred, they began to realize what that occurrence meant. No matter where they might go over the whole face of the globe, they would always be aliens and strangers. If they had been carried away to some unknown shore, some wilderness far from their own land, they might have thought of building ships to return to their homes. They had seen New York vanish before their eyes, however. They had seen their civilization disappear while they watched.

They were in a barbarous world. There was not, for example, a single sulfur match on the whole earth except those in the runaway skyscraper.

IX

Arthur and Van Deventer, in turn with the others of the cooler heads, thundered at the apathetic people, trying to waken them to the necessity for work. They showered promises of inevitable return to modern times, they pledged their honor to the belief that a way would ultimately be found by which they would all yet find themselves safely back home again.

The people, however, had seen New York disintegrate, and Arthur's explanation sounded like some wild dream of an imaginative novelist. Not one person in all the gathering could actually realize that his home might yet be waiting for him, though at the same time he felt a pathetic anxiety for the welfare of its inmates.

Every one was in a turmoil of contradictory beliefs. On the one hand they knew that all of New York could not be actually destroyed and replaced by a splendid forest in the space of a few hours, so the accident or catastrophe must have occurred to those in the tower, and on the other hand, they had seen all of New York vanish by bits and fragments, to be replaced by a smaller and dingier town, had beheld that replaced in turn, and at last had landed in the midst of this forest.

Every one, too, began to feel an unusual and uncomfortable

sensation of hunger. It was a mild discomfort as yet, but few of them had experienced it before without an immediate prospect of assuaging the craving, and the knowledge that there was no food to be had somehow increased the desire for it. They were really in a pitiful state.

Van Deventer spoke encouragingly, and then asked for volunteers for immediate work. There was hardly any response. Every one seemed sunk in despondency. Arthur then began to talk straight from the shoulder and succeeded in rousing them a little, but every one was still rather too frightened to realize that work could help at all.

In desperation the dozen or so men who had gathered in Van Deventer's office went about among the gathering and simply selected men at random, ordering them to follow and begin work. This began to awaken the crowd, but they wakened to fear rather than resolution. They were city-bred, and unaccustomed to face the unusual or the alarming.

Arthur noted the new restlessness, but attributed it to growing uneasiness rather than selfish panic. He was rather pleased that they were outgrowing their apathy. When the meeting had come to an end he felt satisfied that by morning the latent resolution among the people would have crystallized and they would be ready to work earnestly and intelligently on whatever tasks they were directed to undertake.

He returned to the ground floor of the building feeling much more hopeful than before. Two thousand people all earnestly working for one end are hard to down even when faced with such a task as confronted the inhabitants of the runaway skyscraper. Even if they were never able to return to modern times they would still be able to form a community that might do much to hasten the development of civilization in other parts of the world.

His hope received a rude shock when he reached the great hallway on the lower floor. There was a fruit and confectionery stand here, and as Arthur arrived at the spot, he saw a surging mass of men about it. The keeper of the stand looked frightened, but was selling off his stock as fast as he could make change. Arthur forced his way to the counter.

'Here,' he said sharply to the keeper of the stand, 'stop selling this stuff. It's got to be held until we can dole it out where it's needed.'

'I – I can't help myself,' the keeper said. 'They're takin' it anyway.'

'Get back there,' Arthur cried to the crowd. 'Do you call this decent, trying to get more than your share of this stuff? You'll get your portion tomorrow. It is going to be divided up.'

'Go to hell!' someone panted. 'You c'n starve if you want to, but I'm goin' to look out f'r myself.'

The men were not really starving, but had been put into a panic by the plain speeches of Arthur and his helpers, and were seizing what edibles they could lay hands upon in preparation for the hunger they had been warned to expect.

Arthur pushed against the mob, trying to thrust them away from the counter, but his very effort intensified their panic. There was a quick surge and a crash. The glass front of the showcase broke in.

In a flash of rage Arthur struck out viciously. The crowd paid not the slightest attention to him, however. Every man was too panic-stricken, and too intent on getting some of this food before it was all gone to bother with him.

Arthur was simply crushed back by the bodies of the forty or fifty men. In a moment he found himself alone amid the wreckage of the stand, with the keeper wringing his hands over the remnants of his goods.

Van Deventer ran down the stairs.

'What's the matter?' he demanded as he saw Arthur nursing a bleeding hand cut on the broken glass of the showcase.

'Bolsheviki!' answered Arthur with a grim smile. 'We woke up some of the crowd too successfully. They got panic-stricken and started to buy out this stuff here. I tried to stop them, and you see what happened. We'd better look to the restaurant, though I doubt if they'll try anything else just now.'

He followed Van Deventer up to the restaurant floor. There

were picked men before the door, but just as Arthur and the bank president appeared two or three white-faced men went up to the guards and started low-voiced conversations.

Arthur reached the spot in time to forestall bribery.

Arthur collared one man, Van Deventer another, and in a moment the two were sent reeling down the hallway.

'Some fools have got panic-stricken!' Van Deventer explained to the men before the doors in a casual voice, though he was breathing heavily from the unaccustomed exertion. 'They've smashed up the fruit-stand on the ground floor and stolen the contents. It's nothing but blue funk! Only, if any of them start to gather around here, hit them first and talk it over afterward. You'll do that?'

'We will!' the men said heartily.

'Shall we use our guns?' asked another hopefully.

Van Deventer grinned.

'No,' he replied, 'we haven't any excuse for that yet. But you might shoot at the ceiling, if they get excited. They're just frightened!'

He took Arthur's arm, and the two walked toward the stairway again.

'Chamberlain,' he said happily, 'tell me why I've never had as much fun as this before!'

Arthur smiled a bit wearily.

'I'm glad you're enjoying yourself!' he said. 'I'm not. I'm going outside to walk around. I want to see if any cracks have appeared in the earth anywhere. It's dark, and I'll borrow a lantern down in the fire-room, but I want to find out if there are any more developments in the condition of the building.'

X

Despite his preoccupation with his errand, which was to find if there were other signs of the continued activity of the strange forces that had lowered the tower through the Fourth Dimension into the dim and unrecorded years of aboriginal America,

Arthur could not escape the fascination of the sight that met his eyes. A bright moon shone overhead and silvered the white sides of the tower, while the brightly lighted windows of the offices within glittered like jewels set into the shining shaft.

From his position on the ground he looked into the dimness of the forest on all sides. Black obscurity had gathered beneath the dark masses of moonlit foliage. The tiny birch-bark teepees of the now deserted Indian village glowed palely. Above, the stars looked calmly down at the accusing finger of the tower pointing upward, as if in reproach at their indifference to the savagery that reigned over the whole earth.

Like a fairy tower of jewels the building rose. Alone among a wilderness of trees and streams it towered in a strange beauty: moonlit to silver, lighted from within to a mass of brilliant gems, it stood serenely still.

Arthur, carrying his futile lantern about its base, felt his own insignificance as never before. He wondered what the Indians must think. He knew there must be hundreds of eyes fixed upon the strange sight – fixed in awe-stricken terror or superstitious reverence upon this unearthly visitor to their hunting grounds.

A tiny figure, dwarfed by the building whose base he skirted, Arthur moved slowly about the vast pile. The earth seemed not to have been affected by the vast weight of the tower.

Arthur knew, however, that long concrete piles reached far down to bedrock. It was these piles that had sunk into the Fourth Dimension, carrying the building with them.

Arthur had followed the plans with great interest when the Metropolitan was constructed. It was an engineering feat, and in the engineering periodicals, whose study was a part of Arthur's business, great space had been given to the building and the methods of its construction.

While examining the earth carefully he went over his theory of the cause for the catastrophe. The whole structure must have sunk at the same time, or it, too, would have disintegrated, as the other buildings had appeared to disintegrate. Mentally, Arthur likened the submergence of the tower in the oceans of time to an elevator sinking past the different floors of an office building. All about the building the other skyscrapers of New York had seemed to vanish. In an elevator, the floors one passes seem to rise upward.

Carrying out the analogy to its logical end, Arthur reasoned that the building itself had no more cause to disintegrate, as the buildings it passed seemed to disintegrate, than the elevator in the office building would have cause to rise because its surroundings seemed to rise.

Within the building, he knew, there were strange stirrings of emotions. Queer currents of panic were running about, throwing the people to and fro as leaves are thrown about by a current of wind. Yet, underneath all those undercurrents of fear, was a rapidly growing resolution, strengthened by an increasing knowledge of the need to work.

Men were busy even then shifting all possible comfortable furniture to a single story for the women in the building to occupy. The men would sleep on the floor for the present. Beds of boughs could be improvised on the morrow. At sunrise on the following morning many men would go to the streams to fish, guarded by other men. All would be frightened, no doubt, but there would be a grim resolution underneath the fear. Other men would wander about to hunt.

There was little likelihood of Indians approaching for some days, at least, but when they did come Arthur meant to avoid hostilities by all possible means. The Indians would be fearful of their strange visitors, and it should not be difficult to convince them that friendliness was safest, even if they displayed unfriendly desires.

The pressing problem was food. There were two thousand people in the building, soft-bodied and city-bred. They were unaccustomed to hardship, and could not endure what more primitive people would hardly have noticed.

They must be fed, but first they must be taught to feed themselves. The fishermen would help, but Arthur could only hope that they would prove equal to the occasion. He did not know what to expect from them. From the hunters he expected but little. The Indians were wary hunters, and game would be shy if not scarce.

The great cloud of birds he had seen at sunset was a hopeful sign. Arthur vaguely remembered stories of great flocks of wood-pigeons which had been exterminated, as the buffalo was exterminated. As he considered the remembrance became more clear.

They had flown in huge flocks which nearly darkened the sky. As late as the forties of the nineteenth century they had been an important article of food, and had glutted the market at certain seasons of the year.

Estelle had said the birds he had seen at sunset were pigeons. Perhaps this was one of the great flocks. If it were really so, the food problem would be much lessened, provided a way could be found to secure them. The ammunition in the tower was very limited, and a shell could not be found for every bird that was needed, nor even for every three or four. Great traps must be devised, or bird-lime might possibly be produced. Arthur made a mental note to ask Estelle if she knew anything of bird-lime.

A vague, humming roar, altering in pitch, came to his ears. He listened for some time before he identified it as the sound of the wind playing upon the irregular surfaces of the tower. In the city the sound was drowned by the multitude of other noises, but here Arthur could hear it plainly.

He listened a moment, and became surprised at the number of night noises he could hear. In New York he had closed his ears to incidental sounds from sheer self-protection. Somewhere he heard the ripple of a little spring. As the idea of a spring came into his mind, he remembered Estelle's description of the deep-toned roar she had heard.

He put his hand on the cold stone of the building. There was still a vibrant quivering of the rock. It was weaker than before, but was still noticeable.

He drew back from the rock and looked up into the sky. It seemed to blaze with stars, far more stars than Arthur had ever seen in the city, and more than he had dreamed existed.

As he looked, however, a cloud seemed to film a portion of the heavens. The stars still showed through it, but they twinkled in a peculiar fashion that Arthur could not understand.

He watched in growing perplexity. The cloud moved very swiftly. Thin as it seemed to be, it should have been silvery from the moonlight, but the sky was noticeably darker where it moved. It advanced toward the tower and seemed to obscure the upper portion. A confused motion became visible among its parts. Wisps of it whirled away from the brilliantly lighted tower, and then returned swiftly toward it.

Arthur heard a faint tinkle, then a musical scraping, which became louder. A faint scream sounded, then another. The tinkle developed into the sound made by breaking glass, and the scraping sound became that of the broken fragments as they rubbed against the sides of the tower in their fall.

The scream came again. It was the frightened cry of a woman. A soft body struck the earth not ten feet from where Arthur stood, then another, and another.

XI

Arthur urged the elevator boy to greater speed. They were speeding up the shaft as rapidly as possible, but it was not fast enough. When they at last reached the height at which the excitement seemed to be centered, the car was stopped with a jerk and Arthur dashed down the hall.

Half a dozen frightened stenographers stood there, huddled together.

'What's the matter?' Arthur demanded. Men were running from the other floors to see what the trouble was.

'The – the windows broke, and – and something flew in at us!' one of them gasped. There was a crash inside the nearest office and the women screamed again.

Arthur drew a revolver from his pocket and advanced to the door. He quickly threw it open, entered, and closed it behind him. Those left out in the hall waited tensely.

There was no sound. The women began to look even more frightened. The men shuffled their feet uneasily, and looked uncomfortably at one another. Van Deventer appeared on the scene, puffing a little from his haste.

The door opened again and Arthur came out. He was carrying something in his hands. He had put his revolver aside and looked somewhat foolish but very much delighted.

'The food question is settled,' he said happily. 'Look!'

He held out the object he carried. It was a bird, apparently a pigeon of some sort. It seemed to have been stunned, but as Arthur held it out it stirred, then struggled, and in a moment was flapping wildly in an attempt to escape.

'It's a wood-pigeon,' said Arthur. 'They must fly after dark sometimes. A big flock of them ran afoul of the tower and were dazed by the lights. They've broken a lot of windows, I dare say, but a great many of them ran into the stonework and were stunned. I was outside the tower, and when I came in they were dropping to the ground by hundreds. I didn't know what they were then, but if we wait twenty minutes or so I think we can go out and gather up our supper and breakfast and several other meals, all at once.'

Estelle had appeared and now reached out her hands for the bird.

'I'll take care of this one,' she said. 'Wouldn't it be a good idea to see if there aren't some more stunned in the other offices?'

In half an hour the electric stoves of the restaurant were going at their full capacity. Men, cheerfully excited men now, were bringing in pigeons by armfuls, and other men were skinning them. There was no time to pluck them, though a great many of the women were busily engaged in that occupation.

As fast as the birds could be cooked they were served out to the impatient but much cheered castaways, and in a little while nearly every person in the place was walking casually about the halls with a roasted, broiled, or fried pigeon in his hands. The ovens were roasting pigeons, the frying pans were frying them, and the broilers were loaded down with the small but tender birds.

The unexpected solution of the most pressing question cheered everyone amazingly. Many people were still frightened, but less frightened than before. Worry for their families still oppressed a great many, but the removal of the fear of immediate hunger led them to believe that the other problems before them would be solved, too, and in as satisfactory a manner.

Arthur had returned to his office with four broiled pigeons in a sheet of wrapping paper. As he somehow expected, Estelle was waiting there.

'Thought I'd bring lunch up,' he announced. 'Are you hungry?'

'Starving!' Estelle replied, and laughed.

The whole catastrophe began to become an adventure. She bit eagerly into a bird. Arthur began as hungrily on another. For some time neither spoke a word. At last, however, Arthur waved the leg of his second pigeon toward his desk.

'Look what we've got here!' he said.

Estelle nodded. The stunned pigeon Arthur had first picked up was tied by one foot to a paperweight.

'I thought we might keep him for a souvenir,' she suggested.

'You seem pretty confident we'll get back, all right,' Arthur observed. 'It was surely lucky those blessed birds came along. They've heartened up the people wonderfully!'

'Oh, I knew you'd manage somehow!' said Estelle confidently.

'I manage?' Arthur repeated, smiling. 'What have I done?'

'Why, you've done everything,' affirmed Estelle stoutly. 'You've told the people what to do from the very first, and you're going to get us back.'

Arthur grinned, then suddenly his face grew a little more serious.

'I wish I were as sure as you are,' he said. 'I think we'll be all right, though, sooner or later.'

'I'm sure of it,' Estelle declared with conviction. 'Why, you—'

'Why I?' asked Arthur again. He bent forward in his chair and fixed his eyes on Estelle's. She looked up, met his gaze, and stammered.

'You – you do things,' she finished lamely.

'I'm tempted to do something now,' Arthur said. 'Look here, Miss Woodward, you've been in my employ for three or four months. In all that time I've never had anything but the most impersonal comments from you. Why the sudden change?'

The twinkle in his eyes robbed his words of any impertinence.

'Why, I really – I really suppose I never noticed you before,' said Estelle.

'Please notice me hereafter,' said Arthur. 'I have been noticing you. I've been doing practically nothing else.'

Estelle flushed again. She tried to meet Arthur's eyes and failed. She bit desperately into her pigeon drumstick, trying to think of something to say.

'When we get back,' went on Arthur meditatively, 'I'll have nothing to do – no work or anything. I'll be broke and out of a job.'

Estelle shook her head emphatically. Arthur paid no attention.

'Estelle,' he said, smiling, 'would you like to be out of a job with me?'

Estelle turned crimson.

'I'm not very successful,' Arthur went on soberly. 'I'm afraid I wouldn't make a very good husband, I'm rather worthless and lazy!'

'You aren't,' broke in Estelle, 'you're – you're—'

Arthur reached over and took her by the shoulders.

'What?' he demanded.

She would not look at him, but she did not draw away. He held her from him for a moment.

'What am I?' he demanded again. Somehow he found

himself kissing the tips of her ears. Her face was buried against his shoulder.

'What am I?' he repeated sternly.

Her voice was muffled by his coat.

'You're – you're dear!' she said.

There was an interlude of about a minute and a half, then she pushed him away from her.

'Don't!' she said breathlessly. 'Please don't!'

'Aren't you going to marry me?' he demanded.

Still crimson, she nodded shyly. He kissed her again.

'Please don't!' she protested.

She fondled the lapels of his coat, quite content to have his arms about her.

'Why may'n't I kiss you if you're going to marry me?' Arthur demanded.

She looked up at him with an air of demure primness.

'You – you've been eating pigeon,' she told him in mock gravity, 'and – and your mouth is greasy!'

XII

It was two weeks later. Estelle looked out over the now familiar wild landscape. It was much the same when she looked far away, but near by there were great changes.

A cleared trail led through the woods to the waterfront, and a raft of logs extended out into the river for hundreds of feet. Both sides of the raft were lined with busy fishermen – men and women, too. A little to the north of the base of the building a huge mound of earth smoked sullenly. The coal in the cellar had given out and charcoal had been found to be the best substitute they could improvise. The mound was where the charcoal was made.

It was heartbreaking work to keep the fires going with charcoal, because it burned so rapidly in the powerful draft of the furnaces, but the original fire-room gang had been recruited to several times its original number from among the towerites, and the work was divided until it did not seem hard.

As Estelle looked down two tiny figures sauntered across the clearing from the woods with a heavy animal slung between them. One of them was using a gun as a walking-stick. Estelle saw the flash of the sun on its polished metal barrel.

There were a number of Indians in the clearing, watching with wide-open eyes the activities of the whites. Dozens of birch-bark canoes dotted the Hudson, each with its load of fishermen, industriously working for the white people. It had been hard to overcome the fear in the Indians, and they still paid superstitious reverence to the whites, but fair dealings, coupled with a constant readiness to defend themselves, had enabled Arthur to institute a system of trading for food that had so far proved satisfactory.

The whites had found spare light bulbs valuable currency in dealing with the red men. Picture-wire, too, was highly prized. There was not a picture left hanging in any of the offices. Metal paper-knives bought huge quantities of provisions from the eager Indian traders, and the story was current in the tower that Arthur had received eight canoe-loads of corn and vegetables in exchange for a broken-down typewriter. No one could guess what the savages wanted with the typewriter, but they had carted it away triumphantly.

Estelle smiled tenderly to herself as she remembered how Arthur had been the leading spirit in all the numberless enterprises in which the castaways had been forced to engage. He would come to her in a spare ten minutes, and tell her how everything was going. He seemed curiously boylike in those moments.

Sometimes he would come straight from the fire-room – he insisted on taking part in all the more arduous duties – having hastily cleaned himself for her inspection, snatch a hurried kiss, and then go off, laughing, to help chop down trees for the long fishing-raft. He had told them how to make charcoal, had taken a leading part in establishing and maintaining friendly relations with the Indians, and was now down in the deepest sub-basement, working with a gang of volunteers to try to put the building back where it belonged.

Estelle had said, after the collapse of the flooring in the boardroom, that she heard a sound like the rushing of waters. Arthur, on examining the floor where the safe-deposit vault stood, found it had risen an inch. On these facts he had built up his theory. The building, like all modern skyscrapers, rested on concrete piles extending down to bedrock. In the center of one of those piles there was a hollow tube originally intended to serve as an artesian well. The flow had been insufficient and the well had been stopped up.

Arthur, of course, as an engineer, had studied the construction of the building with great care, and happened to remember that this partly hollow pile was the one nearest the safe-deposit vault. The collapse of the boardroom floor had suggested that some change had happened in the building itself, and that was found when he saw that the deposit vault had actually risen an inch.

He at once connected the rise in the flooring above the hollow pile with the pipe in the pile. Estelle had heard liquid sounds. Evidently water had been forced into the hollow artesian pipe under an unthinkable pressure when the catastrophe occurred.

From the rumbling and the suddenness of the whole catastrophe a volcanic or seismic disturbance was evident. The connection of volcanic or seismic action with a flow of water suggested a geyser or a hot spring of some sort, probably a spring which had broken through its normal confines some time before, but whose pressure had been sufficient to prevent the accident until the failure of its flow.

When the flow ceased the building sank rapidly. For the fact that this 'sinking' was in the fourth direction – the Fourth Dimension – Arthur had no explanation. He simply knew that in some mysterious way an outlet for the pressure had developed in that fashion, and that the tower had followed the spring in its fall through time.

The sole apparent change in the building had occurred

above the one hollow concrete pile, which seemed to indicate that if access were to be had to the mysterious, and so far only assumed, spring, it must be through that pile. While the vault retained its abnormal elevation, Arthur believed that there was still water at an immense and incalculable pressure in the pipe. He dared not attempt to tap the pipe until the pressure had abated.

At the end of a week he found the vault slowly settling back into place. When its return to the normal was complete he dared begin boring a hole to reach the hollow tube in the concrete pile.

As he suspected, he found water in the pile – water whose sulfurous and mineral nature confirmed his belief that a geyser reaching deep into the bosom of the earth, as well as far back in the realms of time, was at the bottom of the extraordinary jaunt of the tower.

Geysers were still far from satisfactory things to explain. There are many of their vagaries which we cannot understand at all. We do know a few things which affect them, and one thing is that 'soaping' them will stimulate their flow in an extraordinary manner.

Arthur proposed to 'soap' this mysterious geyser when the renewal of its flow should lift the runaway skyscraper back to the epoch from which the failure of the flow had caused it to fall.

He made his preparations with great care. He confidently expected his plan to work, and to see the skyscraper once more towering over midtown New York as was its wont, but he did not allow the fishermen and hunters to relax their efforts on that account. They labored as before, while deep down in the sub-basement of the colossal building Arthur and his volunteers toiled mightily.

They had to bore through the concrete pile until they reached the hollow within it. Then, when the evidence gained from the water in the pipe had confirmed his surmises, they had to prepare their 'charge' of soapy liquids by which the geyser was to be stirred to renewed activity.

Great quantities of the soap used by the scrubwomen in scrubbing down the floors was boiled with water until a sirupy mess was evolved. Means had then to be provided by which this could be quickly introduced into the hollow pile, the hole then closed, and then braced to withstand a pressure unparalleled in hydraulic science. Arthur believed that from the hollow pile the soapy liquid would find its way to the geyser proper, where it would take effect in stimulating the lessened flow to its former proportions. When that took place he believed that the building would return as swiftly and as surely as it had left them to normal, modern times.

The telephone rang in his office, and Estelle answered it. Arthur was on the wire. A signal was being hung out for all the castaway to return to the building from their several occupations. They were about to soap the geyser.

Did Estelle want to come down and watch? She did! She stood in the main hallway as the excited and hopeful people trooped in. When the last was inside the doors were firmly closed. The few friendly Indians outside stared perplexedly at the mysterious white strangers.

The whites, laughing excitedly, began to wave to the Indians. Their leave-taking was premature.

Estelle took her way down into the cellar. Arthur was awaiting her arrival. Van Deventer stood near, with the grinning, grimy members of Arthur's volunteer work gang. The massive concrete pile stood in the center of the cellar. A big steam-boiler was coupled to a tiny pipe that led into the heart of the mass of concrete. Arthur was going to force the soapy liquid into the hollow pile by steam.

At a signal steam began to hiss in the boiler. Live steam from the fire-room forced the soapy sirup out of the boiler, through the small iron pipe, into the hollow that led to the geyser far underground. Six thousand gallons in all were forced into the opening in a space of three minutes.

Arthur's grimy gang began to work with desperate haste. Quickly they withdrew the iron pipe and inserted a long steel plug, painfully beaten from a bar of solid metal. Then, girding the colossal concrete pile, ring after ring of metal was slipped on, to hold the plug in place.

The last of the safeguards was hardly fastened firmly when Estelle listened intently.

'I hear a rumbling!' she said quietly.

Arthur reached forward and put his hand on the mass of concrete.

'It is quivering!' he reported as quietly. 'I think we'll be on our way in a very little while.'

The group broke for the stairs, to watch the panorama as the runaway skyscraper made its way back through the thousands of years to the times that had built it for a monument to modern commerce.

Arthur and Estelle went high up in the tower. From the window of Arthur's office they looked eagerly, and felt the slight quiver as the tower got under way. Estelle looked up at the sun, and saw it mend its pace toward the west.

Night fell.

The evening sounds became high-pitched and shrill, then seemed to cease altogether.

In a very little while there was light again, and the sun was speeding across the sky. It sank hastily, and returned almost immediately, *via* the east. Its pace became a breakneck rush. Down behind the hills and up in the east. Down in the west, up in the east. Down and up – the flickering began. The race back toward modern times had started.

Arthur and Estelle stood at the window and looked out as the sun rushed more and more rapidly across the sky until it became but a streak of light, shifting first to the right and then to the left as the seasons passed in their turn.

With Arthur's arms about her shoulders, Estelle stared out across the unbelievable landscape, while the nights and days, the winters and summers, and the storms and calms of a thousand years swept past them into the irrevocable past.

Presently Arthur drew her to him and kissed her. While he kissed her, so swiftly did the days and years flee by, three generations were born, grew and begot children, and died again!

Estelle, held fast in Arthur's arms, thought nothing of such trivial things. She put her arms about his neck and kissed him, while the years passed them unheeded.

Of course you know that the building landed safely, in the exact hour, minute, and second from which it started, so that when the frightened and excited people poured out of it to stand in Madison Square and feel that the world was once more right side up, their hilarious and incomprehensible conduct made such of the world as was passing by think a contagious madness had broken out.

Days passed before the story of the two thousand was believed, but at last it was accepted as truth, and eminent scientists studied the matter exhaustively.

There has been one rather queer result of the journey of the runaway skyscraper. A certain Isidore Eckstein, a dealer in jewelry novelties, whose office was in the tower when it disappeared into the past, has entered suit in the courts of the United States against all the holders of land on Manhattan Island. It seems that during the two weeks in which the tower rested in the wilderness he traded independently with one of the Indian chiefs, and in exchange for two near-pearl necklaces, sixteen finger-rings, and one dollar in money, received a title-deed to the entire island. He claims that his deed is a conveyance made previous to all other sales whatever.

Strictly speaking, he is undoubtedly right, as his deed was signed before the discovery of America. The courts, however, are deliberating the question with a great deal of perplexity.

Eckstein is quite confident that in the end his claim will be allowed and he will be admitted as the sole owner of real estate on Manhattan Island, with all occupiers of buildings and territory paying him ground rent at a rate he will fix himself. In the meantime, though the foundations are being reinforced so the catastrophe cannot occur again, his entire office is packed full of articles suitable for trading with the Indians. If the tower makes another trip back through time, Eckstein hopes to become a landholder of some importance.

No less than eighty-seven books have been written by members of the memorable two thousand in description of their trip to the hinterland of time, but Arthur, who could write more intelligently about the matter than anyone else, is so extremely busy that he cannot bother with such things. He has two very important matters to look after. One is, of course, the reinforcement of the foundations of the building so that a repetition of the catastrophe cannot occur, and the other is to convince his wife – who is Estelle, naturally – that she is the most adorable person in the universe. He finds the latter task the more difficult, because she insists that *he* is the most adorable person—

THE MAD PLANET

I

A WORLD INSANE

In all his lifetime of perhaps twenty years, it had never occurred to Burl to wonder what his grandfather had thought about his surroundings. The grandfather had come to an untimely end in a rather unpleasant fashion which Burl remembered vaguely as a succession of screams coming more and more faintly to his ears as he was being carried away at the top speed of which his mother was capable.

Burl had rarely or never thought of the old gentleman since. Surely he had never wondered in the abstract of what his great-grandfather thought, and most surely of all, there had never entered his head such a purely hypothetical question as the one of what his many-times-great-grandfather – say of the year 1920 – would have thought of the scene in which Burl found himself.

He was treading cautiously over a brownish carpet of fungus growth, creeping furtively toward the stream which he knew by the generic title of 'water'. It was the only water he knew. Towering far above his head, three man-heights high, great toadstools hid the grayish sky from his sight. Clinging to the foot-thick stalks of the toadstools were still other fungi, parasites upon the growths that had once been parasites themselves.

Burl himself was a slender young man wearing a single garment twisted about his waist, made from the wing-fabric of a great moth the members of his tribe had slain as it emerged from its cocoon. His skin was fair, without a trace of sunburn. In all his lifetime he had never seen the sun, though the sky was rarely hidden from view save by the giant fungi which, with monster cabbages, were the only growing things he knew. Clouds usually spread overhead, and when they did not, the perpetual haze made the sun but an indefinitely brighter part of the sky, never a sharply edged ball of fire. Fantastic mosses, misshapen fungus growths, colossal molds and yeasts, were the essential parts of the landscape though which he moved.

Once he had dodged through the forest of huge toadstools, his shoulder touched a cream-colored stalk, giving the whole fungus a tiny shock. Instantly, from the umbrella-like mass of pulp overhead, a fine and impalpable powder fell upon him like snow. It was the season when the toadstools send out their spores, or seeds, and they had been dropped upon him at the first sign of disturbance.

Furtive as he was, he paused to brush them from his head and hair. They were deadly poison, as he knew well.

Burl would have been a curious sight to a man of the twentieth century. His skin was pink like that of a child, and there was but little hair upon his body. Even that on top of his head was soft and downy. His chest was larger than his forefathers' had been, and his ears seemed almost capable of independent movement, to catch threatening sounds from any direction. His eyes, large and blue, possessed pupils which could dilate to extreme size, allowing him to see in almost complete darkness.

He was the result of the thirty thousand years' attempt of the human race to adapt itself to the change that had begun in the latter half of the twentieth century.

At about that time, civilization was high, and apparently secure. Mankind had reached a permanent agreement among itself, and all men had equal opportunities to education and leisure. Machinery did most of the labor of the world, and men were only required to supervise its operation. All men were well-fed, all men were well-educated, and it seemed that until the end of time the earth would be the abode of a community of comfortable human beings, pursuing their studies and diversions, their illusions and their truths. Peace, quietness, privacy, freedom were universal.

Then, just as men were congratulating themselves that the Golden Age had come again, it was observed that the planet seemed ill at ease. Fissures opened slowly in the crust, and carbonic acid gas – the carbon dioxide of chemists – began to pour out into the atmosphere. The gas had long been known to be present in the air, and it was considered necessary to plant life. Most of the plants of the world took the gas and absorbed its carbon into themselves, releasing oxygen for use again.

Scientists had calculated that a great deal of the earth's increased fertility was due to the larger quantities of carbon dioxide released by the activities of man in burning his coal and petroleum. Because of those views, for some years no great alarm was caused by the continuous expansion of the world's interior.

Constantly, however, the volume increased. New fissures constantly opened, each one adding a new source of carbon dioxide, and each one pouring into the already laden atmosphere more of the gas – beneficial in small quantities, but as the world learned, deadly in large ones.

The percentage of the heavy, vapor-like gas increased. The whole body of the air became heavier through its admixture. It absorbed more moisture and became more humid. Rainfall increased. Climates grew warmer. Vegetation became more luxuriant – but the air gradually became less exhilarating.

Soon the health of mankind began to be affected. Accustomed through the long ages to breath air rich in oxygen and poor in carbon dioxide, men suffered. Only those who lived on high plateaus or on tall mountain-tops remained unaffected. The plants of the earth, though nourished and increasing in size beyond those ever seen before, were unable to dispose of the continually increasing flood of carbon dioxide exhaled by the weary planet.

By the middle of the twenty-first century it was generally recognized that a new carboniferous period was about to take place, when the earth's atmosphere would be thick and humid, unbreathable by man, when giant grasses and ferns would form the only vegetation.

When the twenty-first century drew to a close the whole

human race began to revert to conditions closely approximating savagery. The lowlands were unbearable. Thick jungles of rank growth covered the ground. The air was depressing and enervating. Men could live there, but it was a sickly, fever-ridden existence. The whole population of the earth desired the high lands, and as the low country became more unbearable, men forgot their two centuries of peace.

They fought destructively, each for a bit of land where he might live and breathe. Then men began to die, men who had persisted in remaining near sea-level. They could not live in the poisonous air. The danger zone crept up as the earth-fissures tirelessly poured out their steady streams of foul gas. Soon men could not live within five hundred feet of sea-level. The lowlands went uncultivated, and became jungles of a thickness comparable only to those of the first carboniferous period.

Then men died of sheer inanition at a thousand feet. The plateaus and mountain-tops were crowded with folk struggling for a foothold beyond the invisible menace that crept up, and up—

These things did not take place in one year, or in ten. Not in one generation, but in several. Between the time when the chemists of the International Geophysical Institute announced that the proportion of carbon dioxide in the air had increased from .04 per cent to .1 percent and the time when at sea-level six per cent of the atmosphere was the deadly gas, more than two hundred years had intervened.

Coming gradually, as it did, the poisonous effects of the deadly stuff increased with insidious slowness. First the lassitude, then the heaviness of the brain, then the weakness of the body. Mankind ceased to grow in numbers. After a long period, the race had fallen to a fraction of its former size. There was room in plenty on the mountain-tops – but the danger-level continued to creep up.

There was but one solution. The human body would have to inure itself to the poison, or it was doomed to extinction. It finally developed a toleration for the gas that had wiped out race after race and nation after nation, but at a terrible cost. Lungs increased in size to secure oxygen on which life depended, but the poison, inhaled at every breath, left the few survivors sickly and filled with perpetual weariness. Their minds lacked the energy to cope with new problems or transmit the knowledge they possessed.

And after thirty thousand years, Burl, a direct descendent of the first president of the United Republic, crept through a forest of toadstools and fungus growths. He was ignorant of fire, of metals, of the uses of stone and wood. A single garment covered him. His language was a scanty group of a few hundred labial sounds, conveying no abstractions and few concrete things.

He was ignorant of the uses of wood. There was no wood in the scanty territory furtively inhabited by his tribe. With the increase in heat and humidity the trees had begun to die out. Those of northern climes went first, the oaks, the cedars, the maples. Then the pines – the beeches went early – the cypresses, and finally even the forests of the jungles vanished. Only grasses and reeds, bamboos and their kin, were able to flourish in the new, steaming atmosphere. The thick jungles gave place to dense thickets of grasses and ferns, now become tree-ferns again.

And then the fungi took their place. Flourishing as never before, flourishing on a planet of torrid heat and perpetual miasma, on whose surface the sun never shone directly because of an ever-thickening bank of clouds that hung sullenly overhead, the fungi sprang up. About the dank pools that festered over the surface of the earth, fungus growths began to cluster. Of every imaginable shade and color, of all monstrous forms and malignant purposes, of huge size and flabby volume, they spread over the land.

The grasses and ferns gave place to them. Squat toadstools, flaking molds, evil-smelling yeasts, vast mounts of fungi inextricably mingled as to species, but growing, forever growing and exhaling an odor of dark places.

The strange growths now grouped themselves in forests, horrible travesties of the vegetation they had succeeded. They grew and grew with feverish intensity beneath a clouded or

haze-obscured sky, while above them fluttered gigantic butterflies and huge moths, sipping daintily of their corruption.

The insects alone of all the animal world above water were
able to endure the change. They multiplied exceedingly, and
enlarged themselves in the thickened air. The solitary vegetation – as distinct from fungus growths – that had survived was
now a degenerate form of the cabbages that had once fed
peasants. On those rank, colossal masses of foliage, the stolid
grubs and caterpillars ate themselves to maturity, then swung
below in strong cocoons to sleep the sleep of metamorphosis
from which they emerged to spread their wings and fly.

The tiniest butterflies from former days had increased their
span until their gaily colored wings should be described in
terms of feet, while the larger emperor moths extended their
purple sails to a breadth of yards upon yards. Burl himself
would have been dwarfed beneath the overshadowing fabric
of their wings.

It was fortunate that they, the largest flying creatures, were
harmless or nearly so. Burl's fellow tribesman sometimes came
upon a cocoon just about to open, and waited patiently beside
it until the beautiful creature within broke through its matted
shell and came out into the sunlight.

Then, before it had gathered energy from the air, and before
its wings had swelled to strength and firmness, the tribesmen
fell upon it, tearing the filmy, delicate wings from its body and
the limbs from its carcass. Then, when it lay helpless before
them, they carried away the juicy, meat-filled limbs to be eaten,
leaving the still living body to stare helplessly at the strange
world through its many-faceted eyes and become a prey to the
voracious ants who would soon clamber upon it, and carry it
away in tiny fragments to their underground city.

Not all the insect world was so helpless or so unthreatening.
Burl knew of wasps almost the length of his own body who
possessed stings that were instantly fatal. To every species of
wasp, however, some other insect is predestined prey and the
furtive members of Burl's tribe feared them but little, as they
sought only the prey to which their instincts led them.

Bees were similarly aloof. They were hard put to it for existence, those bees. Few flowers bloomed and they were reduced to expedients once considered signs of degeneracy in their race. Bubbling yeasts and fouler things, occasionally the nectarless blooms of the rank, giant cabbages. Burl knew the bees. They droned overhead, nearly as large as he was himself, their bulging eyes gazing at him with abstracted preoccupation. And crickets, and beetles, and spiders—

Burl knew spiders! His grandfather had been the prey of one of the hunting tarantulas, which had leaped with incredible ferocity from his excavated tunnel in the earth. A vertical pit in the ground, two feet in diameter, went down for twenty feet. At the bottom of that lair the black-bellied monster waited for the tiny sounds that would warn him of prey approaching his hiding-place.

Burl's grandfather had been careless, and the terrible shrieks he had uttered as the horrible monster darted from the pit and seized him had lingered vaguely in Burl's mind ever since. Burl had seen, too, the monster webs of another species of spider, and watched from a safe distance as the misshapen body of the huge creature sucked the juices from a three-foot cricket that had become entangled in its trap.

Burl had remembered the strange stripes of yellow and black and silver that crossed upon its abdomen. He had been fascinated by the struggles of the imprisoned insect coiled in a hopeless tangle of sticky, gummy ropes the thickness of Burl's finger, cast about its body before the spider made any attempt to approach.

Burl knew these dangers. They were a part of his life. It was his accustomedness to them, and that of his ancestors, that made his existence possible. He was able to evade them; so he survived. A moment of carelessness, an instant's relaxation of his habitual caution, and he would be one with his forebears, forgotten meals of long-dead, inhuman monsters.

Three days before, Burl had crouched behind a bulky, shapeless fungus growth while he watched a furious duel between two huge horned beetles. Their jaws, gaping wide, clicked and clashed upon each other's impenetrable armor. Their legs crashed like so many cymbals as their polished surfaces ground and struck against each other. They were fighting over some particularly attractive bit of carrion.

Burl had watched with all his eyes until a gaping orifice had appeared in the armor of the smaller of the two. It uttered a shrill cry, or seemed to cry out. The noise was actually the tearing of the horny stuff beneath the victorious jaws of the adversary.

The wounded beetle struggled more and more feebly. At last it collapsed, and the conqueror placidly began to eat the conquered before life was extinct.

Burl waited until the meal was finished, and then approached the scene with caution. An ant – the forerunner of many – was already inspecting the carcass.

Burl usually ignored the ants. They were stupid, short-sighted insects, and not hunters. Save when attacked, they offered no injury. They were scavengers, on the lookout for the dead and dying, but they would fight viciously if their prey were questioned, and they were dangerous opponents. They were from three inches, for the tiny black ants, to a foot for the large termites.

Burl was hasty when he heard the tiny clickings of their limbs as they approached. He seized the sharp-pointed snout of the victim, detached from the body, and fled from the scene.

Later, he inspected his find with curiosity. The smaller victim had been a minotaur beetle, with a sharp-pointed horn like that of a rhinoceros to reinforce his offensive armament, already dangerous because of his wide jaws. The jaws of a beetle work from side to side, instead of up and down, and this had made his protection complete in no less than three directions.

Burl inspected the sharp, dagger-like instrument in his hand. He felt its point, and it pricked his finger. He flung it aside as he crept into the hiding-place of his tribe. There were only twenty of them, four or five men, six or seven women, and the rest girls and children.

Burl had been wondering at the strange feelings that came over him when he looked at one of the girls. She was younger than Burl – perhaps eighteen – and fleeter of foot than he. They talked together, sometimes, and once or twice Burl shared with her an especially succulent find of foodstuffs.

The next morning he found the horn where he had thrown it, sticking in the flabby side of a toadstool. He pulled it out, and gradually, far back in his mind, an idea began to take shape. He sat for some time with the thing in his hand, considering it with a far-away look in his eyes. From time to time he stabbed at the toadstool, awkwardly, but with gathering skill. His imagination began to work fitfully. He visualized himself stabbing food with it as the larger beetle had stabbed the former owner of the weapon in his hand.

Burl could not imagine himself coping with one of the fighting insects. He could only picture himself, dimly, stabbing something that was food with his death-dealing thing. It was longer than his arm and though clumsy in his hand, an effective and sharp implement.

He thought. Where was there food, food that lived, that would not fight back? Presently he rose and began to make his way to the tiny river. Yellow-bellied newts swam in its waters. The swimming larvae of a thousand insects floated about its surface or crawled upon its bottom.

There were deadly things there, too. Giant crayfish snapped their horny claws at the unwary. Mosquitos of four-inch wingspread sometimes made their humming way above the river. The last survivors of their race, they were dying out for lack of the plant-juices on which the male of the species lived, but even so they were formidable. Burl had learned to crush them with fragments of fungus.

He crept slowly through the forest of toadstools. Brownish fungus was underfoot. Strange orange, red, and purple molds clustered about the bases of the creamy toadstool stalks. Once Burl paused to run his sharp-pointed weapon through a fleshy stalk and reassure himself that what he planned was practicable.

He made his way furtively through the forest of misshapen growths. Once he heard a tiny clicking, and froze into stillness. It was a troop of four or five ants, each some eight inches long, returning along their habitual pathway to their city. They moved sturdily, heavily laden, along the route marked with the black and odorous formic acid exuded from the bodies of their comrades. Burl waited until they had passed, then went on.

He came to the bank of the river. Green scum covered a great deal of its surface, scum occasionally broken by a slowly enlarging bubble of some gas released from decomposing matter on the bottom. In the center of the placid stream the current ran a little more swiftly, and the water itself was visible.

Over the shining current, water-spiders ran swiftly. They had not shared in the general increase of size that had taken place in the insect world. Depending upon the capillary qualities of the water to support them, an increase in size and weight would have deprived them of the means of locomotion.

From the spot where Burl first peered at the water the green scum spread out for many yards into the stream. He could not see what swam and wriggled and crawled beneath the evil-smelling covering. He peered up and down the banks.

Perhaps a hundred and fifty yards below, the current came near the shore. An outcropping of rock there made a steep descent to the river, from which yellow shelf-fungi stretched out. Dark-red and orange above, they were light-yellow below, and they formed a series of platforms above the smoothly flowing stream. Burl made his way cautiously toward them.

On his way he saw one of the edible mushrooms that formed so large a part of his diet, and paused to break from the flabby flesh an amount that would feed him for many days. It was too often the custom of his people to find a store of food, carry it to their hiding place, and then gorge themselves for days, eating, sleeping, and waking only to eat again until the food was gone.

Absorbed as he was in his plan of trying his new weapon, Burl was tempted to return with his booty. He would give Saya of this food, and they would eat together. Saya was the maiden who roused unusual emotions in Burl. He felt strange impulses stirring within him when she was near, a desire to touch her, to caress her. He did not understand.

He went on, after hesitating. If he brought her food, Saya would be pleased, but if he brought her of the things that swam in the stream, she would be still more pleased. Degraded as his tribe had become, Burl was yet a little more intelligent than they. He was an atavism, a throwback to ancestors who had cultivated the earth and subjugated its animals. He had a vague idea of pride, unformed but potent.

No man within memory had hunted or slain for food. They knew of meat, yes, but it had been the fragments left by an insect-hunter, seized and carried away by the men before the perpetually alert ant colonies had sent their foragers to the scene.

If Burl did what no man before him had done, if he brought a whole carcass to his tribe, they would envy him. They were preoccupied solely with their stomachs, and after that with the preservation of their lives. The perpetuation of the race came third in their consideration.

They were herded together in a leaderless group, coming to the same hiding place that they might share in the finds of the lucky and gather comfort from their numbers. Of weapons, they had none. They sometimes used stones to crack open the limbs of the huge insects they found partly devoured, cracking them open for the sweet meat to be found inside, but they sought safety from their enemies solely in flight and hiding.

Their enemies were not as numerous as might have been imagined. Most of the meat-eating insects have their allotted prey. The sphex – a hunting wasp – feeds solely upon grasshoppers. Other wasps eat flies only. The pirate-bee eats bumblebees only. Spiders were the principal enemies of man, as they devour with a terrifying impartiality all that falls into their clutches.

Burl reached the spot from which he might gaze down into the water. He lay prostrate, staring into the shallow depths. Once a huge crayfish, as long as Burl's body, moved leisurely across his vision. Small fishes and even the huge newts fled before the voracious creature.

After a long time the tide of underwater life resumed its activity. The wriggling grubs of the dragonflies reappeared.

Little flecks of silver swam into view – a school of tiny fish. A larger fish appeared, moving slowly through the water.

Burl's eyes glistened and his mouth watered. He reached down with his long weapon. It barely touched the water. Disappointment filled him, yet the nearness and the apparent practicability of his scheme spurred him on.

He considered the situation. There were the shelf-fungi below him. He rose and moved to a point just above them, then thrust his spear down. They resisted its point. Burl felt them tentatively with his foot, then dared to thrust his weight to them. They held him firmly. He clambered down and lay flat upon them, peering over the edge as before.

The large fish, as long as Burl's arm, swam slowly to and fro below him. Burl had seen the former owner of his spear strive to thrust it into his opponents, and knew that a thrust was necessary. He had tried his weapon upon toadstools – had practiced with it. When the fish swam below him, he thrust sharply downward. The spear seemed to bend when it entered the water, and missed its mark by inches, to Burl's astonishment. He tried again and again.

He grew angry with the fish below him for eluding his efforts to kill it. Repeated strokes had left it untouched, and it was unwary, and did not even try to run away.

Burl became furious. The big fish came to rest directly beneath his hand. Burl thrust downward with all his strength. This time the spear, entering vertically, did not seem to bend. It went straight down. Its point penetrated the scales of the swimmer below, transfixing that lazy fish completely.

An uproar began. The fish, struggling to escape, and Burl, trying to draw it up to his perch, made a huge commotion. In his excitement Burl did not observe a tiny ripple some distance away. The monster crayfish was attracted by the disturbance, and was approaching.

The unequal combat continued. Burl hung on desperately to the end of his spear. Then there was a tremor in Burl's support, it gave way, and fell into the stream with a mighty splash. Burl went under, his eyes open, facing death. And as he sank, his wide-open eyes saw waved before him the gaping claws of the huge crayfish, large enough to sever a limb with a single stroke of their jagged jaws.

II

THE BLACK-BELLIED SPIDER

He opened his mouth to scream – a replica of the terrible screams of his grandfather, seized by a black-bellied tarantula years before – but no sound came forth. Only bubbles floated to the surface of the water. He beat the unresisting fluid with his hands – he did not know how to swim. The colossal creature approached leisurely, while Burl struggled helplessly.

His arms struck a solid object, and grasped it convulsively. A second later he had swung it between himself and the huge crustacean. He felt a shock as the mighty jaws closed upon the corklike fungus, then felt himself drawn upward as the crayfish released his hold and the shelf-fungus floated to the surface. Having given way beneath him, it had been carried below him in his fall, only to rise within his reach just when most needed.

Burl's head popped above water and he saw a larger bit of the fungus floating nearby. Less securely anchored to the rocks of the river bank than the shelf to which Burl had trusted himself, it had been dislodged when the first shelf gave way. It was larger than the fragment to which Burl clung, and floated higher in the water.

Burl was cool with a terrible self-possession. He seized it and struggled to draw himself on top of it. It tilted as his weight came upon it, and nearly overturned, but he paid no heed. With desperate haste, he clawed with hands and feet until he could draw himself clear of the water, of which he would forever retain a slight fear.

As he pulled himself upon the furry, orange-brown upper surface, a sharp blow struck his foot. The crayfish, disgusted at finding only what was to it a tasteless morsel in the shelf-fungus, had made a languid stroke at Burl's wriggling foot in the water. Failing to grasp the fleshy member, the crayfish retreated, disgruntled and annoyed.

And Burl floated downstream, perched, weaponless and alone, frightened and in constant danger, upon a flimsy raft composed of a degenerate fungus floating soggily in the water. He floated slowly down the stream of a river in whose waters death lurked unseen, upon whose banks was peril, and above whose reaches danger fluttered on golden wings.

It was a long time before he recovered his self-possession, and when he did he looked first for his spear. It was floating in the water, still transfixing the fish whose capture had endangered Burl's life. The fish now floated with its belly upward, all life gone.

So insistent was Burl's instinct for food that his predicament was forgotten when he saw his prey just out of his reach. He gazed at it, and his mouth watered, while his cranky craft went downstream, spinning slowly in the current. He lay flat on the floating fungoid, and strove to reach out and grasp the end of the spear.

The raft tilted and nearly flung him overboard again. A little later he discovered that it sank more readily on one side than on the other. That was due, of course, to the greater thickness – and consequently greater buoyancy – of the part which had grown next to the rocks of the river bank.

Burl found that if he lay with his head stretching above that side, it did not sink into the water. He wriggled into this new position, then, and waited until the slow revolution of his vessel brought the spear-shaft near him. He stretched his fingers and his arm, and touched, then grasped it.

A moment later he was tearing strips of flesh from the side of the fish and cramming the oily mess into his mouth with great enjoyment. He had lost his edible mushroom. That danced upon the waves several yards away, but Burl ate contentedly of what he possessed. He did not worry about what was before him. That lay in the future, but suddenly he realized that he was being carried farther and farther from Saya, the maiden of his tribe who caused strange bliss to steal over him when he contemplated her.

The thought came to him when he visualized the delight with which she would receive a gift of part of the fish he had caught. He was suddenly stricken with dumb sorrow. He lifted his head and looked longingly at the river banks.

A long, monotonous row of strangely colored fungus growths. No healthy green, but pallid, cream-colored toadstools, some bright orange, lavender, and purple molds, vivid carmine 'rusts' and mildews, spreading up the banks from the turgid slime. The sun was not a ball of fire, but merely shone as a bright golden patch in the haze-filled sky, a patch whose limits could not be defined or marked.

In the faintly pinkish light that filtered down through the air, a multitude of flying objects could be seen. Now and then a cricket or a grasshopper made its bullet-like flight from one spot to another. Huge butterflies fluttered gayly above the silent, seemingly lifeless world. Bees lumbered anxiously about, seeking the cross-shaped flowers of the monster cabbages. Now and then a slender-waisted, yellow-stomached wasp flew alertly through the air.

Burl watched them with a strange indifference. The wasps were as long as he himself. The bees, on end, could match his height. The butterflies ranged from tiny creatures barely capable of shading his face to colossal things in the folds of whose wings he could have been lost. And above him fluttered dragonflies, whose long, spindle-like bodies were three times the length of his own.

Burl ignored them all. Sitting there, an incongruous creature of pink skin and soft brown hair upon an orange fungus floating in midstream, he was filled with despondency because the current carried him forever farther and farther from a certain slender-limbed maiden of his tiny tribe, whose glances caused an odd commotion in his breast.

The day went on. Once, Burl saw upon the blue-green mold that spread upward from the river, a band of large, red Amazon ants, marching in orderly array, to raid the city of a colony of black ants, and carry away the eggs they would find there. The eggs would be hatched, and the small black creatures made the slaves of the brigands who had stolen them.

The Amazon ants can live only by the labor of their slaves, and for that reason are mighty warriors in their world. Later, etched against the steaming mist that overhung everything as far as the eye could reach, Burl saw strangely shaped, swollen branches rearing themselves from the ground. He knew what they were. A hard-rinded fungus that grew upon itself in peculiar mockery of the vegetation that had vanished from the earth.

And again he saw pear-shaped objects above some of which floated little clouds of smoke. They, too, were fungus growths, puffballs, which when touched emit what seems a puff of vapor. These would have towered above Burl's head, had he stood beside them.

And then, as the day drew to an end, he saw in the distance what seemed a range of purple hills. They were tall hills to Burl, some sixty or seventy feet high, and they seemed to be the agglomeration of a formless growth, multiplying its organisms and forms upon itself until the whole formed an irregular, cone-shaped mound. Burl watched them apathetically.

Presently, he ate again of the oily fish. The taste was pleasant to him, accustomed to feed mostly upon insipid mushrooms. He stuffed himself, though the size of his prey left by far the larger part uneaten.

He still held his spear firmly beside him. It had brought him into trouble, but Burl possessed a fund of obstinacy. Unlike most of his tribe, he associated the spear with the food it had secured, rather than the difficulty into which it had led him. When he had eaten his fill he picked it up and examined it again. The sharpness of its point was unimpaired.

Burl handled it meditatively, debating whether or not to attempt to fish again. The shakiness of his little raft dissuaded him, and he abandoned the idea. Presently he stripped a sinew from the garment about his middle and hung the fish about his neck with it. That would leave him both hands free. Then he sat cross-legged upon the soggily floating fungus, like a pink-skinned Buddha, and watched the shores go by.

Time had passed, and it was drawing near sunset. Burl, never having seen the sun save as a bright spot in the overhanging haze, did not think of the coming of night as 'sunset'. To him it was the letting down of darkness from the sky.

Today happened to be an exceptionally bright day, and the haze was not as thick as usual. Far to the west, the thick mist turned to gold, while the thicker clouds above became blurred masses of dull red. Their shadows seemed like lavender, from the contrast of shades. Upon the still surface of the river, all the myriad tints and shadings were reflected with an incredible faithfulness, and the shining tops of the giant mushrooms by the river brim glowed faintly pink.

Dragonflies buzzed over his head in their swift and angular flight, the metallic luster of their bodies glistening in the rosy light. Great yellow butterflies flew lightly above the stream. Here, there, and everywhere upon the water appeared the shell-formed boats of a thousand caddis flies, floating upon the surface while they might.

Burl could have thrust his hand down into their cavities and seized the white worms that inhabited the strange craft. The huge bulk of a tardy bee droned heavily overhead. Burl glanced upward and saw the long proboscis and the hairy hinder legs with their scanty load of pollen. He saw the great, multiple-lensed eyes with their expression of stupid preoccupation, and even the sting that would mean death alike for him and for the giant insect, should it be used.

The crimson radiance grew dim at the edge of the world. The purple hills had long been left behind. Now the slender stalks of ten thousand round-domed mushrooms lined the river bank and beneath them spread fungi of all colors, from the rawest red to palest blue, but all now fading slowly to a monochromatic background in the growing dusk.

The buzzing, fluttering, and the flapping of the insects of the day died slowly down, while from a million hiding places there crept out into the deep night soft and furry bodies of great moths, who preened themselves and smoothed their feathery antennae before taking to the air. The strong-limbed crickets set up their thunderous noise – grown gravely bass with the increasing size of the organs by which the sound was made – and then there began to gather on the water those slender spirals of tenuous mist that would presently blanket the stream in a mantle of thin fog.

Night fell. The clouds above seemed to lower and grow dark. Gradually, now a drop and then a drop, now a drop and then a drop, the languid fall of large, warm raindrops that would drip from the moisture-laden skies all through the night began. The edge of the stream became a place where great disks of coolly glowing flame appeared.

The mushrooms that bordered on the river were faintly phosphorescent and shone coldly upon the 'rusts' and flake-fungi beneath their feet. Here and there a ball of lambent flame appeared, drifting idly above the steaming, festering earth.

Thirty thousand years before, men had called them 'will-o'-the-wisps', but Burl simply stared at them, accepting them as he accepted all that passed. Only a man attempting to advance in the scale of civilization tries to explain everything that he sees. The savage and the child is most often content to observe without comment, unless he repeats the legends told him by wise folk who are possessed by the itch of knowledge.

Burl watched for a long time. Great fireflies whose beacons lighted up their surroundings for many yards – fireflies Burl knew to be as long as his spear – shed their intermittent glows upon the stream. Softly fluttering wings, in great beats that poured torrents of air upon him, passed above Burl.

The air was full of winged creatures. The night was broken by their cries, by the sound of their invisible wings, by their cries of anguish and their mating calls. Above him and on all sides the persistent, intense life of the insect world went on ceaselessly, but Burl rocked back and forth upon his frail mushroom boat and wished to weep because he was being carried from his tribe, and from Saya – Saya of the swift feet and white teeth, of the shy smile.

Burl may have been homesick, but his principal thoughts were of Saya. He had dared greatly to bring a gift of fresh meat to her, meat captured as meat had never been known to be taken by a member of the tribe. And now he was being carried from her!

He lay, disconsolate, upon his floating atom on the water for a great part of the night. It was long after midnight when the mushroom raft struck gently and remained grounded upon a shallow in the stream.

When the light came in the morning, Burl gazed about him keenly. He was some twenty yards from the shore, and the greenish scum surrounded his now disintegrating vessel. The river had widened out until the other bank was barely to be seen through the haze above the surface of the river, but the nearer shore seemed firm and no more full of dangers than the territory his tribe inhabited. He felt the depth of the water with his spear, then was struck with the multiple usefulness of that weapon. The water would come to but slightly above his ankles.

Shivering a little with fear, Burl stepped down into the water, then made for the bank at the top of his speed. He felt a soft something clinging to one of his bare feet. With an access of terror, he ran faster, and stumbled upon the shore in a panic. He stared down at his foot. A shapeless, flesh-colored pad clung to his heel, and as Burl watched, it began to swell slowly, while the pink of its wrinkled folds deepened.

It was no more than a leech, sharing in the enlargement nearly all the lower world had undergone, but Burl did not know that. He thrust at it with the side of his spear, then scraped frantically at it, and it fell off, leaving a blotch of blood upon the skin where it came away. It lay, writhing and pulsating, upon the ground, and Burl fled from it.

He found himself in one of the toadstool forests with which he was familiar, and finally paused, disconsolately. He knew the nature of the fungus growths about him, and presently fell to eating. In Burl the sight of food always produced hunger – a wise provision of nature to make up for the instinct to store food, which he lacked.

Burl's heart was small within him. He was far from his tribe, and far from Saya. In the parlance of this day, it is probable that no more than forty miles separated them, but Burl did not think of distances. He had come down the river. He was in a land he had never known or seen. And he was alone.

All about him was food. All the mushrooms that surrounded him were edible, and formed a store of sustenance Burl's whole tribe could not have eaten in many days, but that very fact brought Saya to his mind more forcibly. He squatted on the ground, wolfing down the insipid mushroom in great gulps, when an idea suddenly came to him with all the force of inspiration.

He would bring Saya here, where there was food, food in great quantities, and she would be pleased. Burl had forgotten the large and oily fish that still hung down his back from the sinew about his neck, but now he rose, and its flapping against him reminded him again.

He took it and fingered it all over, getting his hands and himself thoroughly greasy in the process, but he could eat no more. The thought of Saya's pleasure at the sight of that, too, reinforced his determination.

With all the immediacy of a child or a savage he set off at once. He had come along the bank of the stream. He would retrace his steps along the bank of the stream.

Through the awkward aisles of the mushroom forest he made his way, eyes and ears open for possibilities of danger. Several times he heard the omnipresent clicking of ants on their multifarious businesses in the wood, but he could afford to ignore them. They were short-sighted at best, and at worst they were foragers rather than hunters. He only feared one kind of ant, the army-ant, which sometimes travels in hordes of millions, eating all that it comes upon. In ages past, when they were tiny creatures not an inch long, even the largest animals fled from them. Now that they measured a foot in length, not even the gorged spiders whose distended bellies were a yard in thickness, dared offer them battle.

The mushroom forest came to an end. A cheerful grasshopper munched delicately at some dainty it had found. Its hind legs were bunched beneath it in perpetual readiness for flight. A monster wasp appeared above – as long as Burl himself – poised an instant, dropped, and seized the luckless feaster.

There was a struggle, then the grasshopper became helpless, and the wasp's flexible abdomen curved delicately. Its sting entered the jointed armor of its prey, just beneath the head. The sting entered with all the deliberate precision of a surgeon's scalpel, and all struggle ceased.

The wasp grasped the paralyzed, not dead, insect and flew away. Burl grunted, and passed on. He had hidden when the wasp darted down from above.

The ground grew rough, and Burl's progress became painful. He clambered arduously up steep slopes and made his way cautiously down their farther sides. Once he had to climb through a tangled mass of mushrooms so closely placed, and so small, that he had to break them apart with blows of his spear before he could pass, when they shed upon him torrents of a fiery red liquid that rolled off his greasy breast and sank into the ground.

A strange self-confidence now took possession of Burl. He walked less cautiously and more boldly. The mere fact that he had struck something and destroyed it provided him with a curious fictitious courage.

He had climbed slowly to the top of a red clay cliff, perhaps a hundred feet high, slowly eaten away by the river when it overflowed. Burl could see the river. At some past floodtime it had lapped at the base of the cliff on whose edge he walked, though now it came no nearer than a quarter-mile.

The cliffside was almost covered with shelf-fungi, large and small, white, yellow, orange, and green, in indescribable confusion and luxuriance. From a point halfway up the cliff the inch-thick cable of a spider's web stretched down to an anchorage on the ground, and the strangely geometrical pattern of the web glistened evilly.

Somewhere among the fungi of the cliffside the huge creature waited until some unfortunate prey should struggle helplessly in its monster snare. The spider waited in a motionless, implacable patience, invincibly certain of prey, utterly merciless to its victims.

Burl strutted on the edge of the cliff, a silly little pink-skinned creature with an oily fish slung about his neck and a draggled fragment of a moth's wing about his middle. In his hand he bore the long spear of a minotaur beetle. He strutted, and looked scornfully down upon the whitely shining trap below him. He struck mushrooms, and they had fallen before him. He feared nothing. He strode fearlessly along. He would go to Saya and bring her to this land where food grew in abundance.

Sixty paces before him, a shaft sank vertically in the sandy, clayey soil. It was a carefully rounded shaft, and lined with silk. It went down for perhaps thirty feet or more, and there enlarged itself into a chamber where the owner and digger of the shaft might rest. The top of the hole was closed by a trap door, stained with mud and earth to imitate with precision the surrounding soil. A keen eye would have been needed to perceive the opening. But a keen eye now peered out from a tiny crack, the eye of the engineer of the underground dwelling.

Eight hairy legs surrounded the body of the creature that hung motionless at the top of the silk-lined shaft. A huge misshapen globe formed its body, colored a dirty brown. Two pairs of ferocious mandibles stretched before its fierce mouth-parts. Two eyes glittered evilly in the darkness of the burrow. And over the whole body spread a rough, mangy fur.

It was a thing of implacable malignance, of incredible ferocity. It was the brown hunting-spider, the American tarantula. Its body was two feet and more in diameter, and its legs, outstretched, would cover a circle three yards across. It watched Burl, its eyes glistening. Slaver welled up and dropped from its jaws.

And Burl strutted forward on the edge of the cliff, puffed up with a sense of his own importance. The white snare of the spinning spider below him impressed him as amusing. He knew the spider would not leave its web to attack him. He reached down and broke off a bit of fungus growing at his feet. Where he broke it, it was oozing a soupy liquid and was full of tiny maggots in a delirium of feasting. Burl flung it down into the web, and then laughed as the black bulk of the hidden spider swung down from its hiding place to investigate.

The tarantula, peering from its burrow, quivered with impatience. Burl drew near, and nearer. He was using his spear as a lever, now, and prying off bits of fungus to fall down the cliffside into the colossal web. The spider, below, went leisurely from one place to another, investigating each new missile with its palpi, then leaving them, as they appeared lifeless and undesirable prey. Burl laughed again as a particularly large lump of shelf-fungus narrowly missed the black-and-silver figure below. Then—

The trap door fell into place with a faint click, and Burl whirled about. His laughter turned to a scream. Moving toward him with incredible rapidity, the monster tarantula opened its dripping jaws. Its mandibles gaped wide. The poison fangs were unsheathed. The creature was thirty paces away, twenty paces – ten. It leaped into the air, eyes glittering, all its eight legs extended to seize, fangs bared—

Burl screamed again, and thrust out his arms to ward off the impact of the leap. In his terror, his grasp upon his spear had become agonized. The spear point shot out, and the tarantula fell upon it. Nearly a quarter of the spear entered the body of the ferocious thing.

It struck upon the spear, writhing horribly, still struggling to reach Burl, who was transfixed with horror. The mandibles clashed, strange sounds came from the beast. Then one of the attenuated, hairy legs rasped across Burl's forearm. He gasped in ultimate fear and stepped backward – and the edge of the cliff gave way beneath him.

He hurtled downward, still clutching the spear which held

the writhing creature from him. Down through space, eyes glassy with panic, the two creatures – the man and the giant tarantula – fell together. There was a strangely elastic crash and crackling. They had fallen into the web beneath them.

Burl had reached the end of terror. He could be no more fear-struck. Struggling madly in the gummy coils of an immense web, which ever bound him more tightly, with a wounded creature shuddering in agony not a yard from him – yet a wounded creature that still strove to reach him with its poison fangs – Burl had reached the limit of panic.

He fought like a madman to break the coils about him. His arms and breast were greasy from the oily fish, and the sticky web did not adhere to them, but his legs and body were inextricably fastened by the elastic threads spread for just such prey as he.

He paused a moment, in exhaustion. Then he saw, five yards away, the silvery and black monster waiting patiently for him to weary himself. It judged the moment propitious. The tarantula and the man were one in its eyes, one struggling thing that had fallen opportunely into its snare. They were moving but feebly now. The spider advanced delicately, swinging its huge bulk nimbly along the web, paying out a cable after as it came inexorably toward him.

Burl's arms were free, because of the greasy coating they had received. He waved them wildly, shrieking at the pitiless monster that approached. The spider paused. Those moving arms suggested mandibles that might wound or slap.

Spiders take few hazards. This spider was no exception to the rule. It drew cautiously near, then stopped. Its spinnerets became busy, and with one of its six legs, used like an arm, it flung a sheet of gummy silk impartially over both the tarantula and the man.

Burl fought against the descending shroud. He strove to thrust it away, but in vain. In a matter of minutes he was completely covered in a silken cloth that hid even the light from his eyes. He and his enemy, the giant tarantula, were beneath the same covering, though the tarantula moved but weakly.

The shower ceased. The web-spider had decided that they were helpless. Then Burl felt the cables of the web give slightly, as the spider approached to sting and suck the sweet juices from its prey.

III

THE ARMY ANTS

The web yielded gently as the added weight of the black-bellied spider approached. Burl froze into stillness under his enveloping covering. Beneath the same silken shroud the tarantula writhed in agony upon the point of Burl's spear. It clashed its jaws, shuddering upon the horny barb.

Burl was quiet in an ecstasy of terror. He waited for the poison-fangs to be thrust into him. He knew the process. He had seen the leisurely fashion in which the giant spiders delicately stung their prey, then withdrew to wait without impatience for the poison to do its work.

When their victim had ceased to struggle, they drew near again, and sucked the sweet juices from the body, first from one point and then another, until what had so recently been a creature vibrant with life became a shrunken, withered husk – to be flung from the web at nightfall. Most spiders are tidy housekeepers, destroying their snares daily to spin anew.

The bloated, evil creature moved meditatively about the shining sheet of silk it had cast over the man and the giant tarantula when they fell from the cliff above. Now only the tarantula moved feebly. Its body was outlined by a bulge in the concealing shroud, throbbing faintly as it still struggled with the spear in its vitals. The irregularly rounded protuberance offered a point of attack for the web spider. It moved quickly forward, and stung.

Galvanized into fresh torment by this new agony, the tarantula writhed in a very hell of pain. Its legs, clustered about the spear still fastened into its body, struck out purposelessly, in horrible gestures of delirious suffering. Burl screamed as one of them touched him, and struggled himself.

His arms and head were free beneath the silken sheet because of the grease and oil that coated them. He clutched at the threads about him and strove to draw himself away from his deadly neighbor. The threads did not break, but they parted one from another, and a tiny opening appeared. One of the tarantula's attenuated limbs touched him again. With the strength of utter panic he hauled himself away, and the opening enlarged. Another struggle, and Burl's head emerged into the open air, and he stared down for twenty feet upon an open space almost carpeted with the chitinous remains of his present captor's former victims.

Burl's head was free, and his breast and arms. The fish slung over his shoulder had shed its oil upon him impartially. But the lower part of his body was held firm by the gummy snare of the web-spider, a snare far more tenacious than any bird-lime ever manufactured by man.

He hung in his tiny window for a moment, despairing. Then he saw, at a little distance, the bulk of the monster spider, waiting patiently for its poison to take effect and the struggling of its prey to be stilled. The tarantula was no more than shuddering now. Soon it would be still, and the black-bellied creature waiting on the web would approach for its meal.

Burl withdrew his head and thrust desperately at the sticky stuff about his loins and legs. The oil upon his hands kept it from clinging to them, and it gave a little. In a flash of inspiration, Burl understood. He reached over his shoulder and grasped the greasy fish; tore it in a dozen places and smeared himself with the now rancid exudation, pushing the sticky threads from his limbs and oiling the surface from which he had thrust it away.

He felt the web tremble. To the spider, its poison seemed to have failed of effect. Another sting seemed to be necessary. This time it would not insert its fangs into the quiescent tarantula, but would sting where the disturbance was manifest – would send its deadly venom into Burl.

He gasped, and drew himself toward his window. It was as if he would have pulled his legs from his body. His head emerged, his shoulders – half his body was out of the hole.

The colossal spider surveyed him, and made ready to cast more of its silken sheet upon him. The spinnerets became active, and the sticky stuff about Burl's feet gave way! He shot out of the opening and fell sprawling, awkwardly and heavily, upon the earth below, crashing upon the shrunken shell of a flying beetle which had fallen into the snare and had not escaped.

Burl rolled over and over, and then sat up. An angry, foot-long ant stood before him, its mandibles extended threateningly, while its antennae waved wildly in the air. A shrill stridulation filled the air.

In ages past, when ants were tiny creatures of lengths to be measured in fractions of an inch, learned scientists debated gravely if their tribe possessed a cry. They believed that certain grooves upon the body of the insects, after the fashion of those upon the great legs of the cricket, might offer the means of uttering an infinitely high-pitched sound too shrill for man's ears to catch.

Burl knew that the stridulation was caused by the doubtful insect before him, though he had never wondered how it was produced. The cry was used to summon others of its city, to help it in its difficulty or good fortune.

Clickings sounded fifty or sixty feet away. Comrades were coming to aid the pioneer. Harmless save when interfered with – all save the army ant, that is – the whole ant tribe was formidable when aroused. Utterly fearless, they could pull down a man and slay him as so many infuriated fox terriers might have done thirty thousand years before.

Burl fled, without debate, and nearly collided with one of the anchoring cables of the web from which he had barely escaped a moment before. He heard the shrill sound behind him suddenly subside. The ant, short-sighted as all ants were, no longer felt itself threatened and went peacefully about the business Burl had interrupted, that of finding among the gruesome relics beneath the spider's web some edible carrion which might feed the inhabitants of its city.

Burl sped on for a few hundred yards, and stopped. It behooved him to move carefully. He was in strange territory, and as even the most familiar territory was full of sudden and implacable dangers, unknown lands were doubly or trebly perilous.

Burl, too, found difficulty in moving. The glutinous stuff from the spider's shroud of silk still stuck to his feet and picked up small objects as he went along. Old ant-gnawed fragments of insect armor pricked him even through his toughened soles.

He looked about cautiously and removed them, took a dozen steps and had to stop again. Burl's brain had been uncommonly stimulated of late. It had gotten him into at least one predicament – due to his invention of a spear – but had no less readily led to his escape from another. But for the reasoning that had led him to use the grease from the fish upon his shoulder in oiling his body when he struggled out of the spider's snare, he would now be furnishing a meal for that monster.

Cautiously, Burl looked all about him. He seemed to be safe. Then, quite deliberately, he sat down to think. It was the first time in his life that he had done such a thing. The people of his tribe were not given to meditation. But an idea had struck Burl with all the force of inspiration – an abstract idea.

When he was in difficulties, something within him seemed to suggest a way out. Would it suggest an inspiration now? He puzzled over the problem. Childlike – and savage-like – the instant the thought came to him, he proceeded to test it out. He fixed his gaze upon his foot. The sharp edges of pebbles, of the remains of insect-armor, of a dozen things, hurt his feet when he walked. They had done so ever since he had been born, but never had his feet been sticky so that the irritation continued with him for more than a single step.

Now he gazed upon his foot, and waited for the thought within him to develop. Meanwhile, he slowly removed the sharp-pointed fragments, one by one. Partly coated as they were with the half-liquid gum from his feet, they clung to his fingers as they had to his feet, except upon those portions where the oil was thick as before.

Burl's reasoning, before, was simple and of the primary order. Where oil covered him, the web did not. Therefore he would coat the rest of himself with oil. Had he been placed in the same predicament again, he would have used the same means of escape. But to apply a bit of knowledge gained in one predicament to another difficulty was something he had not yet done.

A dog may be taught that by pulling on the latchstring of a door he may open it, but the same dog coming to a high and close-barred gate with a latchstring attached, will never think of pulling on this second latchstring. He associates a latchstring with the opening of the door. The opening of a gate is another matter entirely.

Burl had been stirred to one invention by imminent peril. That is not extraordinary. But to reason in cold blood, as he presently did, that oil on his feet would nullify the glue upon his feet and enable him again to walk in comfort – that was a triumph. The inventions of savages are essentially matters of life and death, of food and safety. Comfort and luxury are only produced by intelligence of a high order.

Burl, in safety, had added to his comfort. That was truly a more important thing in his development than almost any other thing he could have done. He oiled his feet.

It was an almost infinitesimal problem, but Burl's struggles with the mental process of reasoning were actual. Thirty thousand years before him, a wise man had pointed out that education is simply training in thought, in efficient and effective thinking. Burl's tribe had been too much preoccupied with food and mere existence to think, and now Burl, sitting at the base of a squat toadstool that all but concealed him, re-exemplified Rodin's 'Thinker' for the first time in many generations.

For Burl to reason that oil upon the soles of his feet would guard him against sharp stones was as much a triumph of intellect as any masterpiece of art in the ages before him. Burl was learning how to think.

He stood up, walked, and crowed in sheer delight, then paused a moment in awe of his own intelligence. Thirty-five miles from his tribe, naked, unarmed, utterly ignorant of fire, of wood, of any weapons save a spear he had experimented with the day before, abysmally uninformed concerning the very existence of any art or science, Burl stopped to assure himself that he was very wonderful.

Pride came to him. He wished to display himself to Saya, these things upon his feet, and his spear. But his spear was gone.

With touching faith in the efficacy of this new pastime, Burl sat promptly down again and knitted his brows. Just as a superstitious person, once convinced that by appeal to a favorite talisman he will be guided aright, will inevitably apply to that talisman on all occasions, so Burl plumped himself down to think.

These questions were easily answered. Burl was naked. He would search out garments for himself. He was weaponless. He would find himself a spear. He was hungry – and would seek food, and he was far from his tribe, so he would go to them. Puerile reasoning, of course, but valuable, because it was consciously reasoning, consciously appealing to his mind for guidance in difficulty, deliberate progress from a mental desire to a mental resolution.

Even in the high civilization of ages before, few men had really used their brains. The great majority of people had depended upon machines and their leaders to think for them. Burl's tribefolk depended on their stomachs. Burl, however, was gradually developing the habit of thinking which makes for leadership and which would be invaluable to his little tribe.

He stood up again and faced upstream, moving slowly and cautiously, his eyes searching the ground before him keenly and his ears alert for the slightest sound of danger. Gigantic butterflies, riotous in coloring, fluttered overhead through the misty haze. Sometimes a grasshopper hurtled through the air like a projectile, its transparent wings beating the air frantically. Now and then a wasp sped by, intent upon its hunting, or a bee droned heavily along, anxious and worried, striving in a nearly flowerless world to gather the pollen that would feed the hive.

Here and there Burl saw flies of various sorts, some no larger than his thumb, but others the size of his whole hand. They fed upon the juices that dripped from the maggot-infested mushrooms, when filth more to their liking was not at hand.

Very far away a shrill roaring sounded faintly. It was like a multitude of clickings blended into a single sound, but was so far away that it did not impress itself upon Burl's attention. He had all the strictly localized vision of a child. What was near was important, and what was distant could be ignored. Only the imminent required attention, and Burl was preoccupied.

Had he listened, he would have realized that army ants were abroad in countless millions, spreading themselves out in a broad array and eating all they came upon far more destructively than so many locusts.

Locusts in past ages had eaten all green things. There were only giant cabbages and a few such tenacious rank growths in the world that Burl knew. The locusts had vanished with civilization and knowledge and the greater part of mankind, but the army ants remained as an invincible enemy to men and insects, and the most of the fungus growths that covered the earth.

Burl did not notice the sound, however. He moved forward, briskly though cautiously, searching with his eyes for garments, food, and weapons. He confidently expected to find all of them within a short distance.

Surely enough he found a thicket – if one might call it so – of edible fungi no more than half a mile beyond the spot where he had improvised his sandals to protect the soles of his feet.

Without especial elation, Burl tugged at the largest until he had broken off a food supply for several days. He went on, eating as he did so, past a broad plain a mile and more across, being broken into odd little hillocks by gradually ripening and suddenly developing mushrooms with which he was unfamiliar.

The earth seemed to be in process of being pushed aside by rounded protuberances of which only the tips showed. Blood-red hemispheres seemed to be forcing aside the earth so they might reach the outer air.

Burl looked at them curiously, and passed among them without touching them. They were strange, and to him most strange things meant danger. In any event, he was full of a new purpose now. He wished garments and weapons.

Above the plain a wasp hovered, a heavy object dangling beneath its black belly, ornamented by a single red band. It was a wasp – the hairy sand-wasp – and it was bringing a paralyzed gray caterpillar to its burrow.

Burl watched it drop down with the speed and sureness of an arrow, pull aside a heavy, flat stone, and descend into the ground. It had a vertical shaft dug down for forty feet or more.

It descended, evidently inspected the interior, reappeared, and vanished into the hole again, dragging the gray worm after it. Burl, marching on over the broad plain that seemed stricken with some erupting disease from the number of red pimples making their appearance, did not know what passed below, but observed the wasp emerge again and busily scratch dirt and stones into the shaft until it was full.

The wasp had paralyzed a caterpillar, taken it to the al-ready prepared burrow, laid an egg upon it, and filled up the entrance. In course of time the egg would hatch into a grub barely as long as Burl's forefinger, which would then feed upon the torpid caterpillar until it had waxed large and fat. Then it would weave itself a chrysalis and sleep a long sleep, only to wake as a wasp and dig its way to the open air.

Burl reached the farther side of the plain and found him-self threading the aisles of one of the fungus forests in which the growths were hideous, misshapen travesties upon the trees they had supplanted. Bloated, yellow limbs branched off from rounded, swollen trunks. Here and there a pear-shaped puff-ball, Burl's height and half as much again, waited craftily until a chance touch should cause it to shoot upward a curling puff of infinitely fine dust.

Burl went cautiously. There were dangers here, but he moved forward steadily, none the less. A great mass of edible mushroom was slung under one of his arms, and from time to time he broke off a fragment and ate of it, while his large eyes searched this way and that for threats of harm.

Behind him, a high, shrill roaring had grown slightly in volume and nearness, but was still too far away to impress Burl. The army ants were working havoc in the distance. By thousands and millions, myriads upon myriads, they were foraging the country, clambering upon every eminence, descending into every depression, their antennae waving restlessly and their mandibles forever threateningly extended. The ground was black with them, each was ten inches and more in length.

A single such creature would be formidable to an unarmed and naked man like Burl, whose wisest move would be flight, but in their thousands and millions they presented a menace from which no escape seemed possible. They were advancing steadily and rapidly, shrill stridulations and a multitude of clickings marking their movements.

The great helpless caterpillars upon the giant cabbages heard the sound of their coming, but were too stupid to flee. The black multitudes covered the rank vegetables, and tiny but voracious jaws began to tear at the flaccid masses of flesh.

Each creature had some futile means of struggling. The caterpillars strove to throw off their innumerable assailants by writhings and contortions, wholly ineffective. The bees fought their entrance to the gigantic hives with stings and wingbeats. The moths took to the air in helpless blindness when discovered by the relentless throngs of small black insects which reeked of formic acid and left the ground behind them denuded of every living thing.

Before the oncoming horde was a world of teeming life, where mushrooms and fungi fought with thinning numbers of giant cabbages for foothold. Behind the black multitude was – nothing. Mushrooms, cabbages, bees, wasps, crickets. Every creeping and crawling thing that did not get aloft before the black tide reached it was lost, torn to bits by tiny mandibles. Even the hunting spiders and tarantulas fell before the host of insects, having killed many in their final struggles, but overwhelmed by sheer numbers. And the wounded and dying army ants made food for their sound comrades.

There is no mercy among insects. Only the web-spiders sat unmoved and immovable in their colossal snares, secure in the knowledge that their gummy webs would discourage attempts at invasion along the slender supporting cables.

Surging onward, flowing like a monstrous, murky tide over the yellow, steaming earth, the army ants advanced. Their vanguard reached the river, and recoiled. Burl was perhaps five miles distant when they changed their course, communicating the altered line of march to those behind them in some mysterious fashion of transmitting intelligence.

Thirty thousand years before, scientists had debated gravely over the means of communication among ants. They had observed that a single ant finding a bit of booty too large for him to handle alone would return to the ant-city and return with others. From that one instance they deduced a language of gestures made with the antennae.

Burl had no wise theories. He merely knew facts, but he knew that the ants had some form of speech or transmission of ideas. Now, however, he was moving cautiously along toward the stamping grounds of his tribe, in complete ignorance of the black blanket of living creatures creeping over the ground toward him.

A million tragedies marked the progress of the insect army. There was a tiny colony of mining bees – Zebra bees – a single mother, some four feet long, had dug a huge gallery with some ten cells, in which she laid her eggs and fed her grubs with hard-gathered pollen. The grubs had waxed fat and large, became bees, and laid eggs in their turn, within the gallery their mother had dug out for them.

Ten such bulky insects now foraged busily for grubs within the ancestral home, while the founder of the colony had grown draggled and wingless with the passing of time. Unable to forage herself, the old bee became the guardian of the nest or hive, as is the custom among the mining bees. She closed the opening of the hive with her head, making a living barrier within the entrance, and withdrawing to give entrance and exit only to duly authenticated members of the extensive colony.

The ancient and draggled concierge of the underground dwelling was at her post when the wave of army ants swept over her. Tiny, evil-smelling feet trampled upon her. She emerged to fight with mandible and sting for the sanctity of the hive. In a moment she was a shaggy mass of biting ants, rending and tearing at her chitinous armor. The old bee fought madly, viciously, sounding a buzzing alarm to the colonists yet within the hive. They emerged, fighting as they came, for the gallery leading down was a dark flood of small insects.

For a few moments a battle such as would make an epic was in progress. Ten huge bees, each four to five feet long, fighting with legs and jaw, wing and mandible, with all the ferocity of as many tigers. The tiny, vicious ants covered them, snapping at their multiple eyes, biting at the tender joints in their armor – sometimes releasing the larger prey to leap upon an injured comrade wounded by the huge creature they battled in common.

The fight, however, could have but one ending. Struggle as the bees might, herculean as their efforts might be, they were powerless against the incredible numbers of their assailants, who tore them into tiny fragments and devoured them. Before the last shred of the hive's defenders had vanished, the hive itself was gutted alike of the grubs it had contained and the food brought to the grubs by such weary effort of the mature bees.

The army ants went on. Only an empty gallery remained, that and a few fragments of tough armor, unappetizing even to the omnivorous ants.

Burl was meditatively inspecting the scene of a recent tragedy, where rent and scraped fragments of a great beetle's shiny casing lay upon the ground. A greater beetle had come upon the first and slain him. Burl was looking upon the remains of the meal.

Three or four minims, little ants barely six inches long, foraged industriously among the bits. A new ant city was to be formed and the queen-ant lay hidden a half-mile away. These were the first hatchlings, who would feed the larger ants on whom would fall the great work of the ant-city. Burl ignored them, searching with his eyes for a spear or weapon.

Behind him the clicking roar, the high-pitched stridulations of the horde of army ants, rose in volume. Burl turned disgustedly away. The best he could find in the way of a weapon was a fiercely toothed hind leg. He picked it up, and an angry whine rose from the ground.

One of the black minims was working busily to detach a fragment of flesh from the joint of the leg, and Burl had snatched the morsel from him. The little creature was hardly half a foot in length, but it advanced upon Burl, shrilling angrily. He struck it with the leg and crushed it. Two of the other minims appeared, attracted by the noise the first had made. Discovering the crushed body of their fellow, they unceremoniously dismembered it and bore it away in triumph.

Burl went on, swinging the toothed limb in his hand. It made a fair club, and Burl was accustomed to use stones to crush the juicy legs of such giant crickets as his tribe sometimes came upon. He formed a half-defined idea of a club. The sharp teeth of the thing in his hand made him realize that a sidewise blow was better than a spear-like thrust.

The sound behind him had become a distant whispering, high-pitched, and growing nearer. The army ants swept over a mushroom forest, and the yellow, umbrella-like growths swarmed with black creatures devouring the substance on which they found a foothold.

A great bluebottle fly, shining with a metallic luster, reposed in an ecstasy of feasting, sipping through its long proboscis the dark-colored liquid that dripped slowly from a mushroom. Maggots filled the mushroom, and exuded a solvent pepsin that liquefied the white firm 'meat'.

They fed upon this soup, this gruel, and a surplus dripped to the ground below, where the bluebottle drank eagerly. Burl drew near, and struck. The fly collapsed into a writhing heap. Burl stood over it for an instant, pondering.

The army ants came nearer, down into a tiny valley,

swarming into and through a little brook over which Burl had leaped. Ants can remain under water for a long time without drowning, so the small stream was but a minor obstacle, though the current of water swept many of them off their feet until they choked the brook-bed, and their comrades passed over their struggling bodies dry-shod. They were no more than temporarily annoyed, however, and presently crawled out to resume their march.

About a quarter of a mile to the left of Burl's line of march, and perhaps a mile behind the spot where he stood over the dead bluebottle fly, there was a stretch of an acre or more where the giant, rank cabbages had so far resisted the encroachments of the ever-present mushrooms. The pale, cross-shaped flowers of the cabbages formed food for many bees, and the leaves fed numberless grubs and worms, and loud-voiced crickets which crouched about on the ground, munching busily at the succulent green stuff. The army ants swept into the green area, ceaselessly devouring all they came upon.

A terrific din arose. The crickets hurtled away in a rocketlike flight, in a dark cloud of wildly beating wings. They shot aimlessly in any direction, with the result that half, or more than half, fell in the midst of the black tide of devouring insects and were seized as they fell. They uttered terrible cries as they were being torn to bits. Horrible inhuman screams reached Burl's ears.

A single such cry of agony would not have attracted Burl's attention – he lived in the very atmosphere of tragedy – but the chorus of creatures in torment made him look up. This was no minor horror. Wholesale slaughter was going on. He peered anxiously in the direction of the sound.

A wild stretch of sickly yellow fungus, here and there interspersed with a squat toadstool or a splash of vivid color where one of the many 'rusts' had found a foothold. To the left a group of awkward, misshapen fungoids clustered in silent mockery of a forest of trees. There a mass of faded green, where the giant cabbages stood.

With the true sun never shining upon them save through a

blanket of thick haze or heavy clouds, they were pallid things, but they were the only green things Burl had seen. Their nodding white flowers with four petals in the form of a cross glowed against the yellowish green leaves. But as Burl gazed toward them, the green became slowly black.

From where he stood, Burl could see two or three great grubs in lazy contentment, eating ceaselessly on the cabbages on which they rested. Suddenly first one and then the other began to jerk spasmodically. Burl saw that about each of them a tiny rim of black had clustered. Tiny black motes milled over the green surfaces of the cabbages. The grubs became black, the cabbages became black. Horrible contortions of the writhing grubs told of the agonies they were enduring. Then a black wave appeared at the further edge of the stretch of the sickly yellow fungus, a glistening, living wave, that moved forward rapidly with the roar of clickings and a persistent overtone of shrill stridulations.

The hair rose upon Burl's head. He knew what this was! He knew all too well the meaning of that tide of shining bodies. With a gasp of terror, all his intellectual preoccupations forgotten, he turned and fled in ultimate panic. And the tide came slowly on after him.

IV

THE RED DEATH

He flung away the great mass of edible mushroom, but clung to his sharp-toothed club desperately, and darted through the tangled aisles of the little mushroom forest with a heedless disregard of the dangers that might await him there. Flies buzzed about him loudly, huge creatures, glittering with a metallic luster. Once he was struck upon the shoulder by the body of one of them, and his skin was torn by the swiftly vibrating wings of the insect, as long as Burl's hand.

Burl thrust it away and sped on. The oil with which he was

partly covered had turned rancid, now, and the odor attracted them, connoisseurs of the fetid. They buzzed over his head, keeping pace even with his headlong flight.

A heavy weight settled upon his head, and in a moment was doubled. Two of the creatures had dropped upon his oily hair, to sip the rancid oil through their disgusting proboscises. Burl shook them off with his hand and ran madly on. His ears were keenly attuned to the sound of the army ants behind him, and it grew but little farther away.

The clicking roar continued, but began to be overshadowed by the buzzing of the flies. In Burl's time the flies had no great heaps of putrid matter in which to lay their eggs. The ants – busy scavengers – carted away the debris of the multitudinous tragedies of the insect world long before it could acquire the gamey flavor beloved by the fly maggots. Only in isolated spots were the flies really numerous, but there they clustered in clouds that darkened the sky.

Such a buzzing, whirling cloud surrounded the madly running figure of Burl. It seemed as though a miniature whirlwind kept pace with the little pink-skinned man, a whirlwind composed of winged bodies and multi-faceted eyes. He twirled his club before him, and almost every stroke was interrupted by an impact against a thinly armored body which collapsed with a spurting of reddish liquid.

An agonizing pain as of a red-hot iron struck upon Burl's back. One of the stinging flies had thrust its sharp-tipped proboscis into Burl's flesh to suck the blood.

Burl uttered a cry and – ran full tilt into the thick stalk of a blackened and draggled toadstool. There was a curious crackling as of wet punk or brittle rotten wood. The toadstool collapsed upon itself with a strange splashing sound. Many flies had laid their eggs in the fungoid, and it was a teeming mass of corruption and ill-smelling liquid.

With the crash of the toadstool's 'head' upon the ground, it fell into a dozen pieces, and the earth for yards around was spattered with a stinking liquid in which tiny, headless maggots twitched convulsively.

The buzzing of the flies took on a note of satisfaction, and they settled by hundreds about the edges of the ill-smelling pools, becoming lost in the ecstasy of feasting while Burl staggered to his feet and darted off again. This time he was but a minor attraction to the flies, and but one or two came near him. From every direction they were hurrying to the toadstool feast, to the banquet of horrible, liquefied fungus that lay spread upon the ground.

Burl ran on. He passed beneath the wide-spreading leaves of a giant cabbage. A great grasshopper crouched upon the ground, its tremendous jaws crunching the rank vegetation voraciously. Half a dozen great worms ate steadily from their resting-places among the leaves. One of them had slung itself beneath an overhanging leaf – which would have thatched a dozen homes for as many men – and was placidly anchoring itself in preparation for the spinning of a cocoon in which to sleep the sleep of metamorphosis.

A mile away, the great black tide of army ants was advancing relentlessly. The great cabbage, the huge grasshopper, and all the stupid caterpillars upon the wide leaves would soon be covered with the tiny biting insects. The cabbage would be reduced to a chewed and destroyed stump, the colossal, furry grubs would be torn into myriad mouthfuls and devoured by the black army ants, and the grasshopper would strike out with terrific, unguided strength, crushing its assailants by blows of its powerful hind legs and bites of its great jaws. But it would die, making terrible sounds of torment as the vicious mandibles of the army ants found crevices in its armor.

The clicking roar of the ants' advance overshadowed all other sounds, now. Burl was running madly, breath coming in great gasps, his eyes wide with panic. Alone of all the world about him, he knew the danger behind. The insects he passed were going about their business with that terrifying efficiency found only in the insect world.

There is something strangely daunting in the actions of an insect. It moves so directly, with such uncanny precision, with such utter indifference to anything but the end in view.

Cannibalism is a rule, almost without exception. The paralysis of prey, so it may remain alive and fresh – though in agony – for weeks on end, is a common practice. The eating piecemeal of still living victims is a matter of course.

Absolute mercilessness, utter callousness, incredible inhumanity beyond anything known in the animal world is the natural and commonplace practice of the insects. And these vast cruelties are performed by armored, machine-like creatures with an abstraction and a routine air that suggests a horrible Nature behind them all.

Burl nearly stumbled upon a tragedy. He passed within a dozen yards of a space where a female dung-beetle was devouring the mate whose honeymoon had begun that same day and ended in that gruesome fashion. Hidden behind a clump of mushrooms, a great yellow-banded spider was coyly threatening a smaller male of her own species. He was discreetly ardent, but if he won the favor of the gruesome creature he was wooing, he would furnish an appetizing meal for her some time within twenty-four hours.

Burl's heart was pounding madly. The breath whistled in his nostrils – and behind him, the wave of army ants was drawing nearer. They came upon the feasting flies. Some took to the air and escaped, but others were too engrossed in their delicious meal. The twitching little maggots, stranded upon the earth by the scattering of their soupy broth, were torn in pieces. The flies who were seized vanished into tiny maws. The serried ranks of black insects went on.

The tiny clickings of their limbs, the perpetual challenges and cross-challenges of crossed antennae, the stridulations of the creatures, all combined to make a high-pitched but deafening din. Now and then another sound pierced the noises made by the ants themselves. A cricket, seized by a thousand tiny jaws, uttered cries of agony. The shrill note of the crickets had grown deeply bass with the increase in size of the organs that uttered it.

There was a strange contrast between the ground before the advancing horde and that immediately behind it. Before, a busy world, teeming with life. Butterflies floating overhead on lazy wings, grubs waxing fat and huge upon the giant cabbages, crickets eating, great spiders sitting quietly in their lairs waiting with invincible patience for prey to draw near their trap doors or fall into their webs, colossal beetles lumbering heavily through the mushroom forests, seeking food, making love in monstrous, tragic fashion.

And behind the wide belt of army ants – chaos. The edible mushrooms gone. The giant cabbages left as mere stumps of unappetizing pulp, the busy life of the insect world completely wiped out save for the flying creatures that fluttered helplessly over an utterly changed landscape. Here and there little bands of stragglers moved busily over the denuded earth, searching for some fragment of food that might conceivably have been overlooked by the main body.

Burl was putting forth his last ounce of strength. His limbs trembled, his breathing was agony, sweat stood out upon his forehead. He ran a little, naked man with the disjointed fragment of a huge insect's limb in his hand, running for his insignificant life, running as if his continued existence among the million tragedies of that single day were the purpose for which the whole of the universe had been created.

He sped across an open space a hundred yards across. A thicket of beautifully golden mushrooms barred his way. Beyond the mushrooms a range of strangely colored hills began, purple and green and black and gold, melting into each other, branching off from each other, inextricably tangled.

They rose to a height of perhaps sixty or seventy feet, and above them a little grayish haze had gathered. There seemed to be a layer of tenuous vapor upon their surfaces, which slowly rose and coiled, and gathered into a tiny cloudlet above their tips.

The hills, themselves, were but masses of fungus, mushrooms and fungoids of every description, yeasts, 'rusts', and every form of fungus growth which had grown within itself and about itself until this great mass of strangely colored, spongy stuff had gathered in a mass that undulated unevenly across the level earth for miles.

Burl burst through the golden thicket and attacked the ascent. His feet sank into the spongy sides of the hillock. Panting, gasping, staggering from exhaustion, he made his way up the top. He plunged into a little valley on the farther side, up another slope. For perhaps ten minutes he forced himself on, then collapsed. He lay, unable to move further, in a little hollow, his sharp-toothed club still clasped in his hands. Above him, a bright yellow butterfly with a thirty-foot spread of wing fluttered lightly.

He lay motionless, breathing in great gasps, his limbs stubbornly refusing to lift him.

The sound of the army ants continued to grow near. At last, above the crest of the last hillock he had surmounted, two tiny antennae appeared, then the black glistening head of an army ant, the forerunner of its horde. It moved deliberately forward, waving its antennae ceaselessly. It made its way toward Burl, tiny clickings coming from the movements of its limbs.

A little wisp of tenuous vapor swirled toward the ant, a wisp of the same vapor that had gathered above the whole range of hills as a thin, low cloud. It enveloped the insect – and the ant seemed to be attacked by a strange convulsion. Its legs moved aimlessly. It threw itself desperately about. If it had been an animal, Burl would have watched with wondering eyes while it coughed and gasped, but it was an insect breathing through air-holes in its abdomen. It writhed upon the spongy fungus growth across which it had been moving.

Burl, lying in an exhausted, panting heap upon the purple mass of fungus, was conscious of a strange sensation. His body felt strangely warm. He knew nothing of fire or the heat of the sun, and the only sensation of warmth he had ever known was that caused when the members of his tribe had huddled together in their hiding place when the damp chill of the night had touched their soft-skinned bodies. Then the heat of their breaths and their bodies had kept out the chill.

This heat that Burl now felt was a hotter, fiercer heat. He moved his body with a tremendous effort, and for a moment the fungus was cool and soft beneath him. Then, slowly, the sensation of heat began again, and increased until Burl's skin was red and inflamed from the irritation.

The thin and tenuous vapor, too, made Burl's lungs smart and his eyes water. He was breathing in great, choking gasps, but the period of rest – short as it was – had enabled him to rise and stagger on. He crawled painfully to the top of the slope, and looked back.

The hill-crest on which he stood was higher than any of those he had passed in his painful run, and he could see clearly the whole of the purple range. Where he was, he was near the farther edge of the range, which was here perhaps half a mile wide.

It was a ceaseless, undulating mass of hills and hollows, ridges and spurs, all of them colored, purple and brown and golden-yellow, deepest black and dingy white. And from the tips of most of the pointed hills little wisps of vapor rose up.

A thin, dark cloud had gathered overhead. Burl could look to the right and left, and see the hills fading into the distance, growing fainter as the haze above them seemed to grow thicker. He saw, too, the advancing cohorts of the army ants, creeping over the tangled mass of fungus growth. They seemed to be feeding as they went, upon the fungus that had gathered into these incredible monstrosities.

The hills were living. They were not upheavals of the ground, they were festering heaps of insanely growing, festering mushrooms and fungus. Upon most of them a purple mold had spread itself so that they seemed a range of purple hills, but here and there patches of other vivid colors showed, and there was a large hill whose whole side was a brilliant golden hue. Another had tiny bright red spots of a strange and malignant mushroom whose properties Burl did not know, scattered all over the purple with which it was covered.

Burl leaned heavily upon his club and watched dully. He could run no more. The army ants were spreading everywhere over the mass of fungus. They would reach him soon.

Far to the right the vapor thickened. A column of smoke arose. What Burl did not know and would never know was that far down in the interior of that compressed mass of fungus, slow oxidization had been going on. The temperature of the interior had been raised. In the darkness and the dampness deep down in the hills, spontaneous combustion had begun.

Just as the vast piles of coal the railroad companies of thirty thousand years before had gathered together sometimes began to burn fiercely in their interiors, and just as the farmers' piles of damp straw suddenly burst into fierce flames from no cause, so these huge piles of tinder-like mushrooms had been burning slowly within themselves.

There had been no flames, because the surface remained intact and nearly air-tight. But when the army ants began to tear at the edible surfaces despite the heat they encountered, fresh air found its way to the smoldering masses of fungus. The slow combustion became rapid combustion. The dull heat became fierce flames. The slow trickle of thin smoke became a huge column of thick, choking, acrid stuff that set the army ants that breathed it into spasms of convulsive writhing.

From a dozen points the flames burst out. A dozen or more columns of blinding smoke rose to the heavens. A pall of fume-laden smoke gathered above the range of purple hills, while Burl watched apathetically. And the serried ranks of army ants marched on to the widening furnaces that awaited them.

They had recoiled from the river, because their instinct had warned them. Thirty thousand years without danger from fire, however, had let their racial fear of fire die out. They marched into the blazing orifices they had opened in the hills, snapping with their mandibles at the leaping flames, springing at the glowing tinder.

The blazing area widened, as the purple surface was under-mined and fell in. Burl watched the phenomenon without com-prehension and even without thankfulness. He stood, panting more and more slowly, breathing more and more easily, until the glow from the approaching flames reddened his skin and the acrid smoke made tears flow from his eyes.

Then he retreated slowly, leaning on his club and looking back. The black wave of the army ants was sweeping into the fire, sweeping into the incredible heat of that carbonized material burning with an open flame. At last there were only the little bodies of stragglers from the great ant-army, scurrying here and there over the ground their comrades had denuded of all living things. The bodies of the main army had vanished – burnt to crisp ashes in the furnace of the hills.

There had been agony in that flame, dreadful agony such as no man would like to dwell upon. The insane courage of the ants, attacking with their horny jaws the burning masses of fungus, rolling over and over with a flaming missile clutched in their mandibles, sounding their shrill war cry while cries of agony came from them – blinded, their antennae burnt off, their lidless eyes scorched by the licking flames, yet going madly forward on flaming feet to attack, ever attack this unknown and unknowable enemy.

Burl made his way slowly over the hills. Twice he saw small bodies of the army ants. They had passed between the widening surfaces their comrades had opened, and they were feeding voraciously upon the hills they trod on. Once Burl was spied, and a shrill war cry was sounded, but he moved on, and the ants were busily eating. A single ant rushed toward him. Burl brought down his club, and a writhing body remained to be eaten later by its comrades when they came upon it.

Again night fell. The skies grew red in the west, though the sun did not shine through the ever-present cloud bank. Darkness spread across the sky. Utter blackness fell over the whole mad world, save where the luminous mushrooms shed their pale light upon the ground and fireflies the length of Burl's arm shed their fitful gleams upon an earth of fungus growths and monstrous insects.

Burl made his way across the range of mushroom hills, picking his path with his large blue eyes whose pupils expanded to great size. Slowly, from the sky, now a drop and then a drop, now a drop and then a drop, the nightly rain that would continue until daybreak began.

Burl found the ground hard beneath his feet. He listened keenly for sounds of danger. Something rustled heavily in a thicket of mushrooms a hundred yards away. There were sounds of preening, and of delicate feet placed lightly here and there upon the ground. Then the throbbing beat of huge wings began suddenly, and a body took to the air.

A fierce, down-coming current of air smote Burl, and he looked upward in time to catch the outline of a huge body – a moth – as it passed above him. He turned to watch the line of its flight, and saw a strange glow in the sky behind him. The mushroom hills were still burning.

He crouched beneath a squat toadstool and waited for the dawn, his club held tightly in his hands, and his ears alert for any sound of danger. The slow-dropping, sodden rain kept on. It fell with irregular, drum-like beats upon the tough top of the toadstool under which he had taken refuge.

Slowly, slowly, the sodden rainfall continued. Drop by drop, all the night long, the warm pellets of liquid came from the sky. They boomed upon the hollow heads of the toadstools, and splashed into the steaming pools that lay festering all over the fungus-covered earth.

And all the night long the great fires grew and spread in the mass of already half-carbonized mushroom. The flare at the horizon grew brighter and nearer. Burl, naked and hiding beneath a huge mushroom, watched it grow near him with wide eyes, wondering what this thing was. He had never seen a flame before.

The overhanging clouds were brightened by the flames. Over a stretch at least a dozen miles in length and from half a mile to three miles across, seething furnaces sent columns of dense smoke up to the roof of clouds, luminous from the glow below them, and spreading out and forming an intermediate layer below the cloudbanks.

It was like the glow of all the many lights of a vast city thrown against the sky – but the last great city had molded into fungus-covered rubbish thirty thousand years before. Like the flitting of airplanes above a populous city, too, was the flitting of fascinated creatures above the glow.

Moths and great flying beetles, gigantic gnats and midges

grown huge with the passing of time, they fluttered and danced the dance of death above the flames. As the fire grew nearer to Burl, he could see them.

Colossal, delicately formed creatures swooped above the strange blaze. Moths with their riotously colored wings of thirty-foot spread beat the air with mighty strokes, and their huge eyes glowed like carbuncles as they stared with the frenzied gaze of intoxicated devotees into the glowing flames below them.

Burl saw a great peacock moth soaring above the burning mushroom hills. Its wings were all of forty feet across, and fluttered like gigantic sails as the moth gazed down at the flaming furnace below. The separate flames had united, now, and a single sheet of white-hot burning stuff spread across the country for miles, sending up its clouds of smoke, in which and through which the fascinated creatures flew.

Feathery antennae of the finest lace spread out before the head of the peacock moth, and its body was softest, richest velvet. A ring of snow-white down marked where its head began, and the red glow from below smote on the maroon of its body with a strange effect.

For one instant it was outlined clearly. Its eyes glowed more redly than any ruby's fire, and the great, delicate wings were poised in flight. Burl caught the flash of the flames upon two great iridescent spots upon the wide-spread wings. Shining purple and vivid red, the glow of opal and the sheen of pearl, all the glory of chalcedony and chrysoprase formed a single wonder in the red glare of burning fungus. White smoke compassed the great moth all about, dimming the radiance of its gorgeous dress.

Burl saw it dart straight into the thickest and brightest of the licking flames, flying madly, eagerly, into the searing, hellish heat as a willing, drunken sacrifice to the god of fire.

Monster flying beetles with their horny wing-cases stiffly stretched, blundered above the reeking, smoking pyre. In the red light from before them they shone like burnished metal, and their clumsy bodies with the spurred and fierce-toothed limbs darted like so many grotesque meteors through the luminous haze of ascending smoke.

Burl saw strange collisions and still stranger meetings. Male and female flying creatures circled and spun in the glare, dancing their dance of love and death in the wild radiance from the funeral pyre of the purple hills. They mounted higher than Burl could see, drunk with the ecstasy of living, then descended to plunge headlong to death in the roaring fires beneath them.

From every side the creatures came. Moths of brightest yellow with soft and furry bodies palpitant with life flew madly into the column of light that reached to the overhanging clouds, then moths of deepest black with gruesome symbols upon their wings came swiftly to dance, like motes in a bath of sunlight, above the glow.

And Burl sat crouched beneath an overshadowing toadstool and watched. The perpetual, slow, sodden raindrops fell. A continual faint hissing penetrated the sound of the fire – the raindrops being turned to steam. The air was alive with flying things. From far away, Burl heard a strange, deep bass muttering. He did not know the cause, but there was a vast swamp, of the existence of which he was ignorant, some ten or fifteen miles away, and the chorus of insect-eating giant frogs reached his ears even at that distance.

The night wore on, while the flying creatures above the fire danced and died, their numbers ever recruited by fresh arrivals. Burl sat tensely still, his wide eyes watching everything, his mind groping for an explanation of what he saw. At last the sky grew dimly gray, then brighter, and day came on. The flames of the burning hills grew faint as the fire died down, and after a long time Burl crept from his hiding place and stood erect.

A hundred yards from where he was, a straight wall of smoke rose from the still smoldering fungus, and Burl could see it stretching for miles in either direction. He turned to continue on his way, and saw the remains of one of the tragedies of the night.

A huge moth had flown into the flames, been horribly scorched, and floundered out again. Had it been able to fly, it would have returned to its devouring deity, but now it lay immovable upon the ground, its antennae seared hopelessly, one beautiful, delicate wing burned in gaping holes, its eyes dimmed by flame and its exquisitely tapering limbs broken and crushed by the force with which it had struck the ground. It lay helpless upon the earth, only the stumps of its antennae moving restlessly, and its abdomen pulsating slowly as it drew pain-racked breaths.

Burl drew near and picked up a stone. He moved on presently, a velvet cloak cast over his shoulders, gleaming with all the colors of the rainbow. A gorgeous mass of soft, blue moth fur was about his middle, and he had bound upon his forehead two yard-long, golden fragments of the moth's magnificent antennae. He strode on, slowly, clad as no man had been clad in all the ages.

After a little he secured a spear and took up his journey to Saya, looking like a prince of Ind upon a bridal journey – though no mere prince ever wore such raiment in days of greatest glory.

V

THE CONQUEROR

For many long miles Burl threaded his way through a single forest of thin-stalked toadstools. They towered three-man-heights high, and all about their bases were streaks and splashes of the 'rusts' and molds that preyed upon them. Twice Burl came to open glades wherein open, bubbling pools of green slime festered in corruption, and once he hid himself fearfully as a monster scarabaeus beetle lumbered within three yards of him, moving heavily onward with a clanking of limbs as of some mighty machine.

Burl saw the mighty armor and the inward-curving jaws of the creature, and envied him his weapons. The time was not yet come, however, when Burl would smile at the great insect and hunt him for the juicy flesh contained in those armored limbs.

Burl was still a savage, still ignorant, still timid. His principal advance had been that whereas he had fled without reasoning, he now paused to see if he need flee. In his hands he bore a long, sharp-pointed chitinous spear. It had been the weapon of a huge, unnamed flying insect scorched to death in the burning of the purple hills, which had floundered out of the flames to die. Burl had worked for an hour before being able to detach the weapon he coveted. It was as long and longer than Burl himself.

He was a strange sight, moving slowly and cautiously through the shadowed lanes of the mushroom forest. A cloak of delicate velvet in which all the colors of the rainbow played in iridescent beauty hung from his shoulders. A mass of soft and beautiful moth fur was about his middle, and in the strip of sinew about his waist the fiercely toothed limb of a fighting beetle was thrust carelessly. He had bound to his forehead twin stalks of a great moth's feathery golden antennae.

Against the play of color that came from his borrowed plumage his pink skin showed in odd contrast. He looked like some proud knight walking slowly through the gardens of a goblin's castle. But he was still a fearful creature, no more than the monstrous creatures about him save in the possession of latent intelligence. He was weak – and therein lay his greatest promise. A hundred thousand years before him his ancestors had been forced by lack of claws and fangs to develop brains.

Burl was sunk as low as they had been, but he had to combat more horrifying enemies, more inexorable threatenings, and many times more crafty assailants. His ancestors had invented knives and spears and flying missiles. The creatures about Burl had knives and spears a thousand times more deadly than the weapons that had made his ancestors masters of the woods and forests.

Burl was in comparison vastly more weak than his forebears had been, and it was that weakness that in times to come would lead him and those who followed him to heights his ancestors had never known. But now—

He heard a discordant, deep bass bellow, coming from a spot not twenty yards away. In a flash of panic he darted behind a clump of mushrooms and hid himself, panting in sheer terror. He waited for an instant in frozen fear, motionless and tense. His wide, blue eyes were glassy.

The bellow came again, but this time with a querulous note. Burl heard a crashing and plunging as of some creature caught in a snare. A mushroom fell with a brittle snapping, and the spongy thud as it fell to the ground was followed by a tremendous commotion. Something was fighting desperately against something else, but Burl did not know what creature or creatures might be in combat.

He waited for a long time, and the noise gradually died away. Presently Burl's breath came more slowly, and his courage returned. He stole from his hiding place, and would have made away, but something held him back. Instead of creeping from the scene, he crept cautiously over toward the source of the noise.

He peered between two cream-colored toadstool stalks and saw the cause of the noise. A wide, funnel-shaped snare of silk was spread out before him, some twenty yards across and as many deep. The individual threads could be plainly seen, but in the mass it seemed a fabric of sheerest, finest texture. Held up by the tall mushrooms, it was anchored to the ground below, and drew away to a tiny point through which a hole gave on some yet unknown recess. And all the space of the wide snare was hung with threads, fine, twisted threads no more than half the thickness of Burl's finger.

This was the trap of a labyrinth spider. Not one of the interlacing threads was strong enough to hold the feeblest of prey, but the threads were there by thousands. A great cricket had become entangled in the maze of sticky lines. Its limbs thrashed out, smashing the snare-lines at every stroke, but at every stroke meeting and becoming entangled with a dozen more. It thrashed about mightily, emitting at intervals the horrible, deep bass cry that the chirping voice of the cricket had become with its increase in size.

Burl breathed more easily, and watched with a fascinated curiosity. Mere death – even tragic death – as among insects held no great interest for him. It was a matter of such common and matter-of-fact occurrence that he was not greatly stirred. But a spider and his prey was another matter.

There were few insects that deliberately sought man. Most insects have their allotted victims, and will touch no others, but spiders have a terrifying impartiality. One great beetle devouring another was a matter of indifference to Burl. A spider devouring some luckless insect was but an example of what might happen to him. He watched alertly, his gaze traveling from the enmeshed cricket to the strange orifice at the rear of the funnel-shaped snare.

The opening darkened. Two shining, glistening eyes had been watching from the rear of the funnel. It drew itself into a tunnel there, in which the spider had been waiting. Now it swung out lightly and came toward the cricket. It was a gray spider, with twin black ribbons upon its thorax, next to the head, and with two stripes of curiously speckled brown and white upon its abdomen. Burl saw, too, two curious appendages like a tail.

It came nimbly out of its tunnel-like hiding place and approached the cricket. The cricket was struggling only feebly now, and the cries it uttered were but feeble, because of the confining threads that fettered its limbs. Burl saw the spider throw itself upon the cricket and saw the final, convulsive shudder of the insect as the spider's fangs pierced its tough armor. The sting lasted a long time, and finally Burl saw that the spider was really feeding. All the succulent juices of the now dead cricket were being sucked from its body by the spider. It had stung the cricket upon the haunch, and presently it went to the other leg and drained that, too, by means of its powerful internal suction-pump. When the second haunch had been sucked dry, the spider pawed the lifeless creature for a few moments and left it.

Food was plentiful, and the spider could afford to be dainty in its feeding. The two choicest titbits had been consumed. The remainder could be discarded.

A sudden thought came to Burl and quite took his breath away. For a second his knees knocked together in self-induced panic. He watched the gray spider carefully with growing determination in his eyes. He, Burl, had killed a hunting-spider upon the red-clay cliff. True, the killing had been an accident, and had nearly cost him his own life a few minutes later in the web-spider's snare, but he had killed a spider, and of the most deadly kind.

Now, a great ambition was growing in Burl's heart. His tribe had always feared spiders too much to know much of their habits, but they knew one or two things. The most important was that the snare-spiders never left their lairs to hunt – never! Burl was about to make a daring application of that knowledge.

He drew back from the white and shining snare and crept softly to the rear. The fabric gathered itself into a point and then continued for some twenty feet as a tunnel, in which the spider waited while dreaming of its last meal and waiting for the next victim to become entangled in the labyrinth in front. Burl made his way to a point where the tunnel was no more than ten feet away, and waited.

Presently, through the interstices of the silk, he saw the gray bulk of the spider. It had left the exhausted body of the cricket, and returned to its resting place. It settled itself carefully upon the soft walls of the tunnel, with its shining eyes fixed upon the tortuous threads of its trap. Burl's hair was standing straight up upon his head from sheer fright, but he was the slave of an idea.

He drew near and poised his spear, his new and sharp spear, taken from the body of an unknown flying creature killed by the burning purple hills. Burl raised the spear and aimed its sharp and deadly point at the thick gray bulk he could see dimly through the threads of the tunnel. He thrust it home with all his strength – and ran away at the top of his speed, glassy-eyed from terror.

A long time later he ventured near again, his heart in his mouth, ready to flee at the slightest sound. All was still. Burl had missed the horrible convulsions of the wounded spider, had not heard the frightful gnashings of its fangs as it tore at the piercing weapon, had not seen the silken threads of the tunnel ripped as the spider – hurt to death – had struggled with insane strength to free itself.

He came back beneath the overshadowing toadstools, stepping quietly and cautiously, to find a great rent in the silken tunnel, to find the great gray bulk lifeless and still, half-fallen through the opening the spear had first made. A little puddle of evil-smelling liquid lay upon the ground below the body, and from time to time a droplet fell from the spear into the puddle with a curious splash.

Burl looked at what he had done, saw the dead body of the creature he had slain, saw the ferocious mandibles, and the keen and deadly fangs. The dead eyes of the creature still stared at him malignantly, and the hairy legs were still braced as if further to enlarge the gaping hole through which it had partly fallen.

Exultation filled Burl's heart. His tribe had been but furtive vermin for thousands of years, fleeing from the mighty insects, hiding from them, and if overtaken but waiting helplessly for death, screaming shrilly in terror.

He, Burl, had turned the tables. He had slain one of the enemies of his tribe. His breast expanded. Always his tribesmen went quietly and fearfully, making no sound. But a sudden, exultant yell burst from Burl's lips – the first hunting cry from the lips of a man in three hundred centuries!

The next second his pulse nearly stopped in sheer panic at having made such a noise. He listened fearfully, but there was no sound. He drew near his prey and carefully withdrew his spear. The viscid liquid made it slimy and slippery, and he had to wipe it dry against a leathery toadstool. Then Burl had to conquer his illogical fear again before daring to touch the creature he had slain.

He moved off presently, with the belly of the spider upon his back and two of the hairy legs over his shoulders. The other limbs of the monster hung limp, and trailed upon the ground. Burl was now a still more curious sight as a gayly colored object with a cloak shining in iridescent colors, the golden antennae of a great moth rising from his forehead, and the hideous bulk of a gray spider for a burden.

He moved through the thin-stalked mushroom forest, and, because of the thing he carried, all creatures fled before him. They did not fear man – their instinct was slow-moving – but during all the millions of years that insects have existed, there have existed spiders to prey upon them. So Burl moved on in solemn state, a brightly clad man bent beneath the weight of a huge and horrible monster.

He came upon a valley full of torn and blackened mushrooms. There was not a single yellow top among them. Every one had been infested with tiny maggots which had liquefied the tough meat of the mushroom and caused it to drip to the ground below. And all the liquid had gathered in a golden pool in the center of the small depression. Burl heard a loud humming and buzzing before he topped the rise that opened the valley for his inspection. He stopped a moment and looked down.

A golden-red lake, its center reflecting the hazy sky overhead. All about, blackened mushrooms, seeming to have been charred and burned by a fierce flame. A slow-flowing golden brooklet trickled slowly over a rocky ledge, into the larger pool. And all about the edges of the golden lake, in ranks and rows, by hundreds, thousands, and by millions, were ranged the green-gold, shining bodies of great flies.

They were small as compared with the other insects. They had increased in size but a fraction of the amount that the bees, for example, had increased; but it was due to an imperative necessity of their race.

The flesh-flies laid their eggs by hundreds in decaying

carcasses. The others laid their eggs by hundreds in the mush-rooms. To feed the maggots that would hatch, a relatively great quantity of food was needed, therefore the flies must remain comparatively small, or the body of a single grasshopper, say, would furnish food for but two or three grubs instead of the hundreds it must support.

Burl stared down at the golden pool. Bluebottles, green-bottles, and all the flies of metallic luster were gathered at the Lucullan feast of corruption. Their buzzing as they darted above the odorous pool of golden liquid made the sound Burl had heard. Their bodies flashed and glittered as they darted back and forth, seeking a place to alight and join in the orgy.

Those which clustered about the banks of the pool were still as if carved from metal. Their huge, red eyes glowed, and their bodies shone with an obscene fatness. Flies are the most disgusting of all insects. Burl watched them a moment, watched the interlacing streams of light as they buzzed eagerly above the pool, seeking a place at the festive board.

A drumming roar sounded in the air. A golden speck appeared in the sky, a slender, needle-like body with trans-parent, shining wings and two huge eyes. It grew nearer and became a dragonfly twenty feet and more in length, its body shimmering, purest gold. It poised itself above the pool and then darted down. Its jaws snapped viciously and repeatedly, and at each snapping the glittering body of a fly vanished.

A second dragonfly appeared, its body a vivid purple, and a third. They swooped and rushed above the golden pool, snap-ping in mid air, turning their abrupt, angular turns, creatures of incredible ferocity and beauty. At the moment they were nothing more or less than slaughtering-machines. They darted here and there, their many-faceted eyes burning with blood-lust. In that mass of buzzing flies even the most voracious appetite must be sated, but the dragonflies kept on. Beautiful, slender, graceful creatures, they dashed here and there above the pond like avenging fiends or the mythical dragons for which they had been named.

And the loud contented buzzing kept on as before. Their

comrades were being slaughtered by hundreds not fifty feet above their heads, but the glittering rows of red-eyed flies gorging themselves on the golden, evil-smelling liquid kept placidly on with their feasting. The dragonflies could contain no more, even of their chosen prey, but they continued to swoop madly above the pool, striking down the buzzing flies even though the bodies must perforce drop uneaten. One or two of the dead flies – crushed to a pulp by the angry jaws of a great dragonfly – dropped among its feasting brothers. They shook themselves.

Presently one of them placed its disgusting proboscis upon the mangled form and sipped daintily of the juices exuding from the broken armor. Another join in, and another. In a little while a cluster of them elbowed and pushed each other for a chance to join in the cannibalistic feast.

Burl turned aside and went on, while the slim forms of the dragonflies still darted here and there above the pool, still striking down the droning flies with vengeful strokes of their great jaws, and while a rain of crushed bodies fell to the contented, glistening horde below.

Only a few miles farther on Burl came upon a familiar landmark. He knew it well, but from a safe distance as always. A mass of rock had heaved itself up from the nearly level plain over which he was traveling, and formed an outjutting cliff. At one point the rock overhung a sheer drop, making an inverted ledge – a roof over nothingness – which had been pre-empted by a hairy creature and made into a fairylike dwelling. A white hemisphere clung tenaciously to the rock above, and long cables anchored it firmly.

Burl knew the place as one to be fearfully avoided. A Clotho spider had built itself a nest there, from which it emerged to hunt the unwary. Within that half-globe there was a monster, resting upon a cushion of softest silk. But if one went too near, one of the little inverted arches, seemingly firmly closed by a wall of silk, would open and a creature out of a dream of hell emerge, to run with fiendish agility toward its prey.

Surely, Burl knew the place. Hung upon the outer walls of the silken palace were stones and tiny boulders, discarded fragments of former meals, and the gutted armor from limbs of ancient prey. But what caused Burl to know the place most surely and most terribly was another decoration that dangled from the castle of this insect ogre. This was the shrunken, desiccated figure of a man, all its juices extracted and the life gone.

The death of that man had saved Burl's life two years before. They had been together, seeking a new source of edible mushrooms for food. The Clotho spider was a hunter, not a spinner of snares. It sprang suddenly from behind a great puff-ball, and the two men froze in terror. Then it came swiftly forward and deliberately chose its victim. Burl had escaped when the other man was seized. Now he looked meditatively at the hiding place of his ancient enemy. Some day—

But now he passed on. He went past the thicket in which the great moths hid during the day, and past the pool – a turgid thing of slime and yeast – in which a monster water snake lurked. He penetrated the little wood of the shining mush-rooms that gave out light at night, and the shadowed place where the truffle-hunting beetles went chirping thunderously during the dark hours.

And then he saw Saya. He caught a flash of pink skin vanishing behind the thick stalk of a squat toadstool, and ran forward, calling her name. She appeared, and saw the figure with the horrible bulk of the spider upon its back. She cried out in horror, and Burl understood. He let his burden fall and then went swiftly toward her.

They met. Saya waited timidly until she saw who this man was, and then astonishment went over her face. Gorgeously attired, in an iridescent cloak from the whole wing of a great moth, with a strip of softest fur from a night-flying creature about his middle, with golden, feathery antennae bound upon his forehead, and a fierce spear in his hands – this was not the Burl she had known.

But then he moved slowly toward her, filled with a fierce delight at seeing her again, thrilling with joy at the slender gracefulness of her form and the dark richness of her tangled hair. He held out his hands and touched her shyly. Then, manlike, he began to babble excitedly of the things that had happened to him, and dragged her toward his great victim, the gray-bellied spider.

Saya trembled when she saw the furry bulk lying upon the ground, and would have fled when Burl advanced and took it upon his back. Then something of the pride that filled him came vicariously to her. She smiled a flashing smile, and Burl stopped short in his excited explanation. He was suddenly tongue-tied. His eyes became pleading and soft. He laid the huge spider at her feet and spread out his hands imploringly.

Thirty thousand years of savagery had not lessened the femininity in Saya. She became aware that Burl was her slave, that these wonderful things he wore and had done were as nothing if she did not approve. She drew away – saw the misery in Burl's face – and abruptly ran into his arms and clung to him, laughing happily. And quite suddenly Burl saw with extreme clarity that all these things he had done, even the slaying of a great spider, were of no importance whatever beside this most wonderful thing that had just happened, and told Saya so quite humbly, but holding her very close to him as he did so.

And so Burl came back to his tribe. He had left it nearly naked, with but a wisp of moth-wing twisted about his middle, a timid, fearful, trembling creature. He returned in triumph, walking slowly and fearlessly down a broad lane of golden mushrooms toward the hiding place of his people.

Upon his shoulders was draped a great and many-colored cloak made from the whole of a moth's wing. Soft fur was about his middle. A spear was in his hand and a fierce club at his waist. He and Saya bore between them the dead body of a huge spider – aforetime the dread of the pink-skinned, naked men. But to Burl the most important thing of all was that Saya walked beside him openly, acknowledging him before all the tribe.

POLITICS

'The War of the Pacific has at least taught one lesson to naval strategists. No naval force can ever be said to be inconsiderable, if officered and manned by a capable and determined personnel.'

Modern Sea Power, Grahame, New York 1932

Lieutenant MacReady saw the enemy from the *Minnesota*'s fighting-top and rejoiced with a bitter rejoicing at the sight. This was in August of 1934, you see, just four days after the Battle of Hungars' Bank, and the *Minnesota*'s whole whole ship-company thirsted for vengeance, both upon the enemy and the politicians who had sacrificed the rest of the fleet to win an election. The politicians were safe, but the enemy was here, and the *Minnesota* tore through the water toward them with the speed and fury of an avenging Nemesis.

'Enemy in sight, sir,' said MacReady crisply into the telephone transmitter strapped to his chest. 'Bearing—'

'*Already reported and ranged*,' said a curt voice in his earphones.

MacReady felt a little shock of surprise. Then he remembered and felt lonely and useless. He looked down. The guns of the top forward turret were winding up to extreme range. The top turret was coming around. He saw monstrous flames. The shock of the discharge reached him even before the blast of the explosion tore past the fighting-top. Three sixteen-inch guns had gone off. It was a ranging salvo. The shells were invisible, screaming demons of steel and explosive; hurtling upward now, but they would descend nearly twenty miles away and it was

168

Lieutenant MacReady's task to watch their fall. Or it had been his task until the new range-finders were installed while the wreckage of that boiler-explosion was being repaired. And at any instant it might be his task again.

He counted the seconds; refocussed his glasses; wet his lips. Somehow he knew that guns were swinging below him. Grim, gray-painted tubes were moving slowly to new positions, pointing ahead. He saw the enemy vessels vaguely. There was what looked like a melee of ships on the horizon's edge. Two huge hulks, one of them listing visibly even at this distance. That would be the *Langley*, the aircraft-carrier. Her sister-ship seemed a shade low in the water, but at this distance one could not be sure. Over and about the distant shapes, tiny motes danced. Aircraft. Army planes from shore, fighting in the place of the naval aircraft that had shared in the disaster of Hungars' Bank. And there was the *Seattle*, on fire but fighting savagely. He saw the flashes of her guns. The *St. Louis* was with her. They were putting up a rear-guard action to enable the aircraft-carriers to get away. Those tiny specks were the destroyers. American destroyers. Half-wrecked and battered but fighting gamely as they limped homeward…

The ranging salvo splashed. Three tremendous water-spouts, rising simultaneously, high above the fighting-top of any ship afloat.

'Right six, up two—' snapped MacReady.

The *Minnesota* burst into flame beneath him. Lieutenant MacReady started at the blast of sound. He was dazed by the mere shock, but he knew that every gun that could be brought to bear ahead had fired in one colossal burst of flame. And before his range-correction was completed!

His ear-phones barked:

'*Range that broadside.*'

'Y-yes, sir,' said Lieutenant MacReady.

He began to count the seconds. The lower forward turret was shifting slightly. Twenty-two, twenty-three – the three guns spouted flame and dingy-brown smoke. This was the very latest constant-pressure powder, guaranteed by the ordnance-department not to vary more than one thousand pounds to the square inch breech-pressure even under service conditions ... Fifty-eight – Fifty-nine ...

The *Minnesota* was making twenty-eight knots. Blue water flowed past her with a deceptive smoothness. One of the distant aircraft-carriers began to spit tiny flames from its anti-torpedo battery. There was a flurry of destroyers – American destroyers meeting an attack. Lieutenant MacReady could see the enemy ships clearly now. Four big ones besides the destroyers. Pocket-battleships, ten thousand tons, with more speed, more armor, more hitting power than anything else twice their size afloat. But the *Minnesota* was a forty-thousand-ton ship, the biggest battleship in the world. She was, incidentally, the only first-line ship left to the American Navy after the Battle of Hungars' Bank.

The broadside struck. A monstrous mound of water rose to an incredible height. The stern of an enemy ship showed from behind it. The rest of the enemy vessel was hidden behind the broadside-splash. It seemed one single, volcanic eruption of water.

'Right one-half,' said Lieutenant MacReady into the transmitter before him. 'Up—'

The mound of water began to fall. The stern of the enemy ship tilted with its descent. It rose upward till the keel showed. It dived slowly ...

'By God, sir!' said Lieutenant MacReady shrilly, 'She's sunk!'

Sixteen-inch shells are not good medicine for pocket battle-ships. MacReady swung his glasses swiftly. There was a ranging salvo of shells still aloft. It was his duty to spot their fall ...

He saw the splashes. Two of them. One was short. One was an over. The third ... The stern of the enemy ship grew suddenly hazy.

'Straddled!' barked Lieutenant MacReady.

But the terrific concussion of the ship's whole forward battery tore at his chest. He felt something warm trickling down his chin. His nose was bleeding. He counted seconds with a strained attention. Another ranging blast below. There was a sudden roaring overhead. Two enemy bombers with six fighting-planes escort were racing toward the ship. The army planes from shore were diving for it... The whole anti-aircraft battery of the *Minnesota* barked savagely, twice, MacReady heard terrific concussions and the sound of a dogfight going on somewhere up aloft.

'I'd be happy,' thought MacReady in savage satisfaction, 'if only some of our politicians were on those ships out there. We're shooting like a streak. We couldn't miss if those damned pol—'

A monster mound of water rose up, obliterating one of the three remaining pocket-battleships. MacReady's lips formed the word 'Straddled!' but there seemed hardly any need. The mound slowly flattened out and the sea was clean where it had been. A pocket-battleship can stand an amazing lot of pounding, but there simply isn't any armor that will keep out a sixteen-inch shell. And when several of them strike at once, the result is deplorable. Seconds later the third pocket-battleship was silhouetted by splashes. The whole fabric of the *Minnesota* shuddered beneath MacReady as for the third time every gun that could be brought to bear was fired in one world-filling blast of sound. And seconds later a fourth ranging salvo...

Splashes began to rise about the *Minnesota* herself. But a ten-thousand-ton ship is not a steady firing-platform, and though it may carry armament far out of proportion to its size, it is really designed for fleet work, with smoke-screens, aircraft spotters and other aids to efficiency. The *Minnesota* was a self-contained fighting unit, capable of fighting like a whirlwind, and it was taking the offensive. Which was an advantage in itself. One shell fell fifty yards from the *Minnesota*'s side. The next salvo from the ship that fired it should have done some damage.

But then the third broadside struck, and when the sea subsided, a pocket-battleship was rolling over with a grave dignity to turn turtle and sink. And seconds later the fourth ranging salvo struck, and as its splashes leaped forward, the *Minnesota* roared for the fourth time...

Lieutenant MacReady was dazed and dizzy. He felt the ship

changing course beneath him. Three broadsides had struck and three ships were sunk! Of course the *Minnesota* carried the heaviest metal of any ship afloat, but it wasn't natural! There'd been no time for the spotting of shells and the correction of range. Just a ranging salvo, and as it sent splashes skyward, the whole forward battery of the *Minnesota* flamed. No delay. No waiting. Above all, no error! The *Minnesota* fired every gun that it could bear. Twenty miles away and a long time later four acres of sea arose mountainously – with scattering splashes outside – and anything afloat in that four acres of sea simply ceased to exist.

It happened again now. The fourth broadside struck, it seemed squarely. When the turmoil of its arrival ceased, the fourth enemy pocket ship was still afloat, but explosions were coming from it with lightning-like rapidity. And suddenly it vomited flame from somewhere amidships, broke jaggedly in half – and the sea was clean.

The *Minnesota* had already changed course. There were only enemy destroyers afloat now, after only four broadsides. The distant American ships drew to one side, fighting savagely as they moved. A torpedo struck home somewhere out there, and a thin sliver of metal which was an American destroyer upended and went down in a clean dive. And the air seemed suddenly full of buzzings as of a myriad mosquitos.

'*Lieutenant MacReady,*' said the curt voice in his headphones. '*You will not be required to spot ranges as long as the new range-finders function. You will, however, search for possible subs, and especially for torpedo-trails.*'

'Yes, sir,' said Lieutenant MacReady exultantly.

He turned to grin at his fellow-spotter in the forward fighting-top. A ringside seat at the big show! Enemy aircraft were racing for the *Minnesota*, but the Army ships from shore were taking a deadly toll. MacReady glanced back at the distant thin line of the coast. Motes were visible in the sky. More army planes, coming out from land. Fighting-planes all, save one squadron of heavy bombers with a haze of tiny pursuit-planes whirling before it, in order to serve as a protection.

A pall of blackness arose far away upon the sea. The enemy destroyers were making a smoke-screen. The *Seattle* and the *St. Louis* were the targets toward which the lengthening spearhead of blackness reached out. They had been under heavy fire from the pocket-ships, before the *Minnesota* came out. If the destroyers could sink them and the aircraft-carriers, it would amount to victory. Destroyer-attacks in daylight against ships like the *Minnesota* are unhealthy, but the lesser and already-crippled American ships might be wiped out.

But the *Minnesota* spouted flame from fifty gun-muzzles. The anti-aircraft guns barked in one monstrous volley. They barked again. There were terrific concussions up aloft, and Lieutenant MacReady saw a huge ball of yellow smoke – T. N.T. smoke – spreading with an enormous velocity in mid-air.

'Got a bomber!' he whispered to himself. He wiped the blood off his face and grinned from ear to ear with sheer excitement.

The broadside landed, fifteen miles away. And it struck, not as a concentrated blast of sheer destruction, but as a barrage. Separate splashes rose in glittering similitude of stalagmites on a lime-cavern floor. But each pinnacle, shining in the sun, represented the point of a six-inch shell – they were small and few – or an eight-inch shell – there were more of them – or of mighty sixteen-inch shells themselves. The broadside of the *Minnesota* had deliberately been spread out to cover a huge area thinly. But a destroyer does not need much pounding to be put out of action. The tip of the spearhead of smoke heading for the American destroyers simply ceased to be. And the *Minnesota* flamed again, and again, and again. Six times, at fifteen-second intervals, she belched out coruscating waves of fire. A long time later the broadsides fell.

The anti-aircraft batteries barked savagely. Firing like the heavy guns; simultaneous salvos at single targets at single instants. Picking out the enemy bombers and leaving the enemy single-seaters to the army ships. Over and above the droning of many motors there was now the intermittent sound of colossal explosions. Enemy two-thousand-pound bombs were going off in mid-air as the bombers that carried them were wrecked by screaming hails of metal.

MacReady fixed his glasses upon the distant smoke-screen. It was ragged and torn. A single enemy destroyer showed clearly for an instant. It was changing course and streaking for the far horizon. The rest were gone! The forward torrent boomed a ranging salvo. MacReady watched feverishly. Army ships coming out from shore in a never-ending stream. Somewhere far aloft – The ranging salvo struck! A quarter-mile over! But the forward battery crashed forth for the tenth time in this action. Every gun bearing ahead crashed...

MacReady was bleeding at the nose and ears from the concussions that had battered at him. He was bruised all over. He was deafened and his bloodshot eyes streamed water, but he sat in a still glow of satisfaction, wishing only that certain politicians could be upon that panic-stricken destroyer that fled from a hail of death.

He saw the shells land. The fleeing destroyer was emitting a dense cloud of smoke to conceal its trail. But it was lifted a hundred and fifty feet, clear, as contact-fused shells went off in an inferno of destruction. It was flung above even its own smoke-screen. MacReady saw it break in pieces and vanish again behind the smoke.

And then there was only the buzzing of a multitude of motors aloft and all around. The tearing, rasping chatter of machine-guns became audible. MacReady gazed upward and saw the Army planes hunt down ruthlessly and relentlessly every enemy plane that was aloft. With bitter satisfaction he watched the flying things go fluttering helplessly downward, or dive as plummets of flame into the sea. His satisfaction was only tempered with a slight regret when the last enemy pilot fought a magnificent lone duel with an Army formation, and entangled two of them in his final, blazing fall.

The *Minnesota* shepherded the other American ships toward the Golden Gate, gleaming and unmarred and belligerent. There were two scout-cruisers under her protection, the *Seattle* and the *St. Louis*. The *Seattle* was still on fire, but was getting it under some control. There were two aircraft-carriers, one of them listing heavily. There were seven half-wrecked destroyers. That was all. They went limping slowly toward the shore, through waters littered for a space with wave-wetted wings...

They went ahead of the *Minnesota* and entered the harbor. They anchored, watched by silent, stunned, almost panic-stricken crowds which thronged the water-front and did not cheer at all.

Because this was four days after the Battle of Hungars' Bank. The enemy fleet held the Pacific. The *Minnesota* alone excepted, the whole first line of the American battlefleet was at the bottom of the sea. Save for a few submarines and perhaps half a dozen still-fugitive destroyers – now being hunted down by the victorious enemy – these limping, shattered carcasses of ships constituted the Navy of the United States of America.

And one day before, the enemy had scornfully broadcast the terms on which it would make peace. Hawaii, Guam, the Philippines, and the Panama Canal were the only territorial demands, but an indemnity was insisted on and the enemy also required the surrender of the *Minnesota* and a pledge that the United States would never build more than a minimum number of small, slow cruisers in the future.

Throughout a panic-stricken nation, strong pacifist political pressure was being brought to bear to force Congress to accept those terms.

'There have been in the past, and there will be in the future, attempts by politicians to dictate naval and military policies for other than naval and military ends. But never again will a civilian official of the United States dare issue a direct order governing naval or military operations! He would be impeached, at least. In the present temper of the populace, he would probably be lynched.'

Addressing to graduating class, U.S. Naval Academy, by the Secretary of the Navy, 1938

Lieutenant MacReady had been at Annapolis with the commander of the torpedo-boat-destroyer, *Wasp*. In those far-off days MacReady had been a lowly plebe, while the destroyer-skipper was an upper-classman, but they foregathered on equal terms in MacReady's quarters on the *Minnesota*. MacReady offered libation and the *Wasp*'s commander raised his arm.

'Here's hell to politicians,' he said grimly. 'They sank our fleet!'

MacReady made an appropriate gesture, accepting the toast.

'Now shoot it,' he commanded. 'What happened?'

'If you want to know,' said the *Wasp*'s commander bitterly, 'they sent the battlefleet out with orders to avoid any action. An election is coming on. Pacifists are strong, politically. If we blew the enemy out of the water, they'd denounce us as murderers, vote against the Administration, and change the political complexion of Congress. Therefore, the Admiral was told to avoid a fleet-action until after elections if he could, and if he couldn't, to make sure it wasn't decisive defeat for the enemy. Isn't that pretty?'

'Dam' pretty,' said MacReady ironically. 'Oh, dam' pretty!'

'The enemy fleet was spoiling for a scrap,' went on the *Wasp*'s commander more bitterly still. 'They've been building pocket battleships, playing with 'em like kids with a new toy. On paper they had more gun-power than we had, in more but smaller ships. We had the weight and the punishment power. They thought they could lick us. They came over to force a fleet action. They ignored Hawaii and came on with a supply-fleet ten miles long behind 'em. And you can't handle a modern fleet, with destroyer-screens and the like, without using wireless. We were picking up their code stuff and trying to decode it. They were doing the same with ours. Both sides were using radio direction-finders, of course. They knew where we were, and we knew where they were. But they wanted a fight, and we were ordered to avoid one. It couldn't be avoided!'

'"Hit first, hit hard, hit often!"' quoted MacReady. 'But tell me, old man, why did the Admiral split his fleet?'

'Direct, specific orders from Washington!' snapped the

Wasp's commander. 'We knew the enemy was determined on a fleet-action and headed straight for us. The Admiral reported to Washington that a general engagement was absolutely unavoidable, and an attempt at anything but a decisive victory was stark madness. He got detailed orders – the plan that sank the fleet! Signed by the President as commander-in-chief. Politics! Arm-chair strategy that looked all right on paper, but – my God! The battlefleet was to proceed northwest, with its radio silent. The two aircraft-carriers, with escorting destroyers, were to proceed southwest. The carriers were to keep planes aloft with their wireless outfits going, simulating a battlefleet in movement. The enemy would head for them. At the logical instant they would cut off their wireless and run. And the battlefleet would make a demonstration proving its actual position to be a thousand miles or so from where the enemy thought it was. A trick to gain time. A trick to postpone a battle until after election. That's all! They say the Admiral cried when he read the order.'

'Here's hell to politicians,' said MacReady morosely. 'Why didn't it work?'

'An air-photo from forty thousand feet,' said the *Wasp*'s commander sardonically, 'is of no ordinary use to anybody. It's taken through an infra-red filter that fog or clouds can't bother, but the Army doesn't use 'em because they don't give enough detail. But they'll tell the difference between a battlefleet and a pair of aircraft-carriers, all right!'

MacReady groaned. The *Wasp*'s skipper went on grimly:

'That must have been how they did it. Silenced high-altitude planes and photos taken through eight miles of haze. Anyhow, six hours after the battlefleet headed northwest, the enemy fleet split up too. They duplicated our maneuver. They sent their supply-fleet to meet us, with its wireless going full blast to simulate a battlefleet, and they sent their battlefleet to meet ours, full speed ahead and with its wireless shut off too. But they didn't leave their carriers behind!'

MacReady groaned again.

'The dirigible *Akron* sighted them,' said the destroyer-skipper coldly. 'They got her in twenty minutes, after she'd sent the alarm back and crashed twelve planes that attacked her. But that was too late. We were eight hundred miles away, with the whole air-service! You should have seen those carriers shoot planes into the air! One – two – three they went up! Streaking for the fight! It'd be four hours before the fastest of them got there, but they went! And the damned thing was nearly over when they arrived. Our ships had gone into action with only the ship-planes to spot and fight for them. The enemy had four carriers – little ones, but they carried a hell of a lot of planes. Twenty minutes after the opening gun, they'd wiped the skies clean above our fleet. There were only six planes spotting for our whole fleet during the second half-hour of the action. With smoke-screens in use, you know what that meant! There were only three during the last hour! The enemy laid down smoke-screens and potted at our ships from behind 'em. Our destroyers went through the screens and tried to do the spotting the air-service should have done. Suicide, but we got two of their pocket-ships and one of their super-dreadnaughts that way. Meanwhile our boats were going to hell and gone. When the airfleet arrived there was only the old *New York* and the *Michigan* above water in the first line, and we'd lost two-thirds of our destroyers. But they stayed afloat, those two old tubs, taking all the punishment the whole enemy fleet could give 'em, and passing out all they had – until our planes ran out of gas! It was all over then! They'd flown eight hundred miles to get to the fight. They were nearly out of fuel when they got there. And the enemy expected to gather them in when they made forced landings. Pretty idea, wasn't it?'

Lieutenant MacReady said pungent words.

'They did get three,' said the commander of the *Wasp*, calmly. 'But the rest somehow got blown up or crashed by their pilots before they jumped for the water. It annoyed the enemy. They left the pilots – in the water.'

Lieutenant MacReady said more pungent words – much more pungent.

'Meanwhile we on the decoy-fleet had been tipped off. Oh, a grand time we had! Orders first were to try to join the battlefleet. An hour later the old Admiral knew he couldn't hold out until the airfleet got there, and ordered us to streak for home. The planes couldn't be turned back. They were gone anyway. He tried to save the carriers and the ships with them. We turned and ran.'

The destroyer-skipper gesticulated bitterly.

'Then the destroyers from the supply-fleet hit us. We'd sent every plane we had to the fleet-action. They'd done nearly the same. So we fought 'em off. For four days we'd been running away from them, fighting night and day, when the *Minnesota* turned up. Those pocket-ships only got here this morning. Four days and nights of fighting, Mac! We sank three of their destroyers for every two of us they got, but there were twenty-four of us when we started out, and there were seven of us who came in, and the pocket-ships would have finished us if the *Minnesota* hadn't come when it did!'

There was silence. There was no noise anywhere on the *Minnesota* except an unplaceable dim whine which was a dynamo running somewhere. Out the porthole of MacReady's cabin could be seen the dim bulks of the two aircraft-carriers that had been brought in port that day. The *Langley* still listed heavily to port, but there were lighters clustered about her side and arc-lamps burned brightly. At three separate points, clusters of arc-lamps burned vividly on the harbor-water.

There was a droning hum overhead. It passed on and out to sea.

'Army planes,' the commander of the *Wasp* said heavily. 'Doing naval patrol. At least the Army can smother their air-force if they try any bombing. But what good'll it do? I haven't got a ship any more. My engines were shot to hell. They're cutting off the bow of the *Wasp* with an underwater torch. They're going to weld it in place of the *Waddy*'s bow, which looks like a full-blown rose. And our stern goes to replace the *Stingray*'s tail. Out of three wrecks they'll make two ships that can steam. It'll take four days, with underwater welding. But what good will it do?'

'It depends,' said MacReady without hope, 'on our shooting. And on politics. You saw our shooting today?'

The *Wasp*'s commander nodded.

'I thought of you up there in the fighting-top, spotting shells. The air was clear and you could do it—'

'I didn't spot a shell,' said MacReady. 'The new range-finders have taken my job away from me and do it ten times as well. We've got fire-power now, old horse! And fire-control! We've got the new range-finders in. Those parallel-beam finders they've been working on for years.'

His companion looked puzzled.

'All electrical,' explained MacReady. 'No observer at all. Two telescopes, one at each end of a base-line, and mounted exactly parallel. Fitted with photoelectric cells instead of eyepieces. You swing the base-line around and they sweep the horizon. And a ship on the horizon changes the amount of light that goes through a narrow slit to the photoelectric cell. It registers the instant the first telescope hits the stern of the ship. A fraction of a second later – because the telescopes are exactly parallel – the ship-image registers on the other cell. Both cells register exactly the same changes in current-output, but one is a fraction of a second behind the other. Knowing the rate of sweep in seconds or mils of arc, if one photoelectric cell lags behind the other one mil, and you know the base-line, you work out the distance in a hurry. See?'

'Complicated,' commented the destroyer-skipper distastefully.

'Complicated, sure,' agreed MacReady readily. 'But man! Does it work? Those range-finders sweep their field ten times per second, ranging each way. We range the enemy ship twenty times per second and get electric impulses to read off. But better than that, we range our own shell-splashes and the target together, with the same instrument, at the same time! See the point?'

'M-m-m-m. That looks good!'

'It's even better!' insisted MacReady. 'We get electric impulses, instantaneous, instead of observer's figures. The impulses go to an integrator that calculates the range and declination. That feeds into a computer that works up the firing-data – barometer, wind, humidity, and so on – and that goes to a relay that lays the gun! All working at the same time! The gun's laid on the target from the first second or two. Constant ranging gives speed and course of the target. The computer dopes 'em out, shifts the gun to where the target will be when the shells land, and we fire a salvo. And then the splashes get ranged by the same outfit in relation to the target! Errors in the firing-data and powder-lot – even wear on the gun-gears – are automatically corrected! Then we let go a broadside. It blows hell out of the target! Gun for gun and ship for ship, the *Minnesota*'s the best fighting-machine in the world! And half our superiority comes from those finders. Why, man! Our anti-aircraft finders range a plane, compute its course and speed in three dimensions, lay twenty guns on its most probable position at the time of shell-burst, and fire the guns – all in two-fifths of a second! They can do everything but play "Home Sweet Home" on a piccolo!'

'Then,' said the commander of the *Wasp*, 'why weren't the other ships fitted with them?'

'Dear heart,' protested MacReady in fine irony, 'haven't you ever heard of politics? We have a few men with guts in Washington. We have also a large number of elderly maiden ladies. The range-finders were in production. They were shipped here to be fitted. War broke out. There was a wave of popular sentiment against the rude and brutal practise of defending one's country against anybody else. The fleet was ordered to sea at once, because if it didn't get to sea, the pacifists might manage to forbid its sailing! With the old range-finders and air spotting we were on equal terms with the enemy. We could fight, anyhow! But even after the fleet had sailed, the political pacifists managed to get those orders issued that you wot of, and which sank our fleet. Politics, you see! It's sweet and pretty? And the *Minnesota* has the range-finders installed simply because one of our boilers blew up. It killed sixteen men. We had to be left in port, and while we were getting the mess cleaned up and repaired the Skipper put in the new finders. That's why we're damned near a match for the whole enemy navy!'

'And what good does it do?' asked the commander of the *Wasp* bitterly. 'You're making 'em a present. The peace terms call for the surrender of the *Minnesota*, and those damned politicians are going to accept 'em!'

Lieutenant MacReady leaned forward confidentially.

'Old boy,' he said under his breath, 'the Secretary of the Navy is not an elderly maiden lady. There has never yet been an American warship surrendered without a fight. Our skipper has told him we can have some destroyers ready to fight again in six days, and asked permission to commit suicide in his own ship. The Army's going to help, by fighting off enemy planes if an action takes place within a hundred miles of shore. So if the enemy wants the *Minnesota*, he'll have to take her! The Secretary thinks he can hold off surrender, in Washington, for those six days. If he can't, we go out before, without the destroyers, and smash our wireless so we can't be ordered to come back. And it will be suicide, and highly immoral to fight against a gallant enemy who has sunk our ships and left our plane-pilots to drown because they blew up their ships rather than hand them over, but – well – it'll be better than the other thing, won't it?'

'You're dam' right!' said the commander of the *Wasp*, hungrily. 'I can shovel coal, or wash mess-dishes, or – or—'

'I think,' said Lieutenant MacReady magnanimously, 'that it can be arranged. The Secretary of the Navy will be fired. The pacifists will write in the school-books that we were murderers. But maybe, if we work it right, the politicians won't object. Because we'll be sunk. I know I'd hate to be a politician and have a Navy man look me in the eye!'

The commander of the *Wasp* stood up.

'I'm going back to slave-drive my men,' he said feverishly, 'We've got to get those destroyers ready.'

'A politician is a man who believes that the greatest catastrophe that can possibly befall his country is the election of
somebody else to the office he wants.'

Politics, Leinster, New York 1931

The *Minnesota* lay at anchor in San Francisco harbor. The sun
shone down placidly upon the scene. There were flags flying
everywhere. Some of them were 'peace-flags' and they flew
brightly. Some were American flags. They were at half-mast.
The city was still and dead. Newspapers came out at frequent
intervals with huge hundred-and-twenty-point headlines and
very nearly identical contents. Two destroyers had made port
in Alaska. They had refueled and gone to sea again. One
destroyer, battered and in a sinking condition, had made the
port of Vancouver, B.C., and was unable to put out again. She
was interned. It was rumored that American submarines had
located the enemy fleet with radio direction-finders and had
submerged in its path. Motors silent and men still as death,
they had allowed the screen of destroyers and light craft to
pass overhead. They had risen among the capital ships of the
enemy navy. They had sunk three ships before they were destroyed. The enemy command denied the rumor. There was
no other war news. Peace news was oratory in print, accounts
of meetings and resolutions and other activities of the persons
opposed to war even in self-defense.

In San Francisco the real sign of life or energy were displayed in two places only. One was the Navy Yard, where
men worked frantically against fate with electric-welding and
oxy-acetylene apparatus, doing work that required months of
time and elaborate equipment in days instead and with makeshift materials. The *Langley* was having a patch made for the
torpedo-blast in her side. It was being welded in one piece on
shore. It would be sunk alongside and welded in place by Ells-
worth underwater torches in the hands of divers. The *Wasp* was
a fragment of herself, her bow and stern cut away and only her
shell-torn middle section beached in shallow water to rust away.
Every one of the returned vessels was aswarm with men. Their

own crews were laboring like madmen to get them in shape to steam. They did not hope to attain to real battle-efficiency. They only hoped to patch them up so they could share in the last foray of the fighting forces of the United States Navy. If they could steam, and if they could fire a gun, the crews of these ships would mutiny if forbidden a place at the suicide of the fleet.

The other spot where activity was in order was the headquarters of those organizations which opposed the prosecution of war against even a declared enemy. Speakers bustled in and out. Banners flew and gaudy placards smote the eye. Orators moved to strategic points to explain to half-stunned crowds that war was evil in itself and that the disaster of Hungars' Bank was the direct act of Providence, disapproving of America. Suitably edited portions of Scripture were available for distribution. And constantly through that activity for the service of abstract good ran the threat of political action, and an insistence upon the power of little mean men at the polls to undo the actions of bigger men who were deaf to the clamor of fanatics.

The orators ranged everywhere. Marine sentries stopped them at the Navy Yard gates, firmly refusing entry even to deputations of sad-eyed, hysterically righteous women intent upon pleading with the sailors not to murder the sons of other women, regardless of the fact that those sons of other women had not hesitated to sink the American battlefleet. It was uncomfortable anywhere to be in a military or naval uniform, because of the reproaches of convinced opponents of war. Pacifism had become respectable within the past four years, and its proponents took full advantage of the immunity accorded to respectable men. An enthusiastic orator even had himself rowed alongside the *Minnesota* and began a moving speech addressed to the sailors, advocating mutiny and the consistent violation of all the articles of war, and was lured below the slopchute by a sergeant of marines. It was pure accident, of course, that the ship's garbage was discharged at just that time, but an indignant protest was immediately telegraphed to the Secretary of the Navy and all other Cabinet officers.

That was in San Francisco. In Washington there were parades in favor of peace. The President – being by American custom not only a government executive but also the leader of a political party – was forced for the sake of his Party's chances in the coming elections to devote four hours in one day to the hearing of spokesmen for different groups of anti-war delegates from anti-war societies throughout the nation. The War and Navy Departments were picketed by determined, passionately sincere advocates of peace at any price. Senators and members of the House of Representatives were besieged by opponents of carnage.

In London, the American Ambassador was drily informed that the British Government, through sympathy with the present embarrassments of the American Government, would delay for the present the taking up of the unquestionably just claims of British subjects against the States which, while in the Confederacy, had sold bonds in England and later repudiated them. The American Ambassador took the hint, and cabled desperately that if the United States announced its renunciation of self-defense, that its standing before the world would be forever gone. In Germany there was laughter and ironically bitter comments in the journals. In France there was alarm and indignation at the threatened disappearance of an ally through what its official press termed national suicide. In Central and South America there was pure panic. Republics which heretofore had maintained a chip-on-the-shoulder attitude toward the United States now made frantic representations that the Monroe Doctrine would be without force behind it.

They begged, they implored, they pleaded with the United States not to adopt a course which would ultimately involve their ruin with its own.

But in the United States, foreign opinion had no weight. Pacifism was an issue which would decide an election. It would determine whether Tweedledum should stay in office or be thrown out for Tweedledee. It was a matter of politics, and therefore much more important than national prestige or national security or the national honor itself to all the Tweedle-dums in office and all the Tweedledees without.

The Secretary of the Navy was fighting for time, with the Secretary for War ably seconding him. These two men, at least, would lose their political status with the triumph of a no-defense attitude in the coming elections. Their place was to be taken – so the righteous had it – by a Secretary for Peace. And they fought tooth and nail, by argument and persuasion and brow-beating and cajoling, to stem the panic of Congress-men in terror of political oblivion. But on the fourth day the Secretary of the Navy wired to San Francisco in code:

'*Peace proposals considered in Congress tomorrow. Will probably be accepted the day after. I take responsibility of ordering you to use your own judgment in operations against the enemy.*'

The Secretary of the Navy would have committed political suicide when the order became known. But he would be able to look at himself in a mirror without shrinking. The captain of the *Minnesota* read the telegram with a grim and weary smile. He tossed it across his desk.

'We'll go out in the morning. The only question is, is that crazy MacReady right?' And how many destroyers will we have?'

'Ten, sir, plus the scout-cruisers and the aircraft carriers. And the planes that went out to try MacReady's idea are due back at any moment, sir.'

The message from the Secretary of the Navy neither inter-rupted nor intensified the feverish labor going on upon the battered ships that had limped into port four days before. An interruption would have slowed things up. An intensification would have been impossible. Repairs were being made with a reckless disregard for mere deficiencies in materials or means. One marvelous assemblage of plates and machinery had parts of six separate vessels in it. Another was repaired from four – one of them a troop-transport stolen from the Army while somebody painstakingly looked the other way. Depth-bomb sowers were being equipped for a new purpose, and a strictly improvised munitions-plant was unloading Army shells of one type and reloading their contents into naval shells of another sort entirely, which lacked full charges.

And Lieutenant MacReady was rapidly attaining to a state approaching heaven. A flight of Navy planes had gone out to sea, far beyond the view of pacifists and politicians. They had laid down a smoke-screen of the thickest and heaviest sort, and made certain tests. Then they laid down a second and made other tests. And they went roaring back to shore with Lieutenant MacReady filled with a quiet rapture.

He found the commander of the *Wasp* in his quarters, picking threads out of one sleeve of his uniform-coat.

'Pulling off some gold braid,' he said ruefully to MacReady. 'Mac, there's no room for me on this damned ship. So I'm pulling some gold braid off. I'll look like a petty officer without it, and I'm stowing away till the action begins.'

'Hold on,' said MacReady unsteadily. 'I'm sort of dizzy with success. But you've a right to share in it. You gave me the idea first. I'll go to the Skipper and ask.'

'What idea? What in hell?'

'You talked about the enemy using an infra-red filter to photograph the battlefleet through eight miles of haze. It made me think. Have you ever seen the sun through a smoke-screen?'

'Of course! It's red.'

'Quite true,' said MacReady. 'The blue rays are filtered out by a smoke-screen or by dust. Only reds remain. The sun gets redder as the smoke-screen gets thicker, because only the very longest of visible rays get through. The question came up, did infra-red rays get stopped at all?'

'Mac!'

'The photoelectric cells in our range-finders,' said MacReady with a strange precision, 'are sensitive to infra-red. We went out to sea with a baby range-finder. We put on camera-filters that shut off everything but the infra-red rays. The range-finder worked perfectly well. Then we laid down a smoke-screen. The finder still worked. Then we laid down another one, thick and wide and deep. And the finder still worked. We're going to fight the last fight of the *Minnesota* that way. We'll be independent of aircraft for spotting, even if we're deep in the middle of a smoke-screen ourselves. And so I'll see if I've got a pull with the Skipper.'

A long time later he came back, his eyes glowing.

'You'll sit up in the fighting-top with me, old horse. We go into action at dawn.'

The commander of the *Wasp* started up.

'Praise God! You're sure?'

'At the present moment,' said MacReady evenly, 'the enemy fleet is bombarding Seattle. The word came through five minutes ago. It's steaming past, on the way south. Every ship, as it passes, flings a few broadsides into the town. The present estimate is that half the civilian population is wiped out, and the fleet is still passing. The enemy intention is evidently to hasten our acceptance of their peace terms.'

The *Wasp*'s commander clenched his fists and swore helplessly.

'We'll sail in time to meet them just after dawn,' said MacReady calmly. 'The *Minnesota* and what destroyers we've patched up, against the battlefleet that sank our own. Old horse, we ought to have a gaudy suicide. And so—' He poured libation. 'Here's hell to politicians!'

'Strategy was defined by General Forrest, C. S. A., as "getting the mostest men there the firstest". Fire superiority may be similarly explained as getting the most shells to the target first. And fire superiority is the lesson to be learned from the Battle of the California Coast.'

Modern Sea Power, Grahame, New York 1937

The dawn came quietly over the hills to eastward. In a vast silence the darkness thinned and the stars paled, and little winking shore-lights faded to obscurity as the sky turned gray, and nearly white, and then took on its normal blueness with only a small pinkish glow above the sun itself.

The *Minnesota* was headed north. Ahead of her there were five destroyers in line, with a scout-cruiser at either end. The monster aircraft-carriers trailed behind her, their decks white with land-planes. More tiny destroyers darted here and there about them. In the rear, again, two fleet-submarines ploughed along at twenty knots. They had come into harbor with their crews bleary-eyed from exhaustion just three hours before the *Minnesota* sailed. And they were going out again, refueled and with their torpedo-racks refilled, with half their crews sleeping the twitching slumber of exhaustion in their bunks. Fresh men would navigate them until the action began. Then the exhausted men would rise and share in it. It was their right, and they had demanded it.

The rim of the sun peered over the eastern horizon. Vividly scarlet, it was not the dull-red ball that presages a sultry morning. It came slowly and heavily up over the edge of the world and like some monstrous balloon broke awkwardly free and swam around into the sky. The sea became abruptly a cerulean blue, and the waves glittered and flashed in the sunshine.

Lieutenant MacReady, up in the *Minnesota*'s fighting-top, turned to the former skipper of the *Wasp*. He pointed to a trailing wake of gulls, fluttering tirelessly after the ship.

'I've watched those things for hours, in my time,' he observed. 'They'll see something, today. Thank God we've got clear weather! Old horse, we've got a fine day to die in!'

The skipper of the *Wasp* was searching the sky ahead through binoculars.

'The enemy,' he said briefly. 'See?'

He pointed. An infinitesimal speck against the pale-blue sky was hovering too steadily to be a gull. Lieutenant MacReady spoke crisply into the transmitter strapped to his chest. There was a sudden flurry over on one of the aircraft carriers. Half a dozen planes shot upward, climbing steeply. They passed nearly over the *Minnesota*. The two in the fighting-top could see the helmeted, goggled head of the last pilot as he went streaking in the wake of the rest.

'Never had much use for the Army,' said MacReady

absently, with his eyes searching the skyline ahead, 'but they're turning out pretty good eggs. They do like a scrap, anyhow.'

The tiny fleet moved steadily onward. The sun shone upon the vessels, and they were gleaming and defiant in its early rays. But the *Minnesota* alone was unblemished. Patches showed clearly on the rest. A sailor was absorbedly engaged in painting something on the *Stingray*. He was trying to cover up a rust-spot that had appeared almost overnight on an unpainted weld.

Silence and stillness. Far overhead, the fighting-planes from the carrier were mere specks, as tiny as the ship they had gone up to destroy. That enemy observation-plane turned tail and fled. The American planes raced after it. They went beyond the horizon and disappeared.

The clamor of a gong sounded below. Lieutenant Mac-Ready turned to his companion and grinned.

'Mess! But they'll send something up for us.'

The fleet went on. Fifteen minutes. Half an hour. An hour. The sea was clean before them. Then tiny pin-points appeared on the horizon.

'Enemy destroyers,' said MacReady. He spoke into his strapped-on transmitters and looked down at the guns. They remained motionless. The *Minnesota* went on steadily, ignoring the distant tiny ships, awaiting enemies worthy of her steel. Her destroyer-escort kept formation. The attitude of the American fleet was that of scorn.

More pin-points. More destroyers. They drew closer, but not too close. They spread about, keeping to a thirty-thousand-yard range. They hemmed in the horizon ahead and to westward. Heavier ships appeared – scout-cruisers. The sea seemed speckled with enemy craft. Light ships closed in the horizon behind the *Minnesota*.

'That's so they can mop up if we try to run for it,' said MacReady. 'Ready for torpedo-attacks at the end of the action. Lord! There's a bunch of them!'

There were a bunch of them. Three-fourths of the destroyer-force that had come across the Pacific. As many as the American battlefleet had taken into the Battle of Hungars'

Bank. They turned the horizon on three sides of the *Minnesota* into something fancifully resembling a picket fence.

Enemy pocket-battleships came into view, steaming at full speed to be in at the death. They deployed in line ahead, cutting off the *Minnesota* from the open sea. But they did not fire a gun. Now little specks began to appear in the air above the enemy fleet, and still there was no offensive movement. Then the six full-sized battleships of the enemy came grandly over the edge of the world. They moved for an apparently pre-determined position.

'This isn't to be a battle,' said MacReady. 'They're figuring it as an execution – a beautiful example of fire-superiority and fire-control. Considering the psychology of our gallant foes, I imagine they'll try to blow us out of the water with a simultaneous broadside from every ship in the fleet. It would be neat, and probably effective. Or do you suppose they think we came out to surrender?'

The ten destroyers with the *Minnesota* suddenly belched forth black smoke from their funnels and shot ahead. Weaving back and forth, darting here and there, they began to make an impenetrable smoke-screen between the *Minnesota* and her enemies. MacReady flung back his head to look at the land. Yes! A long black threadlike line was lengthening from the shore. Army planes. Five miles from the *Minnesota* that line bifurcated – split in two.

'God bless 'em!' said MacReady comfortably, 'they're just on time. They'll give the destroyers a busy morning. Every bomber the Army owns is in that line! We've got air superiority in this action!'

The *Minnesota* was in the center of perhaps a square mile of open sea, with a growing wall of blackness about her. On the fighting-top MacReady saw over it.

He watched the enemy ships building up a precise, ceremonial formation for the destruction of the *Minnesota*. MacReady's eyes gleamed suddenly. The top forward turret swung in place and its guns wound up to nearly maximum elevation.

'They do love ceremony, the enemy,' he said gently. 'They're arranging themselves for our destruction as if it were a review. If I were the Old Man, I'd not bother about ranging salvos after the first spotting. We've got them all ranged, anyhow, and with one salvo for wind and barometer and so on. I'd fire broadsides only.'

The *Minnesota*'s top turret-guns flashed earsplittingly – the first ranging salvo. The destroyers were weaving madly about, extending and thickening the smoke-screen about her. It would have blinded any other ship in the world, and made her utterly dependent upon aircraft observation. But spotting is exacting work, and the Army observers wouldn't be sufficient in spotting for the Navy anyhow. The enemy evidently counted upon it. The smoke-screen was wide and thick. Here and there it billowed upward enough to obscure the horizon. But a long time later MacReady saw three splashes rising mountainously, near one of the pocket-battleships of the enemy. He opened his mouth automatically to telephone a correction, but before he could speak, the *Minnesota* let loose. And this time she was broadside on to her target. Not only her forward battery, but fore and aft, with all her main and secondary battery, she flung a hurtling hell of steel and flame toward the enemy. The recoil made her whole vast fabric shudder. Fifteen seconds later she flamed again. Fifteen seconds; the air split asunder with the same concussion. Fifteen seconds... With unvarying, mathematical precision, she let go twelve broadsides in three minutes. It was impossible to discover that her gun-muzzles shifted.

She came about in a long sweep. MacReady and the skipper of the *Wasp* ignored their bleeding noses and the bruises of sheer concussion. They swept the horizon, quivering like hounds on the scent.

'One – two – three!' MacReady counted in an awed voice. 'Three of them sunk, by God! Thank God for heavy metal! And another one's out of action, or I'm a Swede! – *Ah-h-h!*'

An apparently uninjured speck, against the very edge of the world, tore itself apart with a sudden vehemence. There was a flash and a monstrous ball of dense black smoke. Then there was another gap in the ceremonial formation which was to execute the *Minnesota*. It had either forgotten that the American ship was the most powerful war-vessel in the world, or it had counted upon no more than human accuracy in its shell-fire. But there was no human factor-of-error in the gun-laying on the *Minnesota* now. She was a machine – and the most deadly fighting-machine on earth.

Flashes appeared along that distant line of ships. The *Minnesota* dived into the smoke-screen all about. A destroyer darted aside to give it room. The smoke-screen had been laid in long spreading trails of blackness. From aloft, it would look like a rather untidily-executed maze. MacReady caught a glimpse of the foredeck of the *Langley* – its after deck was blotted out by a hill of densest black – and plane after plane after plane was taking off with the regularity and precision of bullets going out of a machine-gun. He saw a spreading fan of planes rising from another spot – the other carrier. Then the *Minnesota* vanished from beneath him as it went swiftly into darkness. A long distance away he saw the other fighting-top above a sea of black. Black billows rolled lazily about the horizon. He saw a ship on fire, in the enemy line. That was the work of one of the fleet subs. The enemy did not know of their existence or escape. They took a heavy toll, between them, and one of them finally blew itself to atoms beneath the pocket-battleship that rammed it. Which was not healthy for the pocket-battleship.

MacReady heard his companion shouting. He was chattering excitedly into the telephone-transmitter strapped to his chest. A concussion-wave struck him. The ship was firing again. The gas-blasts from the guns blew the smoke-screens crazily about. One; fifteen seconds – two; fifteen seconds – three ... Six broadsides the *Minnesota* fired from the thickest of its own smoke-screen.

Hell broke loose a half-mile astern. A six-inch shell screamed between the fighting-tops of the *Minnesota*. That was a stray. The form of fire from the capital ships of the enemy fleet was pouring into the ocean where the *Minnesota* might have been, but wasn't. They couldn't see her. Her smoke-screen hid her before they had fired ranging salvos. And range-readings by even trained observers are not much good without trial salvos and spottings. The *Minnesota* had started the action on her own terms, which – with air superiority on her side – were much better than the enemy had intended.

Two minutes of silence, save for the screaming of enemy shells searching for the ship. The smoke-screen was lengthening and spreading. The *Minnesota* had four square miles of blackness in which to hide, but it was blackness only to the enemy. MacReady caught a glimpse of a monstrous dogfight going on aloft. Enemy aircraft could not spot the *Minnesota* from above their own ships. So intricately woven was her protecting screen that a position nearly vertically above her was essential. The enemy aircraft were trying to get it. The Army ships were keeping them from it. The solitary American battleship was using tactics which not only were entirely new; they were tactics which were impossible to a ship without control of the air, without eyes to penetrate the screen and prevent collision with her tiny consorts, and without utterly perfect spotting for her shells.

Enemy shells shrieked all about. An eight-incher landed somewhere and burst with a sickening detonation. The whole sea seemed to be boiling. Shell-splashes leaped upward above the smoke-screen, glittering in the sunlight. They were visible to the enemy, but not especially helpful without a sight of their target. There was a flickering ball of madly fighting planes a mile and a half to the right. Something huge and winged burst out of it and raced toward the *Minnesota*'s fighting-tops, with a dozen Army single-seaters pouring lead at it, and two enemy combat planes dying magnificently in the attempt to protect it.

The big ship's anti-aircraft battery crashed venomously. There was a colossal, an incredible explosion. The huge winged thing vanished in an expanding ball of flame. Two combat-ships shriveled and fell with it. Another reeled and a wing came off, and it began to descend, whirling crazily like a maple-seed. The rest of them turned and went madly back toward the ball of roaring, crackling fighting things.

The *Minnesota* shuddered again. And again. And again. Broadsides of every gun that would bear, fired from abysmal blackness into the bright sunshine. Storms of screaming metal, flying shrieking through space, to fall twenty miles away. From the tail of his eye MacReady saw a magnificent duel of two fighting-planes ended in the fraction of a second as the trajectory of some ship's broadside passed through the area of their combat. They were annihilated. But MacReady could not see it all. He was battered at and pounded by waves of sheer concussions. He heard a voice beside him, thinly, and it was the commander of the *Wasp*, but MacReady could not make out what he was saying, and did not try. Then he caught a glimpse of the enemy fleet as the rolling billows of the smoke-screen lowered momentarily.

The noise did not lessen for an instant, and the noise was like the din of all hell let lose. But MacReady did not hear it, because something huge over in the enemy lines was pointing its bow skyward and going down slowly by the stern. A monstrous mound of water rose above it as a broadside struck. The mound subsided, and that monstrous ship was only a third of a ship above water. It was going down and down... A pocket-battleship was on fire. A broadside struck one of the enemy's big ships. Fifteen seconds later, another. Fifteen seconds later still, a third. Fifteen seconds later still, a fourth...

'Fire-power!' cried MacReady exultantly amid the tumult of ten thousand explosions, 'We've got it! The heaviest broadside in the world! Infra-red screens! Beam range-finders that spot our own shells with the targets they strike! Powder that varies less than a thousand pounds pressure at the breech! Six ships we've sunk, old horse! Six ships! And we're barely scratched! – Why doesn't the enemy use his destroyers? Their big ships are no good! If they want to finish us, why don't they bring on their destroyers?'

As if to answer him, he saw. The *Minnesota* ran into an area where its smoke-screen had partly settled down and spread out. It was still not in view of the enemy capital ships. Only the fighting-tops and a quarter of the masts were clear. But the smoke-screen ended a half-mile away and the line of enemy destroyers were in full charge. Full speed ahead, bones in their teeth, straining every nerve for the velocity needed to make a success of their suicidal dash for the *Minnesota*. Twenty of them in a magnificent squadron plunging for the target of their fleet ...

One of them rose and buckled as a thousand-pound bomb exploded in the sea in contact with its hull. The Army bombers were at work. A second lost its tail and came to a halt, spitting smoke and steam and bitterly despairing streams of anti-aircraft shells. A third ran into an aerial bomb and started a dive that ended on the bottom. The *Minnesota*'s anti-torpedo battery exploded thunderously. Again. Again. Again ... Six terrific volleys. Six destroyers died. The bombers got to work again on what were left ... The smoke-screen heaved slowly upward and blotted out the view.

There were twenty square miles of smoke-screen for the *Minnesota* to play in now, and the Army held the air against the most desperate assaults of an enemy now in actually a desperate position. The American battleship was the most powerful battleship on earth – even on paper. She could range her shots and spot them through a smoke-screen that made her invisible to the enemy. The Army had held the air above her from the first. Now it was fighting for the air above the enemy. American air-bombs sank one enemy aircraft-carrier. A pocket-battleship's steering-gear was wrecked by a bombing squadron who went on about their other business and left a flight of torpedo-planes to finish her off. The enemy fleet was in exactly the position into which – with the assistance of American politicians – it had maneuvered the American battlefleet off Hungars' Bank.

The *Minnesota* had control of the air and fought not only behind, but in a smoke-screen. The enemy ships were necessarily firing nearly at random, despite their enormous numerical superiority, while the *Minnesota* fired broadside after broadside with an uncanny accuracy. And its broadside was the heaviest afloat. In this action, because of the unhuman accuracy of its range-finder spotting, it secured a larger percentage of hits than any other vessel had ever made, in action or out of it.

'All they've got left—' panted the commander of the *Wasp*, 'is subs!' He was hoarse, though he could never remember speaking a word, before, and much less shouting. 'They've tried everything else. They'll try their subs now!'

MacReady's nose and ears were bleeding from concussion. His eyes were bloodshot and watering from the same cause. He was gory and horrible to look at, but he grinned exultantly.

'The wind's blowing the smoke-screen southward at fourteen knots. We're moving with it. There's no sub on earth can travel fourteen knots submerged, and you can bet your other collar, old horse, that no sub's going to get to us on the surface!'

A faint howl came up from below. It sounded even above the tumult of explosions all about and the uproar of aircraft aloft. There was no fighting above the *Minnesota* now. The fighting was taking place above the enemy fleet. The howl came up again, thin and reedy but triumphant. MacReady recognized it. It was a simultaneous roar of pure delight from the officers and men of the *Minnesota*. And MacReady's earphones gave him the cause of it an instant later.

'*The enemy has formed a smoke-screen for his own protection from our fire!*'

And Lieutenant MacReady and the commander of the now-trisected *Wasp* arose and danced clumsily about the fighting-top of the *Minnesota* and shrieked themselves shoarse from pure joy.

Because, of course, if the *Minnesota*'s range-finders could range and spot shells through a smoke-screen to direct her fire out of it, they could work through two to direct her fire into another. And the enemy's control of the air was gone forever, so his only possible hope would be to destroy the accuracy of the *Minnesota*'s fire. It was incredible. It was impossible. But it was true.

So the action of the Ninth of August, 1934, more commonly

known as the Battle of the California Coast, was completed with two vast blankets of blackness floating upon the sea. The *Minnesota* remained deep in one mass of impenetrable darkness, and her guns boomed and boomed and boomed, sending shells screaming to the targets futilely hiding in the heart of another darkness, or with even greater futility trying to flee.

The action had started at half-past six in the morning. At three in the afternoon – it was seven o'clock by Washington time – an official order reached the *Minnesota* by wireless and in the official naval code. There had been a stormy, a tumultuous session in Congress. The bombardment of Seattle had had the effect the enemy anticipated. Instead of two days of debate, a conclusion was reached in one. A resolution had been passed accepting the preliminary peace terms of the enemy. The President of the United States was commanded to issue the orders meeting the enemy's requirements for an armistice.

As commander-in-chief of the military and naval forces of the United States, he issued the historic order:

'*To the Senior Officer Commanding American Vessels of War in the Pacific Ocean:*
Immediately on receipt of this order you will surrender all vessels under your command to the officer in command of the enemy battle fleet off our coasts.'

And the captain of the *Minnesota* radioed his even more historic reply:

'*To the President of the United States:*
There is no longer an enemy battle fleet off our coasts. We have destroyed it.'

As a matter of politics, the Battle of the California Coast had the extraordinary result of making pacifism no longer respectable. In any case, it immediately ceased to be a political issue, because Americans instantly backslid into patriotism. Our politicians, in the remaining three days before election, vied with each other in patriotic fervor. Where before they had competed for the noblest expressions of resignation to the will of Providence, now they struggled to outdo each other in the ingenuity of the demands they proposed we should make upon the enemy, as the price of peace. And they were voted for on that basis.

But at any rate – until America forgets – the Army and the Navy are not toys for politicians any longer. They are in the hands of real men.

PROXIMA CENTAURI

I

The *Adastra*, from a little distance, already shone in the light of the approaching sun. The vision disks which scanned the giant space ship's outer skin relayed a faint illumination to the visiplates within. They showed the monstrous, rounded bulk of the metal globe, crisscrossed with girders too massive to be transported by any power less than that of the space ship itself. They showed the whole five-thousand-foot globe as an ever so faintly glowing object, seemingly motionless in mid-space.

In that seeming, they lied. Monstrous as the ship was, and apparently too huge to be stirred by any conceivable power, she was responding to power now. At a dozen points upon her faintly glowing side there were openings. From those openings there flowed out tenuous purple flames – less bright than the star ahead – but they were the disintegration blasts from the rockets which had lifted the *Adastra* from the surface of Earth and for seven years had hurtled it on through interstellar space toward Proxima Centauri, nearest of the fixed stars to humanity's solar system.

Now they hurtled it forward no more. The mighty ship was decelerating. Thirty-two and two-tenths feet per second, losing velocity at the exact rate to maintain the effect of Earth's gravity within its bulk, the huge globe slowed. For months braking had been going on. From a peak-speed measurably near the velocity of light, the first of all vessels to span the distance between two solar systems had slowed and slowed, and would reach a speed of maneuver some sixty million miles from the surface of the star.

Far, far ahead, Proxima Centauri glittered invitingly. The

vision disks that showed its faint glow upon the space ship's hull had counterparts which carried its image within the hull, and in the main control room it appeared enlarged very many times. An old, white-bearded man in uniform regarded it meditatively. He said slowly, as if he had said the same thing often before, 'Quaint, that ring. It is double, like Saturn's. And Saturn has nine moons. One wonders how many planets this sun will have.'

The girl said restlessly, 'We'll find out soon, won't we? We're almost there. And we already know the rotation period of one of them! Jack said that—'

Her father turned deliberately to her. 'Jack?'

'Gary,' said the girl. 'Jack Gary.'

'My dear,' said the old man mildly, 'he seems well-disposed, and his abilities are good, but he is a Mut. Remember!'

The girl bit her lip.

The old man went on, quite slowly and without rancor: 'It is unfortunate that we have had this division among the crew of what should have been a scientific expedition conducted in the spirit of a crusade. You hardly remember how it began. But we officers know only too well how many efforts have been made by the Muts to wreck the whole purpose of our voyage. This Jack Gary is a Mut. He is brilliant, in his way. I would have brought him into the officers' quarters, but Alstair investigated and found undesirable facts which made it impossible.'

'I don't believe Alstair!' said the girl evenly. 'And, anyhow, it was Jack who caught the signals. And he's the one who's working with them, officer or Mut! And he's human, anyhow. It's time for the signals to come again and you depend on him to handle them.'

The old man frowned. He walked with a careful steadiness to a seat. He sat down with an old man's habitual and rather pathetic caution. The *Adastra*, of course, required no such constant vigilance at the controls as the interplanetary space ships require. Out here in emptiness there was no need to watch for meteors, for traffic, or for those queer and yet inexplicable force fields which at first made interplanetary flights so hazardous.

The ship was so monstrous a structure, in any case, that the tinier meteorites could not have harmed her. And at the speed she was now making greater ones would be noticed by the induction fields in time for observation and if necessary the changing of her course.

A door at the side of the control room opened briskly and a man stepped in. He glanced with conscious professionalism at the banks of indicators. A relay clicked, and his eyes darted to the spot. He turned and saluted the old man with meticulous precision. He smiled at the girl.

'Ah, Alstair,' said the old man. 'You are curious about the signals, too?'

'Yes, sir. Of course! And as second in command I rather like to keep an eye on signals. Gary is a Mut, and I would not like him to gather information that might be kept from the officers.'

'That's nonsense!' said the girl hotly.

'Probably,' agreed Alstair. 'I hope so. I even think so. But I prefer to leave out no precaution.'

A buzzer sounded. Alstair pressed a button and a vision plate lighted. A dark, rather grim young face stared out of it.

'Very well, Gary,' said Alstair curtly. He pressed another button. The vision plate darkened and lighted again to show a long corridor down which a solitary figure came. It came close and the same face looked impassively out. Alstair said even more curtly, 'The other doors are open, Gary. You can come straight through.'

'I think that's monstrous!' said the girl angrily as the plate clicked off. 'You know you trust him! You have to! Yet every time he comes into officers' quarters you act as if you thought he had bombs in each hand and all the rest of the men behind him!'

Alstair shrugged and glanced at the old man, who said tiredly, 'Alstair is second in command, my dear, and he will be commander on the way back to Earth. I could wish you would be less offensive.'

But the girl deliberately withdrew her eyes from the brisk figure of Alstair with its smart uniform, and rested her chin in her hands to gaze broodingly at the farther wall. Alstair went to the banks of indicators, surveying them in detail. The ventilator hummed softly. A relay clicked with a curiously smug, self-satisfied note. Otherwise there was no sound.

The *Adastra*, mightiest work of the human race, hurtled on through space with the light of a strange sun shining faintly upon her enormous hull. Twelve lambent purple flames glowed from holes in her forward part. She was decelerating, lessening her speed by thirty-two point two feet per second per second, maintaining the effect of Earth's gravity within her bulk.

Earth was seven years behind and uncounted millions of millions of miles. Interplanetary travel was a commonplace in the solar system now, and a thriving colony on Venus and a precariously maintained outpost on the largest of Jupiter's moons promised to make space commerce thrive even after the dead cities of Mars had ceased to give up their incredibly rich loot. But only the *Adastra* had ever essayed space beyond Pluto.

She was the greatest of ships, the most colossal structure ever attempted by man. In the beginning, indeed, her design was derided as impossible of achievement by the very men who later made her building a fact. Her framework beams were so huge that, once cast, they could not be moved by any lifting contrivance at her builders' disposal. Therefore the molds for them were built and the metal poured in their final position as a part of the ship. Her rocket tubes were so colossal that the necessary supersonic vibrations – to neutralize the disintegration effect of the Caldwell field – had to be generated at thirty separate points on each tube, else the disintegration of her fuel would have spread to the tubes themselves and the big ship afterward, with even the mother planet following in a burst of lambent purple flame. At full acceleration a set of twelve tubes disintegrated five cubic centimeters of water per second.

Her diameter was a shade over five thousand feet. Her air tanks carried a reserve supply which could run her crew of three hundred for ten months without purification. Her stores, her shops, her supplies of raw and finished materials, were in such vast quantities that to enumerate them would be merely to recite meaningless figures.

There were even four hundred acres of food-growing space within her, where crops were grown under sun lamps. Those crops used waste organic matter as fertilizer and restored exhaled carbon dioxide to use, in part as oxygen and in part as carbohydrate foodstuffs.

The *Adastra* was a world in herself. Given power, she could subsist her crew forever, growing her food supplies, purifying her own internal atmosphere without loss and without fail, and containing space within which every human need could be provided, even solitude.

And starting out upon the most stupendous journey in human history, she had formally been given the status of a world, with her commander empowered to make and enforce all needed laws. Bound for a destination four light-years distant, the minimum time for her return was considered to be fourteen years. No crew could possibly survive so long a voyage undecimated. Therefore the enlistments for the voyage had not been by men, but by families.

There were fifty children on board when the *Adastra* lifted from Earth's surface. In the first year of her voyage ten more were born. It had seemed to the people of Earth that not only could the mighty ship subsist her crew forever, but that the crew itself, well-nourished and with more than adequate facilities both for amusement and education, could so far perpetuate itself as to make a voyage of a thousand years as practicable as the mere journey to Proxima Centauri.

And so it could, but for a fact at once so needless and so human that nobody anticipated it. The fact was tedium. In less than six months the journey had ceased to become a great adventure. To the women in particular, the voyage of the big ship became deadly routine.

The *Adastra* itself took on the semblance of a gigantic apartment house without newspapers, department stores, new film plays, new faces, or even the relieving annoyances of changeable weather. The sheer completeness of all preparations for the voyage made the voyage itself uneventful. That meant tedium.

Tedium meant restlessness. And restlessness, with women on board who had envisioned high adventure, meant the devil to pay. Their husbands no longer appeared as glamorous heroes. They were merely human beings. The men encountered similar disillusionments. Pleas for divorce flooded the commander's desk, he being legally the fount of all legal action. During the eighth month there was one murder, and in the three months following, two more.

A year and a half out from Earth, and the crew was in a state of semi-mutiny originating in sheer boredom. By two years out, the officers' quarters were sealed off from the greater part of the *Adastra*'s interior, the crew was disarmed, and what work was demanded of the mutineers was enforced by force guns in the hands of the officers. By three years out, the crew was demanding a return to Earth. But by the time the *Adastra* could be slowed and stopped from her then incredible velocity, she would be so near her destination as to make no appreciable difference in the length of her total voyage. For the rest of the time the members of the crew strove to relieve utter monotony by such vices and such pastimes as could be improvised in the absence of any actual need to work.

The officers referred to their underlings by a contraction of the word 'mutineers' – Muts. The crew came to have a queer distaste for all dealing with the officers. But, despite Alstair, there was no longer much danger of an uprising. A certain mental equilibrium had – very late – developed.

From the nerve-racked psychology of dwellers in an isolated apartment house, the greater number of the *Adastra*'s complement came to have the psychology of dwellers in an isolated village. The difference was profound. In particular the children who had come to maturity during the long journey through space were well adjusted to the conditions of isolation and of routine.

Jack Gary was one of them. He had been sixteen when the trip began, son of a rocket-tube engineer whose death took place the second year out. Helen Bradley was another. She had been fourteen when her father, as designer and commanding officer of the mighty globe, pressed the control key that set the huge rockets into action.

Her father had been past maturity at the beginning. Aged by responsibility for seven uninterrupted years, he was an old man now. And he knew, and even Helen knew without admitting it, that he would never survive the long trip back. Alstair would take his place and the despotic authority inherent in it, and he wanted to marry Helen.

She thought of these things, with her chin cupped in her hand, brooding in the control room. There was no sound save the humming of the ventilator and the infrequent smug click of a relay operating the automatic machinery to keep the *Adastra* a world in which nothing ever happened.

A knock on the door. The commander opened his eyes a trifle vaguely. He was very old now, the commander. He had dozed.

Alstair said shortly, 'Come in!' and Jack Gary entered.

He saluted, pointedly to the commander. Which was according to regulations, but Alstair's eyes snapped.

'Ah, yes,' said the commander. 'Gary. It's about time for more signals, isn't it?'

'Yes, sir.'

Jack Gary was very quiet, very businesslike. Only once, when he glanced at Helen, was there any hint of anything but the formal manner of a man intent on his job. Then his eyes told her something, in an infinitely small fraction of a second, which changed her expression to one of flushed content.

Short as the glance was, Alstair saw it. He said harshly:

'Have you made any progress in deciphering the signals, Gary?'

Jack was setting the dials of a pan-wave receptor, glancing at penciled notes on a calculator pad. He continued to set up the reception pattern.

'No, sir. There is still a sequence of sounds at the beginning which must be a form of call, because a part of the same sequence is used as a signature at the close. With the commander's permission I have used the first part of that call sequence as a signature in our signals in reply. But in looking over the records of the signals I've found something that looks important.'

The commander said mildly, 'What is it, Gary?'

'We've been sending signals ahead of us on a tight beam, sir, for some months. Your idea was to signal ahead, so that if there were any civilized inhabitants on planets about the sun, they'd get an impression of a peaceful mission.'

'Of course!' said the commander. 'It would be tragic for the first of interstellar communications to be unfriendly!'

'We've been getting answers to our signals for nearly three months. Always at intervals of a trifle over thirty hours. We assumed, of course, that a fixed transmitter was sending them, and that it was signaling once a day when the station was in the most favorable position for transmitting to us.'

'Of course,' said the commander gently. 'It gave us the period of rotation of the planet from which the signals come.'

Jack Gary set the last dial and turned on the switch. A low-pitched hum arose, which died away. He glanced at the dials again, checking them.

'I've been comparing the records, sir, making due allowance for our approach. Because we cut down the distance between us and the star so rapidly, our signals today take several seconds less to reach Proxima Centauri than they did yesterday. Their signals should show the same shortening of interval, if they are actually sent out at the same instant of planetary time every day.'

The commander nodded benevolently.

'They did, at first,' said Jack. 'But about three weeks ago the time interval changed in a brand-new fashion. The signal strength changed, and the wave form altered a little, too, as if a new transmitter was sending. And the first day of that change the signals came through one second earlier than our velocity of approach would account for. The second day they were three seconds earlier, the third day six, the fourth day ten, and so on. They kept coming earlier by a period indicating a linear function until one week ago. Then the rate of change began to decrease again.'

'That's nonsense!' said Alstair harshly.

'That's the record,' returned Jack curtly.

'But how do you explain it, Gary?' asked the commander mildly.

'They're sending now from a space ship, sir,' replied Jack briefly, 'which is moving toward us at four times our maximum acceleration. And they're flashing us a signal at the same interval, according to their clocks, as before.'

A pause. Helen Bradley smiled warmly. The commander thought carefully. Then he admitted:

'Very good, Gary! It sounds plausible. What next?'

'Why, sir,' said Jack, 'since the rate of change shifted, a week ago, it looks as if that other space ship started to decelerate again. Here are my calculations, sir. If the signals are sent at the same interval they kept up for over a month, there is another space ship headed toward us, and she is decelerating to stop and reverse and will be matching our course and speed in four days and eighteen hours. They'll meet and surprise us, they think.'

The commander's face lighted up. 'Marvelous, Gary! They must be far advanced indeed in civilization! Intercourse between two such peoples, separated by four light-years of distance! What marvels we shall learn! And to think of their sending a ship far beyond their own system to greet and welcome us!'

Jack's expression remained grim.

'I hope so, sir,' he said dryly.

'What now, Gary?' demanded Alstair angrily.

'Why,' said Jack deliberately, 'they're still pretending that the signals come from their planet, by signaling at what they think are the same times. They could exchange signals for twenty-four hours a day, if they chose, and be working out a code for communication. Instead, they're trying to deceive us. My guess is that they're coming at least prepared to fight. And if I'm right, their signals will begin in three seconds, exactly.'

He stopped, looking at the dials of the receptor. The tape which photographed the waves as they came in, and the other which recorded the modulations, came out of the receptor blank. But suddenly, in just three seconds, a needle kicked over and tiny white lines appeared on the rushing tapes. The speaker uttered sounds.

It was a voice which spoke. So much was clear. It was harsh yet sibilant, more like the stridulation of an insect than anything else. But the sounds it uttered were modulated as no insect can modulate its outcry. They formed what were plainly words, without vowels or consonants, yet possessing expression and varying in pitch and tone quality.

The three men in the control room had heard them many times before, and so had the girl. But for the first time they carried to her an impression of menace, of threat, of a concealed lust for destruction that made her blood run cold.

II

The space ship hurtled on through space, her rocket tubes sending forth small and apparently insufficient purple flames which emitted no smoke, gave off no gas, and were seemingly nothing but small marsh fires inexplicably burning in emptiness.

There was no change in her outer appearance. There had been none to speak of in years. At long, infrequent intervals men had emerged from air locks and moved about her sides, bathing the steel they walked on and themselves alike with fierce glares from heat lamps lest the cold of her plating transmit itself through the material of the suits and kill the men like ants on redhot metal. But for a long time no such expedition had been needed.

Only now, in the distant faint light of Proxima Centauri, a man in a space suit emerged from such a tiny lock. Instantly he shot out to the end of a threadlike life line. The constant deceleration of the ship not only simulated gravity within. Anything partaking of its motion showed the same effect. The man upon its decelerating forward side was flung away from the ship by his own momentum, the same force which, within it, had pressed his feet against the floors.

He hauled himself back laboriously, moving with an

exaggerated clumsiness in his bloated space suit. He clung to handholds and hooked himself in place, while he worked an electric drill. He moved still more clumsily to another place and drilled again. A third, and fourth, and fifth. For half an hour or more, then, he labored to set up on the vast steel surface, which seemed always above him, an intricate array of wires and framework. In the end he seemed content. He hauled himself back to the air lock and climbed within. The *Adastra* hurtled onward, utterly unchanged save for a very tiny fretwork of wire, perhaps thirty feet across, which looked more like a microscopic barbed-wire entanglement than anything else.

Within the *Adastra*, Helen Bradley greeted Jack warmly as he got out of his space suit.

'It was horrible!' she told him, 'to see you dangling like that! With millions of miles of empty space below you!'

'Let's go turn on the inductor and see how the new reception grid works,' said Jack quietly.

He hung up the space suit. As they turned to go through the doorway their hands touched accidentally. They looked at each other and faltered. They stopped, Helen's eyes shining. They all unconsciously swayed toward each other. Jack's hands lifted hungrily.

Footsteps sounded close by. Alstair, second in command of the space ship, rounded a corner and stopped short.

'What's this?' he demanded savagely. 'Just because the commander's brought you into officers' quarters, Gary, it doesn't follow that your Mut methods of romance can come, too!'

'You dare!' cried Helen furiously.

Jack, from a hot dull flush, was swiftly paling to the dead-white of rage.

'You'll take that back,' he said very quietly indeed, 'or I'll show you Mut methods of fighting with a force gun! As an officer, I carry one, too, now!'

Alstair snarled at him.

'Your father's been taken ill,' he told Helen angrily. 'He feels the voyage is about over. Anticipation has kept up his strength for months past, but now he's—'

With a cry, the girl fled.

Alstair swung upon Jack. 'I take back nothing,' he snapped. 'You're an officer, by order of the commander. But you're a Mut besides, and when I'm commander of the *Adastra* you don't stay an officer long! I'm warning you! What were you doing here?'

Jack was deathly pale, but the status of officer on the *Adastra*, with its consequent opportunity of seeing Helen, was far too precious to be given up unless at the last extremity. And, besides, there was the work he had in hand. His work, certainly, could not continue unless he remained an officer.

'I was installing an interference grid on the surface,' he said, 'to try to discover the sending station of the messages we've been getting. It will also act, as you know, as an inductor up to a certain range, and in its range is a good deal more accurate than the main inductors of the ship.'

'Then get to your damned work,' said Alstair harshly, 'and pay full attention to it and less to romance!'

Jack plugged in the lead wire from his new grid to the pan-wave receptor. For an hour he worked more and more grimly. There was something very wrong. The inductors showed blank for all about the *Adastra*. The interference grid showed an object of considerable size not more than two million miles distant and to one side of the *Adastra*'s course. Suddenly, all indication of that object's existence blanked out. Every dial on the pan-wave receptor went back to zero.

'Damnation!' said Jack under his breath.

He set up a new pattern on the controls, calculated a moment and deliberately changed the pattern on the spare bank of the main inductors, and then simultaneously switched both instruments to their new frequencies. He waited, almost holding his breath, for nearly half a minute. It would take so long for the inductor waves of the new frequency to reach out the two million miles and then collapse into the analyzers and give their report of any object in space which had tended to deform them.

Twenty-six, twenty-seven, twenty-eight seconds. Every alarm bell on the monstrous ship clanged furiously! Emergency doors hissed into place all over the vessel, converting every doorway into an air lock. Seconds later, the visiplates in the main control room began to flash alight.

'Reporting, Rocket Control!'

'Reporting, Air Service!'

'Reporting, Power Supply!'

Jack said crisply: 'The main inductors report an object two million miles distant with velocity in our direction. The commander is ill. Please find Vice Commander Alstair.'

Then the door of the control room burst open and Alstair himself raged into the room.

'What the devil!' he gasped. 'Ringing a general alarm? Have you gone mad? The inductors—'

Jack pointed to the main inductor bank. Every dial bore out the message of the still-clanging alarms. Alstair stared blankly at them. As he looked, every dial went back to zero.

And Alstair's face went as blank as the dials.

'They felt out our inductor screens,' said Jack grimly, 'and put out some sort of radiation which neutralized them. So I set up two frequencies, changed both, and they couldn't adjust their neutralizers in time to stop our alarms.'

Alstair stood still, struggling with the rage which still possessed him. Then he nodded curtly.

'Quite right. You did good work. Stand by.'

And, quite cool and composed, he took command of the mighty space ship, even if there was not much for him to do. In five minutes, in fact, every possible preparation for emergency had been made and he turned again to Jack.

'I don't like you,' he said coldly. 'As one man to another, I dislike you intensely. But as vice commander and acting commander at the moment, I have to admit that you did good work in uncovering this little trick of our friends to get within striking distance without our knowing they were anywhere near.'

Jack said nothing. He was frowning, but it was because he was thinking of Helen. The *Adastra* was huge and powerful, but she was not readily maneuverable. She was enormously massive, but she could not be used for ramming. And she possessed within herself almost infinite destructiveness, in the means of producing Caldwell fields for the disintegration of matter, but she contained no weapon more dangerous than a two-thousand-kilowatt vortex gun for the destruction of dangerous animals or vegetation where she might possibly land.

'What's your comment?' demanded Alstair shortly. 'How do you size up the situation?'

'They act as if they're planning hostilities,' replied Jack briefly, 'and they've got four times our maximum acceleration so we can't get away. With that acceleration they ought to be more maneuverable, so we can't dodge them. We've no faintest idea of what weapons they carry, but we know that we can't fight them unless their weapons are very puny indeed. There's just one chance that I can see.'

'What's that?'

'They tried to slip up on us. That looks as if they intended to open fire without warning. But maybe they are frightened and only expected to examine us without our getting a chance to attack them. In that case, our only bet is to swing over our signaling beam to the space ship. When they realize we know they're there and still aren't getting hostile, they may not guess we can't fight. They may think we want to be friendly and they'd better not start anything with a ship our size that's on guard.'

'Very well. You're detailed to communication duty,' said Alstair. 'Go ahead and carry out that program. I'll consult the rocket engineers and see what they can improvise in the way of fighting equipment. Dismiss!'

His tone was harsh. It was arrogant. It rasped Jack's nerves and made him bristle all over. But he had to recognize that Alstair wasn't letting his frank dislike work to the disadvantage of the ship. Alstair was, in fact, one of those ambitious officers who are always cordially disliked by everybody, at all times, until an emergency arises. Then their competence shows up.

Jack went to the communications-control room. It did not take long to realign the transmitter beam. Then the sender began to repeat monotonously the recorded last message from the *Adastra* to the distant and so far unidentified planet of the ringed star. And while the signal went out, over and over again, Jack called on observations control for a sight of the strange ship.

They had a scanner on it now and by stepping up illumination to the utmost, and magnification to the point where the image was as rough as an old-fashioned half-tone cut, they brought the strange ship to the visiplate as a six-inch miniature.

It was egg-shaped and perfectly smooth. There was no sign of external girders, of protruding atmospheric-navigation fins, of escape-boat blisters. It was utterly featureless save for tiny spots which might be portholes, and rocket tubes in which intermittent flames flickered. It was still decelerating to match the speed and course of the *Adastra*.

'Have you got a spectroscope report on it?' asked Jack.

'Yeh,' replied the observations orderly. 'An' I don't believe it. They're using fuel rockets – some organic compound. An' the report says the hull of that thing is cellulose, not metal. It's wood, on the outside.'

Jack shrugged. No sign of weapons. He went back to his own job. The space ship yonder was being penetrated through and through by the message waves. Its receptors could not fail to be reporting that a tight beam was upon it, following its every movement, and that its presence and probable mission were therefore known to the mighty ship from out of space.

But Jack's own receptors were silent. The tape came out of them utterly blank. No – a queer, scrambled, blurry line, as if the analyzers were unable to handle the frequency which was coming through. Jack read the heat effect. The other space ship was sending with a power which meant five thousand kilowatts pouring into the *Adastra*. Not a signal. Grimly, Jack heterodyned the wave on a five-meter circuit and read off its frequency and type. He called the main control.

'They're pouring short stuff into us,' he reported stiffly to Alstair. 'About five thousand kilowatts of thirty-centimeter waves, the type we use on Earth to kill weevils in wheat. It ought to be deadly to animal life, but of course our hull simply absorbs it.'

Helen. Impossible to stop the *Adastra*. They'd started for Proxima Centauri. Decelerating though they were, they couldn't check much short of the solar system, and they were already attacked by a ship with four times their greatest acceleration. Pouring a deadly frequency into them – a frequency used on Earth to kill noxious insects. Helen was—

The G. C. phone snapped suddenly, in Alstair's voice.

'Attention, all officers! The enemy space ship has poured what it evidently considers a deadly frequency into us, and is now approaching at full acceleration! Orders are that absolutely no control of any sort is to be varied by a hair's breadth. Absolutely no sign of living intelligence within the *Adastra* is to be shown. You will stand by all operative controls, prepared for maneuver if it should be necessary. But we try to give the impression that the *Adastra* is operating on automatic controls alone! Understand?'

Jack could imagine the reports from the other control rooms. His own receptor sprang suddenly into life. The almost hooted sounds of the call signal, so familiar that they seemed words. Then an extraordinary jumble of noises – words in a human voice. More stridulent sounds. More words in perfectly accurate English. The English words were in the tones and accents of an officer of the *Adastra*, plainly recorded and retransmitted.

'Communications!' snapped Alstair. 'You will not answer this signal! It is an attempt to find out if we survived their ray attack!'

'Check,' said Jack.

Alstair was right. Jack watched and listened as the receptor babbled on. It stopped. Silence for ten minutes. It began again. The *Adastra* hurtled on. The babble from space came to an end. A little later the G. C. phone snapped once more:

'The enemy space ship has increased its acceleration, evidently convinced that we are all dead. It will arrive in approximately four hours. Normal watches may be resumed for three hours unless an alarm is given.'

Jack leaned back in his chair, frowning. He began to see the tactics Alstair planned to use. They were bad tactics, but the only ones a defenseless ship like the *Adastra* could even contemplate. It was at least ironic that the greeting the *Adastra* received at the end of a seven-years' voyage through empty space be a dose of a type of radiation used on Earth to exterminate vermin.

But the futility of this attack did not mean that all attacks would be similarly useless. And the *Adastra* simply could not be stopped for many millions of miles, yet. Even if Alstair's desperate plan took care of this particular assailant and this particular weapon, it would not mean – it could not! – that the *Adastra* or the folk within had any faintest chance of defending themselves. And there was Helen—

III

The visiplates showed the strange space ship clearly now, even without magnification. It was within five miles of the *Adastra* and it had stopped. Perfectly egg-shaped, without any protuberance whatever except the rocket tubes in its rear, it hung motionless with relation to the Earth ship, which meant that its navigators had analyzed her rate of deceleration long since and had matched all the constants of her course with precision.

Helen, her face still tear-streaked, watched as Jack turned up the magnification, and the illumination with it. Her father had collapsed very suddenly and very completely. He was resting quietly now, dozing almost continuously, with his face wearing an expression of utter contentment.

He had piloted the *Adastra* to its first contact with the civilization of another solar system. His lifework was done and he was wholly prepared to rest. He had no idea, of course, that the first actual contact with the strange space ship was a burst of short waves of a frequency deadly to all animal life.

The space ship swelled on the visiplate as Jack turned the knob. He brought it to an apparent distance of a few hundred yards only. With the illumination turned up, even the starlight on the hull would have been sufficient to show any surface detail. But there was literally none. No rivet, no bolt, no line of joining plates. A row of portholes were dark and dead within.

'And it's wood!' repeated Jack. 'Made out of some sort of cellulose which stands the cold of space!'

Helen said queerly: 'It looks to me as if it had been grown, rather than built.'

Jack blinked. He opened his mouth as if to speak, but the receptor at his elbow suddenly burst into the hootlike stridulations which were the signals from the egglike ship. Then English words, from recordings of previous signals from the *Adastra*. More vowelless, modulated phrases. It sounded exactly as if the beings in the other space ship were trying urgently to open communication and were insisting that they had the key to the *Adastra*'s signals. The temptation to reply was great.

'They've got brains, anyhow,' said Jack.

The signals were cut off. Silence. Jack glanced at the wave tape. It showed the same blurring as before.

'More short stuff. At this distance, it ought not only to kill us, but even sterilize the interior of the whole ship. Lucky our hull is heavy alloy with a high hysteresis-rate. Not a particle of that radiation can get through.'

Silence for a long, long time. The wave tape showed that a terrific beam of thirty-centimeter waves continued to play upon the *Adastra*. Jack suddenly plugged in observations and asked a question. Yes, the outer hull was heating. It had gone up half a degree in fifteen minutes.

'Nothing to worry about in that,' grunted Jack. 'Fifteen degrees will be the limit they can put it up, with this power.'

The tape came out clear. The supposed death radiation was cut off. The egg-shaped ship darted forward. And then for twenty minutes or more Jack had to switch from one outside vision disk to another to keep it in sight. It hovered about the huge bulk of the *Adastra* with a wary inquisitiveness. Now half a mile away, now no more than two hundred yards, the thing darted here and there with an amazing acceleration and as amazing a braking power. It had only the rocket tubes at the smaller end of its egg-shaped form. It was necessary for it to fling its whole shape about to get a new direction, and the gyroscopes within it must have been tremendously powerful. Even so, the abruptness of its turns was startling.

'I wouldn't like to be inside that thing!' said Jack. 'We'd be crushed to a pulp by their normal navigation methods. They aren't men like us. They can stand more than we can.'

The thing outside seemed sentient, seemed alive. And by the eagerness of its movements it seemed the more horrible, flitting about the gigantic space ship it now believed was a monstrous coffin.

It suddenly reversed itself and shot back toward the *Adastra*. Two hundred yards, one hundred yards, a hundred feet. It came to a cushioned stop against the surface of the Earth vessel.

'Now we'll see something of them,' said Jack crisply. 'They landed right at an air lock. They know what that is, evidently. Now we'll see them in their space suits.'

But Helen gasped. A part of the side of the strange ship seemed to swell suddenly. It bulged out like a blister. It touched the surface of the *Adastra*. It seemed to adhere. The point of contact grew larger.

'Good Lord!' said Jack blankly. 'Is it alive? And is it going to try to eat our ship?'

The general-communication phone rasped sharply: 'Officers with arms to the air lock GH41 immediately! The Centaurians are opening the air lock from the outside. Wait orders there! The visiplate in the air lock is working and you will be informed. Go ahead!'

The phone clicked off. Jack seized a heavy gun, one of the force rifles which will stun a man at anything up to eighteen hundred yards and kill at six, when used at full power. His side arm hung in its holster. He swung for the door.

'Jack!' said Helen desperately.

He kissed her. It was the first time their lips had touched, but it seemed the most natural thing in the world, just then. He went racing down the long corridors of the *Adastra* to the rendezvous. And as he raced, his thoughts were not at all those of a scientist and an officer of Earth's first expedition into interstellar space. Jack was thinking of Helen's lips touching his desperately, of her soft body pressed close to him.

A G. C. speaker whispered overhead as he ran: 'They're inside the air lock. They opened it without trouble. They're testing our air, now. Apparently it suits them all.'

The phone fell behind. Jack ran on, panting. Somebody else was running ahead. There were half a dozen, a dozen men grouped at the end of the corridor. A murmur from the side wall.

'... rking at the inner air lock door. Only four or five of them, apparently, will enter the ship. They are to be allowed to get well away from the air lock. You will keep out of sight. When the emergency locks go on, it will be your signal. Use your heavy force guns, increasing power from minimum until they fall paralyzed. It will probably take a good deal of power to subdue them. They are not to be killed if it can be avoided. Ready!'

There were a dozen or more officers on hand. The fat rocket chief. The lean air officer. Subalterns of the other departments. The rocket chief puffed audibly as he wedged himself out of sight. Then the clicking of the inner air lock door. It opened into the anteroom. Subdued, muffled hootings came from that door. The Things – whatever they were – were inspecting the space suits there. The hootings were distinctly separate and distinctly intoned. But they suddenly came as a babble. More than one Thing was speaking at once. There was excitement, eagerness, an extraordinary triumph in these voices.

Then something stirred in the doorway of the air lock anteroom. A shadow crossed the threshold. And then the Earthmen saw the creatures who were invading the ship.

For an instant they seemed almost like men. They had two legs, and two dangling things – tentacles – which apparently served as arms and tapered smoothly to ends which split into movable, slender filaments. The tentacles and the legs alike seemed flexible in their entire lengths. There were no 'joints' such as men use in walking, and the result was that the Centaurians walked with a curiously rolling gait.

Most startling, though, was the fact that they had no heads.

They came wabbling accustomedly out of the air lock, and at the end of one 'arm' each carried a curious, semicylindrical black object which they handled as if it might be a weapon. They wore metallic packs fastened to their bodies. The bodies themselves were queerly 'grained'. There was a tantalizing familiarity about the texture of their skin.

Jack, staring incredulously, looked for eyes, for nostrils, for a mouth. He saw twin slits only. He guessed at them for eyes. He saw no sign of any mouth at all. There was no hair. But he saw a scabrous, brownish substance on the back of one of the Things which turned to hoot excitedly at the rest. It looked like bark, like tree bark. And a light burst upon Jack. He almost cried out, but instead reached down and quietly put the lever of his force gun at full power at once.

The Things moved on. They reached a branching corridor and after much arm waving and production of their apparently articulated sounds they separated into two parties. They vanished. Their voices dwindled. The signal for an attack upon them had not yet been given. The officers, left behind, stirred uneasily. But a G. C. phone whispered.

'Steady! They think we're all dead. They're separating again. We may be able to close emergency doors and have each one sealed off from all the rest and then handle them in detail. You men watch the air lock!'

Silence. The humming of a ventilator somewhere near by. Then, suddenly, a man screamed shrilly a long distance off, and on the heels of his outcry there came a new noise from one of the Things. It was a high-pitched squealing noise, triumphant and joyous and unspeakably horrible.

Other squealings answered it. There were rushing sounds, as if the other Things were running to join the first. And then came a hissing of compressed air and a hum of motors. Doors snapped shut everywhere, sealing off every part of the ship from every other part. And in the dead silence of their own sealed compartment, the officers on guard suddenly heard inquiring hoots.

Two more of the Things came out of the air lock. One of

the men moved. The Thing saw him and turned its half-cylindrical object upon him. The man – it was the communications officer – shrieked suddenly and leaped convulsively. He was stone dead even as his muscles tensed for that incredible leap.

And the Thing emitted a high-pitched, triumphant note which was exactly like the other horrible sound they had heard, and sped eagerly toward the body. One of the long, tapering arms lashed out and touched the dead man's hand.

Then Jack's force gun began to hum. He heard another and another open up. In seconds the air was filled with a sound like that of a hive of angry bees. Three more of the Things came out of the air lock, but they dropped in the barrage of force-gun beams. It was only when there was a sudden rush of air toward the lock, showing that the enemy ship had taken alarm and was darting away, that the men dared cease to fill that doorway with their barrage. Then it was necessary to seal the air lock in a hurry. Only then could they secure the Things that had invaded the *Adastra.*

Two hours later, Jack went into the main control room and saluted with an exact precision. His face was rather white and his expression entirely dogged and resolved. Alstair turned to him, scowling.

'I sent for you,' he said harshly, 'because you're likely to be a source of trouble. The commander is dead. You heard it?'

'Yes, sir,' said Jack. 'I heard it.'

'In consequence, I am commander of the *Adastra,*' said Alstair provocatively. 'I have, you will recall, the power of life and death in cases of mutinous conduct, and it is also true that marriage on the *Adastra* is made legal only by executive order bearing my signature.'

'I am aware of the fact, sir,' said Jack.

'Very well,' said Alstair deliberately. 'For the sake of discipline, I order you to refrain from all association with Miss Bradley. I shall take disobedience of the order as mutiny. I intend to marry her myself. What have you to say to that?'

Jack said as deliberately: 'I shall pay no attention to the order, sir, because you aren't fool enough to carry out such a threat! Are you such a fool that you don't see we've less than one chance in five hundred of coming out of this? If you want to marry Helen, you'd better put all your mind on giving her a chance to live!'

A savage silence held for a moment. The two men glared furiously at each other, the one near middle age, the other still a young man, indeed. Then Alstair showed his teeth in a smile that had no mirth whatever in it.

'As man to man I dislike you extremely,' he said harshly. 'But as commander of the *Adastra* I wish I had a few more like you. We've had seven years of routine on this damned ship, and every officer in quarters is rattled past all usefulness because an emergency has come at last. They'll obey orders, but there's not one fit to give them. The communications officer was killed by one of those devils, wasn't he?'

'Yes, sir.'

'Very well. You're brevet communications officer. I hate your guts, Gary, and I do not doubt that you hate mine, but you have brains. Use them now. What have you been doing?'

'Adjusting a dictawriter, sir, to get a vocabulary of one of these Centaurians' speech, and hooking it up as a two-way translator, sir.'

Alstair stared in momentary surprise, and then nodded. A dictawriter, of course, simply analyzes a word into its phonetic parts, sets up the analysis and picks out a card to match its formula. Normally, the card then actuates a printer. However, instead of a type-choosing record, the card can contain a record of an equivalent word in another language, and then operates a speaker.

Such machines have been of only limited use on Earth because of the need for so large a stock of vocabulary words, but have been used to some extent for literal translations both of print and speech. Jack proposed to record a Centaurian's vocabulary with English equivalents, and the dictawriter, hearing the queer hoots the strange creature uttered, would pick out a card which would then cause a speaker to enunciate its English synonym.

The reverse, of course, would also occur. A conversation could be carried on with such a prepared vocabulary without awaiting practice in understanding or imitating the sounds of another language.

'Excellent!' said Alstair curtly. 'But put someone else on the job if you can. It should be reasonably simple, once it's started. But I need you for other work. You know what's been found out about these Centaurians, don't you?'

'Yes, sir. Their hand weapon is not unlike our force guns, but it seems to be considerably more effective. I saw it kill the communications officer.'

'But the creatures themselves!'

'I helped tie one of them up.'

'What do you make of it? I've a physician's report, but he doesn't believe it himself!'

'I don't blame him, sir,' said Jack grimly. 'They're not our idea of intelligent beings at all. We haven't any word for what they are. In one sense they're plants, apparently. That is, their bodies seem to be composed of cellulose fibers where ours are made of muscle fibers. But they are intelligent, fiendishly intelligent.

'The nearest we have to them on Earth are certain carnivorous plants, like pitcher plants and the like. But they're as far above a pitcher plant as a man is above a sea anemone, which is just as much an animal as a man is. My guess, sir, would be that they're neither plant nor animal. Their bodies are built up of the same materials as earthly plants, but they move about like animals do on Earth. They surprise us, but we may surprise them, too. It's quite possible that the typical animal form on their planet is sessile like the typical plant form on ours.'

Alstair said bitterly: 'And they look on us, animals, as we look on plants!'

Jack said without expression: 'Yes, sir. They eat through holes in their arms. The one who killed the communications officer seized his arm. It seemed to exude some fluid that liquefied his flesh instantly. It sucked the liquid back in at once. If I may make a guess, sir—'

'Go ahead,' snapped Alstair. 'Everybody else is running around in circles, either marveling or sick with terror.'

'The leader of the party, sir, had on what looked like an ornament. It was a band of leather around one of its arms.'

'Now, what the devil—'

'We had two men killed. One was the communications officer and the other was an orderly. When we finally subdued the Centaurian who'd killed that orderly, it had eaten a small bit of him, but the rest of the orderly's body had undergone some queer sort of drying process, from chemicals the Thing seemed to carry with it.'

Alstair's throat worked as if in nausea. 'I saw it.'

'It's a fanciful idea,' said Jack grimly, 'but if a man were in the position of that Centaurian, trapped in a space ship belonging to an alien race, with death very probably before him, well, about the only thing a man would strap to his body, as the Centaurian did the dried, preserved body of that orderly—'

'Would be gold,' snapped Alstair. 'Or platinum, or jewels which he would hope to fight clear with!'

'Just so,' said Jack. 'Now, I'm only guessing, but those creatures are not human, nor even animals. Yet they eat animal food. They treasure animal food as a human being would treasure diamonds. An animal's remains – leather – they wear as an ornament. It looks to me as if animal tissue was rather rare on their planet, to be valued so highly. In consequence—'

Alstair stood up, his features working. 'Then our bodies would be the same as gold to them! As diamonds! Gary, we haven't the ghost of a chance to make friends with these fiends!'

Jack said dispassionately, 'No; I don't think we have. If a race of beings with tissues of metallic gold landed on Earth, I rather think they'd be murdered. But there's another point, too. There's Earth. From our course, these creatures can tell where we came from, and their space ships are rather good. I think I'll put somebody else on the dictawriter job and see if I can flash a message back home. No way to know whether they get it, but they ought to be watching for one by the time it's there. Maybe they've improved their receptors. They intended to try, anyhow.'

'Men could meet these creatures' ships in space,' said Alstair harshly, 'if they were warned. And guns might answer, but if they didn't handle these devils, Caldwell torpedoes would. Or a suicide squad, using their bodies for bait. We're talking like dead men, Gary.'

'I think, sir,' said Jack, 'we are dead men.' Then he added, 'I shall put Helen Bradley on the dictawriter, with a guard to handle the Centaurian. He'll be bound tightly.'

The statement tacitly assumed that Alstair's order to avoid her was withdrawn. It was even a challenge to him to repeat it. And Alstair's eyes glowed and he controlled himself with difficulty.

'Damn you, Gary,' he said savagely, 'get out!'

He turned to the visiplate which showed the enemy ship as Jack left the control room.

The egg-shaped ship was two thousand miles away now, and just decelerating to a stop. In its first flight it had rocketed here and there like a mad thing. It would have been impossible to hit it with any projectile, and difficult in the extreme even to keep radiation on it in anything like a tight beam. Now, stopped stock-still with regard to the *Adastra*, it hung on, observing, very probably devising some new form of devilment. So Alstair considered, anyhow. He watched it somberly.

The resources of the *Adastra*, which had seemed so vast when she took off from Earth, were pitifully inadequate to handle the one situation which had greeted her, hostility. She could have poured out the treasures of man's civilization to the race which ruled this solar system. Savages, she could have uplifted. Even to a race superior to men she could have offered man's friendship and eager pupilage. But these creatures—

The space ship stayed motionless. Probably signaling back to its home planet, demanding orders. Reports came in to the *Adastra*'s main control room and Alstair read them. The Centaurians were unquestionably extracting carbon dioxide from the air. That compound was to their metabolism what oxygen is to men, and in pure air they could not live.

But their metabolic rate was vastly greater than that of any plant on Earth. It compared with the rate of earthly animals. They were not plants by any definition save that of constitution, as a sea anemone is not an animal except by the test of chemical analysis.

The Centaurians had a highly organized nervous system, the equivalent of brains, and both great intelligence and a language. They produced sounds by a stridulating organ in a special body cavity. And they felt emotion.

A captive creature when presented with various objects showed special interest in machinery, showing an acute realization of the purpose of a small sound recorder and uttering into it an entire and deliberate series of sounds. Human clothing it fingered eagerly. Cloth it discarded, when of cotton or rayon, but it displayed great excitement at the feel of a woolen shirt and even more when a leather belt was given to it. It placed the belt about its middle, fastening the buckle without a fumble after a single glance at its working.

It unraveled a thread from the shirt and consumed it, rocking to and fro as if in ecstasy. When meat was placed before it, it seemed to become almost delirious with excitement. A part of the meat it consumed instantly, to ecstatic swayings. The rest it preserved by a curious chemical process, using substances from a small metal pack it had worn and for which it made gestures.

Its organs of vision were behind two slits in the upper part of its body, and no precise examination of the eyes themselves had been made. But the report before Alstair said specifically that the Centaurian displayed an avid eagerness whenever it caught sight of a human being. And that the eagerness was not of a sort to be reassuring.

It was the sort of excitement – only much greater – which it had displayed at the sight of wool and leather. As if by instinct, said the report, the captive Centaurian had several times made a gesture as if turning some weapon upon a human when first it sighted him.

Alstair read this report and others. Helen Bradley reported barely two hours after Jack had assigned her to the work.

'I'm sorry, Helen,' said Alstair ungraciously. 'You shouldn't have been called on for duty. Gary insisted on it. I'd have left you alone.'

'I'm glad he did,' said Helen steadily. 'Father is dead, to be sure, but he was quite content. And he died before he found out what these Centaurians are like. Working was good for me. I've succeeded much better than I even hoped. The Centaurian I worked with was the leader of the party which invaded this ship. He understood almost at once what the dictawriter was doing, and we've a good vocabulary recorded already. If you want to talk to him, you can.'

Alstair glanced at the visiplate. The enemy ship was still motionless. Easily understandable, of course. The *Adastra*'s distance from Proxima Centauri could be measured in hundreds of millions of miles, now, instead of millions of millions, but in another terminology it was light-hours away still. If the space ship had signaled its home planet for orders, it would still be waiting for a reply.

Alstair went heavily to the biology laboratory, of which Helen was in charge, just as she was in charge of the biological specimens – rabbits, sheep, and a seemingly endless array of small animals – which on the voyage had been bred for a food supply and which it had been planned to release should a planet suitable for colonizing revolve about the ringed star.

The Centaurian was bound firmly to a chair with a myriad of cords. He – she – it was utterly helpless. Beside the chair the dictawriter and its speaker were coupled together. From the Centaurian came hooted notes which the machine translated with a rustling sound between words.

'You – are – commander – this – ship?' the machine translated without intonation.

'I am,' said Alstair, and the machine hooted musically.

'This – woman – man – dead,' said the machine tonelessly again, after more sounds from the extraordinary living thing which was not an animal.

Helen interjected swiftly: 'I told him my father was dead.'

The machine went on: 'I – buy – all – dead – man – on – ship – give – metal – gold – you – like—'

Alstair's teeth clicked together. Helen went white. She tried to speak, and choked upon the words.

'This,' said Alstair in mirthless bitterness, 'is the beginning of the interstellar friendship we hoped to institute!'

Then the G. C. phone said abruptly:

'Calling Commander Alstair! Radiation from ahead! Several wave lengths, high intensity! Apparently several space ships are sending, though we can make out no signals!'

And then Jack Gary came into the biology laboratory. His face was set in grim lines. It was very white. He saluted with great precision.

'I didn't have to work hard, sir,' he said sardonically. 'The last communications officer had been taking his office more or less as a sinecure. We'd had no signals for seven years, and he didn't expect any. But they're coming through and have been for months.

'They left Earth three years after we did. A chap named Callaway, it seems, found that a circularly polarized wave makes a tight beam that will hold together forever. They've been sending to us for years past, no doubt, and we're getting some of the first messages now.

'They've built a second *Adastra*, sir, and it's being manned – hell, no! It was manned four years ago! It's on the way out here now! It must be at least three years on the way, and it has no idea of these devils waiting for it. Even if we blow ourselves to bits, sir, there'll be another ship from Earth coming, unarmed as we are, to run into these devils when it's too late to stop—'

The G. C. phone snapped again:

'Commander Alstair! Observations reporting! The external hull temperature has gone up five degrees in the past three minutes and is still climbing. Something's pouring heat into us at a terrific rate!'

Alstair turned to Jack. He said with icy politeness, 'Gary, after all there's no use in our continuing to hate each other.

Here is where we all die together. Why do I still feel inclined to kill you?'

But the question was rhetorical only. The reason was wholly clear. At the triply horrible news, Helen had begun to cry softly. And she had gone blindly into Jack's arms to do it.

IV

The situation was, as a matter of fact, rather worse than the first indications showed. The external hull temperature, for instance, was that of the generalizing thermometer, which averaged for all the external thermometers. A glance at the thermometer bank, through a visiphone connection, showed the rearmost side of the *Adastra* at practically normal. It was the forward hemisphere, the side nearest Proxima Centauri, which was heating. And that hemisphere was not heating equally. The indicators which flashed red lights were closely grouped.

Alstair regarded them with a stony calm in the visiplate.

'Squarely in the center of our disk, as they see it,' he said icily. 'It will be that fleet of space ships, of course.'

Jack Gary said crisply: 'Sir, the ship from which we took prisoners made contact several hours earlier than we expected. It must be that, instead of sending one vessel with a transmitter on board, they sent a fleet, and a scout ship on ahead. That scout ship has reported that we laid a trap for some of her crew, and consequently they've opened fire!'

Alstair said sharply into a G. C. transmitter, 'Sector G90 is to be evacuated at once. It is to be sealed off immediately and all occupants will emerge from air locks. Adjoining sectors are to be evacuated except by men on duty, and they will don space suits immediately.'

He clicked off the phone and added calmly: 'The external temperature over part of G90 is four hundred degrees now. Dull-red heat. In five minutes it should melt. They'll have a hole bored right through us in half an hour.'

Jack said urgently: 'Sir! I'm pointing out that they've attacked because the scout ship reported we laid a trap for some of its crew! We have just the ghost of a chance—'

'What?' demanded Alstair bitterly. 'We've no weapons!'

'The dictawriter, sir!' snapped Jack. 'We can talk to them now!'

Alstair said harshly: 'Very well, Gary. I appoint you ambassador. Go ahead!'

He swung on his heel and went swiftly from the control room. A moment later his voice came out of the G. C. phone: 'Calling the Rocket Chief! Report immediately on personal visiphone. Emergency!'

His voice cut off, but Jack was not aware of it. He was plugging in to communications and demanding full power on the transmission beam and a widening of its arc. He snapped one order after another and explained to Helen in swift asides.

She grasped the idea at once. The Centaurian in the biology laboratory was bound, of course. No flicker of expression could be discovered about the narrow slits which were his vision organs. But Helen – knowing the words of the vocabulary cards – spoke quietly and urgently into the dictawriter microphone. Hootlike noises came out of the speaker in their place, and the Centaurian stirred. Sounds came from him in turn, and the speaker said woodenly, 'I – speak – ship – planet. Yes.'

And as the check-up came through from communications control, the eerie, stridulated, unconsonanted noises of his language filled the biology laboratory and went out on the widened beam of the main transmitter.

Ten thousand miles away the Centaurian scout ship hovered. The *Adastra* bored on toward the ringed sun which had been the goal of mankind's most daring expedition. From ten thousand miles she would have seemed a mere dot, but the telescopes of the Centaurians would show her every detail. From a thousand miles she would seem a toy, perhaps, intricately crisscrossed with strengthening members.

From a distance of a few miles only, though, her gigantic

size could be realized fully. Five thousand feet in diameter, she dwarfed the hugest of those distant, unseen shapes in emptiness which made up a hostile fleet now pouring deadly beams upon her.

From a distance of a few miles, too, the effect of that radiation could be seen. The *Adastra*'s hull was alloy steel; tough and necessarily with a high hysteresis rate. The alternating currents of electricity induced in that steel by the Centaurian radiation would have warmed even a copper hull. But the alloy steel grew hot. It changed color. It glowed faintly red over an area a hundred feet across.

A rocket tube in that area abruptly ceased to emit its purple, lambent flame. It had been cut off. Other rockets increased their power a trifle to make up for it. The dull red glow of the steel increased. It became carmine. Slowly, inexorably, it heated to a yellowish tinge. It became canary in color. It tended toward blue.

Vapor curled upward from its surface, streaming away from the tortured, melting surface as if drawn by the distant sun. That vapor grew thick; dazzlingly bright; a veritable cloud of metallic steam. And suddenly there was a violent eruption from the center of the *Adastra*'s lighted hemisphere. The outer hull was melted through. Air from the interior burst out into the void, flinging masses of molten, vaporizing metal before it. It spread with an incredible rapidity, flaring instantly into the attenuated, faintly glowing mist of a comet's tail.

The visiplate images inside the *Adastra* grew dim. Stars paled ahead. The Earth ship had lost a part of her atmosphere and it fled on before her writhing. Already it had spread into so vast a space that its density was immeasurable, but it was still so much more dense than the infinite emptiness of space that it filled all the cosmos before the *Adastra* with a thinning nebulosity.

And at the edges of the huge gap in the big ship's hull, the thick metal bubbled and steamed, and the interior partitions began to glow with an unholy light of dull-red heat, which swiftly went up to carmine and began to turn faintly yellow.

In the main control room, Alstair watched bitterly until the visiplates showing the interior of section G90 fused. He spoke very calmly into the microphone before him.

'We've got less time than I thought,' he said deliberately. 'You'll have to hurry. It won't be sure at best, and you've got to remember that these devils will undoubtedly puncture us from every direction and make sure there's absolutely nothing living on board. You've got to work something out, and in a hurry, to do what I've outlined!'

A half-hysterical voice came back to him.

'But sir, if I cut the sonic vibrations in the rockets we'll go up in a flare! A single instant! The disintegration of our fuel will spread to the tubes and the whole ship will simply explode! It will be quick!'

'You fool!' snarled Alstair. 'There's another ship from Earth on the way! Unwarned! And unarmed like we are! And from our course these devils can tell where we came from! We're going to die, yes! We won't die pleasantly! But we're going to make sure these fiends don't start out a space fleet for Earth! There's to be no euthanasia for us! We've got to make our dying do some good! We've got to protect humanity!'

Alstair's face, as he snarled into the visiplate, was not that of a martyr or a person making a noble self-sacrifice. It was the face of a man overawing and bullying a subordinate into obedience.

With a beam of radiation playing on his ship which the metal hull absorbed and transformed into heat, Alstair raged at this department and that. A second bulkhead went, and there was a second eruption of vaporized metal and incandescent gas from the monster vessel. Millions of miles away, a wide-flung ring of egg-shaped ships lay utterly motionless, giving no sign of life and looking like monsters asleep. But from them the merciless beams of radiation sped out and focused upon one spot of the *Adastra*'s hull, and it spewed forth frothing metal and writhing gases and now and again some still recognizable object which flared and exploded as it emerged.

And within the innumerable compartments of the mighty ship, human beings reacted to their coming doom in manners as various as the persons themselves. Some screamed. A few of the more sullen members of the crew seemed to go mad, to become homicidal maniacs. Still others broke into the stores and proceeded systematically but in some haste to drink themselves comatose. Some women clutched their children and wept over them. And some of them went mad.

But Alstair's snarling, raging voice maintained a semblance of discipline in a few of the compartments. In a machine shop men worked savagely, cursing, and making mistakes as they worked, which made their work useless. The lean air officer strode about his domain, a huge spanner in his hand, and smote with a righteous anger at any sign of panic. The rocket chief, puffing, manifested an unexpected genius for sustained profanity, and the rockets kept their pale purple flames out in space without a sign of flickering.

But in the biology laboratory the scene was one of quiet, intense concentration. Bound to helplessness, the Centaurian, featureless and inscrutable, filled the room with its peculiar form of speech. The dictawriter rustled softly, senselessly analyzing each of the sounds and senselessly questing for vocabulary cards which would translate them into English wordings. Now and again a single card did match up. Then the machine translated a single word of the Centaurian's speech.

'—ship—' A long series of sounds, varying rapidly in pitch, in intensity, and in emphasis. '—men—' Another long series. '—talk men—'

The Centaurian ceased to make its hootlike noises. Then, very carefully, it emitted new ones. The speaker translated them all. The Centaurian had carefully selected words recorded with Helen.

'He understands what we're trying to do,' said Helen, very pale.

The machine said: 'You – talk – machine – talk – ship.'

Jack said quietly into the transmitter: 'We are friends. We have much you want. We want only friendship. We have killed none of your men except in self-defense. We ask peace. If we do not have peace, we will fight. But we wish peace.' He said under his breath to Helen, as the machine rustled and the speaker hooted: 'Bluff, that war talk. I hope it works!'

Silence. Millions of miles away, unseen space ships aimed a deadly radiation in close, tight beams at the middle of the *Adastra*'s disk. Quaintly enough, that radiation would have been utterly harmless to a man's body. It would have passed through, undetected.

But the steel of the Earth ship's hull stopped and absorbed it as eddy currents. The eddy currents became heat. And a small volcano vomited out into space the walls, the furnishing, the very atmosphere of the *Adastra* through the hole that the heat had made.

It was very quiet indeed in the biology laboratory. The receptor was silent. One minute. Two minutes. Three. The radio waves carrying Jack's voice traveled at the speed of light, but it took no less than ninety seconds for them to reach the source of the beams which were tearing the *Adastra* to pieces. And there was a time loss there, and ninety seconds more for other waves to hurtle through space at one hundred and eighty-six thousand miles each second with the reply.

The receptor hooted unmusically. The dictawriter rustled softly. Then the speaker said without expression, 'We – friends – now – no – fight – ships – come – to – take – you – planet.'

And simultaneously the miniature volcano on the *Adastra*'s hull lessened the violence of its eruption, and slowly its molten, bubbling edges ceased first to steam, and then to bubble, and from the blue-white of vaporizing steel they cooled to yellow, and then to carmine, and more slowly to a dull red, and more slowly still to the glistening, infinitely white metallic surface of steel which cools where there is no oxygen.

Jack said crisply into the control-room microphone: 'Sir, I have communicated with the Centaurians and they have ceased fire. They say they are sending a fleet to take us to their planet.'

'Very good,' said Alstair's voice bitterly, 'especially since nobody seems able to make the one contrivance that would do some good after our death. What next?'

'I think it would be a good idea to release the Centaurian

here,' said Jack. 'We can watch him, of course, and paralyze him if he acts up. It would be a diplomatic thing to do, I believe.'

'You're ambassador,' said Alstair sardonically. 'We've got time to work, now. But you'd better put somebody else on the ambassadorial work and get busy again on the job of sending a message back to Earth, if you think you can adapt a transmitter to the type of wave they'll expect.'

His image faded. And Jack turned to Helen. He felt suddenly very tired.

'That is the devil of it,' he said drearily. 'They'll expect a wave like they sent us, and with no more power than we have, they'll hardly pick up anything else! But we picked up in the middle of a message and just at the end of their description of the sending outfit they're using on Earth. Undoubtedly they'll describe it again, or rather they did describe it again, four years back, and we'll pick it up if we live long enough. But we can't even guess when that will be. You're going to keep on working with this – creature, building up a vocabulary?'

Helen regarded him anxiously. She put her hand upon his arm.

'He's intelligent enough,' she said urgently. 'I'll explain to him and let somebody else work with him. I'll come with you. After all, we – may not have long to be together.'

'Perhaps ten hours,' said Jack tiredly.

He waited, somberly, while she explained in carefully chosen words – which the dictawriter translated – to the Centaurian. She got an assistant and two guards. They released the headless Thing. It offered no violence. Instead, it manifested impatience to continue the work of building up in the translator files a vocabulary through which a complete exchange of ideas could take place.

Jack and Helen went together to the communications room. They ran the Earth message, as received so far. It was an extraordinary hodgepodge. Four years back, Earth had been enthusiastic over the thought of sending word to its most daring adventurers. A flash of immaterial energy could travel tirelessly through uncountable millions of millions of miles of space and overtake the explorers who had started three years before. By its text, this message had been sent some time after the first message of all. In the sending, it had been broadcast all over the Earth, and many millions of people undoubtedly had thrilled to the thought that they heard words which would span the space between two suns.

But the words were not helpful to those on the *Adastra*. The message was a 'cheer-up' program, which began with lusty singing by a popular quartet, continued with wisecracks by Earth's most highly paid comedian – and his jokes were all very familiar to those on the *Adastra* – and then a congratulatory address by an eminent politician, and other drivel. In short, it was a hodgepodge of trash designed to gain publicity by means of the Earth broadcast for those who took part in it.

It was not helpful to those on the *Adastra*, with the hull of the ship punctured, death before them, and probably destruction for the whole human race to follow as a consequence of their voyage.

Jack and Helen sat quietly and listened, their hands clasped unconsciously. Rather queerly, the extreme brevity of the time before them made extravagant expressions of affection seem absurd. They listened to the unspeakably vulgar message from Earth without really hearing it. Now and again they looked at each other.

In the biology laboratory the building-up of a vocabulary went on swiftly. Pictures came into play. A second Centaurian was released, and by his skill in delineation – which proved that the eyes of the plant men functioned almost identically with those of Earth men – added both to the store of definitions and equivalents and to knowledge of the Centaurian civilization.

Piecing the information together, the civilization began to take on a strange resemblance to that of humanity. The Centaurians possessed artificial structures which were undoubtedly dwelling houses. They had cities, laws, arts – the drawing of the second Centaurian was proof of that – and sciences. The science of biology in particular was far advanced, taking to some extent the place of metallurgy in the civilization of men. Their structures were grown, not built. Instead of metals to shape to their own ends, they had forms of protoplasm whose rate and manner of growth they could control.

Houses, bridges, vehicles – even space ships were formed of living matter which was thrown into a quiescent non-living state when it had attained the form and size desired. And it could be caused to become active again at will, permitting such extraordinary features as the blisterlike connection that had been made by the space ship with the hull of the *Adastra*.

So far, the Centaurian civilization was strange enough, but still comprehensible. Even men might have progressed in some such fashion had civilization developed on Earth from a different point of departure. It was the economics of the Centaurians which was both ununderstandable and horrifying to the men who learned of it.

The Centaurian race had developed from carnivorous plants, as men from carnivorous forebears. But at some early date in man's progression, the worship of gold began. No such diversion of interest occurred upon the planets of Proxima Centauri. As men have devastated cities for gold, and have cut down forests and gutted mines and ruthlessly destroyed all things for gold or for other things which could be exchanged for gold, so the Centaurians had quested animals.

As men exterminated the buffalo in America, to trade his hide for gold, so the Centaurians had ruthlessly exterminated the animal life of their planet. But to Centaurians, animal tissue itself was the equivalent of gold. From sheer necessity, ages since, they had learned to tolerate vegetable foodstuffs. But the insensate lust for flesh remained. They had developed methods for preserving animal food for indefinite periods. They had dredged their seas for the last and smallest crustacean. And even space travel became a desirable thing in their eyes, and then a fact, because telescopes showed them vegetation on other planets of their sun, and animal life as a probability.

Three planets of Proxima Centauri were endowed with

climates and atmospheres favorable to vegetation and animal life, but only on one planet now, and that the smallest and most distant, did any trace of animal life survive. And even there the Centaurians hunted feverishly for the last and dwindling colonies of tiny quadrupeds which burrowed hundreds of feet below a frozen continent.

It became clear that the *Adastra* was an argosy of such treasure – in the form of human beings – as no Centaurian could ever have imagined to exist. And it became more than ever clear that a voyage to Earth would command all the resources of the race. Billions of human beings! Trillions of lesser animals! Uncountable creatures in the seas! All the Centaurian race would go mad with eagerness to invade this kingdom of riches and ecstasy, the ecstasy felt by any Centaurian when consuming the prehistoric foodstuff of his race.

V

Egg-shaped, featureless ships of space closed in from every side at once. The thermometer banks showed a deliberate, painstaking progression of alarm signals. One dial glowed madly red and faded, and then another, and yet another, as the Centaurian ships took up their positions. Each such alarm, of course, was from the momentary impact of a radiation beam on the *Adastra*'s hull.

Twenty minutes after the last of the beams had proved the *Adastra*'s helplessness, an egglike ship approached the Earth vessel and with complete precision made contact with its forward side above an air lock. Its hull bellied out in a great blister which adhered to the steel.

Alstair watched the visiplate which showed it, his face very white and his hands clenched tightly. Jack Gary's voice, strained and hoarse, came from the biology-laboratory communicator.

'Sir, a message from the Centaurians. A ship has landed on our hull and its crew will enter through the air lock. A hostile move on our part, of course, will mean instant destruction.'

'There will be no resistance to the Centaurians,' said Alstair harshly. 'It is my order! It would be suicide!'

'Even so, sir,' said Jack's voice savagely, 'I still think it would be a good idea!'

'Stick to your duty!' rasped Alstair. 'What progress has been made in communication?'

'We have vocabulary cards for nearly five thousand words. We can converse on nearly any subject, and all of them are unpleasant. The cards are going through a duplicator now and will be finished in a few minutes. A second dictawriter with the second file will be sent you as soon as the cards are complete.'

In a visiplate, Alstair saw the headless figures of Centaurians emerging from the entrance to an air lock in the *Adastra*'s hull.

'Those Centaurians have entered the ship,' he snapped as an order to Jack. 'You're communications officer! Go meet them and lead their commanding officer here!'

'Check!' said Jack grimly.

It sounded like a sentence of death, that order. In the laboratory he was very pale indeed. Helen pressed close to him.

The formerly captive Centaurian hooted into the dicta-writer, inquiringly. The speaker translated.

'What – command?'

Helen explained. So swiftly does humanity accustom itself to the incredible that it seemed almost natural to address a microphone and hear the hoots and stridulations of a non-human voice fill the room with her meaning.

'I – go – also – they – no – kill – yet.'

The Centaurian rolled on before. With an extraordinary dexterity, he opened the door. He had merely seen it opened. Jack took the lead. His side-arm force gun remained in its holster beside him, but it was useless. He could probably kill the plant man behind him, but that would do no good.

Dim hootings ahead. The plant man made sounds – loud and piercing sounds. Answers came to him. Jack came in view of the new group of invaders. There were twenty or thirty of them, everyone armed with half-cylindrical objects, larger than the first creatures had carried.

At sight of Jack there was excitement. Eager trembling of the armlike tentacles at either side of the headless trunks. There were instinctive, furtive movements of the weapons. A loud hooting as of command. The Things were still. But Jack's flesh crawled from the feeling of sheer, carnivorous lust that seemed to emanate from them.

His guide, the former captive, exchanged incomprehensible noises with the newcomers. Again a ripple of excitement in the ranks of the plant men.

'Come,' said Jack curtly.

He led the way to the main control room. Once they heard someone screaming monotonously. A woman cracked under the coming of doom. A hooting babble broke the silence among the ungainly Things which followed Jack. Again an authoritative note silenced it.

The control room. Alstair looked like a man of stone, of marble, save that his eyes burned with a fierce and almost maniacal flame. A visiplate beside him showed a steady stream of Centaurians entering through a second air lock. There were hundreds of them, apparently. The dictawriter came in, under Helen's care. She cried out in instinctive horror at sight of so many of the monstrous creatures at once in the control room.

'Set up the dictawriter,' said Alstair in a voice so harsh, so brittle that it seemed pure ice.

Trembling, Helen essayed to obey.

'I am ready to talk,' said Alstair harshly into the dictawriter microphone.

The machine, rustling softly, translated. The leader of the new party hooted in reply. An order for all officers to report here at once, after setting all controls for automatic operation of the ship. There was some difficulty with the translation of the Centaurian equivalent of 'automatic'. It was not in the vocabulary file. It took time.

Alstair gave the order. Cold sweat stood out upon his face, but his self-control was iron.

A second order, also understood with a certain amount of difficulty. Copies of all technical records, and all – again it took time to understand – all books bearing on the construction of this ship were to be taken to the air lock by which these plant men had entered. Samples of machinery, generators, and weapons to the same destination.

Again Alstair gave the order. His voice was brittle, was even thin, but it did not falter or break.

The Centaurian leader hooted an order over which the dictawriter rustled in vain. His followers swept swiftly to the doors of the control room. They passed out, leaving but four of their number behind. And Jack went swiftly to Alstair. His force gun snapped out and pressed deep into the commander's middle. The Centaurians made no movement of protest.

'Damn you!' said Jack, his voice thick with rage. 'You've let them take the ship! You plan to bargain for your life! Damn you, I'm going to kill you and fight my way to a rocket tube and send this ship up in a flare of clean flame that'll kill these devils with us!'

But Helen cried swiftly: 'Jack! Don't! I know!'

Like an echo her words – because she was near the dictawriter microphone – were repeated in the hooting sounds of the Centaurian language. And Alstair, livid and near to madness, nevertheless said harshly in the lowest of tones:

'You fool! These devils can reach Earth, now they know it's worth reaching! So even if they kill every man on the ship but the officers – and they may – we've got to navigate to their planet and land there.' His voice dropped to a rasping whisper and he raged almost soundlessly: 'And if you think I want to live through what's coming, shoot!'

Jack stood rigid for an instant. Then he stepped back. A new respect and understanding dawned in his eyes.

'I beg your pardon, sir,' he said unsteadily. 'You can count on me hereafter.'

One of the officers of the *Adastra* stumbled into the control room. Another. Still another. They trickled in. Six officers out of thirty.

A Centaurian entered with the curious rolling gait of his race. He went impatiently to the dictawriter and made noises.

'These – all – officers?' asked the machine tonelessly.

'The air officer shot his family and himself,' gasped a subaltern of the air department. 'A bunch of Muts charged a rocket tube and the rocket chief fought them off. Then he bled to death from a knife in his throat. The stores officer was—'

'Stop!' said Alstair in a thin, high voice. He tore at his collar. He went to the microphone and said thinly: 'These are all the officers still alive. But we can navigate the ship.'

The Centaurian – he wore a wide band of leather about each of his arms and another about his middle – waddled to the G. C. phone. The tendrils at the end of one arm manipulated the switch expertly. He emitted strange, formless sounds – and hell broke loose!

The visiplates all over the room emitted high-pitched, squealing sounds. They were horrible. They were ghastly. They were more terrible than the sounds of a wolf pack hard on the heels of a fear-mad deer. They were the sounds Jack had heard when one of the first invaders of the *Adastra* saw a human being and killed him instantly. And other sounds came out of the visiplates, too. There were human screams. There were even one or two explosions.

But then there was silence. The five Centaurians in the control room quivered and trembled. A desperate blood-lust filled them, the unreasoning, blind, instinctive craving which came of evolution from some race of carnivorous plants become capable of movement through the desperate need for food.

The Centaurian with the leather ornaments went to the dictawriter again. He hooted in it:

'Want – two – men – go – from – ship – learn – from – them – now.'

There was an infinitely tiny sound in the main control room. It was a drop of cold sweat, falling from Alstair's face to the floor. He seemed to have shriveled. His face was an ashy gray. His eyes were closed. But Jack looked steadily from one to the other of the surviving officers.

'That will mean vivisection, I suppose,' he said harshly. 'It's certain they plan to visit Earth, else – intelligent as they are

242

– they wouldn't have wiped out everybody but us. Even for treasure. They'll want to try out weapons on a human body, and so on. Communications is about the most useless of all the departments now, sir. I volunteer.'

Helen gasped: 'No, Jack! No!'

Alstair opened his eyes. 'Gary has volunteered. One more man to volunteer for vivisection.' He said it in the choked voice of one holding to sanity by the most terrible of efforts. 'They'll want to find out how to kill men. Their thirty-centimeter waves didn't work. They know the beams that melted our hull wouldn't kill men. I can't volunteer! I've got to stay with the ship!' There was despair in his voice. 'One more man to volunteer for these devils to kill slowly!'

Silence. The happenings of the past little while, and the knowledge of what still went on within the *Adastra*'s innumerable compartments, had literally stunned most of the six. They could not think. They were mentally dazed, emotionally paralyzed by the sheer horrors they had encountered.

Then Helen stumbled into Jack's arms. 'I'm – going, too!' she gasped. 'We're – all going to die! I'm not needed! And I can – die with Jack.'

Alstair groaned. 'Please!'

'I'm – going!' she panted. 'You can't stop me! With Jack! Whither thou goest—'

Then she choked. She pressed close. The Centaurian of the leather belts hooted impatiently into the dictawriter.

'These – two – come.'

Jack and Helen stood, hands clasped, momentarily dazed. The Centaurian of the leather bands hooted impatiently. He led them, with his queer, rolling gait, toward the air lock by which the plant men had entered. Three times they were seen by roving Things, which emitted that triply horrible shrill squeal. And each time the Centaurian of the leather bands hooted authoritatively and the plant men withdrew.

Once, too, Jack saw four creatures swaying backward and forward about something on the floor. He reached out his hands and covered Helen's eyes until they were past.

They came to the air lock. Their guide pointed through it. The man and the girl obeyed. Long, rubbery tentacles seized them and Helen gasped and was still. Jack fought fiercely, shouting her name. Then something struck him savagely. He collapsed.

He came back to consciousness with a feeling of tremendous weight upon him. He stirred, and with his movement some of the oppression left him. A light burned, not a light such as men know on Earth, but a writhing flare which beat restlessly at the confines of a transparent globe which contained it. There was a queer smell in the air, too, an animal smell. Jack sat up. Helen lay beside him, unconfined and apparently unhurt. None of the Centaurians seemed to be near.

He chafed her wrists helplessly. He heard a stuttering sound and with each of the throbs of noise felt a momentary acceleration. Rockets, fuel rockets.

'We're on one of their damned ships!' said Jack to her. He felt for his force gun. It was gone.

Helen opened her eyes. She stared vaguely about. Her eyes fell upon Jack. She shuddered suddenly and pressed close to him.

'What – what happened?'

'We'll have to find out,' replied Jack grimly.

The floor beneath his feet careened suddenly. Instinctively, he glanced at a porthole which until then he had only subconsciously noted. He gazed out into the utterly familiar blackness of space, illumined by very many tiny points of light which were stars. He saw a ringed sun and points of light which were planets.

One of those points of light was very near. Its disk was perceptible, and polar snow caps, and the misty alternation of greenish areas which would be continents with the indescribable tint which is ocean bottom when viewed from beyond a planet's atmosphere.

Silence. No hootings of that strange language without vowels or consonants which the Centaurians used. No sound of any kind for a moment.

'We're heading for that planet, I suppose,' said Jack quietly. 'We'll have to see if we can't manage to get ourselves killed before we land.'

Then a murmur in the distance. It was a strange, muted murmur, in nothing resembling the queer notes of the plant men. With Helen clinging to him, Jack explored cautiously, out of the cubby-hole in which they had awakened. Silence save for that distant murmur. No movement anywhere. Another faint stutter of the rockets, with a distinct accelerative movement of the whole ship. The animal smell grew stronger. They passed through a strangely shaped opening and Helen cried out:

'The animals!'

Heaped higgledy-piggledy were cages from the *Adastra*, little compartments containing specimens of each of the animals which had been bred for food, and which it had been planned to release if a planet suitable for colonization revolved about Proxima Centauri. Farther on was an indescribable mass of books, machines, cases of all sorts – the materials ordered to be carried to the air lock by the leader of the plant men. Still no sign of any Centaurian.

But the muted murmur, quite incredibly sounding like a human voice, came from still farther ahead. Bewildered, now, Helen followed as Jack went still cautiously toward the source of the sound.

They found it. It came from a bit of mechanism cased in with the same lusterless, dull-brown stuff which composed the floor and walls and every part of the ship about them. And it was a human voice. More, it was Alstair's, racked and harsh and half hysterical.

'—you must have recovered consciousness by now, dammit, and these devils want some sign of it! They cut down your acceleration when I told them the rate they were using would keep you unconscious! Gary! Helen! Set off that signal!'

A pause. The voice again:

'I'll tell it again. You're in a space ship these fiends are guiding by a tight beam which handles the controls. You're going to be set down on one of the planets which once contained animal life. It's empty now, unoccupied except by plants. And you and the space ship's cargo of animals and books and so on are the reserved, special property of the high archfiend of all these devils. He had you sent in an outside-controlled ship because none of his kind could be trusted with such treasure as you and the other animals!

'You're a reserve of knowledge, to translate our books, explain our science, and so on. It's forbidden for any other space ship than his own to land on your planet. Now will you send that signal? It's a knob right above the speaker my voice is coming out of. Pull it three times, and they'll know you're all right and won't send another ship with preservatives for your flesh lest a priceless treasure go to waste!'

The tinny voice – Centaurian receptors were not designed to reproduce the elaborate phonetics of the human voice – laughed hysterically.

Jack reached up and pulled the knob, three times. Alstair's voice went on:

'This ship is hell, now. It isn't a ship any more, but a sort of brimstone pit. There are seven of us alive, and we're instructing Centaurians in the operation of the controls. But we've told them that we can't turn off the rockets to show their inner workings, because to be started they have to have a planet's mass near by, for deformation of space so the reaction can be started. They're keeping us alive until we've shown them that. They've got some method of writing, too, and they write down everything we say, when it's translated by a dictawriter. Very scientific—'

The voice broke off.

'Your signal just came,' it said an instant later. 'You'll find food somewhere about. The air ought to last you till you land. You've got four more days of travel. I'll call back later. Don't worry about navigation. It's attended to.'

The voice died again, definitely.

The two of them, man and girl, explored the Centaurian space ship. Compared to the *Adastra*, it was miniature. A hundred feet long, or more, by perhaps sixty feet at its greatest diameter. They found cubbyholes in which there was now nothing at all, but which undoubtedly at times contained the plant men packed tightly.

These rooms could be refrigerated, and it was probable that at a low temperature the Centaurians reacted like vegetation on Earth in winter and passed into a dormant, hibernating state. Such an arrangement would allow of an enormous crew being carried, to be revived for landing or battle.

'If they refitted the *Adastra* for a trip back to Earth on that basis,' said Jack grimly, 'they'd carry a hundred and fifty thousand Centaurians at least. Probably more.'

The thought of an assault upon mankind by these creatures was an obsession. Jack was tormented by it. Womanlike, Helen tried to cheer him by their own present safety.

'We volunteered for vivisection,' she told him pitifully, the day after their recovery of consciousness, 'and we're safe for a while, anyhow. And – we've got each other—'

'It's time for Alstair to communicate again,' said Jack harshly. It was nearly thirty hours after the last signing off. Centaurian routine, like Earth discipline on terrestrial space ships, maintained a period equal to a planet's daily rotation as the unit of time. 'We'd better go listen to him.'

They did. And Alstair's racked voice came from the queerly shaped speaker. It was more strained, less sane, than the day before. He told them of the progress of the Things in the navigation of the *Adastra*. The six surviving officers already were not needed to keep the ship's apparatus functioning. The air-purifying apparatus in particular was shut off, since in clearing the air of carbon dioxide it tended to make the air unbreathable for the Centaurians.

The six men were now permitted to live that they might satisfy the insatiable desire of the plant men for information. They lived a perpetual third degree, with every resource of their brains demanded for record in the weird notation of their captors. The youngest of the six, a subaltern of the air department, went mad under the strain alike of memory and of anticipation. He screamed senselessly for hours, and was killed and his body promptly mummified by the strange, drying chemicals of the Centaurians. The rest were living shadows, starting at a sound.

'Our deceleration's been changed,' said Alstair, his voice brittle. 'You'll land just two days before we settle down, on the planet these devils call home. Queer they've no colonizing instinct. Another one of us is about to break, I think. They've taken away our shoes and belts now, by the way. They're leather. We'd take a gold band from about a watermelon, wouldn't we? Consistent, these—'

And he raged once, in sudden hysteria:

'I'm a fool! I sent you two off together while I'm living in hell! Gary, I order you to have nothing to do with Helen! I order that the two of you shan't speak to each other! I order that—'

Another day passed. And another. Alstair called twice more. Each time, by his voice, he was more desperate, more nerve-racked, closer to the bounds of madness. The second time he wept, the while he cursed Jack for being where there were none of the plant men.

'We're not interesting to the devils, now, except as animals. Our brains don't count! They're gutting the ship systematically. Yesterday they got the earthworms from the growing area where we grew crops! There's a guard on each of us now. Mine pulled out some of my hair this morning and ate it, rocking back and forth in ecstasy. We've no woolen shirts. They're animal!'

Another day still. Then Alstair was semi-hysterical. There were only three men left alive on the ship. He had instructions to give Jack in the landing of the egg-shaped vessel on the uninhabited world. Jack was supposed to help. His destination was close now. The disk of the planet which was to be his and Helen's prison filled half the heavens. And the other planet toward which the *Adastra* was bound was a full-sized disk to Alstair.

Beyond the rings of Proxima Centaurai there were six planets in all, and the prison planet was next outward from the home of the plant men. It was colder than was congenial to them, though for a thousand years their flesh-hunting expeditions had searched its surface until not a mammal or a bird, no fish or even a crustacean was left upon it. Beyond it again an ice-covered world lay, and still beyond there were frozen shapes whirling in emptiness.

'You know, now, how to take over when the beam releases the atmospheric controls,' said Alstair's voice. It wavered as if he spoke through teeth which chattered from pure nerve strain. 'You'll have quiet. Trees and flowers and something like grass, if the pictures they've made mean anything. We're running into the greatest celebration in the history of all hell. Every space ship called home. There won't be a Centaurian on the planet who won't have a tiny shred of some sort of animal matter to consume. Enough to give him that beastly delight they feel when they get hold of something of animal origin.

'Damn them! Every member of the race! We're the greatest store of treasure ever dreamed of! They make no bones of talking before me, and I'm mad enough to understand a good bit of what they say to each other. Their most high panjandrum is planning bigger space ships than were ever grown before. He'll start out for Earth with three hundred space ships, and most of the crews asleep or hibernating. There'll be three million devils straight from hell on those ships, and they've those damned beams that will fuse an earthly ship at ten million miles.'

Talking helped to keep Alstair sane, apparently. The next day Jack's and Helen's egg-shaped vessel dropped like a plummet from empty space into an atmosphere which screamed wildly past its smooth sides. Then Jack got the ship under control and it descended slowly and ever more slowly and at last came to a cushioned stop in a green glade hard by a forest of strange but wholly reassuring trees. It was close to sunset on this planet, and darkness fell before they could attempt exploration.

They did little exploring, however, either the next day or the day after. Alstair talked almost continuously.

'Another ship coming from Earth,' he said, and his voice

cracked. 'Another ship! She started at least four years ago. She'll get here in four years more. You two may see her, but I'll be dead or mad by tomorrow night! And here's the humorous thing! It seems to me that madness is nearest when I think of you, Helen, letting Jack kiss you! I loved you, you know, Helen, when I was a man, before I became a corpse watching my ship being piloted into hell. I loved you very much. I was jealous, and when you looked at Gary with shining eyes I hated him. I still hate him, Helen! Ah, how I hate him!' But Alstair's voice was the voice of a ghost, now, a ghost in purgatory.

Jack walked about with abstracted, burning eyes. Then he heard Helen at work, somewhere. She seemed to be struggling. It disturbed him. He went to see.

She had just dragged the last of the cages from the *Adastra* out into the open. She was releasing the little creatures within. Pigeons soared eagerly above her. Rabbits, hardly hopping out of her reach, munched delightedly upon the unfamiliar but satisfactory leafed vegetation underfoot.

Sheep browsed. There were six of them besides a tiny, wabbly-legged lamb. Chickens pecked and scratched. But there were no insects on this world. They would find only seeds and green stuff. Four puppies rolled ecstatically on scratchy green things in the sunlight.

'Anyhow,' said Helen defiantly, 'They can be happy for a while! They're not like us! We have to worry! And this world could be a paradise for humans!'

Jack looked somberly out across the green and beautiful world. No noxious animals. No harmful insects. There could be no diseases on this planet, unless men introduced them of set purpose. It would be a paradise.

The murmur of a human voice came from within the space ship. He went bitterly to listen. Helen came after him. They stood in the strangely shaped cubby-hole which was the control room. Walls, floors, ceiling, instrument cases – all were made of the lusterless dark-brown stuff which had grown into the shapes the Centaurians desired. Alstair's voice was strangely more calm, less hysterical, wholly steady.

'I hope you're not off exploring somewhere, Helen and Gary,' it said from the speaker. 'They've had a celebration here today. The *Adastra's* landed. I landed it. I'm the only man left alive. We came down in the center of a city of these devils, in the middle of buildings fit to form the headquarters of hell. The high panjandrum has a sort of palace right next to the open space where I am now.

'And today they celebrated. It's strange how much animal matter there was on the *Adastra*. They even found horsehair stiffening in the coats of our uniforms. Woolen blankets. Shoes. Even some of the soaps had an animal origin, and they "refined" it. They can recover any scrap of animal matter as cleverly as our chemists can recover gold and radium. Queer, eh?'

The speaker was silent a moment.

'I'm sane, now,' the voice said steadily. 'I think I was mad for a while. But what I saw today cleared my brain. I saw millions of these devils dipping their arms into great tanks, great troughs, in which solutions of all the animal tissues from the *Adastra* were dissolved. The high panjandrum kept plenty for himself! I saw the things they carried into his palace, through lines of guards. Some of those things had been my friends. I saw a city gone crazy with beastly joy, the devils swaying back and forth in ecstasy as they absorbed the loot from Earth. I heard the high panjandrum hoot a sort of imperial address from the throne. And I've learned to understand quite a lot of those hootings.

'He was telling them that Earth is packed with animals. Men. Beasts. Birds. Fish in the oceans. And he told them that the greatest space fleet in history will soon be grown, which will use the propulsion methods of men, our rockets, Gary, and the first fleet will carry uncountable swarms of them to occupy Earth. They'll send back treasure, too, so that every one of his subjects will have such ecstasy, frequently, as they had today. And the devils, swaying crazily back and forth, gave out that squealing noise of theirs. Millions of them at once.'

Jack groaned softly. Helen covered her eyes as if to shut out the sight her imagination pictured.

'Now, here's the situation from your standpoint,' said Alstair steadily, millions of miles away and the only human being upon a planet of blood-lusting plant men, 'They're coming here now, their scientists, to have me show them the inside workings of the rockets. Some others will come over to question you two tomorrow. But I'm going to show these devils our rockets. I'm sure – perfectly sure – that every space ship of the race is back on this planet.

'They came to share the celebration when every one of them got as a free gift from the grand panjandrum as much animal tissue as he could hope to acquire in a lifetime of toil. Flesh is a good bit more precious than gold, here. It rates, on a comparative scale, somewhere between platinum and radium. So they all came home. Every one of them! And there's a space ship on the way here from Earth. It'll arrive in four years more. Remember that!'

An impatient, distant hooting came from the speaker.

'They're here,' said Alstair steadily. 'I'm going to show them the rockets. Maybe you'll see the fun. It depends on the time of day where you are. But remember, there's a sister ship to the *Adastra* on the way! And Gary, that order I gave you last thing was the act of a madman, but I'm glad I did it. Good-by, you two!'

Small hooting sounds, growing fainter, came from the speaker. Far, far away, amid the city of fiends, Alstair was going with the plant men to show them the rockets' inner workings. They wished to understand every aspect of the big ship's propulsion, so that they could build – or grow – ships as large to carry multitudes of their swarming myriads to a solar system where animals were to be found.

'Let's go outside,' said Jack at last. 'He said he'd do it, since he couldn't get a bit of a machine made that could be depended on to do it. But I believed he'd go mad. It didn't seem possible to live to their planet. We'll go outside and look at the sky.'

Helen stumbled. They stood upon the green grass, looking up at the firmament above them. They waited, staring. And Jack's mind pictured the great rocket chambers of the *Adastra*. He seemed to see the strange procession enter it; a horde of the ghastly plant men and then Alstair, his face like marble and his hands as steady.

He'd open up the breech of one of the rockets. He'd explain the disintegration field, which collapses the electrons of hydrogen so that it rises in atomic weight to helium, and the helium to lithium, while the oxygen of the water is split literally into neutronium and pure force. Alstair would answer hooted questions. The supersonic generators he would explain as controls of force and direction. He would not speak of the fact that only the material of the rocket tubes, when filled with exactly the frequency those generators produced, could withstand the effect of the disintegration field.

He would not explain that a tube started without those generators in action would catch from the fuel and disintegrate, and that any other substance save one, under any other condition save that one rate of vibration, would catch also and that tubes, ship, and planet alike would vanish in a lambent purple flame.

No; Alstair would not explain that. He would show the Centaurians how to start the Caldwell field.

The man and the girl looked at the sky. And suddenly there was a fierce purple light. It dwarfed the reddish tinge of the ringed sun overhead. For one second, for two, for three, the purple light persisted. There was no sound. There was a momentary blast of intolerable heat. Then all was as before.

The ringed sun shone brightly. Clouds like those of Earth floated serenely in a sky but a little less blue than that of home. The small animals from the *Adastra* munched contentedly at the leafy stuff underfoot. The pigeons soared joyously, exercising their wings in full freedom.

'He did it,' said Jack. 'And every space ship was home. There aren't any more plant men. There's nothing left of their planet, their civilization, or their plans to harm our Earth.'

Even out in space, there was nothing where the planet of the Centaurians had been. Not even steam or cooling gases. It was gone as if it had never existed. And the man and woman of Earth stood upon a planet which could be a paradise for human beings, and another ship was coming presently, with more of their kind.

'He did it!' repeated Jack quietly. 'Rest his soul! And we – we can think of living, now, instead of death.'

The grimness of his face relaxed slowly. He looked down at Helen. Gently, he put his arm about her shoulders.

She pressed close, gladly, thrusting away all thoughts of what had been. Presently she asked softly: 'What was that last order Alstair gave you?'

'I never looked,' said Jack.

He fumbled in his pocket. Pocketworn and frayed, the order slip came out. He read it and showed it to Helen. By statues passed before the *Adastra* left Earth, laws and law enforcement on the artificial planet were intrusted to the huge ship's commander. It had been specially provided that a legal marriage on the *Adastra* would be constituted by an official order of marriage signed by the commander. And the slip handed to Jack by Alstair, as Jack went to what he'd thought would be an agonizing death, was such an order. It was, in effect, a marriage certificate.

They smiled at each other, those two.

'It – wouldn't have mattered,' said Helen uncertainly. 'I love you. But I'm glad!'

One of the freed pigeons found a straw upon the ground. He tugged at it. His mate inspected it solemnly. They made pigeon noises to each other. They flew away with the straw. After due discussion, they had decided that it was an eminently suitable straw with which to begin the building of a nest.

FIRST CONTACT

Tommy Dort went into the captain's room with his last pair of stereophotos and said:

'I'm through, sir. These are the last two pictures I can take.'

He handed over the photographs and looked with professional interest at the visiplates which showed all space outside the ship. Subdued, deep-red lighting indicated the controls and such instruments as the quartermaster on duty needed for navigation of the spaceship *Llanvabon*. There was a deeply cushioned control chair. There was the little gadget of oddly angled mirrors – remote descendant of the back-view mirrors of twentieth-century motorists – which allowed a view of all the visiplates without turning the head. And there were the huge plates which were so much more satisfactory for a direct view of space.

The *Llanvabon* was a long way from home. The plates, which showed every star of visual magnitude and could be stepped up to any desired magnification, portrayed stars of every imaginable degree of brilliance, in the startlingly different colors they show outside of atmosphere. But every one was unfamiliar. Only two constellations could be recognized as seen from Earth, and they were shrunken and distorted. The Milky Way seemed vaguely out of place. But even such oddities were minor compared to a sight in the forward plates.

There was a vast, vast mistiness ahead. A luminous mist. It seemed motionless. It took a long time for any appreciable nearing to appear in the vision plates, though the spaceship's velocity indicator showed an incredible speed. The mist was the Crab Nebula, six light-years long, three and a half light-years thick, with outward-reaching members that in the telescopes of Earth gave it some resemblance to the creature for which it was named. It was a cloud of gas, infinitely tenuous, reaching half again as far as from Sol to its nearest neighbor-sun. Deep within it burned two stars; a double star; one component the familiar yellow of the sun of Earth, the other an unholy white.

Tommy Dort said meditatively:

'We're heading into a deep, sir?'

The skipper studied the last two plates of Tommy's taking, and put them aside. He went back to his uneasy contemplation of the vision plates ahead. The *Llanvabon* was decelerating at full force. She was a bare half light-year from the nebula. Tommy's work was guiding the ship's course, now, but the work was done. During all the stay of the exploring ship in the nebula, Tommy Dort would loaf. But he'd more than paid his way so far.

He had just completed a quite unique first – a complete photographic record of the movement of a nebula during a period of four thousand years, taken by one individual with the same apparatus and with control exposures to detect and record any systematic errors. It was an achievement in itself worth the journey from Earth. But in addition, he had also recorded four thousand years of the history of a double star, and four thousand years of the history of a star in the act of degenerating into a white dwarf.

It was not that Tommy Dort was four thousand years old. He was, actually, in his twenties. But the Crab Nebula is four thousand light-years from Earth, and the last two pictures had been taken by light which would not reach Earth until the sixth millennium A.D.. On the way here – at speeds incredible multiples of the speed of light – Tommy Dort had recorded each aspect of the nebula by the light which had left it from forty centuries since to a bare six months ago.

The *Llanvabon* bored on through space. Slowly, slowly, slowly, the incredible luminosity crept across the vision plates. It blotted out half the universe from view. Before was glowing mist, and behind was a star-studded emptiness. The mist shut off three-fourths of all the stars. Some few of the brightest shone dimly through it near its edge, but only a few. Then there was only an irregularly shaped patch of darkness astern against which stars shone unwinking. The *Llanvabon* dived into the nebula, and it seemed as if it bored into a tunnel of darkness with walls of shining fog.

Which was exactly what the spaceship was doing. The most distant photographs of all had disclosed structural features in the nebula. It was not amorphous. It had form. As the *Llanvabon* drew nearer, indications of structure grew more distinct, and Tommy Dort had argued for a curved approach for photographic reasons. So the spaceship had come up to the nebula on a vast logarithmic curve, and Tommy had been able to take successive photographs from slightly different angles and get stereopairs which showed the nebula in three dimensions; which disclosed billowings and hollows and an actually complicated shape. In places, the nebula displayed convolutions like those of a human brain. It was into one of those hollows that the spaceship now plunged. They had been called 'deeps' by analogy with crevasses in the ocean floor. And they promised to be useful.

The skipper relaxed. One of a skipper's functions, nowadays, is to think of things to worry about, and then worry about them. The skipper of the *Llanvabon* was conscientious. Only after a certain instrument remained definitely non-registering did he ease himself back in his seat.

'It was just barely possible,' he said heavily, 'that those deeps might be non-luminous gas. But they're empty. So we'll be able to use overdrive as long as we're in them.'

It was a light-year-and-a-half from the edge of the nebula to the neighborhood of the double star which was its heart. That was the problem. A nebula is a gas. It is so thin that a comet's tail is solid by comparison, but a ship traveling on overdrive – above the speed of light – does not want to hit even a merely hard vacuum. It needs pure emptiness, such as exists between the stars. But the *Llanvabon* could not do much in this expanse of mist if it was limited to speeds a merely hard vacuum would permit.

The luminosity seemed to close in behind the spaceship, which slowed and slowed and slowed. The overdrive went off with the sudden *pinging* sensation which goes all over a person when the overdrive field is released.

Then, almost instantly, bells burst into clanging, strident uproar all through the ship. Tommy was almost deafened by the alarm bell which rang in the captain's room before the quartermaster shut it off with a flip of his hand. But other bells could be heard ringing throughout the rest of the ship, to be cut off as automatic doors closed one by one.

Tommy Dort stared at the skipper. The skipper's hands clenched. He was up and staring over the quartermaster's shoulder. One indicator was apparently having convulsions. Others strained to record their findings. A spot on the diffusedly bright mistiness of a bow-quartering visiplate grew brighter as the automatic scanner focused on it. That was the direction of the object which had sounded collision-alarm. But the object locator itself – according to its reading, there was one solid object some eighty thousand miles away – an object of no great size. But there was another object whose distance varied from extreme range to zero, and whose size shared its impossible advance and retreat.

'Step up the scanner,' snapped the skipper.

The extra-bright spot on the scanner rolled outward, obliterating the undifferentiated image behind it. Magnification increased. But nothing appeared. Absolutely nothing. Yet the radio locator insisted that something monstrous and invisible made lunatic dashes toward the *Llanvabon*, at speeds which inevitably implied collision, and then fled coyly away at the same rate.

The visiplate went up to maximum magnification. Still nothing. The skipper ground his teeth. Tommy Dort said meditatively:

'D'you know, sir, I saw something like this on a liner on the Earth–Mars run once, when we were being located by another ship. Their locator beam was the same frequency as ours, and every time it hit, it registered like something monstrous, and solid.'

'That,' said the skipper savagely, 'is just what's happening now. There's something like a locator beam on us. We're getting that beam and our own echo besides. But the other ship's invisible! Who is out here in an invisible ship with locator devices? Not men, certainly!'

He pressed the button in his sleeve communicator and snapped:

'Action stations! Man all weapons! Condition of extreme alert in all departments immediately!'

His hands closed and unclosed. He stared again at the visiplate, which showed nothing but a formless brightness.

'Not men?' Tommy Dort straightened sharply. 'You mean—'

'How many solar systems in our galaxy?' demanded the skipper bitterly. 'How many planets fit for life? And how many kinds of life could there be? If this ship isn't from Earth – and it isn't – it has a crew that isn't human. And things that aren't human but are up to the level of deep-space travel in their civilization could mean anything!'

The skipper's hands were actually shaking. He would not have talked so freely before a member of his own crew, but Tommy Dort was of the observation staff. And even a skipper whose duties include worrying may sometimes need desperately to unload his worries. Sometimes, too, it helps to think aloud.

'Something like this has been talked about and speculated about for years,' he said softly. 'Mathematically, it's been an odds-on bet that somewhere in our galaxy there'd be another race with a civilization equal to or further advanced than ours. Nobody could ever guess where or when we'd meet them. But it looks like we've done it now!'

Tommy's eyes were very bright.

'D'you suppose they'll be friendly, sir?'

The skipper glanced at the distance indicator. The phantom object still made its insane, nonexistent swoops toward and away from the *Llanvabon*. The secondary indication of an object at eighty thousand miles stirred ever so slightly.

'It's moving,' he said curtly. 'Heading for us. Just what we'd do if a strange spaceship appeared in our hunting grounds! Friendly? Maybe! We're going to try to contact them. We have to. But I suspect this is the end of this expedition. Thank God for the blasters!'

The blasters are those beams of ravening destruction which take care of recalcitrant meteorites in a spaceship's course when the deflectors can't handle them. They are not designed as weapons, but they can serve as pretty good ones. They can go into action at five thousand miles, and draw on the entire power output of a whole ship. With automatic aim and a traverse of five degrees, a ship like the *Llanvabon* can come very close to blasting a hole through a small-sized asteroid which gets in its way. But not on overdrive, of course.

Tommy Dort had approached the bow-quartering visiplate. Now he jerked his head around.

'Blasters, sir? What for?'

The skipper grimaced at the empty visiplate.

'Because we don't know what they're like and can't take a chance! I know!' he added bitterly. 'We're going to make contacts and try to find out all we can about them – especially where they come from. I suppose we'll try to make friends – but we haven't much chance. We can't trust them a fraction of an inch. We daren't! They've locators. Maybe they've tracers better than any we have. Maybe they could trace us all the way home without our knowing it! We can't risk a nonhuman race knowing where Earth is unless we're sure of them! And how can we be sure? They could come to trade, of course – or they could swoop down on overdrive with a battle fleet that could wipe us out before we knew what happened. We wouldn't know which to expect, or when!'

Tommy's face was startled.

'It's all been thrashed out over and over, in theory,' said the skipper. 'Nobody's ever been able to find a sound answer, even on paper. But you know, in all their theorizing, no one considered the crazy, rank impossibility of a deep-space contact, with neither side knowing the other's home world! But we've got to find an answer in fact! What are we going to do about them? Maybe these creatures will be aesthetic marvels, nice and friendly and polite – and, underneath, with the sneaking brutal ferocity of a Japanese. Or maybe they'll be crude and gruff as a Swedish farmer – and just as decent underneath. Maybe they're something in between. But am I going to risk the possible future of the human race on a guess that it's safe to trust them? God knows it would be worthwhile to make friends with a new civilization! It would be bound to stimulate our own, and maybe we'd gain enormously. But I can't take chances. The one thing I won't risk is having them know how to find Earth! Either I know they can't follow me, or I don't go home! And they'll probably feel the same way!'

He pressed the sleeve-communicator button again.

'Navigation officers, attention! Every star map on this ship is to be prepared for instant destruction. This includes photographs and diagrams from which our course or starting point could be deduced. I want all astronomical data gathered and arranged to be destroyed in a split second, on order. Make it fast and report when ready!'

He released the button. He looked suddenly old. The first contact of humanity with an alien race was a situation which had been foreseen in many fashions, but never one quite so hopeless of solution as this. A solitary Earth-ship and a solitary alien, meeting in a nebula which must be remote from the home planet of each. They might wish peace, but the line of conduct which best prepared a treacherous attack was just the seeming of friendliness. Failure to be suspicious might doom the human race – and a peaceful exchange of the fruits of civilization would be the greatest benefit imaginable. Any mistake would be irreparable, but a failure to be on guard would be fatal.

The captain's room was very, very quiet. The bow-quartering visiplate was filled with the image of a very small section of the nebula. A very small section indeed. It was all diffused, featureless, luminous mist. But suddenly Tommy Dort pointed.

'There, sir!'

There was a small shape in the mist. It was far away. It was a black shape, not polished to mirror-reflection like the hull of the *Llanvabon*. It was bulbous – roughly pear-shaped. There was much thin luminosity between, and no details could be observed, but it was surely no natural object. Then Tommy looked at the distance indicator and said quietly:

'It's headed for us at very high acceleration, sir. The odds are that they're thinking the same thing, sir, that neither of us will dare let the other go home. Do you think they'll try a contact with us, or let loose with their weapons as soon as they're in range?'

The *Llanvabon* was no longer in a crevasse of emptiness in the nebula's thin substance. She swam in luminescence. There were no stars save the two fierce glows in the nebula's heart. There was nothing but an all-enveloping light, curiously like one's imagining of underwater in the tropics of Earth.

The alien ship had made one sign of less than lethal intention. As it drew near the *Llanvabon*, it decelerated. The *Llanvabon* itself had advanced for a meeting and then come to a dead stop. Its movement had been a recognition of the nearness of the other ship. Its pausing was both a friendly sign and a precaution against attack. Relatively still, it could swivel on its own axis to present the least target to a slashing assault, and it would have a longer firing-time than if the two ships flashed past each other at their combined speeds.

The moment of actual approach, however, was tenseness itself. The *Llanvabon*'s needle-pointed bow aimed unwaveringly at the alien bulk. A relay to the captain's room put a key under his hand which would fire the blasters with maximum power. Tommy Dort watched, his brow wrinkled. The aliens must be of a high degree of civilization if they had spaceships, and civilization does not develop without the development of foresight. These aliens must recognize all the implications of this first contact of two civilized races as fully as did the humans on the *Llanvabon*.

The possibility of an enormous spurt in the development of both, by peaceful contact and exchange of their separate technologies, would probably appeal to them as to man. But when dissimilar human cultures are in contact, one must usually be subordinate or there is war. But subordination between races arising on separate planets could not be peacefully arranged. Men, at least, would never consent to subordination, nor was it likely that any highly developed race would agree. The benefits to be derived from commerce could never make up for a condition of inferiority. Some races – men, perhaps – would prefer commerce to conquest. Perhaps – perhaps! – these aliens would also. But some types even of human beings would have craved red war. If the alien ship now approaching the *Llanvabon* returned to its home base with news of humanity's existence and of ships like the *Llanvabon*, it would give its race the choice of trade or battle. They might want trade, or they might want war. But it takes two to make trade, and only one to make war. They could not be sure of men's peacefulness, nor could men be sure of theirs. The only safety for either civilization would lie in the destruction of one or both of the two ships here and now.

But even victory would not be really enough. Men would need to know where this alien race was to be found, for avoidance if not for battle. They would need to know its weapons, and its resources, and if it could be a menace and how it could be eliminated in case of need. The aliens would feel the same necessities concerning humanity.

So the skipper of the *Llanvabon* did not press the key which might possibly have blasted the other ship to nothingness. He dared not. But he dared not not fire either. Sweat came out on his face.

A speaker muttered. Someone from the range room.

'The other ship's stopped, sir. Quite stationary. Blasters are centered on it, sir.'

It was an urging to fire. But the skipper shook his head, to himself. The alien ship was no more than twenty miles away. It was dead-black. Every bit of its exterior was an abysmal, nonreflecting sable. No details could be seen except by minor variations in its outline against the misty nebula.

'It's stopped dead, sir,' said another voice. 'They've sent a modulated short wave at us, sir. Frequency modulated. Apparently a signal. Not enough power to do any harm.'

The skipper said through tight-locked teeth:

'They're doing something now. There's movement on the outside of their hull. Watch what comes out. Put the auxiliary blasters on it.'

Something small and round came smoothly out of the oval outline of the black ship. The bulbous hulk moved.

'Moving away, sir,' said the speaker. 'The object they let out is stationary in the place they've left.'

Another voice cut in:

'More frequency modulated stuff, sir. Unintelligible.'

Tommy Dort's eyes brightened. The skipper watched the visiplate, with sweat-droplets on his forehead.

'Rather pretty, sir,' said Tommy, meditatively. 'If they sent anything toward us, it might seem a projectile or a bomb. So they came close, let out a lifeboat, and went away again. They figure we can send a boat or a man to make contact without risking our ship. They must think pretty much as we do.'

The skipper said, without moving his eyes from the plate:

'Mr Dort, would you care to go out and look the thing over? I can't order you, but I need all my operating crew for emergencies. The observation staff—'

'Is expendable. Very well, sir,' said Tommy briskly. 'I won't take a lifeboat, sir. Just a suit with a drive in it. It's smaller and the arms and legs will look unsuitable for a bomb. I think I should carry a scanner, sir.'

The alien ship continued to retreat. Forty, eighty, four hundred miles. It came to a stop and hung there, waiting. Climbing into his atomic-driven spacesuit just within the *Llanvabon*'s air lock, Tommy heard the reports as they went over the speakers throughout the ship. That the other ship had stopped its retreat at four hundred miles was encouraging. It might not have weapons effective at a greater distance than that, and so felt safe. But just as the thought formed itself in his mind, the alien retreated precipitately still farther. Which, as Tommy reflected as he emerged from the lock, might be because the aliens had realized they were giving themselves away, or might be because they wanted to give the impression that they had done so.

He swooped away from the silvery-mirror *Llanvabon*, through a brightly glowing emptiness which was past any previous experience of the human race. Behind him, the *Llanvabon* swung about and darted away. The skipper's voice came in Tommy's helmet phones.

'We're pulling back, too, Mr Dort. There is a bare possibility that they've some explosive atomic reaction they can't use from their own ship, but which might be destructive even as far as this. We'll draw back. Keep your scanner on the object.'

The reasoning was sound, if not very comforting. An explosive which would destroy anything within twenty miles was theoretically possible, but humans didn't have it yet. It was decidedly safest for the *Llanvabon* to draw back.

But Tommy Dort felt very lonely. He sped through emptiness toward the tiny black speck which hung in incredible brightness. The *Llanvabon* vanished. Its polished hull would merge with the glowing mist at a relatively short distance, anyhow. The alien ship was not visible to the naked eye, either. Tommy swam in nothingness, four thousand light-years from home, toward a tiny black spot which was the only solid object to be seen in all of space.

It was a slightly distorted sphere, not much over six feet in diameter. It bounced away when Tommy landed on it, feet-first. There were small tentacles, or horns, which projected in every direction. They looked rather like the detonating horns of a submarine mine, but there was a glint of crystal at the tip-end of each.

'I'm here,' said Tommy into his helmet phone.

He caught hold of a horn and drew himself to the object. It was all metal, dead-black. He could feel no texture through his space gloves, of course, but he went over and over it, trying to discover its purpose.

'Deadlock, sir,' he said presently. 'Nothing to report that the scanner hasn't shown you.'

Then, through his suit, he felt vibrations. They translated themselves as clankings. A section of the rounded hull of the object opened out. Two sections. He worked his way around to look in and see the first nonhuman civilized beings that any man had ever looked upon.

But what he saw was simply a flat plate on which dim-red glows crawled here and there in seeming aimlessness. His helmet phones emitted a startled exclamation. The skipper's voice:

'Very good, Mr Dort. Fix your scanner to look into that plate. They dumped out a robot with an infra-red visiplate for communication. Not risking any personnel. Whatever we might do would damage only machinery. Maybe they expect us to bring it on board – and it may have a bomb charge that can be detonated when they're ready to start for home. I'll send a plate to face one of its scanners. You return to the ship.'

'Yes, sir,' said Tommy. 'But which way is the ship, sir?'

There were no stars. The nebula obscured them with its light. The only thing visible from the robot was the double star at the nebula's center. Tommy was no longer oriented. He had but one reference point.

'Head straight away from the double star,' came the order in his helmet phone. 'We'll pick you up.'

He passed another lonely figure, a little later, headed for the alien sphere with a vision plate to set up. The two spaceships, each knowing that it dared not risk its own race by the slightest lack of caution, would communicate with each other through this small round robot. Their separate vision systems would enable them to exchange all the information they dared give, while they debated the most practical way of making sure that their own civilization would not be endangered by this first contact with another. The truly most practical method would be the destruction of the other ship in a swift and deadly attack – in self-defense.

The *Llanvabon*, thereafter, was a ship in which there were two separate enterprises on hand at the same time. She had come out from Earth to make close-range observations on the smaller component of the double star at the nebula's center. The nebula itself was the result of the most titanic explosion of which men have any knowledge. The explosion took place some time in the year 2946 B.C., before the first of the seven cities of long-dead Ilium was even thought of. The light of that explosion reached Earth in the year 1054 A.D., and was duly recorded in ecclesiastical annals and somewhat more reliably by Chinese court astronomers. It was bright enough to be seen in daylight for twenty-three successive days. Its light – and it was four thousand light-years away – was brighter than that of Venus.

From these facts, astronomers could calculate nine hundred years later the violence of the detonation. Matter blown away from the center of the explosion would have traveled outward at the rate of two million three hundred thousand miles an hour; more than thirty-eight thousand miles a minute; something over six hundred thirty-eight miles per second. When twentieth-century telescopes were turned upon the scene of this vast explosion, only a double star remained – and the nebula. The brighter star of the doublet was almost unique in having so high a surface temperature that it showed no spectrum lines at all. It had a continuous spectrum. Sol's surface temperature is about 7,000° Absolute. That of the hot white star is 500,000 degrees. It has nearly the mass of the sun, but only one fifth its diameter, so that its density is one hundred seventy-three times that of water, sixteen times that of lead, and eight times that of iridium – the heaviest substance known on Earth. But even this density is not that of a dwarf white star like the companion of Sirius. The white star in the Crab Nebula is an incomplete dwarf; it is a star still in the act of collapsing. Examination – including the survey of a four-thousand-year column of its light – was worthwhile. The *Llanvabon* had come to make that examination. But the finding of an alien spaceship upon a similar errand had implications which overshadowed the original purpose of the expedition.

A tiny bulbous robot floated in the tenuous nebular gas. The normal operating crew of the *Llanvabon* stood at their posts with a sharp alertness which was productive of tense nerves. The observation staff divided itself, and a part went half-heartedly about the making of the observations for which the *Llanvabon* had come. The other half applied itself to the problem the spaceship offered.

It represented a culture which was up to space travel on an interstellar scale. The explosion of a mere five thousand years since must have blasted every trace of life out of existence in the area now filled by the nebula. So the aliens of the black spaceship came from another solar system. Their trip must have been, like that of the Earth ship, for purely scientific purposes. There was nothing to be extracted from the nebula.

They were, then, at least near the level of human civilization, which meant that they had or could develop arts and articles of commerce which men would want to trade for, in friendship. But they would necessarily realize that the existence and civilization of humanity was a potential menace to their own race. The two races could be friends, but also they could be deadly enemies. Each, even if unwillingly, was a monstrous menace to the other. And the only safe thing to do with a menace is to destroy it.

In the Crab Nebula the problem was acute and immediate. The future relationship of the two races would be settled here and now. If a process for friendship could be established, one race, otherwise doomed, would survive and both would benefit immensely. But that process had to be established, and confidence built up, without the most minute risk of danger from treachery. Confidence would need to be established upon a foundation of necessarily complete distrust. Neither dared return to its own base if the other could do harm to its race. Neither dared risk any of the necessities to trust. The only safe thing for either to do was destroy the other or be destroyed.

But even for war, more was needed than mere destruction of the other. With interstellar traffic, the aliens must have atomic power and some form of overdrive for travel above the speed of light. With radio location and visiplates and short-wave communication, they had, of course, many other devices.

What weapons did they have? How widely extended was their culture? What were their resources? Could there be a development of trade and friendship, or were the two races so unlike that only war could exist between them? If peace was possible, how could it be begun?

The men on the *Llanvabon* needed facts – and so did the crew of the other ship. They must take back every morsel of information they could. The most important information of all would be of the location of the other civilization, just in case of war. That one bit of information might be the decisive factor in an interstellar war. But other facts would be enormously valuable.

The tragic thing was that there could be no possible information which could lead to peace. Neither ship could stake its own race's existence upon any conviction of the good will or the honor of the other.

So there was a strange truce between the two ships. The alien went about its work of making observations, as did the *Llanvabon*. The tiny robot floated in bright emptiness. A scanner from the *Llanvabon* was focussed upon a vision plate from the alien. A scanner from the alien regarded a vision plate from the *Llanvabon*. Communication began.

It progressed rapidly. Tommy Dort was one of those who made the first progress report. His special task on the expedition was over. He had now been assigned to work on the problem of communication with the alien entities. He went with the ship's solitary psychologist to the captain's room to convey the news of success. The captain's room, as usual, was a place of silence and dull-red indicator lights and the great bright visiplates on every wall and on the ceiling.

'We've established fairly satisfactory communication, sir,' said the psychologist. He looked tired. His work on the trip was supposed to be that of measuring personal factors of error in the observation staff, for the reduction of all observations to the nearest possible decimal to the absolute. He had been pressed into service for which he was not especially fitted, and it told upon him. 'That is, we can say almost anything we wish to them, and can understand what they say in return. But of course we don't know how much of what they say is the truth.'

The skipper's eyes turned to Tommy Dort.

'We've hooked up some machinery,' said Tommy, 'that amounts to a mechanical translator. We have vision plates, of course, and then short-wave beams direct. They use frequency-modulation plus what is probably variations in wave forms – like our vowel and consonant sounds in speech. We've never had any use for anything like that before, so our coils won't handle it, but we've developed a sort of code which isn't the language of either set of us. They shoot over short-wave stuff with frequency-modulation, and we record it as sound. When we shoot it back, it's reconverted into frequency-modulation.'

The skipper said, frowning:

'Why wave-form changes in short waves? How do you know?'

'We showed them our recorder in the vision plates, and they showed us theirs. They record the frequency-modulation direct. I think,' said Tommy carefully, 'they don't use sound at all, even in speech. They've set up a communications room, and we've watched them in the act of communicating with us. They made no perceptible movement of anything that corresponds to a speech organ. Instead of a microphone, they simply stand near something that would work as a pick-up antenna. My guess, sir, is that they use microwaves for what you might call person-to-person conversation. I think they make short-wave trains as we make sounds.'

The skipper stared at him:

'That means they have telepathy?'

'M-m-m. Yes, sir,' said Tommy. 'Also it means that we have telepathy too, as far as they are concerned. They're probably deaf. They've certainly no idea of using sound waves in air for communication. They simply don't use noises for any purpose.'

The skipper stored the information away.

'What else?'

'Well, sir,' said Tommy doubtfully, 'I think we're all set. We agreed on arbitrary symbols for objects, sir, by way of the visiplates, and worked out relationships and verbs and so on with diagrams and pictures. We've a couple of thousand words that have mutual meanings. We set up an analyzer to sort out their short-wave groups, which we feed into a decoding machine. And then the coding end of the machine picks out recordings to make the wave groups we want to send back. When you're ready to talk to the skipper of the other ship, sir, I think we're ready.'

'Hm-m-m. What's your impression of their psychology?' The skipper asked the question of the psychologist.

'I don't know, sir,' said the psychologist harassedly. 'They seem to be completely direct. But they haven't let slip even a hint of the tenseness we know exists. They act as if they were simply setting up a means of communication for friendly conversation. But there is ... well ... an overtone—'

The psychologist was a good man at psychological mensuration, which is a good and useful field. But he was not equipped to analyze a completely alien thought-pattern.

'If I may say so, sir—' said Tommy uncomfortably.

'What?'

'They're oxygen breathers,' said Tommy, 'and they're not too dissimilar to us in other ways. It seems to me, sir, that parallel evolution has been at work. Perhaps intelligence evolves in parallel lines, just as ... well ... basic bodily functions. I mean,' he added conscientiously, 'any living being of any sort must ingest, metabolize, and excrete. Perhaps any intelligent brain must perceive, apperceive, and find a personal reaction. I'm sure I've detected irony. That implies humor, too. In short, sir, I think they could be likable.'

The skipper heaved himself to his feet.

'H-m-m,' he said profoundly, 'we'll see what they have to say.'

He walked to the communications room. The scanner for the vision plate in the robot was in readiness. The skipper walked in front of it. Tommy Dort sat down at the coding machine and tapped at the keys. Highly improbable noises came from it, went into a microphone, and governed the frequency-modulation of a signal sent through space to the other spaceship. Almost instantly the vision screen which with one relay – in the robot – showed the interior of the other ship lighted up. An alien came before the scanner and seemed to look inquisitively out of the plate. He was extraordinarily manlike, but he was not human. The impression he gave was of extreme baldness and a somehow humorous frankness.

'I'd like to say,' said the skipper heavily, 'the appropriate things about this first contact of two dissimilar civilized races, and of my hopes that a friendly intercourse between the two peoples will result.'

Tommy Dort hesitated. Then he shrugged and tapped expertly upon the coder. More improbable noises.

The alien skipper seemed to receive the message. He made a gesture which was wryly assenting. The decoder on the *Llanvabon* hummed to itself and word-cards dropped into the message frame. Tommy said dispassionately:

'He says, sir, "That is all very well, but is there any way for us to let each other go home alive? I would be happy to hear of such a way if you can contrive it. At the moment it seems to me that one of us must be killed."'

The atmosphere was of confusion. There were too many questions to be answered all at once. Nobody could answer any of them. And all of them had to be answered.

The *Llanvabon* could start for home. The alien ship might or might not be able to multiply the speed of light by one more unit than the Earth vessel. If it could, the *Llanvabon* would get close enough to Earth to reveal its destination – and then have to fight. It might or might not win. Even if it did win, the aliens might have a communication system by which the *Llanvabon*'s destination might have been reported to the aliens' home planet before battle was joined. But the *Llanvabon* might lose in such a fight. If she were to be destroyed, it would be better to be destroyed here, without giving any clue to where human beings might be found by a forewarned, forearmed alien battle fleet.

The black ship was in exactly the same predicament. It, too, could start for home. But the *Llanvabon* might be faster, and an overdrive field can be trailed, if you set to work on it soon enough. The aliens, also, would not know whether the *Llanvabon* could report to its home base without returning. If the alien were to be destroyed, it also would prefer to fight it out here, so that it could not lead a probable enemy to its own civilization.

Neither ship, then, could think of flight. The course of the *Llanvabon* into the nebula might be known to the black ship, but it had been the end of a logarithmic curve, and the aliens could not know its properties. They could not tell from that from what direction the Earth ship had started. As of the moment, then, the two ships were even. But the question was and remained, 'What now?'

There was no specific answer. The aliens traded information for information – and did not always realize what information they gave. The humans traded information for information – and Tommy Dort sweated blood in his anxiety not to give any clue to the whereabouts of Earth.

The aliens saw by infrared light, and the vision plates and scanners in the robot communication-exchange had to adapt their respective images up and down an optical octave each, for them to have any meaning at all. It did not occur to the aliens that their eyesight told that their sun was a red dwarf, yielding light of greatest energy just below the part of the spectrum visible to human-eyes. But after that fact was realized on the *Llanvabon*, it was realized that the aliens, also, should be able to deduce the Sun's spectral type by the light to which men's eyes were best adapted.

There was a gadget for the recording of short-wave trains which was as casually in use among the aliens as a sound-recorder is among men. The humans wanted that, badly. And the aliens were fascinated by the mystery of sound. They were able to perceive noise, of course, just as a man's palm will perceive infrared light by the sensation of heat it produces, but they could no more differentiate pitch or tone-quality than a man is able to distinguish between two frequencies of heat-radiation even half an octave apart. To them, the human science of sound was a remarkable discovery. They would find uses for noises which humans had never imagined – if they lived.

But that was another question. Neither ship could leave without first destroying the other. But while the flood of information was in passage, neither ship could afford to destroy the other. There was the matter of the outer coloring of the two ships. The *Llanvabon* was mirror-bright exteriorly. The alien ship was dead-black by visible light. It absorbed heat to perfection, and should radiate it away again as readily. But it did not. The black coating was not a 'black body' color or lack of color. It was a perfect reflector of certain infrared wave lengths while simultaneously it fluoresced in just those wave bands. In practice, it absorbed the higher frequencies of heat, converted them to lower frequencies it did not radiate – and stayed at the desired temperature even in empty space.

Tommy Dort labored over his task of communications. He found the alien thought-processes not so alien that he could not follow them. The discussion of technics reached the matter of interstellar navigation. A star map was needed to illustrate the process. It would have been logical to use a star map from the chart room – but from a star map one could guess the point from which the map was projected. Tommy had a map made specially, with imaginary but convincing star images upon it. He translated directions for its use by the coder and decoder. In return, the aliens presented a star map of their own before the visiplate. Copied instantly by photograph, the Nav officers labored over it, trying to figure out from what spot in the galaxy the stars and Milky Way would show at such an angle. It baffled them.

It was Tommy who realized finally that the aliens had made a special star map for their demonstration too, and that it was a mirror-image of the faked map Tommy had shown them previously.

Tommy could grin at that. He began to like these aliens. They were not humans, but they had a very human sense of the ridiculous. In course of time Tommy essayed a mild joke. It had to be translated into code numerals, these into quite cryptic groups of short-wave, frequency-modulated impulses, and these went to the other ship and into heaven knew what to become intelligible. A joke which went through such formalities would not seem likely to be funny. But the alien did see the point.

There was one of the aliens to whom communication became as normal a function as Tommy's own code-handlings. The two of them developed a quite insane friendship, conversing by coder, decoder, and short-wave trains. When technicalities in the official messages grew too involved, that alien sometimes threw in strictly nontechnical interpolations akin to slang. Often, they cleared up the confusion. Tommy, for no reason whatever, had filed a code-name of 'Buck' which the decoder picked out regularly when this particular one signed his own symbol to a message.

In the third week of communication, the decoder suddenly presented Tommy with a message in the message frame:

You are a good guy. It is too bad we have to kill each other. – BUCK.

Tommy had been thinking much the same thing. He tapped off the rueful reply:

We can't see any way out of it. Can you?

There was a pause, and the message frame filled up again:

If we could believe each other, yes. Our skipper would like it. But we can't believe you, and you can't believe us. We'd trail you home if we got a chance, and you'd trail us. But we feel sorry about it. – BUCK.

Tommy Dort took the messages to the skipper.

'Look here, sir!' he said urgently. 'These people are almost human, and they're likable cusses.'

The skipper was busy about his important task of thinking

275

of things to worry about, and worrying about them. He said tiredly:

'They're oxygen breathers. Their air is twenty-eight percent oxygen instead of twenty, but they could do very well on Earth. It would be a highly desirable conquest for them. And we still don't know what weapons they've got or what they can develop. Would you tell them how to find Earth?'

'N-no,' said Tommy, unhappily.

'They probably feel the same way,' said the skipper dryly. 'And if we did manage to make a friendly contact, how long would it stay friendly? If their weapons were inferior to ours, they'd feel that for their own safety they had to improve them. And we, knowing they were planning to revolt, would crush them while we could – for our own safety! If it happened to be the other way about, they'd have to smash us before we could catch up to them.'

Tommy was silent, but he moved restlessly.

'If we smash this black ship and get home,' said the skipper, 'Earth Government will be annoyed if we don't tell them where it came from. But what can we do? We'll be lucky enough to get back alive with our warning. It isn't possible to get out of those creatures any more information than we give them, and we surely won't give them our address! We've run into them by accident. Maybe – if we smash this ship – there won't be another contact for thousands of years. And it's a pity, because trade could mean so much! But it takes two to make a peace, and we can't risk trusting them. The only answer is to kill them if we can, and if we can't, to make sure that when they kill us they'll find out nothing that will lead them to Earth. I don't like it,' added the skipper tiredly, 'but there simply isn't anything else to do!'

On the *Llanvabon*, the technicians worked frantically in two divisions. One prepared for victory, and the other for defeat. The ones working for victory could do little. The main blasters were the only weapons with any promise. Their mountings were cautiously altered so that they were no longer fixed nearly dead ahead, with only a 5° traverse. Electronic controls which followed a radio-locator master-finder would keep them trained with absolute precision upon a given target regardless of its maneuverings. More, a hitherto unsung genius in the engine room devised a capacity-storage system by which the normal full output of the ship's engines could be momentarily accumulated and released in surges of stored power far above normal. In theory, the range of the blasters should be multiplied and their destructive power considerably stepped up. But there was not much more that could be done.

The defeat crew had more leeway. Star charts, navigational instruments carrying telltale notations, the photographic record Tommy Dort had made on the six-months' journey from Earth, and every other memorandum offering clues to Earth's position, were prepared for destruction. They were put in sealed files, and if any one of them was opened by one who did not know the exact, complicated process, the contents of all the files would flash into ashes and the ash be churned past any hope of restoration. Of course, if the *Llanvabon* should be victorious, a carefully not-indicated method of re-opening them in safety would remain.

There were atomic bombs placed all over the hull of the ship. If its human crew should be killed without complete destruction of the ship, the atomic-power bombs should detonate if the *Llanvabon* was brought alongside the alien vessel. There were no ready-made atomic bombs on board, but there were small spare atomic-power units on board. It was not hard to trick them so that when they were turned on, instead of yielding a smooth flow of power they would explode. And four men of the Earth ship's crew remained always in spacesuits with closed helmets, to fight the ship should it be punctured in many compartments by an unwarned attack.

Such an attack, however, would not be treacherous. The alien skipper had spoken frankly. His manner was that of one who wryly admits the uselessness of lies. The skipper and the *Llanvabon*, in turn, heavily admitted the virtue of frankness. Each insisted – perhaps truthfully – that he wished for friendship between the two races. But neither could trust the other not to make every conceivable effort to find out the one thing he needed most desperately to conceal – the location of his home planet. And neither dared believe that the other was unable to trail him and find out. Because each felt it his own duty to accomplish that unbearable – to the other – act, neither could risk the possible existence of his race by trusting the other. They must fight because they could not do anything else.

They could raise the stakes of the battle by an exchange of information beforehand. But there was a limit to the stake either would put up. No information on weapons, population, or resources would be given by either. Not even the distance of their home bases from the Crab Nebula would be told. They exchanged information, to be sure, but they knew a battle to the death must follow, and each strove to represent his own civilization as powerful enough to give pause to the other's ideas of possible conquest – and thereby increased its appearance of menace to the other, and made battle more unavoidable.

It was curious how completely such alien brains could mesh, however. Tommy Dort, sweating over the coding and decoding machines, found a personal equation emerging from the at first stilted arrays of word-cards which arranged themselves. He had seen the aliens only in the vision screen, and then only in light at least one octave removed from the light they saw by. They, in turn, saw him very strangely, by transposed illumination from what to them would be the far ultra-violet. But their brains worked alike. Amazingly alike. Tommy Dort felt an actual sympathy and even something close to friendship for the gill-breathing, bald, and dryly ironic creatures of the black space vessel.

Because of that mental kinship he set up – though hopelessly – a sort of table of the aspects of the problem before them. He did not believe that the aliens had any instinctive desire to destroy man. In fact, the study of communications from the aliens had produced on the *Llanvabon* a feeling of tolerance not unlike that between enemy soldiers during a truce on Earth. The men felt no enmity, and probably neither did the aliens. But they had to kill or be killed for strictly logical reasons.

Tommy's table was specific. He made a list of objectives the men must try to achieve, in the order of their importance. The first was the carrying back of news of the existence of the alien culture. The second was the location of that alien culture in the galaxy. The third was the carrying back of as much information as possible about that culture. The third was being worked on, but the second was probably impossible. The first – and all – would depend on the result of the fight which must take place.

The aliens' objectives would be exactly similar, so that the men must prevent, first, news of the existence of Earth's culture from being taken back by the aliens; second, alien discovery of the location of Earth; and third, the acquiring by the aliens of information which would help them or encourage them to attack humanity. And again the third was in train, and the second was probably taken care of, and the first must await the battle.

There was no possible way to avoid the grim necessity of the destruction of the black ship. The aliens would see no solution to their problems but the destruction of the *Llanvabon*. But Tommy Dort, regarding his tabulation ruefully, realized that even complete victory would not be a perfect solution. The ideal would be for the *Llanvabon* to take back the alien ship for study. Nothing less would be a complete attainment of the third objective. But Tommy realized that he hated the idea of so complete a victory, even if it could be accomplished. He would hate the idea of killing even non-human creatures who understood a human joke. And beyond that, he would hate the idea of Earth fitting out a fleet of fighting ships to destroy an alien culture because its existence was dangerous. The pure accident of this encounter, between peoples who could like each other, had created a situation which could only result in wholesale destruction.

Tommy Dort soured on his own brain which could find no answer which would work. But there had to be an answer! The gamble was too big! It was too absurd that two spaceships should fight – neither one primarily designed for fighting – so that the survivor could carry back news which would set one race to frenzied preparation for war against the unwarned other.

If both races could be warned, though, and each knew that the other did not want to fight, and if they could communicate with each other but not locate each other until some grounds for mutual trust could be reached—

It was impossible. It was chimerical. It was a daydream. It was nonsense. But it was such luring nonsense that Tommy Dort ruefully put it into the coder to his gill-breathing friend Buck, then some hundred thousand miles off in the misty brightness of the nebula.

'Sure,' said Buck, in the decoder's word-cards flicking into place in the message frame. 'That is a good dream. But I like you and still won't believe you. If I said that first, you would like me but not believe me, either. I tell you the truth more than you believe, and maybe you tell me the truth more than I believe. But there is no way to know. I am sorry.'

Tommy Dort stared gloomily at the message. He felt a very horrible sense of responsibility. Everyone did, on the *Llanvabon*. If they failed in this encounter, the human race would run a very good chance of being exterminated in time to come. If they succeeded, the race of the aliens would be the one to face destruction, most likely. Millions or billions of lives hung upon the actions of a few men.

Then Tommy Dort saw the answer.

It would be amazingly simple, if it worked. At worst it might give a partial victory to humanity and the *Llanvabon*. He sat quite still, not daring to move lest he break the chain of thought that followed the first tenuous idea. He went over and over it, excitedly finding objections here and meeting them, and overcoming impossibilities there. It was the answer! He felt sure of it.

He felt almost dizzy with relief when he found his way to the captain's room and asked leave to speak.

It is the function of a skipper, among others, to find things to worry about. But the *Llanvabon*'s skipper did not have to look. In the three weeks and four days since the first contact with the alien black ship, the skipper's face had grown lined and old. He had not only the *Llanvabon* to worry about. He had all of humanity.

'Sir,' said Tommy Dort, his mouth rather dry because of his enormous earnestness, 'may I offer a method of attack on the black ship? I'll undertake it myself, sir, and if it doesn't work our ship won't be weakened.'

The skipper looked at him unseeingly.

'The tactics are all worked out, Mr Dort,' he said heavily. 'They're being cut on tape now, for the ship's handling. It's a terrible gamble, but it has to be done.'

'I think,' said Tommy carefully, 'I've worked out a way to take the gamble out. Suppose, sir, we send a message to the other ship, offering—'

His voice went on in the utterly quiet captain's room, with the visiplates showing only a vast mistiness outside and the two fiercely burning stars in the nebula's heart.

The skipper himself went through the air lock with Tommy. For one reason, the action Tommy had suggested would need his authority behind it. For another, the skipper had worried more intensely than anybody else on the *Llanvabon*, and he was tired of it. If he went with Tommy. he would do the thing himself, and if he failed he would be the first one killed – and the tape for the Earth ship's maneuvering was already fed into the control board and correlated with the master-timer. If Tommy and the skipper were killed, a single control pushed home would throw the *Llanvabon* into the most furious possible all-out attack, which would end in the complete destruction of one ship or the other – or both. So the skipper was not deserting his post.

The outer air lock door swung wide. It opened upon that shining emptiness which was the nebula. Twenty miles away, the little round robot hung in space, drifting in an incredible orbit about the twin central suns, and floating ever nearer and nearer. It would never reach either of them, of course. The white star alone was so much hotter than Earth's sun that its heat-effect would produce Earth's temperature on an object five times as far from it as Neptune is from Sol. Even removed to the distance of Pluto, the little robot would be raised to cherry-red heat by the blazing white dwarf. And it could not possibly approach to the ninety-odd million miles which is the Earth's distance from the sun. So near, its metal would melt and boil away as vapor. But, half a light-year out, the bulbous object bobbed in emptiness.

The two spacesuited figures soared away from the *Llanvabon*. The small atomic drives which made them minute spaceships on their own had been subtly altered, but the change did not interfere with their functioning. They headed for the communication robot. The skipper, out in space, said gruffly:

'Mr Dort, all my life I have longed for adventure. This is the first time I could ever justify it to myself.'

His voice came through Tommy's space-phone receivers. Tommy wet his lips and said:

'It doesn't seem like adventure to me, sir. I want terribly for the plan to go through. I thought adventure was when you didn't care.'

'Oh, no,' said the skipper. 'Adventure is when you toss your life on the scales of chance and wait for the pointer to stop.'

They reached the round object. They clung to its short, scanner-tipped horns.

'Intelligent, those creatures,' said the skipper heavily. 'They must want desperately to see more of our ship than the communication room, to agree to this exchange of visits before the fight.'

'Yes, sir,' said Tommy. But privately, he suspected that Buck – his gill-breathing friend – would like to see him in the flesh before one or both of them died. And it seemed to him that between the two ships had grown up an odd tradition of courtesy, like that between two ancient knights before a tourney, when they admired each other wholeheartedly before hacking at each other with all the contents of their respective armories.

They waited.

Then, out of the mist, came two other figures. The alien spacesuits were also power-driven. The aliens themselves were shorter than men, and their helmet openings were coated with a filtering material to cut off visible and ultraviolet rays which to them would be lethal. It was not possible to see more than the outline of the heads within.

Tommy's helmet phone said, from the communication room on the *Llanvabon:*

'They say that their ship is waiting for you, sir. The air lock door will be open.'

The skipper's voice said heavily:

'Mr Dort, have you seen their spacesuits before? If so, are you sure they're not carrying anything extra, such as bombs?'

'Yes, sir,' said Tommy. 'We've showed each other our space equipment. They've nothing but regular stuff in view, sir.'

The skipper made a gesture to the two aliens. He and Tommy Dort plunged on for the black vessel. They could not make out the ship very clearly with the naked eye, but directions for change of course came from the communication room.

The black ship loomed up. It was huge, as long as the *Llanvabon* and vastly thicker. The air lock did stand open. The two spacesuited men moved in and anchored themselves with magnetic-soled boots. The outer door closed. There was a rush of air and simultaneously the sharp quick tug of artificial gravity. Then the inner door opened.

All was darkness. Tommy switched on his helmet light at the same instant as the skipper. Since the aliens saw by infrared, a white light would have been intolerable to them. The men's helmet lights were, therefore, of the deep-red tint used to illuminate instrument panels so there will be no dazzling of eyes that must be able to detect the minutest specks of white light on a navigating vision plate. There were aliens waiting to receive them. They blinked at the brightness of the helmet lights. The space-phone receivers said in Tommy's ear:

'They say, sir, their skipper is waiting for you.'

Tommy and the skipper were in a long corridor with a soft flooring underfoot. Their lights showed details of which every one was exotic.

'I think I'll crack my helmet, sir,' said Tommy.

He did. The air was good. By analysis it was thirty percent oxygen instead of twenty for normal air on Earth, but the pressure was less. It felt just right. The artificial gravity, too, was less than that maintained on the *Llanvabon*. The home planet of the aliens would be smaller than Earth, and – by the infrared data – circling close to a nearly dead, dull-red sun. The air had smells in it. They were utterly strange, but not unpleasant.

An arched opening. A ramp with the same soft stuff underfoot. Lights which actually shed a dim, dull-red glow about. The aliens had stepped up some of their illuminating equipment as an act of courtesy. The light might hurt their eyes, but it was a gesture of consideration which made Tommy even more anxious for his plan to go through.

The alien skipper faced them with what seemed to Tommy a gesture of wryly humorous deprecation. The helmet phones said:

'He says, sir, that he greets you with pleasure, but he has been able to think of only one way in which the problem created by the meeting of these two ships can be solved.'

'He means a fight,' said the skipper. 'Tell him I'm here to offer another choice.'

The *Llanvabon*'s skipper and the skipper of the alien ship were face to face, but their communication was weirdly indirect. The aliens used no sound in communication. Their talk, in fact, took place on microwaves and approximated telepathy. But they could not hear, in any ordinary sense of the word, so the skipper's and Tommy's speech approached telepathy, too, as far as they were concerned. When the skipper spoke, his space phone sent his words back to the *Llanvabon*, where the words were fed into the coder and short-wave equivalents sent back to the black ship. The alien skipper's reply went to the *Llanvabon* and through the decoder, and was retransmitted by space phone in words read from the message frame. It was awkward, but it worked.

The short and stocky alien skipper paused. The helmet phones relayed his translated, soundless reply.

'He is anxious to hear, sir.'

The skipper took off his helmet. He put his hands at his belt in a belligerent pose.

'Look here!' he said truculently to the bald, strange creature in the unearthly red glow before him. 'It looks like we have to fight and one batch of us get killed. We're ready to do it if we have to. But if you win, we've got it fixed so you'll never find out where Earth is, and there's a good chance we'll get you anyhow! If we win, we'll be in the same fix. And if we win and go back home, our government will fit out a fleet and start hunting your planet. And if we find it we'll be ready to blast it to hell! If you win, the same thing will happen to us! And it's all foolishness! We've stayed here a month, and we've swapped information, and we don't hate each other. There's no reason for us to fight except for the rest of our respective races!'

The skipper stopped for breath, scowling. Tommy Dort inconspicuously put his own hands on the belt of his spacesuit. He waited, hoping desperately that the trick would work.

'He says, sir,' reported the helmet phones, 'that all you say is true. But that his race has to be protected, just as you feel that yours must be.'

'Naturally,' said the skipper angrily, 'but the sensible thing to do is to figure out how to protect it! Putting its future up as a gamble in a fight is not sensible. Our races have to be warned of each other's existence. That's true. But each should have proof that the other doesn't want to fight, but wants to be friendly. And we shouldn't be able to find each other, but we should be able to communicate with each other to work out grounds for a common trust. If our governments want to be fools, let them! But we should give them the chance to make friends, instead of starting a space war out of mutual funk!'

Briefly, the space phone said:

'He says that the difficulty is that of trusting each other now. With the possible existence of his race at stake, he cannot take any chance, and neither can you, of yielding an advantage.'

'But my race,' boomed the skipper, glaring at the alien captain, 'my race has an advantage now. We came here to your ship in atom-powered spacesuits! Before we left, we altered the drives! We can set off ten pounds of sensitized fuel apiece, right here in this ship, or it can be set off by remote control from our ship! It will be rather remarkable if your fuel store doesn't blow up with us! In other words, if you don't accept my proposal for a commonsense approach to this predicament, Dort and I blow up in an atomic explosion, and your ship will be wrecked if not destroyed – and the *Llanvabon* will be attacking with everything it's got within two seconds after the blast goes off!'

The captain's room of the alien ship was a strange scene, with its dull-red illumination and the strange, bald, gill-breathing aliens watching the skipper and waiting for the inaudible translation of the harangue they could not hear. But a sudden tensity appeared in the air. A sharp, savage feeling of strain. The alien skipper made a gesture. The helmet phones hummed.

'He says, sir, what is your proposal?'

'Swap ships!' roared the skipper. 'Swap ships and go on home! We can fix our instruments so they'll do no trailing, he can do the same with his. We'll each remove our star maps and records. We'll each dismantle our weapons. The air will serve, and we'll take their ship and they'll take ours, and neither one can harm or trail the other, and each will carry home more information than can be taken otherwise! We can agree on this same Crab Nebula as a rendezvous when the double-star has made another circuit, and if our people want to meet then they can do it, and if they are scared they can duck it! That's my proposal! And he'll take it, or Dort and I blow up their ship and the *Llanvabon* blasts what's left!'

He glared about him while he waited for the translation to reach the tense small stocky figures about him. He could tell when it came because the tenseness changed. The figures stirred. They made gestures. One of them made convulsive movements. It lay down on the soft floor and kicked. Others leaned against the walls and shook.

The voice in Tommy Dort's helmet phones had been strictly crisp and professional, before, but now it sounded blankly amazed.

'He says, sir, that it is a good joke. Because the two crew

members he sent to our ship, and that you passed on the way, have their spacesuits stuffed with atomic explosives too, sir, and he intended to make the very same offer and threat! Of course he accepts, sir. Your ship is worth more to him than his own, and his is worth more to you than the *Llanvabon*. It appears, sir, to be a deal.'

Then Tommy Dort realized what the convulsive movements of the aliens were. They were laughter.

It wasn't quite as simple as the skipper had outlined it. The actual working-out of the proposal was complicated. For three days the crews of the two ships were intermingled, the aliens learning the workings of the *Llanvabon*'s engines, and the men learning the controls of the black spaceship. It was a good joke – but it wasn't all a joke. There were men on the black ship, and aliens on the *Llanvabon*, ready at an instant's notice to blow up the vessels in question. And they would have done it in case of need, for which reason the need did not appear. But it was, actually, a better arrangement to have two expeditions return to two civilizations, under the current arrangement, than for either to return alone.

There were differences, though. There was some dispute about the removal of records. In most cases the dispute was settled by the destruction of the records. There was more trouble caused by the *Llanvabon*'s books, and the alien equivalent of a ship's library, containing works which approximated the novels of Earth. But those items were valuable to possible friendship, because they would show the two cultures, each to the other, from the viewpoint of normal citizens and without propaganda.

But nerves were tense during those three days. Aliens unloaded and inspected the foodstuffs intended for the men on the black ship. Men transshipped the foodstuffs the aliens would need to return to their home. There were endless details, from the exchange of lighting equipment to suit the eyesight of the exchanging crews, to a final check-up of apparatus. A joint inspection party of both races verified that all detector devices

287

had been smashed but not removed, so that they could not be used for trailing and had not been smuggled away. And of course, the aliens were anxious not to leave any useful weapon on the black ship, nor the men upon the *Llanvabon*. It was a curious fact that each crew was best qualified to take exactly the measures which made an evasion of the agreement impossible.

There was a final conference before the two ships parted, back in the communication room of the *Llanvabon*.

Tell the little runt,' rumbled the *Llanvabon*'s former skipper, 'that he's got a good ship and he'd better treat her right.'

The message frame flicked word-cards into position.

'I believe,' it said on the alien skipper's behalf, 'that your ship is just as good. I will hope to meet you here when the double star has turned one turn.'

The last man left the *Llanvabon*. It moved away into the misty nebula before they had returned to the black ship. The vision plates in that vessel had been altered for human eyes, and human crewmen watched jealously for any trace of their former ship as their new craft took a crazy, evading course to a remote part of the nebula. It came to a crevasse of nothingness, leading to the stars. It rose swiftly to clear space. There was the instant of breathlessness which the overdrive field produces as it goes on, and then the black ship whipped away into the void at many times the speed of light.

Many days later, the skipper saw Tommy Dort poring over one of the strange objects which were the equivalent of books. It was fascinating to puzzle over. The skipper was pleased with himself. The technicians of the *Llanvabon*'s former crew were finding out desirable things about the ship almost momently. Doubtless the aliens were as pleased with their discoveries in the *Llanvabon*. But the black ship would be enormously worthwhile – and the solution that had been found was by any standard much superior even to combat in which the Earthmen had been overwhelmingly victorious.

'Hm-m-m. Mr Dort,' said the skipper profoundly, 'you've no equipment to make another photographic record on the way back. It was left on the *Llanvabon*. But fortunately, we have your record taken on the way out, and I shall report most favorably on your suggestion and your assistance in carrying it out. I think very well of you, sir.'

'Thank you, sir,' said Tommy Dort.

He waited. The skipper cleared his throat.

'You ... ah ... first realized the close similarity of mental processes between the aliens and ourselves,' he observed. 'What do you think of the prospects of a friendly arrangement if we keep a rendezvous with them at the nebula as agreed?'

'Oh, we'll get along all right, sir,' said Tommy. 'We've got a good start toward friendship. After all, since they see by infrared, the planets they'd want to make use of wouldn't suit us. There's no reason why we shouldn't get along. We're almost alike in psychology.'

'Hm-m-m. Now just what do you mean by that?' demanded the skipper.

'Why, they're just like us, sir!' said Tommy. 'Of course they breathe through gills and they see by heat waves, and their blood has a copper base instead of iron and a few little details like that. But otherwise we're just alike! There were only men in their crew, sir, but they have two sexes as we have, and they have families, and ... er ... their sense of humor – in fact—'

Tommy hesitated.

'Go on, sir,' said the skipper.

'Well – there was the one I called Buck, sir, because he hasn't any name that goes into sound waves,' said Tommy. 'We got along very well. I'd really call him my friend, sir. And we were together for a couple of hours just before the two ships separated and we'd nothing in particular to do. So I became convinced that humans and aliens are bound to be good friends if they have only half a chance. You see, sir, we spent those two hours telling dirty jokes.'

A LOGIC NAMED JOE

It was on the third day of August that Joe come off the assembly-line, and on the fifth Laurine come into town, an' that afternoon I save civilization. That's what I figure, anyhow. Laurine is a blonde that I was crazy about once – and crazy is the word – and Joe is a Logic that I have stored away down in the cellar right now. I had to pay for him because I said I busted him, and sometimes I think about turning him on and sometimes I think about taking an axe to him. Sooner or later I'm gonna do one or the other. I kinda hope it's the axe. I could use a couple million dollars – sure! – an' Joe'd tell me how to get or make 'em. He can do plenty! But so far I been scared to take a chance. After all, I figure I really saved civilization by turnin' him off.

The way Laurine fits in is that she makes cold shivers run up an' down my spine when I think about her. You see, I've got a wife which I acquired after I had parted from Laurine with much romantic despair. She is a reasonable good wife, and I have some kids which are hellcats but I value 'em. If I have sense enough to leave well enough alone, sooner or later I will retire on a pension an' Social Security an' spend the rest of my life fishin' contented an' lyin' about what a great guy I used to be. But there's Joe. I'm worried about Joe.

I'm a maintenance man for the Logics Company. My job is servicing Logics, and I admit modestly that I am pretty good. I was servicing televisions before that guy Carson invented his trick circuit that will select any of 'steenteen million other circuits – in theory there ain't no limit – and before the Logics

Company hooked it into the Tank-and-Integrator set-up they were usin' 'em as business-machine service. They added a vision-screen for speed – an' they found out they'd made Logics. They were surprised an' pleased. They're still findin' out what Logics will do, but everybody's got 'em.

I got Joe, after Laurine nearly got me. You know the Logics set-up. You got a Logic in your house. It looks like a vision-receiver used to, only it's got keys instead of dials and you punch the keys for what you wanna get. It's hooked in to the Tank, which has the Carson Circuit all fixed up with relays. Say you punch 'Station SNAFU' on your Logic. Relays in the Tank take over an' whatever vision-program SNAFU is telecastin' comes on your Logic's screen. Or you punch 'Sally Hancock's Phone' an' the screen blinks an' sputters an' you're hooked up with the Logic in her house an' if somebody answers you got a vision-phone connection. But besides that, if you punch for the weather forecast or who won today's race at Hialeah or who was mistress of the White House durin' Garfield's administration or what is PDQ and R sellin' for today, that comes on the screen too. The relays in the Tank do it. The Tank is a big buildin' full of all the facts in creation an' all the recorded telecasts that ever was made – an' it's hooked in with all the other Tanks all over the country – an' everything you wanna know or see or hear, you punch for it an' you get it. Very convenient. Also it does math for you, an' keeps books, an' acts as consultin' chemist, physicist, astronomer an' tea-leaf reader, with 'Advice to the Lovelorn' thrown in. The only thing it won't do is tell you exactly what your wife meant when she said, 'Oh, you think so, do you?' in that peculiar kinda voice. Logics don't work good on women. Only on things that make sense.

Logics are all right, though. They changed civilization, the highbrows tell us. All on accounta the Carson Circuit. And Joe shoulda been a perfectly normal Logic, keeping some family or other from wearin' out its brains doin' the kids' homework for 'em. But something went wrong in the assembly-line. It was somethin' so small that precision-gauges didn't measure it, but it made Joe a individual. Maybe he didn't know it at first. Or maybe, bein' logical, he figured out that if he was to show he was different from other Logics they'd scrap him. Which woulda been a brilliant idea. But anyhow, he come off the assembly-line, an' he went through the regular tests without anybody screamin' shrilly on findin' out what he was. And he went right on out an' was duly installed in the home of Mr Thaddeus Korlanovitch at 119 East Seventh Street, second floor front. So far, everything was serene.

The installation happened late Saturday night. Sunday mornin' the Korlanovitch kids turned him on an' seen the Kiddie Shows. Around noon their parents peeled 'em away from him an' piled 'em in the car. Then they come back into the house for the lunch they'd forgot an' one of the kids sneaked back an' they found him punchin' keys for the Kiddie Shows of the week before. They dragged him out an' went off. But they left Joe turned on.

That was noon. Nothin' happened until two in the afternoon. It was the calm before the storm. Laurine wasn't in town yet, but she was comin'. I picture Joe sittin' there all by himself, buzzing meditative. Maybe he run Kiddie Shows in the empty apartment for a while. But I think he went kinda remote-control exploring in the Tank. There ain't any fact that can be said to be a fact that ain't on a data-plate in some Tank somewhere – unless it's one the technicians are diggin' out an' puttin' on a data-plate now. Joe had plenty of material to work on. An' he musta started workin' right off the bat.

Joe ain't vicious, you understand. He ain't like one of these ambitious robots you read about that make up their minds the human race is inefficient and has got to be wiped out an' replaced by thinkin' machines. Joe's just got ambition. If you were a machine, you'd wanna work right, wouldn't you? That's Joe. He wants to work right. An' he's a Logic. An' Logics can do a lotta things that ain't been found out yet. So Joe, discoverin' the fact, begun to feel restless. He selects some things us dumb humans ain't thought of yet, an' begins to arrange so Logics will be called on to do 'em.

That's all. That's everything. But, brother, it's enough!

Things are kinda quiet in the Maintenance Department about two in the afternoon. We are playing pinochle. Then one of the guys remembers he has to call up his wife. He goes to one of the bank of Logics in Maintenance and punches the keys for his house. The screen sputters. Then a flash comes on the screen.

'Announcing new and improved Logics service! Your Logic is now equipped to give you not only consultive but directive service. If you want to do something and don't know how to do it – Ask your Logic!'

There's a pause. A kinda expectant pause. Then, as if reluctantly, his connection comes through. His wife answers an' gives him hell for somethin' or other. He takes it an' snaps off.

'Whadda you know?' he says when he comes back. He tells us about the flash. 'We shoulda been warned about that. There's gonna be a lotta complaints. Suppose a fella asks how to get ridda his wife an' the censor circuits block the question?'

Somebody melds a hundred aces an' says:

'Whyn't punch for it an' see what happens?'

It's a gag, o'course. But the guy goes over. He punches keys. In theory, a censor block is gonna come on an' the screen will say severely, 'Public Policy Forbids This Service'. You hafta have censor blocks or the kiddies will be askin' detailed questions about things they're too young to know. And there are other reasons. As you will see.

This fella punches, 'How can I get rid of my wife?' Just for the hell of it. The screen is blank for a half a second. Then comes a flash. 'Service question; is she blonde or brunette?' He hollers to us an' we come look. He punches 'Blonde'. There's another brief pause. Then the screen says, 'Hexymetacrylo-aminoacetine is a constituent of green shoe-polish. Take home a frozen meal including dried-pea soup. Color the soup with green shoe-polish. It will appear to be green-pea soup. Hexy-metacryloaminoacetine is a selective poison which is fatal to blonde females but not to brunettes or males of any coloring. This fact has not been brought out by human experiment but is a product of Logics service. You cannot be convicted of murder. It is improbable that you will be suspected.'

The screen goes blank, and we stare at each other. It's bound to be right. A Logic workin' the Carson Circuit can no more make a mistake than any other kinda computin' machine. I call the Tank in a hurry.

'Hey, you guys!' I yell. 'Somethin's happened! Logics are givin' detailed instructions for wife-murder! Check your censor-circuits – but quick!'

That was close, I think. But little do I know. At that precise instant, over on Monroe Avenue, a drunk starts mournful to punch for somethin' on a Logic. The screen says, 'Announcing new and improved Logics service!... If you want to do something and don't know how to do it – Ask your Logic!' And the drunk says owlish, 'I'll do it!' So he cancels his first punching and fumbles around and says, 'How can I keep my wife from finding out I've been drinking?' And the screen says, prompt, 'Buy a bottle of Franine hair shampoo. It is harmless but contains a detergent which will neutralize ethyl alcohol immediately. Take one teaspoonful for each jigger of hundred-proof you have consumed.'

This guy was plenty plastered – just plastered enough to stagger next-door and obey instructions. An' five minutes later he was cold sober and writing down the information so he couldn't forget it. It was new, and it was big! He got rich offa that memo. He patented 'SOBUH, *The Drink that Makes Happy Homes!*' You can top off any souse with a slug or two of it an' go home sober as a judge. The guy's cussin' income-taxes right now!

You can't kick on stuff like that. But an ambitious young fourteen-year-old wanted to buy some kid stuff and his pop wouldn't fork over. He called up a friend to tell his troubles. And his Logic says, 'If you want to do something and don't know how to do it – Ask your Logic!' So this kid punches, 'How can I make a lotta money, fast?'

His Logic comes through with the simplest, neatest, and most efficient counterfeitin' device yet known to science.

You see, all the data was in the Tank. The Logic – since Joe had closed some relays here an' there in the Tank – simply integrated the facts. That's all. The kid got caught up with three days later, havin' already spent two thousand credits an' havin' plenty more on hand. They hadda heluva time tellin' his counterfeits from the real stuff, an' the only way they done it was that he changed his printer, kid fashion, not bein' able to let somethin' that was workin' right alone.

Those are what you might call samples. Nobody knows all that Joe done. But there was the bank-president who got humorous when his Logic flashed that 'Ask your Logic' spiel on him, and jestingly asked how to rob his own bank. An' the Logic told him, brief and explicit but good! The bank-president hit the ceiling, hollering for cops. There musta been plenty of that sorta thing. There was fifty-four more robberies than usual in the next twenty-four hours, all of them planned astute an' perfect. Some of 'em they never did figure out how they'd been done. Joe, he'd gone exploring in the Tank and closed some relays like a Logic is supposed to do – but only when required – and blocked all censor-circuits an' fixed up this Logics Service which planned perfect crimes, nourishing an' attractive meals, counterfeitin' machines, an' new industries with a fine impartiality. He musta been plenty happy, Joe must. He was functionin' swell, buzzin' along to himself while the Korlanovitch kids were off ridin' with their ma an' pa.

They come back at seven o'clock, the kids all happily wore out with their afternoon of fightin' each other in the car. Their folks put 'em to bed an' sat down to rest. They saw Joe's screen flickerin' meditative from one subject to another an' old man Korlanovitch had had enough excitement for one day. He turned Joe off.

An' at that instant the pattern of relays that Joe had turned on snapped off, all the offers of directive service stopped flashin' on Logic screens everywhere, an' peace descended on the earth.

For everybody else. But for me – Laurine come to town. I have often thanked Gawd fervent that she didn't marry me when I thought I wanted her to. In the intervenin' years she had progressed. She was blonde an' fatal to begin with. She had got blonder and fataler an' had had four husbands and one acquittal for homicide an' had acquired a air of enthusiasm and self-confidence. That's just a sketch of the background. Laurine was not the kinda former girl-friend you like to have turning up in the same town with your wife. But she come to town, an' on Monday morning she tuned right into the middle of Joe's second spasm of activity.

The Korlanovitch kids had turned him on again – I got these details later and kinda pieced 'em together – an' every Logic in town was dutifully flashin, 'If you want to do something and don't know how to do it – Ask your Logic!' every time they was turned on for use. More'n that, when people punched for the morning news, they got a full account of the previous afternoon's doin's. Which put 'em in a frame of mind to share in the party. One bright fella demands, 'How can I make a perpetual motion machine?' And his Logic sputters a while an' then comes up with a set-up usin' the Brownian movement to turn little wheels. If the wheels ain't bigger'n a eighth of an inch, they'll turn, all right, an' practically it's perpetual motion. Another one asks for the secret of transmuting metals. The Logic rakes back in the data-plates an' integrates a strictly practical answer. It does take so much power that you can't make no profit except on radium, but that pays off good. An' from the fact that for a coupla years to come the police were turnin' up new and improved jimmies, knob-claws for getting at safe-innards, and all-purpose keys that'd open any known lock – why there must have been other inquirers with a strictly practical viewpoint. Joe done a lot for technical progress!

But he done more in other lines. Educational, say. None of my kids are old enough to be interested, but Joe by-passed all censor-circuits because they hampered the service he figured Logics should ought to give humanity. So the kids an' teenagers who wanted to know what comes after the bees an' flowers found out. And there is certain facts which men hope their

296

wives won't do more'n suspect, an' these facts are just what their wives are really curious about. So when a woman dials: 'How can I tell if Oswald is true to me?' and her Logic tells her – you can figure out how many rows got started that night when the men came home!

All this while Joe goes on buzzin' happy to himself, showin' the Korlanovitch kids the animated funnies with one circuit while with the others he remote-controls the tank so that all the other Logics can give people what they ask for and thereby raise merry hell.

An' then Laurine gets onto the new service. She turns on the Logic in her hotel room, prob'ly to see the week's style-forecast. But the Logic says, dutiful: 'If you want to do something and don't know how to do it – Ask your Logic!' So Laurine prob'ly looks enthusiastic – she would! – and tries to figure out something to ask. She already knows all about everything she cares about – ain't she had four husbands and shot one? – so I occur to her. She knows this is the town I live in. So she punches, 'How can I find Ducky?'

O.K., guy! But that is what she used to call me. She gets a service question, 'Is Ducky known by any other name?' So she gives my regular name. And the Logic can't find me. Because my Logic ain't listed under my name on account of I'm in Maintenance and don't want to be pestered when I'm home, and there ain't any data-plates on code-listed Logics, because the codes get changed so often – like a guy gets plastered an' tells a redhead to call him up, an' on gettin' sober hurriedly has the code changed before she reaches his wife on the screen.

Well! Joe is stumped. That's probtly the first question Logics Service hasn't been able to answer. 'How can I locate Ducky?' Quite a problem! So Joe broods over it while showin' the Korlanovitch kids the animated comic about the cute little boy who carries sticks of dynamite in his hip pocket an' plays practical jokes on everybody. Then he gets the trick. Laurine's screen suddenly flashes: 'Logics special service will work upon your question. Please punch your Logic designation and leave it turned on. You will be called back.'

Laurine is merely mildly interested, but she punches her hotel-room number and has a drink and takes a nap. Joe sets to work. He has been given an idea.

My wife calls me at Maintenance and hollers. She is fit to be tied. She says I got to do something. She was gonna make a call to the butcher shop. Instead of the butcher or even the 'If you want to do something' flash, she got a new one. The screen says, 'Service question: What is your name?' She is kinda puzzled, but she punches it. The screen sputters an' then says: 'Secretarial Service Demonstration! You—' It reels off her name, address, age, sex, coloring, the amounts of all her charge accounts in all the stores, my name as her husband, how much I get a week, the fact that I've been pinched three times – twice was traffic stuff, and once for a argument I got in with a guy – and the interestin' item that once when she was mad with me she left me for three weeks an' had her address changed to her folks' home. Then it says, brisk: 'Logics Service will hereafter keep your personal accounts, take messages, and locate persons you may wish to get in touch with. This demonstration is to introduce the service.' Then it connects her with the butcher. But she don't want meat, then. She wants blood. She calls me.

'If it'll tell me all about myself,' she says, fairly boilin', 'it'll tell anybody else who punches my name! You've got to stop it!'

'Now, now, honey!' I says. 'I didn't know about all this! It's new! But they musta fixed the tank so it won't give out information except to the Logic where a person lives!'

'Nothing of the kind!' she tells me, furious. 'I tried! And you know that Blossom woman who lives next door! She's been married three times and she's forty-two years old and she says she's only thirty! And Mrs Hudson's had her husband arrested four times for non-support and once for beating her up. And—'

'Hey!' I says. 'You mean the Logic told you all this?'

'Yes!' she wails. 'It will tell anybody anything! You've got to stop it! How long will it take?'

'I'll call up the Tank,' I says. 'It can't take long.'

'Hurry!' she says, desperate, 'before somebody punches my name! I'm going to see what it says about that hussy across the street.'

She snaps off to gather what she can before it's stopped. So I punch for the Tank and I get this new 'What is your name?' flash. I got a morbid curiosity and I punch my name, and the screen says: 'Were you ever called Ducky?' I blink. I ain't got no suspicions. I say, 'Sure!' And the screen says, 'There is a call for you.'

Bingo! There's the inside of a hotel room and Laurine is reclinin' asleep on the bed. She'd been told to leave her Logic turned on an' she'd done it. It is a hot day and she is trying to be cool. I would say that she oughta not suffer from the heat. Me, being human, I do not stay as cool as she looks. But there ain't no need to go into that. After I get my breath I say, 'For Heaven's sake!' and she opens her eyes.

At first she looks puzzled, like she was thinking is she getting absent-minded and is this guy somebody she married lately. Then she grabs a sheet and drapes it around herself and beams at me.

'Ducky!' she says. 'How marvelous!'

I say something like 'Ugmph!' I am sweating.

She says: 'I put in a call for you, Ducky, and here you are! Isn't it romantic? Where are you really, Ducky? And when can you come up? You've no idea how often I've thought of you!'

I am probably the only guy she ever knew real well that she has not been married to at some time or another.

I say 'Ugmph!' again, and swallow.

'Can you come up instantly?' asks Laurine brightly.

'I'm ... workin',' I say. 'I'll ... uh ... call you back.'

'I'm terribly lonesome,' says Laurine. 'Please make it quick, Ducky! I'll have a drink waiting for you. Have you ever thought of me?'

'Yeah,' I say, feeble. 'Plenty!'

'You darling!' says Laurine. 'Here's a kiss to go on with until you get here! Hurry, Ducky!'

Then I sweat! I still don't know nothing about Joe,

understand. I cuss out the guys at the Tank because I blame them for this. If Laurine was just another blonde – well – when it comes to ordinary blondes I can leave 'em alone or leave 'em alone, either one. A married man gets that way or else. But Laurine has a look of unquenched enthusiasm that gives a man very strange weak sensations at the back of his knees. And she's had four husbands and shot one and got acquitted.

So I punch the keys for the Tank technical room, fumbling. And the screen says: 'What is your name?' but I don't want any more. I punch the name of the old guy who's stock clerk in Maintenance. And the screen gives me some pretty interestin' dope – I never woulda thought the old fella had ever had that much pep – and winds up by mentionin' an unclaimed deposit now amountin' to two hundred eighty credits in the First National Bank, which he should look into. Then it spiels about the new secretarial service and gives me the Tank at last.

    I start to swear at the guy who looks at me. But he says, tired:

    'Snap it off, fella. We got troubles an' you're just another. What are the Logics doin' now?'

    I tell him, and he laughs a hollow laugh.

    'A light matter, fella,' he says. 'A very light matter! We just managed to clamp off all the data-plates that give information on high explosives. The demand for instructions in counterfeiting is increasing minute by minute. We are also trying to shut off, by main force, the relays that hook in to data-plates that just barely might give advice on the fine points of murder. So if people will only keep busy getting the goods on each other for a while, maybe we'll get a chance to stop the circuits that are shifting credit-balances from bank to bank before everybody's bankrupt except the guys who thought of askin' how to get big bank-accounts in a hurry.'

    'Then,' I says hoarse, 'shut down the Tank! Do somethin'!'

    'Shut down the Tank?' he says, mirthless. 'Does it occur to you, fella, that the Tank has been doin' all the computin' for every business office for years? It's been handlin' the distribution of ninety-four per cent of all telecast programs, has given out all information on weather, plane schedules, special sales, employment opportunities and news; has handled all person-to-person contacts over wires and recorded every damned business conversation and agreement... Listen, fella! Logics changed civilization. Logics *are* civilization! If we shut off Logics, we go back to a kind of civilization we have forgotten how to run! I'm getting hysterical myself and that's why I'm talkin' like this! If my wife finds out my pay-check is thirty credits a week more than I told her and starts hunting for that red-head—'

He smiles a haggard smile at me and snaps off. And I sit down and put my head in my hands. It's true. If something had happened back in cave days and they'd hadda stop usin' fire – if they'd hadda stop usin' steam in the nineteenth century or electricity in the twentieth – it's like that. We got a very simple civilization. Where in the nineteen hundreds a man would have to make use of a typewriter, radio, telephone, teletypewriter, newspaper, reference library, encyclopaedias, office-files, directories, plus messenger service and consulting lawyers, chemists, doctors, dieticians, filing-clerks, secretaries, an' Gawd knows what all – all to put down what he wanted to remember an' tell him what other people had put down that he wanted to know; to report what he said to somebody else and to report to him what they said back. All we have to have is Logics. Anything we want to know or see or hear, or anybody we want to talk to, we punch keys on a Logic. Shut off Logics and everything goes skiddoo. But Laurine...

Somethin' had happened. I still didn't know what it was. Nobody else knows, even yet. What had happened was Joe. What was the matter with him was that he wanted to work good. All this hell he was raisin' was, actual, nothin' but stuff we shoulda thought of ourselves. Directive advice, tellin' us what we wanted to know to solve a problem, wasn't but a slight extension of logical integrator service. Figurin' out a good way to poison a fella's wife was only different in degree from figurin' out a cube root or a guy's bank balance. It was gettin' the answer to a question. But things was goin' to pot because there was too many answers being given to too many questions.

One of the Logics in Maintenance lights up. I go over, weary, to answer it. I punch the answer key. Laurine says:

'Ducky!'

It's the same hotel-room. There's two glasses on the table with drinks in them. One is for me. Laurine's got on some kinda frothy hangin'-around-the-house-with-the-boy-friend outfit on that automatic makes you strain your eyes to see if you actual see what you think. Laurine looks at me enthusiastic.

'Ducky!' says Laurine. 'I'm lonesome! Why haven't you come up?'

'I ... been busy,' I say, strangling slightly.

'*Pooh!*' says Laurine. 'Listen, Ducky! Do you remember how much in love we used to be?'

I gulp.

'Are you doin' anything this evening?' says Laurine.

I gulp again, because she is smiling at me in a way that a single man would maybe get dizzy, but it gives a old married man like me cold chills. When a dame looks at you possessive—

'Ducky!' says Laurine, impulsive. 'I was so mean to you! Let's get married!'

Desperation gives me a voice.

'I ... got married,' I tell her, hoarse.

Laurine blinks. Then she says, courageous:

'Poor boy! But we'll get you outa that! Only it would be nice if we could be married today. Now we can only be engaged!'

'I ... can't—'

'I'll call up your wife,' says Laurine, happy, 'and have a talk with her. You must have a code signal for your Logic, darling. I tried to ring your house and noth—'

Click! That's my Logic turned off. I turned it off. And I feel faint all over. I got nervous prostration. I got combat fatigue. I got anything you like. I got cold feet.

I beat it outta Maintenance, yellin' to somebody I got a emergency call. I'm gonna get out in a Maintenance car an' cruise around until it's plausible to go home. Then I'm gonna take the wife an' kids an' beat it for somewheres that Laurine won't never find me. I don't wanna be fifth in Laurine's series of husbands and maybe the second one she shoots in a moment of boredom. I got experience of blondes. I got experience of Laurine! And I'm scared to death!

I beat it out into traffic in the Maintenance car. There was a disconnected Logic in the back, ready to substitute for one that hadda burned-out coil or something that it was easier to switch and fix back in the Maintenance shop. I drove crazy but automatic. It was kinda ironic, if you think of it. I was goin' hoopla over a strictly personal problem, while civilization was crackin' up all around me because other people were havin' their personal problems solved as fast as they could state 'em. It is a matter of record that part of the Mid-Western Electric research guys had been workin' on cold electron-emission for thirty years, to make vacuum-tubes that wouldn't need a power-source to heat the filament. And one of those fellas was intrigued by the 'Ask your Logic' flash. He asked how to get cold emission of electrons. And the Logic integrates a few squintillion facts on the physics data-plates and tells him. Just as casual as it told somebody over in the Fourth Ward how to serve left-over soup in a new attractive way, and somebody else on Mason Street how to dispose of a torso that somebody had left careless in his cellar after ceasing to use same.

Laurine wouldn't never have found me if it hadn't been for this new hell-raisin' Logics Service. But now that it was started – Zowie! She'd shot one husband and got acquitted. Suppose she got impatient because I was still married an' asked Logics Service how to get me free an' in a spot where I'd have to marry her by eight thirty P.M.? It woulda told her! Just like it told that woman out in the suburbs how to make sure her husband wouldn't run around no more. *Br-r-r-r!* An' like it told that kid how to find some buried treasure. Remember? He was happy totin' home the gold reserve of the Hanoverian Bank and Trust Company when they caught onto it. The Logic had told him how to make some kinda machine that nobody has been able to figure how it works even yet, only they guess it dodges around a couple extra dimensions. If Laurine was to start askin' questions with a technical aspect to them, that would be Logics Service meat! And fella, I was scared! If you think a he-man oughtn't to be scared of just one blonde – you ain't met Laurine!

I'm drivin' blind when a social-conscious guy asks how to bring about his own particular system of social organization at once. He don't ask if it's best or if it'll work. He just wants to get it started. And the Logic – or Joe – tells him! Simultaneous, there's a retired preacher asks how can the human race be cured of concupiscence. Bein' seventy, he's pretty safe himself, but he wants to remove the peril to the spiritual welfare of the rest of us. He finds out. It involves constructin' a sort of broadcastin' station to emit a certain wave-pattern an' turnin' it on. Just that. Nothing more. It's found out afterward, when he is solicitin' funds to construct it. Fortunate, he didn't think to ask Logics how to finance it, or it woulda told him that, too, an' we woulda all been cured of the impulses we maybe regret afterward but never at the time. And there's another group of serious thinkers who are sure the human race would be a lot better off if everybody went back to nature an' lived in the woods with the ants an' poison ivy. They start askin' questions about how to cause humanity to abandon cities and artificial conditions of living. They practically got the answer in Logics Service!

Maybe it didn't strike you serious at the time, but while I was drivin' aimless, sweatin' blood over Laurine bein' after me, the fate of civilization hung in the balance. I ain't kiddin'. For instance, the Superior Man gang that sneers at the rest of us was quietly asking questions on what kinda weapons could be made by which Superior Men could take over and run things...

But I drove here an' there, sweatin' an' talkin' to myself.

'My Gawd!' I says. 'What I oughta do is ask this whacky Logics Service how to get outa this mess. But it'd just tell me an intricate an' fool-proof way to bump Laurine off. I wanna have peace! I wanna grow comfortably old and brag to other old guys about what a hellion I used to be, without havin' to go through it an' lose my chance of livin' to be a elderly liar.'

I turn a corner at random, there in the Maintenance car.

'It was a nice kinda world once,' I says, bitter. 'I could go home peaceful and not have belly-cramps wonderin' if a blonde has called up my wife to announce my engagement to her. I could punch keys on a Logic without gazing into some-body's bedroom while she is giving her epidermis an air-bath and being led to think things I gotta take out in thinkin'. I could—'

Then I groan, rememberin' that my wife, naturally, is gonna blame me for the fact that our private life ain't private any more if anybody has tried to peek into it.

'It was a swell world,' I says, homesick for the dear dead days-before-yesterday. 'We was playin' happy with our toys like little innocent children until somethin' happened. Like a guy named Joe come in and squashed all our mud-pies.'

Then it hit me. I got the whole thing in one flash. There ain't nothing in the Tank set-up to start relays closin'. Relays are closed exclusive by Logics, to get the information the keys are punched for. Nothin' but a Logic coulda cooked up the relay-patterns that constituted Logics Service. Humans wouldn't ha' been able to figure it out! Only a Logic could integrate all the stuff that woulda made all the other Logics work like this—

There was one answer. I drove into a restaurant and went over to a pay-Logic an' dropped in a coin.

'Can a Logic be modified,' I spell out, 'to cooperate in long-term planning which human brains are too limited in scope to do?'

The screen sputters. Then it says:

'Definitely yes.'

'How great will the modifications be?' I punch.

'Microscopically slight. Changes in dimensions,' says the screen. 'Even modern precision gauges are not exact enough to check them, however. They can only come about under present manufacturing methods by an extremely improbable accident, which has only happened once.'

'How can one get hold of that one accident which can do this highly necessary work?' I punch.

The screen sputters. Sweat broke out on me. I ain't got it figured out close, yet, but what I'm scared of is that whatever is Joe will be suspicious. But what I'm askin' is strictly logical. And Logics can't lie. They gotta be accurate. They can't help it.

'A complete Logic capable of the work required,' says the screen, 'is now in ordinary family use in—'

And it gives me the Korlanovitch address and do I go over there! Do I go over there fast! I pull up the Maintenance car in front of the place, and I take the extra Logic outa the back, and I stagger up to the Korlanovitch flat and I ring the bell. A kid answers the door.

'I'm from Logics Maintenance,' I tell the kid. 'An inspection record has shown that your Logic is apt to break down any minute. I come to put in a new one before it does.'

The kid says, 'O.K.!' real bright and runs back to the livin' room where Joe – I got the habit of callin' him Joe later, through just meditatin' about him – is runnin' somethin' the kids wanna look at. I hook in the other Logic an' turn it on, conscientious makin' sure it works. Then I say:

'Now kiddies, you punch this one for what you want. I'm gonna take the old one away before it breaks down.'

And I glance at the screen. The kiddies have apparently said they wanna look at some real cannibals. So the screen is presenting a anthropological-expedition scientific record film of the fertility dance of the Huba-Jouba tribe of West Africa. It is supposed to be restricted to anthropological professors an' post-graduate medical students. But there ain't any censor-blocks workin' any more and it's on. The kids are much interested. Me, bein' a old married man, I blush.

I disconnect Joe. Careful. I turn to the other Logic and punch keys for Maintenance. I do not get a Service flash. I get Maintenance. I feel very good. I report that I am goin' home because I fell down a flight of steps an' hurt my leg. I add, inspired:

'An' say, I was carryin' the Logic I replaced an' it busted all to hell. I left it for the dustman to pick up.'

'If you don't turn 'em in,' says Stock, 'you gotta pay for 'em.'

'Cheap at the price,' I say.

I go home. Laurine ain't called. I put Joe down in the cellar, careful. If I turned him in, he'd be inspected an' his parts salvaged even if I busted somethin' on him. Whatever part was off-normal might be used again and everything start all over. I can't risk it. I pay for him and leave him be.

That's what happened. You might say I saved civilization an' not be far wrong. I know I ain't goin' to take a chance on havin' Joe in action again. Not while Laurine is livin'. An' there are other reasons. With all the nuts who wanna change the world to their own line o' thinkin', an' the ones that wanna bump people off, an' generally solve their problems – yeah! Problems are bad, but I figure I better let sleepin' problems lie.

But on the other hand, if Joe could be tamed, somehow, and got to work just reasonable . . . He could make me a couple million dollars, easy. But even if I got sense enough not to get rich, an' if I get retired and just loaf around fishin' an' lyin' to other old duffers about what a great guy I used to be – maybe I'll like it, but maybe I won't. And after all, if I get fed up with bein' old and confined strictly to thinking – why – I could hook Joe in long enough to ask, 'How can a old guy not stay old?' Joe'll be able to find out. An' he'll tell me.

That couldn't be allowed out general, of course. You gotta make room for kids to grow up. But it's a pretty good world, now Joe's turned off. Maybe I'll turn him on long enough to learn how to stay in it. But on the other hand, maybe—

DE PROFUNDIS

I, Sard, make report to the Shadi during Peace Tides. I have made a journey of experiment suggested by the scientist Morpt after discussing with me an Object fallen into Honda from the Surface. I fear that my report will not be accepted as true. I therefore await the consensus on my sanity, offering this report to be judged science or delirium as the Shadi may elect...

I was present when the Object fell. At the moment I was in communication with the scientist Morpt as he meditated upon the facts of the universe. He was rather drowsy, and his mind was more conscientious than inspiring as he reflected – for the benefit of us, his students – upon the evidence of the Caluphian theory of the universe, that it is a shell of solid matter filled with water, which being naturally repelled from the center, acquires pressure, and that we, the Shadi, live in the region of greatest pressure. He almost dozed off as he reflected for our instruction that this theory accounts for all known physical phenomena, except the existence of the substance gas, which is neither solid nor liquid and is found only in our swim-bladders. For this reason, it is commonly assumed to be our immortal part, rising to the center of the universe when our bodies are consumed, and there exists forever.

As he meditated, I recalled the Morpt exercises by which a part of this gas may be ejected from a Shadi body and kept in an inverted receptacle while the body forms a new supply in the swim-bladder. I waited anxiously for Morpt's trenchant reasoning which denies that a substance – however rare and singular – which can be kept in a receptacle or replaced by the body can constitute its vital essence.

These experiments of Morpt's have caused great disturbances among scientific circles.

At the moment, however, he was merely a drowsy instructor, sleepily thinking a lecture he had thought a hundred times before. He was a little annoyed by a sharp rock sticking into his seventh tentacle, which was not quite uncomfortable enough to make him stir.

I lay in my cave, attending anxiously. Then, abruptly, I was aware that something was descending from above. The instinct of our race to block out thought-transference and seize food before anyone else can know of it operated instantly. I flowed out of my cave and swept to the space below the Object. I raised my tentacles to snatch it. The whole process was automatic – mind-block on, spatial sensation extended to the fullest, full focused reception of mental images turned upon the sinking Object to foresee its efforts to escape so that I could anticipate them – but every Shadi knows what one does by pure instinct when a moving thing comes within one's ken.

There were two causes for my behavior after that automatic reaction, however. One was that I had fed, and lately. The other was that I received mental images from within the Object which were startlingly tuned to the subject of Morpt's lecture and my own thoughts of the moment. As my first tentacle swooped upon the descending thing, instead of thoughts of fright or battle, I intercepted the message of an entity, cogitating despairingly, to another.

'My dear, we will never see the Surface again,' it was thinking.

And I received a dazzling impression of what the Surface was like. Since I shall describe the Surface later, I omit a description of the mental picture I then received. But it gave me to pause, I believe fortunately. For one thing, had I swept the Object into my maw as instinct impelled, I believe I would have had trouble digesting it. The Object, as I soon discovered, was made of that rare solid substance which only appears in the form of artifacts. One such specimen has been repeatedly described by Glor. It is about half the length of a Shadi's body, hollow, pointed at one end, with one of its sides curiously flat with strangely shaped excrescences, openings, and two shafts and one hollow tube sticking out of it.

As I said, the Object was made of this rare solid material. My spatial sense immediately told me that it was hollow. Further, that it was filled with gas! And then I received conflicting mental images which told me that there were two living creatures within it! Let me repeat – there were two living entities within the Object, and they lived in gas instead of water!

I was stunned. For a long time I was not really aware of anything at all save the thoughts of the creatures within the Object. I held the Object firmly between two of my tentacles, dazed by the impossible facts I faced. I was most incautious. I could have been killed and consumed in the interval of my bewilderment. But I came to myself and returned swiftly to my cave, carrying the Object with me. As I did so, I was aware of startled thoughts.

'We've hit bottom – no! Something has seized us. It must be monstrous in size. It will soon be over, now ...'

Not in answer, but separately, the other entity thought only emotional things I cannot describe. I do not understand them at all. They represent a psychology so alien to ours that there is no way to express them. I can only say that the second entity was in complete despair, and therefore desired intensely to be clasped firmly in the other entity's two tentacles. This would constitute complete helplessness, but it was what the second creature craved. I report the matter with no attempt to explain it.

While flowing into my cave, I knocked the Object against the top of the opening. It was a sharp blow. I had again an impression of despair.

'This is it!' the first creature thought, and looked with dread for an inpouring of water into the gas-filled Object.

Since the psychology of these creatures is so completely

inexplicable, I merely summarize the few mental images I received during the next short period which served to explain the history of the Object.

To begin with, it had been a scientific experiment. The Object was created to contain the gas in which the creatures lived, and to allow the gas to be lowered into the regions of pressure. The creatures themselves were of the same species, but different in a fashion for which we have no thought. One thought of itself as 'man', the other as 'woman'. They did not fear each other. They had accompanied the b.ject for the purpose of recording their observations in regions of pressure. To make their observations, the Object was suspended by a long tentacle from an artifact like the one of Glor's description.

When they had observed, they were to have been returned to the artifact. Then the gas was to be released, and they would rejoin their fellows. The fact that two creatures could remain together with safety for both is strange enough. But their thoughts told me that forty or fifty others of the same species awaited them on the artifact, all equally devoid of the instinct to feed upon each other.

This appears impossible, of course, and I merely report the thought-images I received. However, while at the full length of the tentacle which held it, the tentacle broke. The Object therefore sank down into the regions of pressure in which we Shadi live. As it neared solidity, I reached up and grasped it and miraculously did not swallow it. I could have done so with ease.

When, in my cave, I had attended for some time to the thoughts coming from within the Object, I tried to communicate. First, of course, I attempted to paralyze the creatures with fear. They did not seem to be aware of the presence of mind. I then attempted, more gently, to converse with them. But they seemed to be devoid of the receptive faculty. They are rational creatures, but even with no mind-block up, they are completely unaware of the thoughts of others. In fact, their thoughts were plainly secret from each other.

I tried to understand all this, and failed. At long last a proper humility came to me, and I sent out a mental call to Morpt. He was still drowsily detailing the consequences of the Caluph theory – that in the center of the universe the gas which has escaped from the swim-bladders of dead Shadi has gathered to form a vast bubble, and that the border between the central bubble and the water is the legendary Surface.

Legends of the Surface are well-known. Morpt reflected, in sleepy irony, that if gas is the immortal part of Shadi, then since two Shadi who see each other instantly fight to the death, the bubble at the center of the universe must be the scene of magnificent combat. But his irony was lost upon me. I interrupted to tell him of the Object and what I had already learned from it.

I immediately felt other minds crowd me. All of Morpt's pupils were instantly alert. I blanked out my mind with more than usual care – to avoid giving any clue to the whereabouts of my cave – and served science to the best of my ability. I told, freely, everything I knew.

Under other conditions, I would have been proud of the furor I created. It seemed that every Shadi in the Honda joined the discussion. Many, of course, said that I lied. But I was fed, and filled with curiosity. I did not reveal my whereabouts to those challengers. I waited. Even Morpt tried to taunt me into an incautious revelation and went into a typical Shadi rage when he failed. But Morpt is experienced and huge. I could not hope to be the one to live, did we meet each other outside of the Peace Tides.

Once I had proved I could not be lured out, however, Morpt discussed the matter dispassionately and in the end suggested the journey from which I have just returned. If, despite my caution where other Shadi were concerned – all of Morpt's pupils will recognize the challenging irony with which he thought this – if, despite my caution, I was not afraid to serve science, he advised me to carry the Object back to the Heights. From the creatures within it I should receive directions. From their kind I had my strength and ferocity as protections. From the Heights themselves, Morpt urged his exercises as the only possible safeguards.

As I knew, said Morpt, the gas in our swim-bladders expands as pressure lessens. Normally, we have muscles which control it so that we can float in pursuit of our prey or sink to solidity at will. But he told me that as I neared the Heights I would find the pressure growing so small that in theory even my muscles would be unable to control the gas. Under such conditions I must use the Morpt exercises and release a portion of it. Then I could descend again.

Otherwise, I might actually be carried up by my own expanding gas, it might rupture my swim-bladder and invade other body cavities and expand still further, and finally carry me with it up to the Surface and the central bubble of Caluph's theory.

In such a case, Morpt assured me wittily, I would become one Shadi who knew whether Caluph was right or not, but I would not be likely to return to tell about it. Still, he insisted, if I paused to use his exercises whenever I felt unusually buoyant, I would certainly carry the Object quite near the Surface without danger and so bring back conclusive evidence of the truth or error of the entire Caluphian cosmology, thus rendering a great service to science. The thoughts coming from within the Object should be of great assistance in the enterprise.

I immediately determined to make the journey. For one thing, I was not too sure that I could keep my whereabouts hidden, if continually probed by older and more experienced minds. Only exceedingly powerful minds, like those of Morpt and the other instructors, can risk exposure to constant hungry inspection. Of course, they find the profit in their instructorships in such slips among their students . . .

It would be distinctly wise for me to leave my cave, now that I had called attention to myself. So I put up my mind-block tightly, and with the Object clutched in one tentacle, I flowed swiftly up the slope which surrounds Honda before other Shadi should think of patrolling it for me – and each other.

I went far above my usual level before I paused. I went so

high that the gas in my swim-bladder was markedly uncomfortable. I did the Morpt exercises until it was released. It was strange that I did this with complete calm. But my curiosity was involved now, and we Shadi are inveterate seekers. So I found it possible to perform an act – the deliberate freeing of a part of the contents of my swim-bladder – which would have filled past generations of Shadi with horror.

Morpt was right. I was able to continue my ascent without discomfort. More, with increasing Height, I had much for my mind to think of. The two creatures – the man and the woman – in the Object were bewildered by what had happened to their container.

'We have risen two thousand feet from our greatest depth,' the man said to the woman.

'My dear, you don't have to lie to make me brave,' the woman said. 'I don't mind. I couldn't have kept you out of the bathysphere, and I'd rather die with you than live without you.'

Such thoughts do not seem compatible with intelligence. A race with such a psychology would die out. But I do not pretend to understand.

I continued upward until it was necessary to perform the Morpt exercises again. The necessary movements shook the Object violently. The creatures within speculated hopelessly upon the cause. These creatures not only lack the receptive faculty, so that their thoughts are secret from each other, but apparently they have no spatial sense, no sense of pressure, and apparently fail of the cycle of instincts which is so necessary to us Shadi.

In all the time of my contact with their minds, I found no thought of anything approximating the Peace Tides, when we Shadi cease altogether to feed and, therefore, instinctively cease to fear each other and intermingle freely to breed. One wonders how their race can continue without Peace Tides, unless their whole lives are passed in a sort of Peace Tide. In that case, since no one feeds during the Peace Tides, why are they not starved to death? They are inexplicable.

They watched their instruments as the ascent went on.

Instruments are artifacts which they use to supplement their defective senses.

'Four thousand feet up,' said the man to the woman. 'Only heaven knows what has happened!'

'Do you think there's a chance for us?' the woman said yearningly.

'How could there be?' the man demanded bitterly. 'We sank to eighteen thousand feet. There is still almost three miles of water over our heads, and the oxygen won't last forever. I wish I hadn't let you come. If only you were safe!'

Four thousand feet – whatever that term may mean – above the Honda, the character of living things had changed. All forms of life were smaller, and their spatial sense seemed imperfect. They were not aware of my coming until I was actually upon them. I kept two tentacles busy snatching them as I passed. Their body lights were less brilliant than those of the lesser creatures of the Honda.

I continued my flowing climb toward the Surface. From time to time, I paused to perform the Morpt exercises. The volume of gas I released from my swim-bladder was amazing. I remember thinking, in somewhat the ironic manner of Morpt himself, that if ever Shadi possessed so vast an immortal part, the central bubble must be greater than Honda itself! The creatures inside the Object now watched their instruments incredulously.

'We are up to nine thousand feet,' said the man dazedly. 'We dropped to eighteen thousand, the greatest depth in this part of the world.'

The thought 'world' approximates the Shadi conception of 'universe', but there are puzzling differences.

'We've risen half of it again,' the man added.

'Do you think that the ballast dropped off and we will float to the Surface?' asked the woman anxiously.

The thought of 'ballast' was of things fastened to the Object to make it descend, and that if they were detached, the Object would rise. This would seem to be nonsense, because all substances descend, except gas. However, I report only what I sensed.

'But we're not floating,' said the man. 'If we were, we'd rise steadily. As it is, we go up a thousand feet or so and then we're practically shaken to death. Then we go up another thousand feet. We're not floating. We're being carried. But only the fates know by what or why.'

This, I point out, is rationality. They knew that their rise was unreasonable. My curiosity increased. I should explain how the creatures knew of their position. They have no spatial sense or any sense of pressure. For the latter they used instruments – artifacts – which told of their ascent. The remarkable thing is that they inspected those instruments by means of a light which they did not make themselves. The light was also made by an artifact. And this artificial light was strong enough to be reflected, not only perceptibly, but distinctly, so that the instruments were seen by reflection only.

I fear that Kanth, whose discovery that light is capable of reflection made his scientific reputation, will deny that any light could be powerful enough to make unlighted objects appear to have light, but I must go even further. As I learned to share not only consciously formed thoughts but sense-impressions of the creatures in the Object, I learned that to them, light has different qualities. Some lights have qualities which to them are different from other lights.

The light we know they speak of as 'bluish'. They know additional words which they term 'red' and 'white' and 'yellow' and other terms. As we perceive differences in the solidity of rocks and ooze, they perceive differences in objects by the light they reflect. Thus, they have a sense which we Shadi have not. I am aware that Shadi are the highest possible type of organism, but this observation – if not insanity – is important matter for meditation.

But I continued to flow steadily upward, pausing only to perform the necessary Morpt exercises to release gas from my swim-bladder when its expansion threatened to become uncontrollable. As I went higher and ever higher, the man and woman were filled with emotions of a quite extraordinary nature. These emotions were unbearably poignant to them, and it is to be doubted that any Shadi has ever sensed such sensations before. Certainly the emotion they call 'love' is inconceivable to Shadi, except by reception from such a creature. It led to peculiar vagaries. For example, the woman put her twin tentacles about the man and clung to him with no effort to rend or tear.

The idea of two creatures of the same species pleasurably anticipating being together without devouring each other – except during the Peace Tides, of course – is almost inconceivable to a Shadi. However, it appeared to be part of their normal psychology.

But this report grows long. I flowed upward and upward. The creatures in the Object experienced emotions which were stronger and ever stronger, and more and more remarkable. Successively the man reported to the woman that they were but four thousand of their 'feet' below the Surface, then two thousand, and then one. I was now completely possessed by curiosity. I had barely performed what turned out to be the last needed Morpt exercise and was moving still higher when my spatial sense suddenly gave me a new and incredible message. Above me, there was a barrier to its operation.

I cannot convey the feeling of finding a barrier to one's spatial sense. I was aware of my surroundings in every direction, but at a certain point above me there was suddenly – nothing! Nothing! At first it was alarming. I flowed up half my length, and the barrier grew nearer. Cautiously – even timorously – I flowed slowly nearer and nearer.

'Five hundred feet,' said the man inside the Object. 'My heavens, only five hundred feet! We should see glimmers of light through the ports. No, it's night now.'

I paused, debating. I was close enough to this barrier to reach up my first tentacle and touch it. I hesitated a long time. Then I did touch it. Nothing happened. I thrust my tentacle boldly through it. It went into Nothingness. Where it was there was no water. With an enormous emotion, I realized that above me was the central bubble and that I alone of living Shadi had reached and dared to touch it. The sensation in my tentacle within the bubble, above the Surface, was that of an enormous weight, as if the gas of departed Shadi would have thrust me back. But they did not attack, they did not even attempt to injure me.

Yes, I was splendidly proud. I felt like one who has overcome and consumed a Shadi of greater size than himself. And as I exulted, I became aware of the emotions of the creatures within the Object.

'Three hundred feet!' said the man frantically. 'It can't stop here! It can't! My dear, fate could not be so cruel!'

I found pleasure in the emotions of the two creatures. They felt a new emotion, now, which was as strange as any of my other experiences with them. It was an emotion which was the anticipation of other emotions. The woman named it.

'It is insane,' she told the man, 'but somehow I feel hope again.'

And in my pleasure and intellectual interest it seemed a very small thing for one who had already dared so greatly to continue the pleasures I felt. I flowed further up the slope. The barrier to my spatial sense – the Surface – came closer and ever closer.

'A hundred feet,' said the man in an emotion which to him was agony, but because of its novelty was a source of intellectual pleasure to me.

I transferred the Object to a forward tentacle and thrust it ahead. It bumped upon the solidity which here approached and actually penetrated the Surface. The man experienced a passion of the strong emotion called 'hope.'

'Twenty-five feet!' he cried. 'Darling, if we start to go down again, I'll open the hatch, and we'll go out as the bathysphere floods. I don't know whether we're near shore or not, but we'll try.'

The woman was pressed close against him. The agony of hope which filled her was a sensation which mingled with the high elation I felt over my own daring and achievement. I thrust the Object forward yet again. Here the Surface was so near the solidity under it that a part of my tentacle went above the Surface. And the emotions within the Object reached a climax. I thrust on, powerfully, against the weight within the Bubble, until the Object broke the surface, and then on and on until it was no longer in water but in gas, resting upon solidity which was itself touched only by gas.

The man and woman worked frantically within the Object. A part of it detached itself. They climbed out of it. They opened their maws and uttered cries. They wrapped their tentacles about each other and touched their maws together, not to devour but to express their emotions. They looked about them dazed with relief, and I saw through their eyes. The Surface stretched away for as far as their senses reported, moving and uneven, and yet flat. They stood upon solidity from which things projected upward. Overhead was a vast blackness, penetrated by innumerable small bright sources of light.

'Thank God!' said the man. 'To see trees and the stars again.'

They felt absolutely secure and at peace, as if in a Peace Tides enhanced a thousand fold. And perhaps I was intoxicated by my own daring or perhaps by the emotions I received from them. I thrust my tentacles through the Surface. Their weight was enormous, but my strength is great also.

Daringly I heaved up my body. I thrust my entire forepart through the Surface and into the central bubble. I was in the central bubble while still alive! My weight increased beyond computation, but for a long, proud interval I loomed above the Surface. I saw with my own eyes – all eighty of them – the Surface beneath me and the patch of solidity on which the man and the woman stood. I, Sard, did this!

As I dipped below the Surface again I received the astounded thoughts of the creatures.

'A sea-serpent,' thought the man, and doubted his own sanity as I fear mine will be doubted. 'That's what did it.'

'Why not, darling?' the woman said calmly. 'It was a miracle, but people who love each other as we do simply couldn't be allowed to die.'

But the man stared at the Surface where I had vanished. I had caught his troubled thought.

'No one would believe it. They'd say we're insane. But confound it, here's the bathysphere, and our cable did break when we were above the Deep. When we're found, we'll simply say we don't know what happened and let them try to figure it out.'

I lay resting, close to the Surface, thinking many things. After a long time there was light. Fierce, unbearable light. It grew stronger and yet stronger. It was unbearable. It flowed down into the nearer depths.

That was many tides ago, because I dared not return to Honda with so vast a proportion of the gas in my swim-bladder released to the central bubble. I remained not too far below the Surface until my swim-bladder felt normal. I descended again and again waited until my 'immortal part' had replenished itself. It is difficult to feed upon such small creatures as inhabit the Heights. It took a long time for me to make the descent which by Morpt's discovery had been made so readily as an ascent. All my waking time was spent in the capture of food, and I had little time for meditation. I was never once full-fed in all the periods I paused to wait for my swim-bladder to be replenished. But when I returned to my cave, it had been occupied in my absence by another Shadi. I fed well.

Then came the Peace Tides. And now, having bred, I lay my report of my journey to the Surface at the service of all the Shadi. If I am decreed insane, I shall say no more. But this is my report. Now determine, O Shadi: am I mad?

I, Morpt, in Peace Tides, have heard the report of Sard and having consulted with others of the Shadi, do declare that he has plainly confounded the imagined with the real.

His description of the scientific aspects of his journey, and which are not connected with the assumed creatures in the Object, are consistent with science. But it is manifestly impossible that any creature could live with its fellows permanently without the instinct to feed. It is manifestly impossible that creatures could live in gas. Distinction between light and light is patent nonsense. The psychology of such creatures as described by Sard is of the stuff of dreams.

Therefore, it is the consensus that Sard's report is not science. He may not be insane, however. The physiological effects of his admitted journey to great Heights have probably caused disorders in his body which have shown themselves in illusions. The scientific lesson to be learned from this report is that journeys to the Heights, though possible because of the exercises invented by myself, are extremely unwise and should never be made by Shadi. Given during the Peace Tides...

IF YOU WAS A MOKLIN

Up to the very last minute, I can't imagine that Moklin is going to be the first planet that humans get off of, moving fast, breathing hard, and sweating awful copious. There ain't any reason for it. Humans have been on Moklin for more than forty years, and nobody ever figures there is anything the least bit wrong until Brooks works it out. When he does, nobody can believe it. But it turns out bad. Plenty bad. But maybe things are working out all right now.

Maybe! I hope so.

At first, even after he's sent off long reports by six ships in a row, I don't see the picture beginning to turn sour. I don't get it until after the old *Palmyra* comes and squats down on the next to the last trip a Company ship is ever going to make to Moklin.

Up to that very morning everything is serene, and that morning I am sitting on the trading post porch, not doing a thing but sitting there and breathing happy. I'm looking at a Moklin kid. She's about the size of a human six-year-old and she is playing in a mud puddle while her folks are trading in the post. She is a cute kid – mighty human-looking. She has long whiskers like Old Man Bland, who's the first human to open a trading post and learn to talk to Moklins.

Moklins think a lot of Old Man Bland. They build him a big tomb, Moklin-style, when he dies, and there is more Moklin kids born with long whiskers than you can shake a stick at. And everything looks okay. *Everything!*

Sitting there on the porch, I hear a Moklin talking inside

the trade room. Talking English just as good as anybody. He says to Deeth, our Moklin trade-clerk, 'But Deeth, I can buy this cheaper over at the other trading post! Why should I pay more here?'

Deeth says, in English too, 'I can't help that. That's the price here. You pay it or you don't. That's all.'

I just sit there breathing complacent, thinking how good things are. Here I'm Joe Brinkley, and me and Brooks are the Company on Moklin – only humans rate as Company employees and get pensions, of course – and I'm thinking sentimental about how much humaner Moklins are getting every day and how swell everything is.

The six-year-old kid gets up out of the mud puddle, and wrings out her whiskers – they are exactly like the ones on the picture of Old Man Bland in the trade room – and she goes trotting off down the road after her folks. She is mighty human-looking, that one.

The wild ones don't look near so human. Those that live in the forest are greenish, and have saucer eyes, and their noses can wiggle like an Earth rabbit. You wouldn't think they're the same breed as the trading post Moklins at all, but they are. They crossbreed with each other, only the kids look humaner than their parents and are mighty near the same skin color as Earthmen, which is plenty natural when you think about it, but nobody does. Not up to then.

I don't think about that then, or anything else. Not even about the reports Brooks keeps sweating over and sending off with every Company ship. I am just sitting there contented when I notice that Sally, the tree that shades the trading post porch, starts pulling up her roots. She gets them coiled careful and starts marching off. I see the other trees are moving off, too, clearing the landing field. They're waddling away to leave a free space, and they're pushing and shoving, trying to crowd each other, and the little ones sneak under the big ones and they all act peevish. Somehow they know a ship is coming in. That's what their walking off means, anyhow. But there ain't a ship due in for a month, yet.

They're clearing the landing field, though, so I start listening for a ship's drive, even if I don't believe it. At first I don't hear a thing. It must be ten minutes before I hear a thin whistle, and right after it the heavy drone that's the ground-repulsor units pushing against bedrock underground. Lucky they don't push on wet stuff, or a ship would sure mess up the local countryside!

I get off my chair and go out to look. Sure enough, the old *Palmyra* comes bulging down out of the sky, a month ahead of schedule, and the trees over at the edge of the field shove each other all round to make room. The ship drops, hangs anxious ten feet up, and then kind of sighs and lets down. Then there's Moklins running out of everywhere, waving cordial.

They sure do like humans, these Moklins! Humans are their idea of what people should be like! Moklins will wrestle the freight over to the trading post while others are climbing over everything that's waiting to go off, all set to pass it up to the ship and hoping to spot friends they've made in the crew. If they can get a human to go home with them and visit while the ship is down, they brag about it for weeks. And do they treat their guests swell!

They got fancy Moklin clothes for them to wear – soft, silky guest garments – and they got Moklin fruits and Moklin drinks – you ought to taste them! And when the humans have to go back to the ship at takeoff time, the Moklins bring them back with flower wreaths all over them.

Humans is tops on Moklin. And Moklins get humaner every day. There's Deeth, our clerk. You couldn't hardly tell him from human, anyways. He looks like a human named Casey that used to be at the trading post, and he's got a flock of brothers and sisters as human-looking as he is. You'd swear—

But this is the last time but one that a Earth ship is going to land on Moklin, though nobody knows it yet. Her passenger port opens up and Captain Haney gets out. The Moklins yell cheerful when they see him. He waves a hand and helps a human girl out. She has red hair and a sort of businesslike air about her. The Moklins wave and holler and grin. The girl looks at them funny, and Cap Haney explains something, but she sets her lips. Then the Moklins run out a freight-truck, and Haney and the girl get on it, and they come racing over to the post, the Moklins pushing and pulling them and making a big fuss of laughing and hollering – all so friendly, it would make anybody feel good inside. Moklins like humans! They admire them tremendous! They do everything they can think of to be human, and they're smart, but sometimes I get cold shivers when I think how close a thing it turns out to be.

Cap Haney steps off the freight-truck and helps the girl down. Her eyes are blazing. She is the maddest-looking female I ever see, but pretty as they make them, with that red hair and those blue eyes staring at me hostile.

'Hiya, Joe,' says Cap Haney. 'Where's Brooks?'

I tell him. Brooks is poking around in the mountains up back of the post. He is jumpy and worried and peevish, and he acts like he's trying to find something that ain't there, but he's bound he's going to find it regardless.

'Too bad he's not here,' says Haney. He turns to the girl. 'This is Joe Brinkley,' he says. 'He's Brooks' assistant. And, Joe, this is Inspector Caldwell – Miss Caldwell.'

'Inspector will do,' says the girl, curt. She looks at me accusing. 'I'm here to check into this matter of a competitive trading post on Moklin.'

'Oh,' I says. 'That's bad business. But it ain't cut into our trade much. In fact, I don't think it's cut our trade at all.'

'Get my baggage ashore, Captain,' says Inspector Caldwell, imperious. 'Then you can go about your business. I'll stay here until you stop on your return trip.'

I call, 'Hey, Deeth!' But he's right behind me. He looks respectful and admiring at the girl. You'd swear he's human! He's the spit and image of Casey, who used to be on Moklin until six years back.

'Yes, sir,' says Deeth. He says to the girl, 'Yes, ma'am. I'll show you your quarters, ma'am, and your baggage will get there right away. This way, ma'am.'

He leads her off, but he don't have to send for her baggage. A pack of Moklins come along, dragging it, hopeful of having her say 'Thank you' to them for it. There hasn't ever been a human woman on Moklin before, and they are all excited. I bet if there had been women around before, there'd have been hell loose before, too. But now the Moklins just hang around, admiring.

There are kids with whiskers like Old Man Bland, and other kids with mustaches – male and female both – and all that sort of stuff. I'm pointing out to Cap Haney some kids that bear a remarkable resemblance to him and he's saying, 'Well, what do you know!' when Inspector Caldwell comes back.

'What are you waiting for, Captain?' she asks, frosty.

'The ship usually grounds a few hours,' I explain. 'These Moklins are such friendly critters, we figure it makes good will for the trading post for the crew to be friendly with 'em.'

'I doubt,' says Inspector Caldwell, her voice dripping icicles, 'that I shall advise that that custom be continued.'

Cap Haney shrugs his shoulders and goes off, so I know Inspector Caldwell is high up in the Company. She ain't old, maybe in her middle twenties, I'd say, but the Caldwell family practically owns the Company, and all the nephews and cousins and so on get put into a special school so they can go to work in the family firm. They get taught pretty good, and most of them really rate the good jobs they get. Anyhow, there's plenty of good jobs. The Company runs twenty or thirty solar systems and it's run pretty tight. Being a Caldwell means you get breaks, but you got to live up to them.

Cap Haney almost has to fight his way through the Moklins who want to give him flowers and fruits and such. Moklins are sure crazy about humans! He gets to the entry port and goes in, and the door closes and the Moklins pull back. Then the *Palmyra* booms. The ground-repulsor unit is on. She heaves up, like she is grunting, and goes bulging up into the air, and the humming gets deeper and deeper, and fainter and fainter – and suddenly there's a keen whistling and she's gone. It's all very normal. Nobody would guess that this is the last time but one a Earth ship will ever lift off Moklin!

Inspector Caldwell taps her foot, icy. 'When will you send for Mr Brooks?' she demands.

'Right away,' I says to her. 'Deeth—'

'I sent a runner for him, ma'am,' says Deeth. 'If he was in hearing of the ship's landing, he may be on the way here now.'

He bows and goes in the trade room. There are Moklins that came to see the ship land, and now have tramped over to do some trading. Inspector Caldwell jumps.

'Wh-what's that?' she asks, tense.

The trees that crowded off the field to make room for the *Palmyra* are waddling back. I realize for the first time that it might look funny to somebody just landed on Moklin. They are regular-looking trees, in a way. They got bark and branches and so on. Only they can put their roots down into holes they make in the ground, and that's the way they stay, mostly, but they can move. Wild ones, when there's a water shortage or they get too crowded or mad with each other, they pull up their roots and go waddling around looking for a better place to take root in.

The trees on our landing field have learned that every so often a ship is going to land and they've got to make room for it. But now the ship is gone, and they're lurching back to their places. The younger ones are waddling faster than the big ones, though, and taking the best places, and the old grunting trees are waving their branches indignant and puffing after them mad as hell.

I explain what is happening. Inspector Caldwell just stares. Then Sally comes lumbering up. I got a friendly feeling for Sally. She's pretty old – her trunk is all of three feet thick – but she always puts out a branch to shade my window in the morning, and I never let any other tree take her place. She comes groaning up, and uncoils her roots, and sticks them down one by one into the holes she'd left, and sort of scrunches into place and looks peaceful.

'Aren't they – dangerous?' asks Inspector Caldwell, pretty uneasy.

'Not a bit,' I says. 'Things can change on Moklin. They

don't have to fight. Things fight in other places because they can't change and they get crowded, and that's the only way they can meet competition. But there's a special kind of evolution on Moklin. Cooperative, you might call it. It's a nice place to live. Only thing is everything matures so fast. Four years and a Moklin is grown up, for instance.'

She sniffs. 'What about that other trading post?' she says, sharp. 'Who's back of it? The Company is supposed to have exclusive trading rights here. Who's trespassing?'

'Brooks is trying to find out,' I says. 'They got a good complete line of trade goods, but the Moklins always say the humans running the place have gone off somewhere, hunting and such. We ain't seen any of them.'

'No?' says the girl, short. 'I'll see them! We can't have competition in our exclusive territory! The rest of Mr Brooks' reports—' She stops. Then she says, 'That clerk of yours reminds me of someone I know.'

'He's a Moklin,' I explain, 'but he looks like a Company man named Casey. Casey's Area Director over on Khatim Two now, but he used to be here, and Deeth is the spit and image of him.'

'Outrageous!' says Inspector Caldwell, looking disgusted.

There's a couple of trees pushing hard at each other. They are fighting, tree-fashion, for a specially good place. And there's others waddling around, mad as hell, because somebody else beat them to the spots they liked. I watch them. Then I grin, because a couple of young trees duck under the fighting big ones and set their roots down in the place the big trees was fighting over.

'I don't like your attitude!' says Inspector Caldwell, furious.

She goes stamping into the post, leaving me puzzled. What's wrong with me smiling at those kid trees getting the best of their betters?

That afternoon Brooks comes back, marching ahead of a pack of woods-Moklins with greenish skins and saucer eyes that've been guiding him around. He's a good-looking kind of fellow, Brooks is, with a good build and a solid jaw.

When he comes out of the woods on the landing field – the trees are all settled down by then – he's striding impatient and loose-jointed. With the woods-Moklins trailing him, he looks plenty dramatic, like a visi-reel picture of a explorer on some unknown planet, coming back from the dark and perilous forests, followed by the strange natives who do not yet know whether this visitor from outer space is a god or what. You know the stuff.

I see Inspector Caldwell take a good look at him, and I see her eyes widen. She looks like he is a shock, and not a painful one.

He blinks when he sees her. He grunts, 'What's this? A she-Moklin?'

Inspector Caldwell draws herself up to her full five-foot-three. She bristles.

I say quick, 'This here is Inspector Caldwell that the *Palmyra* dumped off here today. Uh – Inspector, this is Brooks, the Head Trader.'

They shake hands. He looks at her and says, 'I'd lost hope my reports would ever get any attention paid to them. You've come to check my report that the trading post on Moklin has to be abandoned?'

'I have not!' says Inspector Caldwell, sharp. 'That's absurd! This planet has great potentialities, this post is profitable and the natives are friendly, and the trade should continue to increase. The Board is even considering the introduction of special crops.'

That strikes me as a bright idea. I'd like to see what would happen if Moklins started cultivating new kinds of plants! It would be a thing to watch – with regular Moklin plants seeing strangers getting good growing places and special attention! I can't even guess what'll happen, but I want to watch!

'What I want to ask right off,' says Inspector Caldwell, fierce, 'is why you have allowed a competitive trading post to be established, why you did not report it sooner, and why you haven't identified the company back of it?'

Brooks stares at her. He gets mad.

'Hell!' he says. 'My reports cover all that! Haven't you read them?'

'Of course not,' says Inspector Caldwell. 'I was given an outline of the situation here and told to investigate and correct it.'

'Oh!' says Brooks. 'That's it!'

Then he looks like he's swallowing naughty words. It is funny to see them glare at each other, both of them looking like they are seeing something that interests them plenty, but throwing off angry sparks just the same.

'If you'll show me samples of their trade goods,' says Inspector Caldwell, arrogant, 'and I hope you can do *that* much, I'll identify the trading company handling them!'

He grins at her without amusement and leads the way to the inside of the trading post. We bring out the stuff we've had some of our Moklins go over and buy for us. Brooks dumps the goods on a table and stands back to see what she'll make of them, grinning with the same lack of mirth. She picks up a visi-reel projector.

'Hmm,' she says, scornful. 'Not very good quality. It's . . .' Then she stops. She picks up a forest knife. 'This,' she says, 'is a product of—' Then she stops again. She picks up some cloth and fingers it. She really steams. 'I see!' she says, angry. 'Because we have been on this planet so long and the Moklins are used to our goods, the people of the other trading post *duplicate* them! Do they cut prices?'

'Fifty per cent,' says Brooks.

I chime in, 'But we ain't lost much trade. Lots of Moklins still trade with us, out of friendship. Friendly folks, these Moklins.'

Just then Deeth comes in, looking just like Casey that used to be here on Moklin. He grins at me.

'A girl just brought you a compliment,' he lets me know.

'Shucks!' I says, embarrassed and pleased. 'Send her in and get a present for her.'

Deeth goes out. Inspector Caldwell hasn't noticed. She's seething over that other trading company copying our trade goods and underselling us on a planet we're supposed to have exclusive. Brooks looks at her grim.

'I shall look over their post,' she announces, fierce, 'and if they want a trade war, they'll get one! We can cut prices if we need to – we have all the resources of the Company behind us!'

Brooks seems to be steaming on his own, maybe because she hasn't read his reports. But just then a Moklin girl comes in. Not bad-looking, either. You can see she is a Moklin – she ain't as convincing human as Deeth is, say – but she looks pretty human, at that. She giggles at me.

'Compliment,' she says, and shows me what she's carrying.

I look. It's a Moklin kid, a boy, just about brand-new. And it has my shape ears, and its nose looks like somebody had stepped on it – my nose is that way – and it looks like a very small-sized working model of me. I chuck it under the chin and say, 'Kitchy-coo!' It gurgles at me.

'What's your name?' I ask the girl.

She tells me. I don't remember it, and I don't remember ever seeing her before, but she's paid me a compliment, all right – Moklin-style.

'Mighty nice,' I say. 'Cute as all get-out. I hope he grows up to have more sense than I got, though.' Then Deeth comes in with a armload of trade stuff like Old Man Bland gave to the first Moklin kid that was born with long whiskers like his, and I say, 'Thanks for the compliment. I am greatly honored.'

She takes the stuff and giggles again, and goes out. The kid beams at me over her shoulder and waves its fist. Mighty humanlike. A right cute kid, anyway you look at it.

Then I hear a noise. Inspector Caldwell is regarding me with loathing in her eyes.

'Did you say they were friendly creatures?' she asks, bitter. 'I think affectionate would be a better word!' Her voice shakes. 'You are going to be transferred out of here the instant the *Palmyra* gets back!'

'What's the matter?' I ask, surprised. 'She paid me a compliment and I gave her a present. It's a custom. She's satisfied. I never see her before that I remember.'

'You *don't*,' she says. 'The – the *callousness!* You're revolting!'

Brooks begins to sputter, then he snickers, and all of a sudden he's howling with laughter. He is laughing at Inspector Caldwell. Then I get it, and I snort. Then I hoot and holler. It gets funnier when she gets madder still. She near blows up from being mad!

We must look crazy, the two of us there in the post, just hollering with laughter while she gets furiouser and furiouser. Finally I have to lay down on the floor to laugh more comfortable. You see, she doesn't get a bit of what I've told her about there being a special kind of evolution on Moklin. The more disgusted and furious she looks at me, the harder I have to laugh. I can't help it.

When we set out for the other trading post next day, the atmosphere ain't what you'd call exactly cordial. There is just the Inspector and me, with Deeth and a couple of other Moklins for the look of things. She has on a green forest suit, and with her red hair she sure looks good! But she looks at me cold when Brooks says I'll take her over to the other post, and she doesn't say a word the first mile or two.

We trudge on, and presently Deeth and the others get ahead so they can't hear what she says. And she remarks indignant, 'I must say Mr Brooks isn't very cooperative. Why didn't he come with me? Is he afraid of the men at the other post?'

'Not him,' I says. 'He's a good guy. But you got authority over him and you ain't read his reports.'

'If I have authority,' she says, sharp, 'I assure you it's because I'm competent!'

'I don't doubt it,' I says. 'If you wasn't cute, he wouldn't care. But a man don't want a good-looking girl giving him orders. He wants to give them to her. A homely woman, it don't matter.'

She tosses her head, but it don't displease her. Then she says, 'What's in the reports that I should have read?'

'I don't know,' I admit. 'But he's been sweating over them. It makes him mad that nobody bothered to read 'em.'

'Maybe,' she guesses, 'it was what I need to know about this other trading post. What do you know about it, Mr Brinkley?'

I tell her what Deeth has told Brooks. Brooks found out about it because one day some Moklins come in to trade and ask friendly why we charge so much for this and that. Deeth told them we'd always charged that, and they say the other trading post sells things cheaper, and Deeth says what trading post? So they up and tell him there's another post that sells the same kind of things we do, only cheaper. But that's all they'll say.

So Brooks tells Deeth to find out, and he scouts around and comes back. There is another trading post only fifteen miles away, and it is selling stuff just like ours. And it charges only half price. Deeth didn't see the men – just the Moklin clerks. We ain't been able to see the men either.

'Why haven't you seen the men?'

'Every time Brooks or me go over,' I explain, 'the Moklins they got working for them say the other men are off somewhere. Maybe they're starting some more posts. We wrote 'em a note, asking what the hell they mean, but they never answered it. Of course, we ain't seen their books or their living quarters—'

'You could find out plenty by a glimpse at their books!' she snaps. 'Why haven't you just marched in and made the Moklins show you what you want to know, since the men were away?'

'Because,' I says, patient, 'Moklins imitate humans. If we start trouble, they'll start it too. We can't set a example of rough stuff like burglary, mayhem, breaking and entering, manslaughter, or bigamy, or those Moklins will do just like us.'

'Bigamy!' She grabs on that sardonic. 'If you're trying to make me think you've got enough moral sense—'

I get a little mad. Brooks and me, we've explained to her, careful, how it is admiration *and* the way evolution works on Moklin that makes Moklin kids get born with long whiskers and that the compliment the Moklin girl has paid me is just exactly that. But she hasn't listened to a word.

'Miss Caldwell,' I says, 'Brooks and me told you the facts.

333

We tried to tell them delicate, to spare your feelings. Now if you'll try to spare mine, I'll thank you.'

'If you mean your finer feelings,' she says, sarcastic, 'I'll spare them as soon as I find some!'

So I shut up. There's no use trying to argue with a woman. We tramp on through the forest without a word. Presently we come on a nest-bush. It's a pretty big one. There are a couple dozen nests on it, from the little-bitty bud ones no bigger than your fist, to the big ripe ones lined with soft stuff that have busted open and have got cacklebirds housekeeping in them now.

There are two cacklebirds sitting on a branch by the nest that is big enough to open up and have eggs laid in it, only it ain't. The cacklebirds are making noises like they are cussing it and telling it to hurry up and open, because they are in a hurry.

'That's a nest-bush,' I says. 'It grows nests for the cacklebirds. The birds – uh – fertilize the ground around it. They're sloppy feeders and drop a lot of stuff that rots and is fertilizer too. The nest-bush and the cacklebirds kind of cooperate. That's the way evolution works on Moklin, like Brooks and me told you.'

She tosses that red head of hers and stamps on, not saying a word. So we get to the other trading post. And there she gets one of these slow-burning, long-lasting mads on that fill a guy like me with awe.

There's only Moklins at the other trading post, as usual. They say the humans are off somewhere. They look at her admiring and polite. They show her their stock. It is practically identical with ours – only they admit that they've sold out of some items because their prices are low. They act most respectful and pleased to see her.

But she don't learn a thing about where their stuff comes from or what company is horning in on Moklin trade. And she looks at their head clerk and she burns and burns.

When we get back, Brooks is sweating over memorandums he has made, getting another report ready for the next Company ship. Inspector Caldwell marches into the trade room and gives orders in a controlled, venomous voice. Then she marches right in on Brooks.

'I have just ordered the Moklin sales force to cut the price on all items on sale by seventy-five per cent,' she says, her voice trembling a little with fury. 'I have also ordered the credit given for Moklin trade goods to be doubled. They want a trade war? They'll get it!'

She is madder than business would account for. Brooks says, tired, 'I'd like to show you some facts. I've been over every inch of territory in thirty miles, looking for a place where a ship could land for that other post. There isn't any. Does that mean anything to you?'

'The post is there, isn't it?' she says. 'And they have trade goods, haven't they? And we have exclusive trading rights on Moklin, haven't we? That's enough for me. Our job is to drive them out of business!'

But she is a *lot* madder than business would account for. Brooks says, very weary, 'There's nearly a whole planet where they could have put another trading post. They could have set up shop on the other hemisphere and charged any price they pleased. But they set up shop right next to us? Does that make sense?'

'Setting up close,' she says, 'would furnish them with customers already used to human trade goods. And it furnished them with Moklins trained to be interpreters and clerks! And—' Then it come out, what she's raging, boiling, steaming, burning up about. 'And,' she says, furious, 'it furnished them with a Moklin head-clerk who is a very handsome young man, Mr Brooks! He not only resembles you in every feature, but he even has a good many of your mannerisms. You should be very proud!'

With this she slams out of the room. Brooks blinks.

'She won't believe anything,' he says, sour, 'except only that man is vile. Is that true about a Moklin who looks like me?'

I nod.

'Funny his folks never showed him to me for a compliment

present!' Then he stares at me, hard. 'How good is the likeness?'

'If he is wearing your clothes,' I tell him, truthful, 'I'd swear he is you.'

Then Brooks – slow, very slow – turns white. 'Remember the time you went off with Deeth and his folks hunting? That was the time a Moklin got killed. You were wearing guest garments, weren't you?'

I feel queer inside, but I nod. Guest garments, for Moklins, are like the best bedroom and the drumstick of the chicken among humans. And a Moklin hunting party is something. They go hunting *garlikthos*, which you might as well call dragons, because they've got scales and they fly and they are tough babies.

The way to hunt them is you take along some cacklebirds that ain't nesting – they are no good for anything while they're honeymooning – and the cacklebirds go flapping around until a *garlikthos* comes after them, and then they go jet-streaking to where the hunters are, cackling a blue streak to say, 'Here I come, boys! Hold everything until I get past!' Then the *garlikthos* dives after them and the hunters get it as it dives.

You give the cacklebirds its innards, and they sit around and eat, cackling to each other, zestful, like they're bragging about the other times they done the same thing, only better.

'You were wearing guest garments?' repeats Brooks, grim.

I feel very queer inside, but I nod again. Moklin guest garments are mighty easy on the skin and feel mighty good. They ain't exactly practical hunting clothes, but the Moklins feel bad if a human that's their guest don't wear them. And of course he has to shed his human clothes to wear them.

'What's the idea?' I want to know. But I feel pretty unhappy inside.

'You didn't come back for one day, in the middle of the hunt, after tobacco and a bath?'

'No,' I says, beginning to get rattled. 'We were way over at the Thunlib Hills. We buried the dead Moklin over there and had a hell of a time building a tomb over him. Why?'

'During that week,' says Brooks, grim, 'and while you were off wearing Moklin guest garments, somebody came back wearing your clothes – and got some tobacco and passed the time of day and went off again. Joe, just like there's a Moklin you say could pass for me, there's one that could pass for you. In fact, he did. Nobody suspected either.'

I get panicky. 'But what'd he do that for?' I want to know. 'He didn't steal anything! Would he have done it just to brag to the other Moklins that he fooled you?'

'He might,' says Brooks, 'have been checking to see if he could fool me. Or Captain Haney of the *Palmyra*. Or—'

He looks at me. I feel myself going numb. This can mean one hell of a mess!

'I haven't told you before,' says Brooks, 'but I've been guessing at something like this. Moklins like to be human, and they get human kids – kids that look human, anyway. Maybe they can want to be smart like humans, and they are.' He tries to grin, and can't. 'That rival trading post looked fishy to me right at the start. They're practicing with that. It shouldn't be there at all, but it is. You see?'

I feel weak and sick all over. This is a dangerous sort of thing! But I say quick, 'If you mean they got Moklins that could pass for you and me, and they're figuring to bump us off and take our places – I don't believe that! Moklins *like* humans! They wouldn't harm humans for *anything!*'

Brooks don't pay any attention. He says, harsh, 'I've been trying to persuade the Company that we've got to get out of here, fast! And they send this Inspector Caldwell who's not only female, but a redhead to boot! All they think about is a competitive trading post! And all she sees is that we're a bunch of lascivious scoundrels, and since she's a woman there's nothing that'll convince her otherwise!'

Then something hits me. It looks hopeful.

'She's the first human woman to land on Moklin. And she has got red hair. It's the first red hair the Moklins ever saw. Have we got time?'

He figures. Then he says, 'With luck, it ought to turn up!

You've hit it!' And then his expression sort of softens. 'If that happens – poor kid, she's going to take it hard! Women hate to be wrong. Especially redheads! But that might be the saving of – of humanity, when you think of it.'

I blink at him. He goes on, fierce, 'Look, I'm no Moklin! You know that. But if there's a Moklin that looks enough like me to take my place ... You see? We got to think of Inspector Caldwell, anyhow. If you ever see me cross my fingers, you wiggle your little finger. Then I know it's you. And the other way about. Get it? You swear you'll watch over Inspector Caldwell?'

'Sure!' I say. 'Of course!'

I wiggle my little finger. He crosses his. Its a signal nobody but us two would know. I feel a lot better.

Brooks goes off next morning, grim, to visit the other trading post and see the Moklin that looks so much like him. Inspector Caldwell goes along, fierce, and I'm guessing it's to see the fireworks when Brooks sees his Moklin double that she thinks is more than a coincidence. Which she is right, only not in the way she thinks.

Before they go, Brooks crosses his fingers and looks at me significant. I wiggle my little finger back at him. They go off.

I sit down in the shade of Sally and try to think things out. I am all churned up inside, and scared as hell. It's near two weeks to landing time, when the old *Palmyra* ought to come bulging down out of the sky with a load of new trade goods. I think wistful about how swell everything has been on Moklin up to now, and how Moklins admire humans, and how friendly everything has been, and how it's a great compliment for Moklins to want to be like humans and to get like them, and how no Moklin would ever dream of hurting a human and how they imitate humans joyous and reverent and happy. Nice people, Moklins. But—

The end of things is in sight. Liking humans has made Moklins smart, but now there's been a slip-up. Moklins will do anything to produce kids that look like humans. That's a compliment. But no human ever sees a Moklin that's four or five years old and all grown up and looks so much like him that nobody can tell them apart. That ain't scheming. It's just that Moklins like humans, but they're scared the humans might not like to see themselves in a sort of Moklin mirror. So if they did that at all, they'd maybe keep it a secret, like children keep secrets from grownups.

Moklins are a lot like kids. You can't help liking them. But a human can get plenty panicky if he thinks what would happen if Moklins get to passing for humans among humans, and want their kids to have top-grade brains, and top-grade talents, and so on...

I sweat, sitting there. I can see the whole picture. Brooks is worrying about Moklins loose among humans, outsmarting them as their kids grow up, being the big politicians, the bosses, the planetary pioneers, the prettiest girls and the handsomest guys in the Galaxy – everything humans want to be themselves. Just thinking about it is enough to make any human feel like he's going nuts. But Brooks is also worrying about Inspector Caldwell, who is five foot three and red-headed and cute as a bug's ear and riding for a bad fall.

They come back from the trip to the other trading post. Inspector Caldwell is baffled and mad. Brooks is sweating and scared. He slips me the signal and I wiggle my little finger back at him, just so I'll know he didn't get substituted for without Inspector Caldwell knowing it, and so he knows nothing happened to me while he was gone. They didn't see the Moklin that looks like Brooks. They didn't get a bit of information we didn't have before – which is just about none at all.

Things go on. Brooks and me are sweating it out until the *Palmyra* lets down out of the sky again, meanwhile praying for Inspector Caldwell to get her ears pinned back so proper steps can be taken, and every morning he crosses his fingers at me, and I wiggle my little finger back at him... And he watches over Inspector Caldwell tender.

*

339

The other trading post goes on placid. They sell their stuff at half the price we sell ours for. So, on Inspector Caldwell's orders, we cut ours again to half what they sell theirs for. So they sell theirs for half what we sell ours for, so we sell ours for half what they sell theirs for. And so on. Meanwhile we sweat.

Three days before the *Palmyra* is due, our goods are marked at just exactly one per cent of what they was marked a month before, and the other trading post is selling them at half that. It looks like we are going to have to pay a bonus to Moklins to take goods away for us to compete with the other trading post.

Otherwise, everything looks normal on the surface. Moklins hang around as usual, friendly and admiring. They'll hang around a couple of days just to get a look at Inspector Caldwell, and they regard her respectful.

Brooks looks grim. He is head over heels crazy about her now and she knows it, and she rides him hard. She snaps at him, and he answers her patient and gentle – because he knows that when what he hopes is going to happen, she is going to need him to comfort her. She has about wiped out our stock, throwing bargain sales. Our shelves are almost bare. But the other trading post still has plenty of stock.

'Mr Brooks,' says Inspector Caldwell, bitter, at breakfast, 'we'll have to take most of the *Palmyra*'s cargo to fill up our inventory.'

'Maybe,' he says, tender, 'and maybe not.'

'But we've got to drive that other post out of business!' she says, desperate. Then she breaks down. 'This – this is my first independent assignment. I've got to handle it successfully!'

He hesitates. But just then Deeth comes in. He beams friendly at Inspector Caldwell.

'A compliment for you, ma'am. Three of them.'

She goggles at him. Brooks says, gentle, 'It's all right. Deeth, show them in and get some presents.'

Inspector Caldwell splutters incredulous, 'But – but—'

'Don't be angry,' says Brooks. 'They mean it as a compliment. It is, actually, you know.'

Three Moklin girls come in, giggling. They are not

bad-looking at all. They look as human as Deeth, but one of them has a long, droopy mustache like a mate of the *Palmyra* – that's because they hadn't even seen a human woman before Inspector Caldwell come along. They sure have admired her, though! And Moklin kids get born fast. Very fast.

They show her what they are holding so proud and happy in their arms. They have got three little Moklin kids, one apiece. And every one of them has red hair, just like Inspector Caldwell, and every one of them is a girl that is the spit and image of her. You would swear they are human babies, and you'd swear they are hers. But of course they ain't. They make kid noises and wave their little fists.

Inspector Caldwell is just plain paralyzed. She stares at them, and goes red as fire and white as chalk, and she is speechless. So Brooks has to do the honors. He admires the kids extravagant, and the Moklin girls giggle, and take the compliment presents Deeth brings in, and they go out happy.

When the door closes, Inspector Caldwell wilts.

'Oh-h!' she wails. 'It's true! You didn't – you haven't – they can make their babies look like anybody they want!'

Brooks puts his arms around her and she begins to cry against his shoulder. He pats her and says, 'They've got a queer sort of evolution on Moklin, darling. Babies here inherit desired characteristics. Not *acquired* characteristics, but *desired* ones! And what could be more desirable than you?'

I am blinking at them. He says to me, cold, 'Will you kindly get the hell out of here and stay out?'

I come to. I says, 'Just one precaution.'

I wiggle my little finger. He crosses his fingers at me.

'Then,' I says, 'since there's no chance of a mistake, I'll leave you two together.'

And I do.

The *Palmyra* booms down out of the sky two days later. We are all packed up. Inspector Caldwell is shaky, on the porch of the post, when Moklins come hollering and waving friendly over from the landing field pulling a freight-truck with Cap

Haney on it. I see the other festive groups around members of the crew that – this being a scheduled stop – have been given ship-leave for a couple hours to visit their Moklin friends.

'I've got the usual cargo—' begins Cap Haney.

'Don't discharge it,' says Inspector Caldwell, firm. 'We are abandoning this post. I have authority and Mr Brooks has convinced me of the necessity for it. Please get our baggage to the ship.'

He gapes at her. 'The Company don't like to give in to competition—'

'There isn't any competition,' says Inspector Caldwell. She gulps. 'Darling, you tell him,' she says to Brooks.

He says, lucid, 'She's right, Captain. The other trading post is purely a Moklin enterprise. They like to do everything that humans do. Since humans were running a trading post, they opened one too. They bought goods from us and pretended to sell them at half price, and we cut our prices, and they bought more goods from us and pretended to sell at half the new prices . . . Some Moklin or other must've thought it would be nice to be a smart businessman, so his kids would be smart businessmen. Too smart! We close up this post before Moklins think of other things . . .'

He means, of course, that if Moklins get loose from their home planet and pass as humans, their kids can maybe take over human civilization. Human nature couldn't take that! But it is something to be passed on to the high brass, and not told around general.

'Better sound the emergency recall signal,' says Inspector Caldwell, brisk.

We go over to the ship and the *Palmyra* lets go that wailing siren that'll carry twenty miles. Any crew member in hearing is going to beat it back to the ship full-speed. They come running from every which way, where they been visiting their Moklin friends. And then, all of a sudden, here comes a fellow wearing Moklin guest garments, yelling, 'Hey! Wait! I ain't got my clothes—'

And then there is what you might call a dead silence.

Because lined up for checkoff is another guy that comes running at the recall signal, and he is wearing ship's clothes, and you can see that him and the guy in Moklin guest garments are just exactly alike. Twins. Identical. The spit and image of each other. And it is for sure that one of them is a Moklin. But which?

Cap Haney's eyes start to pop out of his head. But then the guy in *Palmyra* uniform grins and says, 'Okay, I'm a Moklin. But us Moklins like humans so much, I thought it would be nice to make a trip to Earth and see more humans. My parents planned it five years ago, made me look like this wonderful human, and hid me for this moment. But we would not want to make any difficulties for humans, so I have confessed and I will leave the ship.'

He takes it as a joke on him. He talks English as good as anybody. I don't know how anybody could tell which was the human guy and which one the Moklin, but this Moklin grins and steps down, and the other Moklins admire him enormous for passing even a few minutes as human among humans.

We get away from there so fast, he is allowed to keep the human uniform.

Moklin is the first planet that humans ever get off of, moving fast, breathing hard, and sweating copious. It's one of those things that humans just can't take. Not that there's anything wrong with Moklins. They're swell folks. They like humans. But humans just can't take the idea of Moklins passing for human and being all the things humans want to be themselves. I think it's really a false alarm. I'll find out pretty soon.

Inspector Caldwell and Brooks get married, and they go off to a post on Briarius Four – a swell place for a honeymoon if there ever was one – and I guess they are living happy ever after. Me, I go to the new job the Company assigns me – telling me stern not to talk about Moklin, which I don't – and the Space Patrol orders no human ship to land on Moklin for any reason.

But I've been saving money and worrying. I keep thinking

of those three Moklin kids that Inspector Caldwell knows she ain't the father of. I worry about those kids. I hope nothing's happened to them. Moklin kids grow up fast, like I told you. They'll be just about grown now.

I'll tell you. I've bought me a little private spacecruiser, small but good. I'm shoving off for Moklin next week. If one of those three ain't married, I'm going to marry her, Moklin-style, and bring her out to a human colony planet. We'll have some kids. I know just what I want my kids to be like. They'll have plenty of brains – *top-level brains* – and the girls will be *real* good-looking!

But besides that, I've got to bring some other Moklins out and start them passing for human, too. Because my kids are going to need other Moklins to marry, ain't they? It's not that I don't like humans. I do! If the fellow I look like – Joe Brinkley – hadn't got killed accidental on that hunting trip with Deeth, I never would have thought of taking his place and being Joe Brinkley. But you can't blame me for wanting to live among humans.

Wouldn't you, if you was a Moklin?

EXPLORATION TEAM

The nearer moon went by overhead. It was jagged and irregular in shape, probably a captured asteroid. Huyghens had seen it often enough, so he did not go out of his quarters to watch it hurtle across the sky with seemingly the speed of an atmosphere-flier, occulting the stars as it went. Instead, he sweated over paperwork, which should have been odd because he was technically a felon and all his labors on Loren Two felonious. It was odd, too, for a man to do paperwork in a room with steel shutters and a huge bald eagle – untethered – dozing on a three-inch perch set in the wall. But paperwork was not Huyghens' real task. His only assistant had tangled with a night-walker, and the furtive Kodius Company ships had taken him away to where Kodius Company ships came from. Huyghens had to do two men's work in loneliness. To his knowledge, he was the only man in this solar system.

Below him, there were snufflings. Sitka Pete got up heavily and padded to his water-pan. He lapped the refrigerated water and sneezed violently. Sourdough Charley waked and complained in a rumbling growl. There were divers other rumblings and mutterings below. Huyghens called reassuringly, 'Easy there!' and went on with his work. He finished a climate report, and fed figures to a computer. While it hummed over them he entered the inventory totals in the station log, showing what supplies remained. Then he began to write up the log proper.

'*Sitka Pete,*' he wrote, '*has apparently solved the problem of killing individual sphexes. He has learned that it doesn't do to hug them and that his claws can't penetrate their hide, not the top-hide, anyhow. Today Semper notified us that a pack of sphexes had found the scent-trail to the station. Sitka hid downwind until they arrived. Then he charged from the rear and brought his paws together on both sides of a sphex's head in a terrific pair of slaps. It must have been like two twelve-inch shells arriving from opposite directions at the same time. It must have scrambled the sphex's brains as if they were eggs. It dropped dead. He killed two more with such mighty pairs of wallops. Sourdough Charley watched, grunting, and when the sphexes turned on Sitka, he charged in his turn. I, of course, couldn't shoot too close to him, so he might have fared badly except that Faro Nell came pouring out of the bear-quarters to help. The diversion enabled Sitka Pete to resume the use of his new technique, towering on his hind legs and swinging his paws in the new and grisly fashion. The fight ended promptly. Semper flew and screamed above the scrap, but as usual did not join in. Note: Nugget, the cub, tried to mix in but his mother cuffed him out of the way. Sourdough and Sitka ignored him as usual. Kodius Champion's genes are sound!'*

The noises of the night went on outside. There were notes like organ-tones – song-lizards. There were the tittering, giggling cries of night-walkers. There were sounds like tack-hammers, and doors closing, and from every direction came noises like hiccoughs in various keys. These were made by the improbable small creatures which on Loren Two took the place of insects.

Huyghens wrote out:

'Sitka seemed ruffled when the fight was over. He used his trick on the head of every dead or wounded sphex, except those he'd killed with it, lifting up their heads for his pile-driver-like blows from two directions at once, as if to show Sourdough how it was done. There was much grunting as they hauled the carcasses to the incinerator. It almost seemed—'

The arrival-bell clanged, and Huyghens jerked up his head to stare at it. Semper, the eagle, opened icy eyes. He blinked.

Noises. There was a long, deep, contented snore from below. Something shrieked, out in the jungle. Hiccoughs, clatterings, and organ-notes...

The bell clanged again. It was a notice that an unscheduled ship aloft somewhere had picked up the beacon-beam – which only Kodius Company ships should know about – and was communicating for a landing. But there shouldn't be any ships in this solar system just now! The Kodius Company's colony was completely illegal, and there were few graver crimes than unauthorized occupation of a new planet.

The bell clanged a third time. Huyghens swore. His hand went out to cut off the beacon, and then stopped. That would be useless. Radar would have fixed it and tied it in with physical features like the nearby sea and the Sere Plateau. The ship could find the place, anyhow, and descend by daylight.

'The devil!' said Huyghens. But he waited yet again for the bell to ring. A Kodius Company ship would double-ring to reassure him. But there shouldn't be a Kodius Company ship for months.

The bell clanged singly. The space-phone dial flickered and a voice came out of it, tinny from stratospheric distortion:

'Calling ground. Calling ground. Crete Line ship Odysseus calling ground on Loren Two. Landing one passenger by boat. Put on your field lights.'

Huyghens' mouth dropped open. A Kodius Company ship would be welcome. A Colonial Survey ship would be extremely unwelcome, because it would destroy the colony and Sitka and Sourdough and Faro Nell and Nugget – and Semper – and carry Huyghens off to be tried for unauthorized colonization and all that it implied.

But a commercial ship, landing one passenger by boat... There were simply no circumstances under which that could happen. Not to an unknown, illegal colony. Not to a furtive station!

Huyghens flicked on the landing-field lights. He saw the glare over the field half a mile away. Then he stood up and prepared to take the measures required by discovery. He packed the paperwork he'd been doing into the disposal-safe. He gathered up all personal documents and tossed them in. Every record, every bit of evidence that the Kodius Company maintained this station went into the safe. He slammed the door. He moved his finger toward the disposal-button, which would destroy the contents and melt down even the ashes past their possible use for evidence in court.

Then he hesitated. If it were a Survey ship, the button had to be pressed and he must resign himself to a long term in prison. But a Crete Line ship – if the space-phone told the truth – was not threatening. It was simply unbelievable.

He shook his head. He got into travel garb, armed himself, and went down into the bear-quarters, turning on lights as he went. There were startled snufflings, and Sitka Pete reared himself to a sitting position to blink at him. Sourdough Charley lay on his back with his legs in the air. He'd found it cooler, sleeping that way. He rolled over with a thump, and made snorting sounds which somehow sounded cordial. Faro Nell padded to the door of her separate apartment, assigned her so that Nugget would not be underfoot to irritate the big males.

Huyghens, as the human population of Loren Two, faced the work-force, fighting-force, and – with Nugget – four-fifths of the terrestrial non-human population of the planet. They were mutated Kodiak bears, descendants of that Kodius Champion for whom the Kodius Company was named. Sitka Pete was a good twenty-two hundred pounds of lumbering, intelligent carnivore. Sourdough Charley would weigh within a hundred pounds of that figure. Faro Nell was eighteen hundred pounds of female charm and ferocity. Then Nugget poked his muzzle around his mother's furry rump to see what was toward, and he was six hundred pounds of ursine infancy. The animals looked at Huyghens expectantly. If he'd had Semper riding on his shoulder they'd have known what was expected of them.

'Let's go,' said Huyghens. 'It's dark outside, but somebody's coming. And it may be bad!'

He unfastened the outer door of the bear-quarters. Sitka Pete went charging clumsily through it. A forthright charge was the best way to develop any situation – if one was an oversize male Kodiak bear. Sourdough went lumbering after him. There was nothing hostile immediately outside. Sitka stood up on his hind legs – he reared up a solid twelve feet – and sniffed the air. Sourdough methodically lumbered to one side and then the other, sniffing in his turn. Nell came out, nine-tenths of a ton of daintiness, and rumbled admonitorily at Nugget, who trailed her closely. Huyghens stood in the doorway, his night-sighted gun ready. He felt uncomfortable at sending the bears ahead into a Loren Two jungle at night, but they were qualified to scent danger, and he was not.

The illumination of the jungle in a wide path toward the landing-field made for weirdness in the look of things. There were arching giant ferns and columnar trees which grew above them, and the extraordinary lanceolate underbrush of the jungle. The flood-lamps, set level with the ground, lighted everything from below. The foliage, then, was brightly lit against the black night-sky, brightly enough lit to dim the stars.

'On ahead!' commanded Huyghens, waving. 'Hup!'

He swung the bear-quarters door shut, and moved toward the landing-field through the lane of lighted forest. The two giant male Kodiaks lumbered ahead. Sitka Pete dropped to all fours and prowled. Sourdough Charley followed closely, swinging from side to side. Huyghens came behind the two of them, and Faro Nell brought up the rear with Nugget nudging her.

It was an excellent military formation for progress through dangerous jungle. Sourdough and Sitka were advance guard and point, respectively, while Faro Nell guarded the rear. With Nugget to look after, she was especially alert against attack from behind. Huyghens was, of course, the striking force. His gun fired explosive bullets which would discourage even sphexes, and his night-sight – a cone of light which went on when he took up the trigger-slack – told exactly where they would strike. It was not a sportsmanlike weapon, but the creatures of Loren Two were not sportsmanlike antagonists. The night-walkers, for example. But night-walkers feared light. They attacked only in a species of hysteria if it were too bright.

Huyghens moved toward the glare at the landing field. His mental state was savage. The Kodius Company on Loren Two was completely illegal. It happened to be necessary, from one point of view, but it was still illegal. The tinny voice on the space-phone was not convincing, in ignoring that illegality. But if a ship landed, Huyghens could get back to the station before men could follow, and he'd have the disposal-safe turned on in time to protect those who'd sent him here.

Then he heard the far-away and high harsh roar of a landing boat rocket – not a ship's bellowing tubes – as he made his way through the unreal-seeming brush. The roar grew louder as he pushed on, the three big Kodiaks padding here and there, sniffing for danger.

He reached the edge of the landing field, and it was blindingly bright, with the customary divergent beams slanting skyward so a ship could check its instrument-landing by sight. Landing fields like this had been standard, once upon a time. Nowadays all developed planets had landing-grids – monstrous structures which drew upon ionospheres for power and lifted and drew down star-ships with remarkable gentleness and unlimited force. This sort of landing field would now be found only where a survey-team was at work, or where some strictly temporary investigation of ecology or bacteriology was under way, or where a newly authorized colony had not yet been able to build its landing-grid. Of course, it was unthinkable that anybody would attempt a settlement in defiance of the law!

Already, as Huyghens reached the edge of the scorched open space, the night-creatures had rushed to the light, like moths on Earth. The air was misty with crazily gyrating, tiny flying things. They were innumerable and of every possible form and size, from the white midges of the night and multi-winged flying worms to those revoltingly naked-looking larger creatures which might have passed for plucked flying monkeys if they had not been carnivorous and worse. The flying things soared and whirred and danced and spun insanely in the glare, making peculiarly plaintive humming noises. They almost formed a lamp-lit ceiling over the cleared space, and actually did hide the stars. Staring upward, Huyghens could just barely make out the blue-white flame of the space-boat's rockets through the fog of wings and bodies.

The rocket-flame grew steadily in size. Once it tilted to

adjust the boat's descending course. It went back to normal. A speck of incandescence at first, it grew until it was like a great star, then a more-than-brilliant moon, and then it was a pitiless glaring eye. Huyghens averted his gaze from it. Sitka Pete sat lumpily and blinked at the dark jungle away from the light. Sourdough ignored the deepening, increasing rocket-roar. He sniffed the air. Faro Nell held Nugget firmly under one huge paw and licked his head as if tidying him up to be seen by company. Nugget wriggled.

The roar became that of ten thousand thunders. A warm breeze blew outward from the landing field. The rocket-boat hurtled downward, and as its flame touched the mist of flying things, they shriveled and burned. Then there were churning clouds of dust everywhere, and the center of the field blazed terribly – and something slid down a shaft of fire, squeezed it flat, and sat on it – and the flame went out. The rocket-boat sat there, resting on its tail-fins, pointing toward the stars from which it came.

There was a terrible silence after the tumult. Then, very faintly, the noises of the night came again. There were sounds like those of organ-pipes, and very faint and apologetic noises like hiccoughs. All these sounds increased, and suddenly Huyghens could hear quite normally. As he watched, a side-port opened with a clattering, something unfolded from where it had been inset into the hull of the space-boat, and there was a metal passageway across the flame-heated space on which the boat stood.

A man came out of the port. He reached back in and shook hands. Then he climbed down the ladder-rungs to the walk-way, and marched above the steaming baked area, carrying a traveling bag. At the end of the walk he stepped to the ground, and moved hastily to the edge of the clearing. He waved to the space-boat. The walk-way folded briskly back up to the hull and vanished in it, and almost at once a flame exploded into being under the tail-fins. There were fresh clouds of monstrous, choking dust, a brightness like that of a sun, and noise past the possibility of endurance. Then the light rose swiftly through the dust-cloud, sprang higher, and climbed more swiftly still. When Huyghens' ears again permitted him to hear anything, there was only a diminishing mutter in the heavens and a faint bright speck of light ascending to the sky, swinging eastward as it rose to intercept the ship from which it had descended.

The night-noises of the jungle went on, even though there was a spot of incandescence in the day-bright clearing, and steam rolled up in clouds at the edge of the hottest area. Beyond that edge, a man with a traveling bag in his hand looked about him.

Huyghens advanced toward him as the incandescence dimmed. Sourdough and Sitka preceded him. Faro Nell trailed faithfully, keeping a maternal eye on her offspring. The man in the clearing stared at the parade they made. It would be upsetting, even after preparation, to land at night on a strange planet, to have the ship's boat and all links with the rest of the cosmos depart, and then to find oneself approached – it might seem stalked – by two colossal male Kodiak bears, with a third bear and a cub behind them. A single human figure in such company might seem irrelevant.

The new arrival gazed blankly. He moved back a few steps. Then Huyghens called:

'Hello, there! Don't worry about the bears! They're friends!'

Sitka reached the newcomer. He went warily downwind from him and sniffed. The smell was satisfactory. Man-smell. Sitka sat down with the solid impact of more than a ton of bear-meat landing on packed dirt, and regarded the man. Sourdough said '*Whoosh!*' and went on to sample the air beyond the clearing. Huyghens approached. The newcomer wore the uniform of the Colonial Survey. That was bad. It bore the insignia of a senior officer. Worse.

'Hah!' said the just-landed man. 'Where are the robots? What in all the nineteen hells are these creatures? Why did you shift your station? I'm Bordman, here to make a progress-report on your colony.'

Huyghens said:

'What colony?'

'Loren Two Robot Installation—' then Bordman said indignantly, 'Don't tell me that that idiot skipper can have dropped me at the wrong place! This is Loren Two, isn't it! And this is the landing field. But where are your robots? You should have the beginning of a grid up! What the devil's happened here and what are these beasts?'

Huyghens grimaced.

'This,' he said, 'is an illegal, unlicensed settlement. I'm a criminal. These beasts are my confederates. If you don't want to associate with criminals you needn't, of course, but I doubt if you'll live till morning unless you accept my hospitality while I think over what to do about your landing. In reason, I ought to shoot you.'

Faro Nell came to a halt behind Huyghens, which was her proper post in all out-door movement. Nugget, however, saw a new human. Nugget was a cub, and therefore friendly. He ambled forward. He wriggled bashfully as he approached Bordman. He sneezed, because he was embarrassed.

His mother overtook him and cuffed him to one side. He wailed. The wail of a six-hundred-pound Kodiak bear-cub is a remarkable sound. Bordman gave ground a pace.

'I think,' he said carefully, 'that we'd better talk things over. But if this is an illegal colony, of course you're under arrest and anything you say will be used against you.'

Huyghens grimaced again.

'Right,' he said. 'But now if you'll walk close to me, we'll head back to the station. I'd have Sourdough carry your bag – he likes to carry things – but he may need his teeth. We've half a mile to travel.' He turned to the animals. 'Let's go!' he said commandingly. 'Back to the station! Hup!'

Grunting, Sitka Pete arose and took up his duties as advanced point of a combat-team. Sourdough trailed, swinging widely to one side and another. Huyghens and Bordman moved together. Faro Nell and Nugget brought up the rear.

There was only one incident on the way back. It was a night-walker, made hysterical by the lane of light. It poured through the underbrush, uttering cries like maniacal laughter.

Sourdough brought it down, a good ten yards from Huyghens.

When it was all over, Nugget bristled up to the dead creature, uttering cub-growls. He feigned to attack it.

His mother whacked him soundly.

There were comfortable, settling-down noises below, as the bears grunted and rumbled, and ultimately were still. The glare from the landing field was gone. The lighted lane through the jungle was dark again. Huyghens ushered the man from the space-boat up into his living quarters. There was a rustling stir, and Semper took his head from under his wing. He stared coldly at the two humans, spread monstrous, seven-foot wings, and fluttered them. He opened his beak and closed it with a snap.

'That's Semper,' said Huyghens. 'Semper Tyrannis. He's the rest of the terrestrial population here. Not being a fly-by-night sort of creature, he didn't come out to welcome you.'

Bordman blinked at the huge bird, perched on a three-inch-thick perch set in the wall.

'An eagle?' he demanded. 'Kodiak bears – mutated ones, but still bears – and now an eagle? You've a very nice fighting unit in the bears—'

'They're pack animals too,' said Huyghens. 'They can carry some hundreds of pounds without losing too much combat efficiency. And there's no problem of supply. They live off the jungle. Not sphexes, though. Nothing will eat a sphex.'

He brought out glasses and a bottle and indicated a chair. Bordman put down his traveling bag, took a glass, and sat down.

'I'm curious,' he observed. 'Why Semper Tyrannis? I can understand Sitka Pete and Sourdough Charley as fighters. But why Semper?'

'He was bred for hawking,' said Huyghens. 'You sic a dog on something. You sic Semper Tyrannis. He's too big to ride on a hawking-glove, so the shoulders of my coats are padded to let him ride there. He's a flying scout. I've trained him to notify us of sphexes, and in flight he carries a tiny television camera. He's useful, but he hasn't the brains of the bears.'

Bordman sat down and sipped at his glass.

'Interesting, very interesting! – Didn't you say something about shooting me?'

'I'm trying to think of a way out,' Huyghens said. 'Add up all the penalties for illegal colonization and I'd be in a very bad fix if you got away and reported this set-up. Shooting you would be logical.'

'I see that,' said Bordman reasonably. 'But since the point has come up – I have a blaster trained on you from my pocket.'

Huyghens shrugged.

'It's rather likely that my human confederates will be back here before your friends. You'd be in a very tight fix if my friends came back and found you more or less sitting on my corpse.'

Bordman nodded.

'That's true, too. Also it's probable that your fellow-terrestrials wouldn't cooperate with me as they have with you. You seem to have the whip hand, even with my blaster trained on you. On the other hand, you could have killed me quite easily after the boat left, when I'd first landed. I'd have been quite unsuspicious. Therefore you may not really intend to murder me.'

Huyghens shrugged again.

'So,' said Bordman, 'since the secret of getting along with people is that of postponing quarrels, suppose we postpone the question of who kills whom? Frankly, I'm going to send you to prison if I can. Unlawful colonization is very bad business. But I suppose you feel that you have to do something perman-ent about me. In your place I probably should, too. Shall we declare a truce?'

Huyghens indicated indifference.

'Then I do,' Bordman said. 'I have to! So—'

He pulled his hand out of his pocket and put a pocket blaster on the table. He leaned back.

'Keep it,' said Huyghens. 'Loren Two isn't a place where you live long unarmed.' He turned to a cupboard. 'Hungry?'

'I could eat,' admitted Bordman.

Huyghens pulled out two meal-packs from the cupboard and inserted them in the readier below. He set out plates.

'Now, what happened to the official, licensed, authorized colony here?' asked Bordman briskly. 'License issued eighteen months ago. There was a landing of colonists with a drone-fleet of equipment and supplies. There've been four ship-contacts since. There should be several thousand robots being industrious under adequate human supervision. There should be a hundred-mile-square clearing, planted with food-plants for later human arrivals. There should be a landing-grid at least half-finished. Obviously there should be a space-beacon to guide ships to a landing. There isn't. There's no clearing visible from space. That Crete Line ship has been in orbit for three days, trying to find a place to drop me. Her skipper was fuming. Your beacon is the only one on the planet, and we found it by accident. What happened?'

Huyghens served the food. He said drily:

'There could be a hundred colonies on this planet without any one knowing of any other. I can only guess about your robots, but I suspect they ran into sphexes.'

Bordman paused, with his fork in his hand.

'I read up on this planet, since I was to report on its colony. A sphex is part of the inimical animal life here. Cold-blooded belligerent carnivore, not a lizard but a genus all its own. Hunts in packs. Seven to eight hundred pounds, when adult. Lethally dangerous and simply too numerous to fight. They're why no license was ever granted to human colonists. Only robots could work here, because they're machines. What animal attacks machines?'

Huyghens said:

'What machine attacks animals? The sphexes wouldn't bother robots, of course, but would robots bother the sphexes?'

Bordman chewed and swallowed.

'Hold it! I'll agree that you can't make a hunting-robot. A machine can discriminate, but it can't decide. That's why there's no danger of a robot revolt. They can't decide to do something for which they have no instructions. But this colony was planned with full knowledge of what robots can and can't do. As ground was cleared, it was enclosed in an electrified fence which no sphex could touch without frying.'

Huyghens thoughtfully cut his food. After a moment:

'The landing was in the winter time,' he observed. 'It must have been, because the colony survived a while. And at a guess, the last ship-landing was before thaw. The years are eighteen months long here, you know.'

'It was in winter that the landing was made,' Bordman admitted. 'And the last ship-landing was before spring. The idea was to get mines in operation for material, and to have ground cleared and enclosed in sphex-proof fence before the sphexes came back from the tropics. They winter there, I understand.'

'Did you ever see a sphex?' asked Huyghens. Then he said, 'No, of course not. But if you took a spitting cobra and crossed it with a wild-cat, painted it tan-and-blue and then gave it hydrophobia and homicidal mania at once, you might have one sphex. But not the race of sphexes. They can climb trees, by the way. A fence wouldn't stop them.'

'An electrified fence,' said Bordman. 'Nothing could climb that!'

'No one animal,' Huyghens told him. 'But sphexes are a race. The smell of one dead sphex brings others running with blood in their eyes. Leave a dead sphex alone for six hours and you've got them around by dozens. Two days and there are hundreds. Longer, and you've got thousands of them! They gather to caterwaul over their dead pal and hunt for whoever or whatever killed him.'

He returned to his meal. A moment later he said:

'No need to wonder what happened to your colony. During the winter the robots burned out a clearing and put up an electrified fence according to the book. Come spring, the sphexes come back. They're curious, among their other madnesses. A sphex would try to climb the fence just to see what was behind it. He'd be electrocuted. His carcass would bring others, raging because a sphex was dead. Some of them would try to climb the fence, and die. And their corpses would bring others. Presently the fence would break down from the bodies hanging on it, or a bridge of dead beasts' carcasses would be built across it – and from as far downwind as the scent carried there'd be loping, raging, scent-crazed sphexes racing to the spot. They'd pour into the clearing through or over the fence, squalling and screeching for something to kill. I think they'd find it.'

Bordman ceased to eat. He looked sick.

'There were pictures of sphexes in the data I read. I suppose that would account for – everything.'

He tried to lift his fork. He put it down again.

'I can't eat,' he said abruptly.

Huyghens made no comment. He finished his own meal, scowling. He rose and put the plates into the top of the cleaner.

'Let me see those reports, eh?' he asked dourly. 'I'd like to see what sort of a set-up they had, those robots.'

Bordman hesitated and then opened his traveling bag. There was a microviewer and reels of films. One entire reel was labeled 'Specifications for Construction, Colonial Survey', which would contain detailed plans and all requirements of material and workmanship for everything from desks, office, administrative personnel, for use of, to landing-grids, heavy-gravity planets, lift-capacity 100,000 Earth-tons. But Huyghens found another. He inserted it and spun the control swiftly here and there, pausing only briefly at index-frames until he came to the section he wanted. He began to study the information with growing impatience.

'Robots, robots, robots!' he snapped. 'Why don't they leave them where they belong – in cities to do the dirty work, and on airless planets where nothing unexpected ever happens! Robots don't belong in new colonies. Your colonists depended on them for defense! Dammit, let a man work with robots long enough and he thinks all nature is as limited as they are! This is a plan to set up a controlled environment – on Loren Two! Controlled environment—' He swore. 'Complacent, idiotic, desk-bound half-wits!'

'Robots are all right,' said Bordman. 'We couldn't run civilization without them.'

'But you can't tame a wilderness with 'em,' snapped Huyghens. 'You had a dozen men landed, with fifty assembled robots to start with. There were parts for fifteen hundred more, and I'll bet anything I've got the ship-contacts landed more still!'

'They did,' admitted Bordman.

'I despise 'em,' growled Huyghens. 'I feel about 'em the way the old Greeks felt about slaves. They're for menial work – the sort of work a man will perform for himself, but that he won't do for another man for pay. Degrading work!'

'Quite aristocratic!' said Bordman with a touch of irony. 'I take it that robots clean out the bear-quarters downstairs.'

'No!' snapped Huyghens. 'I do. They're my friends. They fight for me. No robot would do the job right!'

He growled, again. The noises of the night went on outside. Organ-tones and hiccoughings and the sound of tack-hammers and slamming doors. Somewhere there was a singularly exact replica of the discordant squeakings of a rusty pump.

'I'm looking,' said Huyghens at the microviewer, 'for the record of their mining operations. An open-pit operation would not mean a thing. But if they had driven a tunnel, and somebody was there supervising the robots when the colony was wiped out, there's an off-chance he survived a while.'

Bordman regarded him with suddenly intent eyes.

'And—'

'Dammit,' snapped Huyghens, 'if so I'll go see! He'd – they'd have no chance at all, otherwise. Not that the chance is good in any case.'

Bordman raised his eyebrows.

'I've told you I'll send you to prison if I can,' he said. 'You've risked the lives of millions of people, maintaining non-quarantined communication with an unlicensed planet. If you did rescue somebody from the ruins of the robot colony – does it occur to you that they'd be witnesses to your unauthorized presence here?'

359

Huyghens spun the viewer again. He stopped, switched back and forth, and found what he wanted. He muttered in satisfaction: 'They did run a tunnel!' Aloud he said, 'I'll worry about witnesses when I have to.'

He pushed aside another cupboard door. Inside it were the odds and ends a man makes use of to repair the things about his house that he never notices until they go wrong. There was an assortment of wires, transistors, bolts, and similar stray items.

'What now?' asked Bordman mildly.

'I'm going to try to find out if there's anybody left alive over there. I'd have checked before if I'd known the colony existed. I can't prove they're all dead, but I may prove that somebody's still alive. It's barely two weeks' journey away from here. Odd that two colonies picked spots so near!'

He picked over the oddments he'd selected.

'Confound it!' Bordman said. 'How can you check somebody's alive some hundreds of miles away?'

Huyghens threw a switch and took down a wall-panel, exposing electronic apparatus and circuits behind. He busied himself with it.

'Ever think about hunting for a castaway?' he asked over his shoulder. 'Here's a planet with some tens of millions of square miles on it. You know there's a ship down. You've no idea where. You assume the survivors have power – no civilized man will be without power very long, so long as he can smelt metals! – but making a space-beacon calls for high-precision measurements and workmanship. It's not to be improvised. So what will your shipwrecked civilized man do, to guide a rescue-ship to the one or two square miles he occupies among some tens of millions on the planet?'

'What?'

'He's had to go primitive, to begin with,' Huyghens explained. 'He cooks his meat over a fire, and so on. He has to make a strictly primitive signal. It's all he can do without gauges and micrometers and special tools. But he can fill all the planet's atmosphere with a signal that searchers for him can't miss. You see?'

Bordman thought irritably. He shook his head.

'He'll make,' said Huyghens, 'a spark transmitter. He'll fix its output at the shortest frequency he can contrive, somewhere in the five-to-fifty-meter wave-band, but it will tune very broad – and it will be a plainly human signal. He'll start it broadcasting. Some of those frequencies will go all around the planet under the ionosphere. Any ship that comes in under the radio roof will pick up his signal, get a fix on it, move and get another fix, and then go straight to where the castaway is waiting placidly in a hand-braided hammock, sipping whatever sort of drink he's improvised out of the local vegetation.'

Bordman said grudgingly:

'Now that you mention it, of course ...'

'My space-phone picks up microwaves,' said Huyghens. 'I'm shifting a few elements to make it listen for longer stuff. It won't be efficient, but it will catch a distress-signal if one's in the air. I don't expect it, though.'

He worked. Bordman sat still a long time, watching him. Down below, a rhythmic sort of sound arose. It was Sourdough Charley, snoring.

Sitka Pete grunted in his sleep. He was dreaming. In the general room of the station Semper blinked his eyes rapidly and then tucked his head under a gigantic wing and went to sleep. The noises of the Loren Two jungle came through the steel-shuttered windows. The nearer moon – which had passed overhead not long before the ringing of the arrival-bell – again came soaring over the eastern horizon. It sped across the sky.

Inside the station, Bordman said angrily:

'See here, Huyghens! You've reason to kill me. Apparently you don't intend to. You've excellent reason to leave that robot colony strictly alone. But you're preparing to help, if there's anybody alive to need it. And yet you're a criminal, and I mean a criminal! There've been some ghastly bacteria exported from planets like Loren Two. There've been plenty of lives lost in consequence, and you're risking more. Why the hell do you do it? Why do you do something that could produce monstrous results to other human beings?'

Huyghens grunted.

'You're only assuming there are no sanitary and quarantine precautions taken by my partners. As a matter of fact, there are. They're taken, all right! As for the rest, you wouldn't understand.'

'I don't understand,' snapped Bordman, 'but that's no proof I can't! Why are you a criminal?'

Huyghens painstakingly used a screwdriver inside the wall-panel. He lifted out a small electronic assembly, and began to fit in a spaghettied new assembly with larger units.

'I'm cutting my amplification here to hell-and-gone,' he observed, 'but I think it'll do ... I'm doing what I'm doing,' he added calmly, 'because it seems to me it fits what I think I am. Everybody acts according to his own real notion of himself. You're a conscientious citizen, a loyal official, a well-adjusted personality. You act that way. You consider yourself an intelligent rational animal. But you don't act that way! You're reminding me of my need to shoot you or something similar, which a merely rational animal would try to make me forget. You happen, Bordman, to be a man. So am I. But I'm aware of it. Therefore I deliberately do things a merely rational animal wouldn't, because they're my notion of what a man who's more than a rational animal should do.'

He tightened one small screw after another.

Bordman said:

'Oh. Religion.'

'Self-respect,' corrected Huyghens. 'I don't like robots. They're too much like rational animals. A robot will do whatever it can that its supervisor requires it to do. A merely rational animal will do whatever circumstances require it to do. I wouldn't like a robot unless it had some idea of what was fitting and would spit in my eye if I tried to make it do something else. The bears downstairs, now ... They're no robots! They are loyal and honorable beasts, but they'd turn and tear me to bits if I tried to make them do something against their nature.

Faro Nell would fight me and all creation together, if we tried to harm Nugget. It would be unintelligent and unreasonable and irrational. She'd lose out and get killed. But I like her that way! And I'll fight you and all creation when you make me try to do something against my nature. I'll be stupid and unreasonable and irrational about it.' Then he grinned over his shoulder. 'So will you. Only you don't realize it.'

He turned back to his task. After a moment he fitted a manual-control knob over a shaft in his haywire assembly.

'What did somebody try to make you do?' asked Bordman shrewdly. 'What was demanded of you that turned you into a criminal? What are you in revolt against?'

Huyghens threw a switch. He began to turn the knob which controlled the knob of his makeshift receiver.

'Why,' he said, 'when I was young the people around me tried to make me into a conscientious citizen and a loyal employee and a well-adjusted personality. They tried to make me into a highly intelligent rational animal and nothing more. The difference between us, Bordman, is that I found it out. Naturally, I rev—'

He stopped short. Faint, crackling, frying sounds came from the speaker of the space-phone now modified to receive what once were called short waves.

Huyghens listened. He cocked his head intently. He turned the knob very, very slowly. Bordman made an arrested gesture, to call attention to something in the sibilant sound. Huyghens nodded. He turned the knob again, with infinitesimal increments.

Out of the background noise came a patterned mutter. As Huyghens shifted the tuning, it grew louder. It reached a volume where it was unmistakable. It was a sequence of sounds like a discordant buzzing. There were three half-second buzzings with half-second pauses between. A two-second pause. Three full-second buzzings with half-second pauses between. Another two-second pause and three half-second buzzings, again. Then silence for five seconds. Then the pattern repeated.

'The devil!' said Huyghens. 'That's a human signal!

363

Mechanically made, too. In fact, it used to be a standard distress call. It was termed an SOS, though I've no idea what that meant. Anyhow, somebody must have read old-fashioned novels some time, to know about it. And so someone is still alive over at your licensed but now smashed-up robot colony. And they're asking for help. I'd say they're likely to need it.'

He looked at Bordman.

'The intelligent thing to do is sit back and wait for a ship, either my friends' or yours. A ship can help survivors or castaways much better than we can. It could even find them more easily. But maybe time is important to the poor devils. So I'm going to take the bears and see if I can reach him. You can wait here, if you like. What say?'

Bordman snapped angrily:

'Don't be a fool! Of course I'm coming! What do you take me for? And two of us should have four times the chance of one!'

Huyghens grinned.

'Not quite. You forget Sitka Pete and Sourdough Charley and Faro Nell. There'll be five of us if you come, instead of four. And, of course, Nugget has to come – and he'll be no help – but Semper may make up for him. You won't quadruple our chances, Bordman, but I'll be glad to have you if you want to be stupid and unreasonable and not at all rational, and come with me.'

There was a jagged spur of stone looming precipitously over a river-valley. A thousand feet below, a broad stream ran westward to the sea. Twenty miles to the east, a wall of mountains rose sheer against the sky, its peaks seeming to blend to a remarkable evenness of height. Rolling, tumbled ground lay between for as far as the eye could see.

A speck in the sky came swiftly downward. Great pinions spread and flapped, and icy eyes surveyed the rocky space. With more great flappings, Semper the eagle came to ground. He folded his huge wings and turned his head jerkily, his eyes unblinking. A tiny harness held a miniature camera against his chest. He strutted over the bare stone to the highest point and stood there, a lonely and arrogant figure in the vastness.

Crashings and rustlings, and snuffling sounds, and Sitka Pete came lumbering out into the clear space. He wore a harness too, and a pack. The harness was complex, because it had to hold a pack not only in normal travel, but when he stood on his hind legs, and it must not hamper the use of his forepaws in combat.

He went cagily all over the open area. He peered over the edge of the spur's farthest tip, and prowled to the other side and looked down. Once he moved close to Semper and the eagle opened his great curved beak and uttered an indignant noise. Sitka paid no attention.

He relaxed, satisfied. He sat down untidily, his hind legs sprawling. He wore an air approaching benevolence as he surveyed the landscape about and below him.

More snufflings and crashings. Sourdough Charley came into view with Huyghens and Bordman behind him. Sourdough carried a pack, too. Then there was a squealing and Nugget scurried up from the rear, impelled by a whack from his mother. Faro Nell appeared, with the carcass of a stag-like animal lashed to her harness.

'I picked this place from a space-photo,' said Huyghens, 'to make a directional fix from you. I'll get set up.'

He swung his pack from his shoulders to the ground, and extracted an obviously self-constructed device which he set on the ground. It had a whip aerial, which he extended. Then he plugged in a considerable length of flexible wire and unfolded a tiny, improvised directional aerial with an even tinier booster at its base. Bordman slipped his pack from his shoulders and watched. Huyghens put a pair of head-phones over his ears. He looked up and said sharply:

'Watch the bears, Bordman. The wind's blowing up the way we came. Anything that trails us will send its scent on before. The bears will tell us.'

He busied himself with the instruments he'd brought. He heard the hissing, frying, background noise which could be anything at all except a human signal. He reached out and swung the small aerial around. Rasping, buzzing tones came in, faintly and then loudly. This receiver, though, had been made for this particular wave-band. It was much more efficient than the modified space-phone had been. It picked up three short buzzes, three long ones, and three short ones again. Three dots, three dashes, and three dots. Over and over again. SOS. SOS. SOS.

Huyghens took a reading and moved the directional aerial a carefully measured distance. He took another reading, shifted it yet again and again, carefully marking and measuring each spot and taking notes of the instrument readings. When he finished, he had checked the direction of the signal not only by loudness but by phase, and had as accurate a fix as could possibly be made with portable apparatus.

Sourdough growled softly. Sitka Pete whiffed the air and arose from his sitting position. Faro Nell whacked Nugget, sending him whimpering to the farthest corner of the flat place. She stood bristling, facing downhill the way they'd come.

'Damn!' said Huyghens.

He got up and waved his arm at Semper, who had turned his head at the stirrings. Semper squawked and dived off the spur, and was immediately fighting the down-draught beyond it. As Huyghens readied his weapon, the eagle came back overhead. He went magnificently past, a hundred feet high, careening and flapping in the tricky currents. He screamed, abruptly, and screamed again. Huyghens swung a tiny vision-plate from its strap to where he could look into it. He saw, of course, what the tiny camera on Semper's chest could see – reeling, swaying terrain as Semper saw it, though of course without his breadth of field. There were moving objects to be seen through the shifting trees. Their coloring was unmistakable.

'Sphexes,' said Huyghens dourly. 'Eight of them. Don't look for them to follow our track, Bordman. They run parallel to a trail on either side. That way they attack in breadth and all at once when they catch up. And listen! The bears can handle

366

anything they tangle with – it's our job to pick off the loose ones. And aim for the body! The bullets explode.'

He threw off the safety of his weapon. Faro Nell, uttering thunderous growls, went padding to a place between Sitka Pete and Sourdough. Sitka glanced at her and made a whuffing noise, as if derisive of her bloodcurdling sounds. Sourdough grunted. He and Sitka moved farther away from Nell to either side. They would cover a wider front.

There was no other sign of life than the shrillings of the incredibly tiny creatures which on this planet were birds, and Faro Nell's deep-bass, raging growls, and then the click of Bordman's safety going off as he got ready to use the weapon Huyghens had given him.

Semper screamed again, flapping low above the tree-tops, following parti-colored, monstrous shapes beneath.

Eight blue-and-tan fiends came racing out of the underbrush. They had spiny fringes, and horns, and glaring eyes, and they looked as if they had come straight out of hell. On the instant of their appearance they leaped, emitting squalling, spitting squeals that were like the cries of fighting tomcats ten thousand times magnified. Huyghens' rifle cracked, and its sound was wiped out in the louder detonation of its bullet in Sphexian flesh. A tan-and-blue monster tumbled over, shrieking. Faro Nell charged, the very impersonation of white-hot fury. Bordman fired, and his bullet exploded against a tree. Sitka Pete brought his massive forepaws in a clapping, monstrous ear-boxing motion. A sphex died.

Then Bordman fired again. Sourdough Charley whuffed. He fell forward upon a spitting bi-colored fiend, rolled him over, and raked with his hind-claws. The belly-hide of the sphex was tenderer than the rest. The creature rolled away, snapping at its own wounds. Another sphex found itself shaken loose from the tumult about Sitka Pete. It whirled to leap on him from behind, and Huyghens fired. Two plunged upon Faro Nell, and Bordman blasted one and Faro Nell disposed of the other in awesome fury. Then Sitka Pete heaved himself erect – seeming to drip sphexes – and Sourdough waddled over and pulled one off and killed it and went back for another. Then both rifles cracked together and there was suddenly nothing left to fight.

The bears prowled from one to another of the corpses. Sitka Pete rumbled and lifted up a limp head. Crash! Then another. He went over the lot, whether or not they showed signs of life. When he had finished, they were wholly still.

Semper came flapping down out of the sky. He had screamed and fluttered overhead as the fight went on. Now he landed with a rush. Huyghens went soothingly from one bear to another, calming them with his voice. It took longest to calm Faro Nell, licking Nugget with impassioned solicitude and growling horribly as she licked.

'Come along, now,' said Huyghens, when Sitka showed signs of intending to sit down again. 'Heave these carcasses over a cliff. Come along! Sitka! Sourdough! Hup!'

He guided them as the two big males somewhat fastidiously lifted up the nightmarish creatures and carried them to the edge of the spur of stone. They let the beasts go bouncing and sliding down into the valley.

'That,' said Huyghens, 'is so their little pals will gather round them and caterwaul their woe where there's no trail of ours to give them ideas. If we'd been near a river I'd have dumped them in to float downstream and gather mourners wherever they stranded. Around the station I incinerate them. If I had to leave them, I'd make tracks away. About fifty miles upwind would be a good idea.'

He opened the pack Sourdough carried and extracted giant-sized swabs and some gallons of antiseptic. He tended the three Kodiaks in turn, swabbing not only the cuts and scratches they'd received, but deeply soaking their fur where there could be suspicion of spilled sphex-blood.

'This antiseptic deodorizes, too,' he told Bordman. 'Or we'd be trailed by any sphex who passed to leeward of us. When we start off, I'll swab the bears' paws for the same reason.'

Bordman was very quiet. He'd missed his first shot, but the last few seconds of the fight he'd fired very deliberately and every bullet hit. Now he said bitterly:

'If you're instructing me so I can carry on should you be killed, I doubt that it's worthwhile!'

Huyghens felt in his pack and unfolded the enlargements he'd made of the space-photos of this part of the planet. He carefully oriented the map with distant landmarks, and drew a line across the photo.

'The SOS signal comes from somewhere close to the robot colony,' he reported. 'I think a little to the south of it. Probably from a mine they'd opened up, on the far side of the Sere Plateau. See how I've marked this map? Two fixes, one from the station and one from here. I came away off-course to get a fix here so we'd have two position-lines to the transmitter. The signal could have come from the other side of the planet. But it doesn't.'

'The odds would be astronomical against other castaways,' protested Bordman.

'No,' said Huyghens. 'Ships have been coming here. To the robot-colony. One could have crashed. And I have friends, too.'

He repacked his apparatus and gestured to the bears. He led them beyond the scene of combat and carefully swabbed off their paws, so they could not possibly leave a train of sphex-blood scent behind them. He waved Semper, the eagle, aloft.

'Let's go,' he told the Kodiaks. 'Yonder! Hup!'

The party headed downhill and into the jungle again. Now it was Sourdough's turn to take the lead, and Sitka Pete prowled more widely behind him. Faro Nell trailed the men, with Nugget. She kept a sharp eye upon the cub. He was a baby, still; he only weighed six hundred pounds. And of course she watched against danger from the rear.

Overhead, Semper fluttered and flew in giant circles and spirals, never going very far away. Huyghens referred constantly to the screen which showed what the air-borne camera saw. The image tilted and circled and banked and swayed. It was by no means the best air-reconnaissance that could be imagined, but it was the best that would work. Presently Huyghens said:

'We swing to the right, here. The going's bad straight ahead, and it looks like a pack of sphexes has killed and is feeding.'

Bordman said:

'It's against reason for carnivores to be as thick as you say! There has to be a certain amount of other animal life for every meat-eating beast. Too many of them would eat all the game and starve.'

'They're gone all winter,' explained Huyghens, 'which around here isn't as severe as you might think. And a good many animals seem to breed just after the sphexes go south. Also, the sphexes aren't around all the warm weather. There's a sort of peak, and then for a matter of weeks you won't see one of them, and suddenly the jungle swarms with them again. Then, presently, they head south. Apparently they're migratory in some fashion, but nobody knows.' He said drily: 'There haven't been many naturalists around on this planet. The animal life's inimical.'

Bordman fretted. He was accustomed to arrival at a partly or completely finished colonial set-up, and to pass upon the completion or non-completion of the installation as designed. Now he was in an intolerably hostile environment, depending upon an illegal colonist for his life, engaged upon a demoralizingly indefinite enterprise – because the mechanical spark-signal could be working long after its constructors were dead – and his ideas about a number of matters were shaken. He was alive, for example, because of three giant Kodiak bears and a bald eagle. He and Huyghens could have been surrounded by ten thousand robots, and they'd have been killed. Sphexes and robots would have ignored each other, and sphexes would have made straight for the men, who'd have had less than four seconds in which to discover for themselves that they were attacked, prepare to defend themselves, and kill the eight sphexes.

Bordman's convictions as a civilized man were shaken. Robots were marvelous contrivances for doing the expected, accomplishing the planned, coping with the predicted. But they also had defects. Robots could only follow instructions. If this thing happens, do this, if that thing happens, do that. But before something else, neither this or that, robots were helpless.

So a robot civilization worked only in an environment where nothing unanticipated ever turned up, and human supervisors never demanded anything unexpected. Bordman was appalled.

He found Nugget, the cub, ambling uneasily in his wake. The cub flattened his ears miserably when Bordman glanced at him. It occurred to the man that Nugget was receiving a lot of disciplinary thumpings from Faro Nell. He was knocked about psychologically. His lack of information and unfitness for independent survival in this environment was being hammered into him.

'Hi, Nugget,' said Bordman ruefully. 'I feel just about the way you do!'

Nugget brightened visibly. He frisked. He tended to gambol. He looked hopefully up into Bordman's face.

The man reached out and patted Nugget's head. It was the first time in all his life that he'd ever petted an animal.

He heard a snuffling sound behind him. Skin crawled at the back of his neck. He whirled.

Faro Nell regarded him – eighteen hundred pounds of she-bear only ten feet away and looking into his eyes. For one panicky instant Bordman went cold all over. Then he realized that Faro Nell's eyes were not burning. She was not snarling, nor did she emit those blood-curdling sounds which the bare prospect of danger to Nugget had produced up on the rocky spur. She looked at him blandly. In fact, after a moment she swung off on some independent investigation of a matter that had aroused her curiosity.

The traveling-party went on, Nugget frisking beside Bordman and tending to bump into him out of pure cub-clumsiness. Now and again he looked adoringly at Bordman, in the instant and overwhelming affection of the very young.

Bordman trudged on. Presently he glanced behind again. Faro Nell was now ranging more widely. She was well satisfied to have Nugget in the immediate care of a man. From time to time he got on her nerves.

A little while later, Bordman called ahead.

'Huyghens! Look here! I've been appointed nursemaid to Nugget!'

Huyghens looked back.

'Oh, slap him a few times and he'll go back to his mother.'

'The devil I will!' said Bordman querulously. 'I like it!'

The traveling-party went on.

When night fell, they camped. There could be no fire, of course, because all the minute night-things about would come to dance in the glow. But there could not be darkness, equally, because night-walkers hunted in the dark. So Huyghens set out barrier-lamps which made a wall of twilight about their halting-place, and the stag-like creature Faro Nell had carried became their evening meal. Then they slept – at least the men did – and the bears dozed and snorted and waked and dozed again. Semper sat immobile with his head under his wing on a tree-limb. Presently there was a glorious cool hush and all the world glowed in morning-light diffused through the jungle by a newly risen sun. Then they arose and pushed on.

This day they stopped stock-still for two hours while sphexes puzzled over the trail the bears had left. Huyghens discoursed on the need for an anti-scent, to be used on the boots of men and the paws of bears, which would make the following of their trails unpopular with sphexes. Bordman seized upon the idea and suggested that a sphex-repellent odor might be worked out, which would make a human revolting to a sphex. If that were done, humans could go freely about, unmolested.

'Like stink-bugs,' said Huyghens, sardonically. 'A very intelligent idea! Very rational! You can feel proud!'

And suddenly Bordman was not proud of the idea at all.

They camped again. On the third night they were at the base of that remarkable formation, the Sere Plateau, which from a distance looked like a mountain range but was actually a desert table-land. It was not reasonable for a desert to be raised high, while lowlands had rain, but on the fourth morning they found out why. They saw, far, far away, a truly monstrous mountain-mass at the end of the long expanse of the plateau.

It was like the prow of a ship. It lay, so Huyghens observed, directly in line with the prevailing winds, and divided them as a ship's prow divides the waters. The moisture-bearing air-currents flowed beside the plateau, not over it, and its interior was desert in the unscreened sunshine of the high altitudes.

It took them a full day to get half-way up the slope. And here, twice, as they climbed, Semper flew screaming over aggregations of sphexes to one side of them or the other. These were much larger groups than Huyghens had ever seen before, fifty to a hundred monstrosities together, where a dozen was a large hunting-pack elsewhere. He looked in the screen which showed him what Semper saw, four to five miles away. The sphexes padded uphill toward the Sere Plateau in a long line. Fifty – sixty – seventy tan-and-azure beasts out of hell.

'I'd hate to have that bunch jump us,' he said candidly to Bordman. 'I don't think we'd stand a chance.'

'Here's where a robot tank would be useful,' Bordman observed.

'Anything armored,' conceded Huyghens. 'One man in an armored station like mine would be safe. But if he killed a sphex he'd be besieged. He'd have to stay holed up, breathing the smell of dead sphex, until the odor'd gone away. And he mustn't kill any others or he'd be besieged until winter came.'

Bordman did not suggest the advantages of robots in other directions. At that moment, for example, they were working their way up a slope which averaged fifty degrees. The bears climbed without effort despite their burdens. For the men it was infinite toil. Semper, the eagle, manifested impatience with bears and men alike, who crawled so slowly up an incline over which he soared.

He went ahead up the mountainside and teetered in the air-currents at the plateau's edge. Huyghens looked in the vision-plate by which he reported.

'How the devil,' panted Bordman – they had stopped for a breather, and the bears waited patiently for them – 'how do you train bears like these? I can understand Semper.'

'I don't train them,' said Huyghens, staring into the plate.

373

'They're mutations. In heredity the sex-linkage of physical characteristics is standard stuff. There's also been some sound work done on the gene-linkage of psychological factors. There was need, on my home planet, for an animal who could fight like a fiend, live off the land, carry a pack and get along with men at least as well as dogs do. In the old days they'd have tried to breed the desired physical properties in an animal who already had the personality they wanted. Something like a giant dog, say. But back home they went at it the other way about. They picked the wanted physical characteristics and bred for the personality, the psychology. The job got done over a century ago. A Kodiak bear named Kodius Champion was the first real success. He had everything that was wanted. These bears are his descendants.'

'They look normal,' commented Bordman.

'They are!' said Huyghens warmly. 'Just as normal as an honest dog! They're not trained, like Semper. They train themselves!' He looked back into the plate in his hands, which showed the ground six or seven thousand feet higher. 'Semper, now, is a trained bird without too much brain. He's educated – a glorified hawk. But the bears want to get along with men. They're emotionally dependent on us. Like dogs. Semper's a servant, but they're companions and friends. He's trained, but they're loyal. He's conditioned. They love us. He'd abandon me if he ever realized he could; he thinks he can only eat what men feed him. But the bears wouldn't want to. They like us. I admit I like them. Maybe because they like me.'

Bordman said deliberately:

'Aren't you a trifle loose-tongued, Huyghens? You've told me something that will locate and convict the people who set you up here. It shouldn't be hard to find where bears were bred for psychological mutations, and where a bear named Kodius Champion left descendants. I can find out where you came from now, Huyghens!'

Huyghens looked up from the plate with its tiny swaying television image.

'No harm done,' he said amiably. 'I'm a criminal there,

too. It's officially on record that I kidnapped these bears and escaped with them. Which, on my home planet, is about as heinous a crime as a man can commit. It's worse than horse-theft back on Earth in the old days. The kin and cousins of my bears are highly thought of. I'm quite a criminal, back home.'

Bordman stared.

'Did you steal them?' he demanded.

'Confidentially,' said Huyghens. 'No. But prove it!' Then he said: 'Take a look in this plate. See what Semper can see up at the plateau's edge.'

Bordman squinted aloft, where the eagle flew in great sweeps and dashes. Somehow, by the experience of the past few days, Bordman knew that Semper was screaming fiercely as he flew. He made a dart toward the plateau's border.

Bordman looked at the transmitted picture. It was only four inches by six, but it was perfectly without grain and accurate in color. It moved and turned as the camera-bearing eagle swooped and circled. For an instant the screen showed the steeply sloping mountainside, and off at one edge the party of men and bears could be seen as dots. Then it swept away and showed the top of the plateau.

There were sphexes. A pack of two hundred trotted toward the desert interior. They moved at leisure, in the open. The viewing camera reeled, and there were more. As Bordman watched and as the bird flew higher, he could see still other sphexes moving up over the edge of the plateau from a small erosion-defile here and another one there. The Sere Plateau was alive with the hellish creatures. It was inconceivable that there should be game enough for them to live on. They were visible as herds of cattle would be visible on grazing planets.

It was simply impossible.

'Migrating,' observed Huyghens. 'I said they did. They're headed somewhere. Do you know, I doubt that it would be healthy for us to try to cross the Plateau through such a swarm of sphexes!'

Bordman swore, in abrupt change of mood.

'But the signal's still coming through. Somebody's alive over at the robot colony. Must we wait till the migration's over?'

'We don't know,' Huyghens pointed out, 'that they'll stay alive. They may need help badly. We have to get to them. But at the same time—'

He glanced at Sourdough Charley and Sitka Pete, clinging patiently to the mountainside while the men rested and talked. Sitka had managed to find a place to sit down, one massive paw anchoring him in place.

Huyghens waved his arm, pointing in a new direction.

'Let's go!' he called briskly. 'Let's go! Yonder! Hup!'

They followed the slopes of the Sere Plateau, neither ascending to its level top – where sphexes congregated – nor descending into the foothills where sphexes assembled. They moved along hillsides and mountain-flanks which sloped anywhere from thirty to sixty degrees, and they did not cover much territory. They practically forgot what it was to walk on level ground.

At the end of the sixth day, they camped on the top of a massive boulder which projected from a mountainous stony wall. There was barely room on the boulder for all the party. Faro Nell fussily insisted that Nugget should be in the safest part, which meant near the mountain-flank. She would have crowded the men outward, but Nugget whimpered for Bordman. Wherefore, when Bordman moved to comfort him, Faro Nell drew back and snorted at Sitka and Sourdough and they made room for her near the edge.

It was a hungry camp. They had come upon tiny rills upon occasion, flowing down the mountainside. Here the bears had drunk deeply and the men had filled canteens. But this was the third night on the mountainside, and there had been no game at all. Huyghens made no move to bring out food for Bordman or himself. Bordman made no comment. He was beginning to participate in the relationship between bears and men, which was not the slavery of the bears but something more. It was two-way. He felt it.

'You'd think,' he said, 'that since the sphexes don't seem to hunt on their way uphill, there should be some game. They ignore everything as they file up.'

This was true enough. The normal fighting formation of sphexes was line abreast, which automatically surrounded anything which offered to flee and outflanked anything which offered fight. But here they ascended the mountain in long files, one after the other, apparently following long-established trails. The wind blew along the slopes and carried scent sidewise. But the sphexes were not diverted from their chosen paths. The long processions of hideous blue-and-tawny creatures – it was hard to think of them as natural beasts, male and female and laying eggs like reptiles on other planets – the long processions simply climbed.

'There've been other thousands of beasts before them,' said Huyghens. 'They must have been crowding this way for days or even weeks. We've seen tens of thousands in Semper's camera. They must be uncountable, altogether. The first-comers ate all the game there was, and the last-comers have something else on whatever they use for minds.'

Bordman protested:

'But so many carnivores in one place is impossible! I know they are here, but they can't be!'

'They're cold-blooded,' Huyghens pointed out. 'They don't burn food to sustain body-temperature. After all, lots of creatures go for long periods without eating. Even bears hibernate. But this isn't hibernation – or estivation, either.'

He was setting up the radiation-wave receiver in the darkness. There was no point in attempting a fix here. The transmitter was on the other side of the sphex-crowded Sere Plateau. The men and bears would commit suicide by crossing here.

Even so, Huyghens turned on the receiver. There came the whispering, scratchy sound of background-noise, and then the signal. Three dots, three dashes, three dots. Huyghens turned it off. Bordman said:

'Shouldn't we have answered that signal before we left the station? To encourage them?'

'I doubt they have a receiver,' said Huyghens. 'They won't expect an answer for months, anyhow. They'd hardly listen all the time, and if they're living in a mine-tunnel and trying to sneak out for food to stretch their supplies, they'll be too busy to try to make complicated recorders or relays.'

Bordman was silent for a moment or two.

'We've got to get food for the bears,' he said presently. 'Nugget's weaned, and he's hungry.'

'We will,' Huyghens promised. 'I may be wrong, but it seems to me that the number of sphexes climbing the mountain is less than yesterday and the day before. We may have just about crossed the path of their migration. They're thinning out. When we're past their trail, we'll have to look out for night-walkers and the like again. But I think they wiped out all animal life on their migration-route.'

He was not quite right. He was waked in darkness by the sound of slappings and the grunting of bears. Feather-light puffs of breeze beat upon his face. He struck his belt-lamp sharply and the world was hidden by a whitish film which snatched itself away. Something flapped. Then he saw the stars and the emptiness on the edge of which they camped. Then big white things flapped toward him.

Sitka Pete whuffed mightily and swatted. Faro Nell grunted and swung. She caught something in her claws.

'Watch this!' said Huyghens.

More things strangely-shaped and pallid like human skin reeled and flapped crazily toward him.

A huge hairy paw reached up into the light-beam and snatched a flying thing out of it. Another great paw. The three great Kodiaks were on their hind legs, swatting at creatures which flittered insanely, unable to resist the fascination of the glaring lamp. Because of their wild gyrations it was impossible to see them in detail, but they were those unpleasant night-creatures which looked like plucked flying monkeys but were actually something quite different.

The bears did not snarl or snap. They swatted, with a

remarkable air of business-like competence and purpose. Small mounds of broken things built up about their feet.

Suddenly there were no more. Huyghens snapped off the light. The bears crunched and fed busily in the darkness.

'Those things are carnivores *and* blood-suckers, Bordman,' said Huyghens calmly. 'They drain their victims of blood like vampire-bats – they've some trick of not waking them – and when they're dead the whole tribe eats. But bears have thick fur, and they wake when they're touched. And they're omnivorous. They'll eat anything but sphexes, and like it. You might say that those night-creatures came to lunch. They *are* it, for the bears, who are living off the country as usual.'

Bordman uttered a sudden exclamation. He made a tiny light, and blood flowed down his hand. Huyghens passed over his pocket kit of antiseptic and bandages. Bordman stanched the bleeding and bound up his hand. Then he realized that Nugget chewed on something. When he turned the light, Nugget swallowed convulsively. It appeared that he had caught and devoured the creature which had drawn blood from Bordman. But he'd lost none to speak of, at that.

In the morning they started along the sloping scarp of the plateau once more. After marching silently for awhile, Bordman said:

'Robots wouldn't have handled those vampire-things, Huyghens.'

'Oh, they could be built to watch for them,' said Huyghens, tolerantly. 'But you'd have to swat for yourself. I prefer the bears.'

He led the way on. Twice Huyghens halted to examine the ground about the mountains' bases through binoculars. He looked encouraged as they went on. The monstrous peak which was like the bow of a ship at the end of the Sere Plateau was visibly nearer. Toward midday, indeed, it loomed high above the horizon, no more than fifteen miles away. And at midday Huyghens called a final halt.

'No more congregations of sphexes down below,' he said cheerfully, 'and we haven't seen a climbing line of them in miles.' The crossing of a sphex-trail had meant simply waiting until one party had passed, and then crossing before another came in view. 'I've a hunch we've left their migration route behind. Let's see what Semper tells us!'

He waved the eagle aloft. Like all creatures other than men, the bird normally functioned only for the satisfaction of his appetite, and then tended to loaf or sleep. He had ridden the last few miles perched on Sitka Pete's pack. Now he soared upward and Huyghens watched in the small vision-plate.

Semper went soaring. The image on the plate swayed and turned, and in minutes was above the plateau's edge. Here there were some patches of brush and the ground rolled a little. But as Semper towered higher still, the inner desert appeared. Nearby, it was clear of beasts. Only once, when the eagle banked sharply and the camera looked along the long dimension of the plateau, did Huyghens see any sign of the blue-and-tan beasts. There he saw what looked like masses amounting to herds. Incredible, of course; carnivores do not gather in herds.

'We go straight up,' said Huyghens in satisfaction. 'We cross the Plateau here, and we can edge downwind a bit, even. I think we'll find something interesting on our way to your robot colony.'

He waved to the bears to go ahead uphill.

They reached the top hours later, barely before sunset. And they saw game. Not much, but game at the grassy, brushy border of the desert. Huyghens brought down a shaggy ruminant which surely would not live on a desert. When night fell there was an abrupt chill in the air. It was much colder than night temperatures on the slopes. The air was thin. Bordman thought and presently guessed at the cause. In the lee of the prow-mountain the air was calm. There were no clouds. The ground radiated its heat to empty space. It could be bitterly cold in the night-time, here.

'And hot by day,' Huyghens agreed when he mentioned it. 'The sunshine's terrifically hot where the air is thin, but on most mountains there's wind. By day, here, the ground will tend to heat up like the surface of a planet without atmosphere. It may be a hundred and forty or fifty degrees on the sand at midday. But it should be cold at night.'

It was. Before midnight Huyghens built a fire. There could be no danger of night-walkers where the temperature dropped to freezing.

In the morning the men were stiff with cold, but the bears snorted and moved about briskly. They seemed to revel in the morning chill. Sitka and Sourdough Charley, in fact, became festive and engaged in a mock fight, whacking each other with blows that were only feigned, but would have crushed the skull of any man. Nugget sneezed with excitement as he watched them. Faro Nell regarded them with female disapproval.

They started on. Semper seemed sluggish. After a single brief flight he descended and rode on Sitka's pack, as on the previous day. He perched there, surveying the landscape as it changed from semi-arid to pure desert in their progress. He would not fly. Soaring birds do not like to fly when there are no winds to make currents of which they can take advantage.

Once Huyghens stopped and pointed out to Bordman exactly where they were on the enlarged photograph taken from space, and the exact spot from which the distress-signal seemed to come.

'You're doing it in case something happens to you,' said Bordman. 'I admit it's sense, but – what could I do to help those survivors even if I got to them, without you?'

'What you've learned about sphexes would help,' said Huyghens. 'The bears would help. And we left a note back at my station. Whoever grounds at the landing field back there – and the beacon's working – will find instructions to come to the place we're trying to reach.'

They started walking again. The narrow patch of non-desert border of the Sere Plateau was behind them, now, and they marched across powdery desert sand.

'See here,' said Bordman. 'I want to know something. You tell me you're listed as a bear-thief on your home planet. You tell me it's a lie, to protect your friends from prosecution by the

Colonial Survey. You're on your own, risking your life every minute of every day. You took a risk in not shooting me. Now you're risking more in going to help men who'd have to be witnesses that you were a criminal. What are you doing it for?'

Huyghens grinned.

'Because I don't like robots. I don't like the fact that they're subduing men, making men subordinate to them.'

'Go on,' insisted Bordman. 'I don't see why disliking robots should make you a criminal! Nor men subordinating themselves to robots, either.'

'But they are,' said Huyghens mildly. 'I'm a crank, of course. But – I live like a man on this planet. I go where I please and do what I please. My helpers are my friends. If the robot colony had been a success, would the humans in it have lived like men? Hardly. They'd have to live the way robots let them! They'd have to stay inside a fence the robots built. They'd have to eat foods that robots could raise, and no others. Why, a man couldn't move his bed near a window, because if he did the house-tending robots couldn't work! Robots would serve them – the way the robots determined – but all they'd get out of it would be jobs servicing the robots!'

Bordman shook his head.

'As long as men want robot service, they have to take the service that robots can give. If you don't want those services—'

'I want to decide what I want,' said Huyghens, again mildly, 'instead of being limited to choose what I'm offered. In my home planet we half-way tamed it with dogs and guns. Then we developed the bears, and we finished the job with them. Now there's population-pressure and the room for bears and dogs – and men! – is dwindling. More and more people are being deprived of the power of decision, and being allowed only the power of choice among the things robots allow. The more we depend on robots, the more limited those choices become. We don't want our children to limit themselves to wanting what robots can provide! We don't want them shrivelling to where they abandon everything robots can't give, or won't. We want them to be men and women. Not damned

382

automatons who live *by* pushing robot-controls so they can live *to* push robot-controls. If that's not subordination to robots—'

'It's an emotional argument,' protested Bordman. 'Not everybody feels that way.'

'But I feel that way,' said Huyghens. 'And so do a lot of others. This is a damned big galaxy and it's apt to contain some surprises. The one sure thing about a robot and a man who depends on them is that they can't handle the unexpected. There's going to come a time when we need men who can. So on my home planet, some of us asked for Loren Two, to colonize. It was refused – too dangerous. But men can colonize anywhere if they're men. So I came here to study the planet. Especially the sphexes. Eventually, we expected to ask for a license again, with proof that we could handle even those beasts. I'm already doing it in a mild way. But the Survey licensed a robot colony – and where is it?'

Bordman made a sour face.

'You took the wrong way to go about it, Huyghens. It was illegal. It is. It was the pioneer spirit, which is admirable enough, but wrongly directed. After all, it was pioneers who left Earth for the stars. But—'

Sourdough raised up on his hind-legs and sniffed the air. Huyghens swung his rifle around to be handy. Bordman slipped off the safety-catch of his own. Nothing happened.

'In a way,' said Bordman, 'you're talking about liberty and freedom, which most people think is politics. You say it can be more. In principle, I'll concede it. But the way you put it, it sounds like a freak religion.'

'It's self-respect,' corrected Huyghens.

'You may be—'

Faro Nell growled. She bumped Nugget with her nose, to drive him closer to Bordman. She snorted at him, and trotted swiftly to where Sitka and Sourdough faced toward the broader, sphex-filled expanse of the Sere Plateau. She took up her position between them.

Huyghens gazed sharply beyond them and then all about.

'This could be bad!' he said softly. 'But luckily there's no wind. Here's a sort of hill. Come along, Bordman!'

He ran ahead, Bordman following and Nugget plumping heavily with him. They reached the raised place, actually a mere hillock no more than five or six feet above the surrounding sand, with a distorted cactus-like growth protruding from the ground. Huyghens stared again. He used his binoculars.

'One sphex,' he said curtly. 'Just one! And it's out of all reason for a sphex to be alone. But it's not rational for them to gather in hundreds of thousands, either!' He wetted his finger and held it up. 'No wind at all.'

He used the binoculars again.

'It doesn't know we're here,' he added. 'It's moving away. Not another one in sight...' He hesitated, biting his lips. 'Look here, Bordman! I'd like to kill that one lone sphex and find out something. There's a fifty percent chance I could find out something really important. But – I might have to run. If I'm right...' Then he said grimly, 'It'll have to be done quickly. I'm going to ride Faro Nell, for speed. I doubt Sitka or Sourdough will stay behind. But Nugget can't run fast enough. Will you stay here with him?'

Bordman drew in his breath. Then he said calmly:

'You know what you're doing, I hope.'

'Keep your eyes open. If you see anything, even at a distance, shoot and we'll be back, fast! Don't wait until something's close enough to hit. Shoot the instant you see anything, if you do!'

Bordman nodded. He found it peculiarly difficult to speak again. Huyghens went over to the embattled bears and climbed up on Faro Nell's back, holding fast by her shaggy fur.

'Let's go!' he snapped. 'That way! Hup!'

The three Kodiaks plunged away at a dead run, Huyghens lurching and swaying on Faro Nell's back. The sudden rush dislodged Semper from his perch. He flapped wildly and got aloft. Then he followed effortfully, flying low.

It happened very quickly. A Kodiak bear can travel as fast as a race-horse on occasion. These three plunged arrow-straight for a spot perhaps half a mile distant, where a blue-and-tawny shape whirled to face them. There was the crash of Huyghens' weapon from where he rode on Faro Nell's back; the explosions of the weapon and the bullet were one sound. The monster leaped and died.

Huyghens jumped down from Faro Nell. He became feverishly busy at something on the ground. Semper banked and whirled and landed. He watched, with his head on one side.

Bordman stared. Huyghens was doing something to the dead sphex. The two male bears prowled about, while Faro Nell regarded Huyghens with intense curiosity. Back at the hillock Nugget whimpered a little, and Bordman patted him. Nugget whimpered more loudly. In the distance, Huyghens straightened up and mounted Faro Nell's back. Sitka looked back toward Bordman. He reared upward. He made a noise, apparently, because Sourdough ambled to his side. The two great beasts began to trot back. Semper flapped wildly and – lacking wind – lurched crazily in the air. He landed on Huyghens' shoulder and clung there with his talons.

Then Nugget howled hysterically and tried to swarm up Bordman, as a cub tries to swarm up the nearest tree in time of danger. Bordman collapsed, and the cub upon him – and there was a flash of stinking scaly hide, while the air was filled with the snarling, spitting squeals of a sphex in full leap. The beast had over-jumped, aiming at Bordman and the cub while both were upright and arriving when they had fallen. It went tumbling.

Bordman heard nothing but the fiendish squalling, but in the distance Sitka and Sourdough were coming at rocket-ship speed. Faro Nell let out a roar that fairly split the air. And then there was a furry streaking toward her, bawling, while Bordman rolled to his feet and snatched up his gun. He raged through pure instinct. The sphex crouched to pursue the cub and Bordman swung his weapon as a club. He was literally too close to shoot – and perhaps the sphex had only seen the fleeing bear-cub. But he swung furiously—

And the sphex whirled. Bordman was toppled from his feet. An eight-hundred-pound monstrosity straight out of hell – half wildcat and half spitting cobra with hydrophobia and homicidal mania added – such a monstrosity is not to be withstood when in whirling its body strikes one in the chest.

That was when Sitka arrived, bellowing. He stood on his hind legs, emitting roars like thunder, challenging the sphex to battle. He waddled forward. Huyghens approached, but he could not shoot with Bordman in the sphere of an explosive bullet's destructiveness. Faro Nell raged and snarled, torn between the urge to be sure that Nugget was unharmed, and the frenzied fury of a mother whose offspring has been endangered.

Mounted on Faro Nell, with Semper clinging idiotically to his shoulder, Huyghens watched helplessly as the sphex spat and squalled at Sitka, having only to reach out one claw to let out Bordman's life.

They got away from there, though Sitka seemed to want to lift the limp carcass of his victim in his teeth and dash it repeatedly to the ground. He seemed doubly raging because a man – with whom all Kodius Champion's descendants had an emotional relationship – had been mishandled. But Bordman was not grievously hurt. He bounced and swore as the bears raced for the horizon. Huyghens had flung him up on Sourdough's back and snapped for him to hold on. He shouted:

'Damn it, Huyghens! This isn't right! Sitka got some deep scratches! That horror's claws may be poisonous!'

But Huyghens snapped 'Hup! Hup!' to the bears, and they continued their race against time. They went on for a good two miles, when Nugget wailed despairingly of his exhaustion and Faro Nell halted firmly to nuzzle him.

'This may be good enough,' said Huyghens. 'Considering that there's no wind and the big mass of beasts is down the plateau and there were only those two around here. Maybe they're too busy to hold a wake, even. Anyhow—'

He slid to the ground and extracted the antiseptic and swabs. 'Sitka first,' snapped Bordman. 'I'm all right!'

Huyghens swabbed the big bear's wounds. They were trivial,

because Sitka Pete was an experienced sphex-fighter. Then Bordman grudgingly let the curiously-smelling stuff – it reeked of ozone – be applied to the slashes on his chest. He held his breath as it stung. Then he said:

'It was my fault, Huyghens. I watched you instead of the landscape. I couldn't imagine what you were doing.'

'I was doing a quick dissection,' Huyghens told him. 'By luck, that first sphex was a female, as I hoped. And she was about to lay her eggs. Ugh! And now I know why the sphexes migrate, and where, and how it is that they don't need game up here.'

He slapped a quick bandage on Bordman, then led the way eastward, still putting distance between the dead sphexes and his party.

'I'd dissected them before,' said Huyghens. 'Not enough's been known about them. Some things needed to be found out if men were ever to be able to live here.'

'With bears?' asked Bordman ironically.

'Oh, yes,' said Huyghens. 'But the point is that sphexes come to the desert here to breed, to mate and lay their eggs for the sun to hatch. It's a particular place. Seals return to a special place to mate – and the males, at least, don't eat for weeks on end. Salmon return to their native streams to spawn. They don't eat, and they die afterward. And eels – I'm using Earth examples, Bordman – travel some thousands of miles to the Sargasso to mate and die. Unfortunately, sphexes don't appear to die, but it's clear that they have an ancestral breeding-place and that they come to the Sere Plateau to deposit their eggs!'

Bordman plodded onward. He was angry; angry with himself because he hadn't taken elementary precautions; because he'd felt too safe, as a man in a robot-served civilization forms the habit of doing; because he hadn't used his brain when Nugget whimpered, with even a bear-cub's awareness that danger was near.

'And now,' Huyghens added, 'I need some equipment that the robot colony has. With it, I think we can make a start toward turning this into a planet that man can live like men on!'

Bordman blinked.

'What's that?'

'Equipment,' said Huyghens impatiently. 'It'll be at the robot colony. Robots were useless because they wouldn't pay attention to sphexes. They'd still be. But take out the robot controls and the machines will do! They shouldn't be ruined by a few months' exposure to weather!'

Bordman marched on and on. Presently he said:

'I never thought you'd want anything that came from that colony, Huyghens!'

'Why not?' demanded Huyghens impatiently. 'When men make machines do what they want, that's all right. Even robots, when they're where they belong. But men will have to handle flame-casters in the job I want them for. There have to be some, because there was a hundred-mile clearing to be burned off for the colony. And earth-sterilizers, intended to kill the seeds of any plants that robots couldn't handle. We'll come back up here, Bordman, and at the least we'll destroy the spawn of these infernal beasts! If we can't do more than that, just doing that every year will wipe out the race in time. There are probably other hordes than this, with other breeding-places. But we'll find them too. We'll make this planet into a place where men from my world can come and still be men!'

Bordman said sardonically:

'It was sphexes that beat the robots. Are you sure you aren't planning to make this world safe for robots?' '

Huyghens laughed.

'You've only seen one night-walker,' he said. 'And how about those things on the mountain-slope, which would have drained you of blood? Would you care to wander about this planet with only a robot body-guard, Bordman? Hardly! Men can't live on this planet with only robots to help them. You'll see!'

They found the colony after only ten days' more travel and after many sphexes and more than a few stag-like creatures and shaggy ruminants had fallen to their weapons and the bears. And they found survivors.

There were three of them, hard-bitten and bearded and deeply embittered. When the electrified fence went down, two of them were away at a mine tunnel, installing a new control panel for the robots who worked in it. The third was in charge of the mining operation. They were alarmed by the stopping of communication with the colony and went back in a tank-truck to find out what had happened, and only the fact that they were unarmed saved them. They found sphexes prowling and caterwauling about the fallen colony, in numbers they still did not wholly believe. The sphexes smelled men inside the armored vehicle, but couldn't break in. In turn, the men couldn't kill them, or they'd have been trailed to the mine and besieged there for as long as they could kill an occasional monster.

The survivors stopped all mining, of course, and tried to use remote-controlled robots for revenge and to get supplies for them. Their mining-robots were not designed for either task. And they had no weapons. They improvised miniature throwers of burning rocket-fuel, and they sent occasional prowling sphexes away screaming with scorched hides. But this was useful only because it did not kill the beasts. And it cost fuel. In the end they barricaded themselves and used the fuel only to keep a spark-signal going against the day when another ship came to seek the colony. They stayed in the mine as in a prison, on short rations, without real hope. For diversion they could only contemplate the mining-robots they could not spare fuel to run and which could not do anything but mine.

When Huyghens and Bordman reached them, they wept. They hated robots and all things robotic only a little less than they hated sphexes. But Huyghens explained, and, armed with weapons from the packs of the bears, they marched to the dead colony with the male Kodiaks as point and advance-guard, and with Faro Nell bringing up the rear. They killed sixteen sphexes on the way. In the now overgrown clearing there were four more. In the shelters of the colony they found only foulness and the fragments of what had been men. But there was some food — not much, because the sphexes clawed at anything that smelled of men, and had ruined the plastic packets of radiation-sterilized food. But there were some supplies in metal containers which were not destroyed.

And there was fuel, which men could use when they got to the control-panels of the equipment. There were robots everywhere, bright and shining and ready for operation, but immobile, with plants growing up around and over them.

They ignored those robots, and instead fueled tracked flame-casters – after adapting them to human rather than robot operation – and the giant soil-sterilizer which had been built to destroy vegetation that robots could not be made to weed out or cultivate. Then they headed back for the Sere Plateau.

As time passed Nugget became a badly spoiled bear-cub, because the freed men approved passionately of anything that would even grow up to kill sphexes. They petted him to excess when they camped.

Finally they reached the plateau by a sphex-trail to the top and sphexes came squalling and spitting to destroy them. While Bordman and Huyghens fired steadily, the great machines swept up with their special weapons. The earth-sterilizer, it developed, was deadly against animal life as well as seeds, when its diathermic beam was raised and aimed.

Presently the bears were not needed, because the scorched corpses of sphexes drew live ones from all parts of the plateau even in the absence of noticeable breezes. The official business of the sphexes was presumably finished, but they came to caterwaul and seek vengeance – which they did not find. After a while the survivors of the robot colony drove the machines in great circles around the huge heap of slaughtered fiends, destroying new arrivals as they came. It was such a killing as men had never before made on any planet, and there would be very few left of the sphex-horde which had bred in this particular patch of desert.

Nor would more grow up, because the soil-sterilizer would go over the dug-up sand where the sphex-spawn lay hidden for the sun to hatch. And the sun would never hatch them.

Huyghens and Bordman, by that time, were camped on

the edge of the plateau with the Kodiaks. Somehow it seemed more befitting for the men of the robot colony to conduct the slaughter. After all, it was those men whose companions had been killed.

There came an evening when Huyghens cuffed Nugget away from where he sniffed too urgently at a stag-steak cooking on the campfire. Nugget ambled dolefully behind the protecting form of Bordman and sniveled.

'Huyghens,' said Bordman, 'we've got to come to a settlement of our affairs. You're an illegal colonist, and it's my duty to arrest you.'

Huyghens regarded him with interest.

'Will you offer me lenience if I tell on my confederates?' he asked. 'Or may I plead that I can't be forced to testify against myself?'

Bordman said:

'It's irritating! I've been an honest man all my life, but – I don't believe in robots as I did, except in their place. And their place isn't here! Not as the robot colony was planned, anyhow. The sphexes are nearly wiped out, but they won't be extinct and robots can't handle them. Bears and men will have to live here or else the people who do will have to spend their lives behind sphex-proof fences, accepting only what robots can give them. And there's much too much on this planet for people to miss it! To live in a robot-managed environment on a planet like Loren Two wouldn't – it wouldn't be self-respecting!'

'You wouldn't be getting religious, would you?' asked Huyghens drily. 'That was your term for self-respect before.'

'You don't let me finish!' protested Bordman. 'It's my job to pass on the work that's done on a planet before any but the first-landed colonists may come there to live. And of course to see that specifications are followed. Now, the robot colony I was sent to survey was practically destroyed. As designed, it wouldn't work. It couldn't survive.'

Huyghens grunted. Night was falling. He turned the meat over the fire.

'In emergencies,' said Bordman, 'colonists have the right to call on any passing ship for aid. Naturally! So my report will be that the colony as designed was impractical, and that it was overwhelmed and destroyed except for three survivors who holed up and signaled for help. They did, you know!'

'Go on,' grunted Huyghens.

'So,' said Bordman, 'it just happened – just happened, mind you – that a ship with you and the bears and the eagle on board picked up the distress-call. So you landed to help the colonists. That's the story. Therefore it isn't illegal for you to be here. It was only illegal for you to be here when you were needed. But we'll pretend you weren't.'

Huyghens glanced over his shoulder in the deepening night. He said:

'I wouldn't believe that if I told it myself. Do you think the Survey will?'

'They're not fools,' said Bordman tartly. 'Of course they won't! But when my report says that because of this unlikely series of events it is practical to colonize the planet, whereas before it wasn't, and when my report proves that a robot colony alone is stark nonsense, but that with bears and men from your world added, so many thousand colonists can be received per year... And when that much is true, anyhow...'

Huyghens seemed to shake a little as a dark silhouette against the flames.

'My reports carry weight,' insisted Bordman. 'The deal will be offered, anyhow! The robot colony organizers will have to agree or they'll have to fold up. And your people can hold them up for nearly what terms they choose.'

Huyghens' shaking became understandable. It was laughter.

'You're a lousy liar, Bordman,' he said. 'Isn't it unintelligent and unreasonable to throw away a lifetime of honesty just to get me out of a jam? You're not acting like a rational animal, Bordman. But I thought you wouldn't, when it came to the point.'

Bordman squirmed.

'That's the only solution I can think of,' he said. 'But it'll work.'

'I accept it,' said Huyghens, grinning. 'With thanks. If only because it means another few generations of men can live like men on a planet that is going to take a lot of taming. And – if you want to know – because it keeps Sourdough and Sitka and Nell and Nugget from being killed because I brought them here illegally.'

Something pressed hard against Bordman. Nugget, the cub, pushed urgently against him in his desire to get closer to the fragrantly cooking meat. He edged forward. Bordman toppled from where he squatted on the ground. He sprawled. Nugget sniffed luxuriously.

'Slap him,' said Huyghens. 'He'll move back.'

'I won't!' said Bordman indignantly from where he lay. 'I won't do it. He's my friend!'

Murray Leinster was the pen name of William Fitzgerald Jenkins – an author whose career spanned the first six decades of the 20th Century. From mystery and adventure stories in the earliest years to science fiction in his later years, he worked steadily and at a highly professional level of craftsmanship longer than most writers of his generation. He won a Hugo Award in 1956 for his novella *Exploration Team*, and in 1995 the Sidewise Award for Alternate History took its name from his classic story, *Sidewise in Time*. His last original work appeared in 1967.